HONOR BOUND: BOOK FIVE

ANGEL PAYNE

wet

HONOR BOUND: BOOK FIVE

ANGEL PAYNE

WATERHOUSE PRESS

For my Mau Loa...my forever love.

*You are the most amazing husband and father
a woman could ask for.*

CHAPTER ONE

"Perhaps I didn't make myself clear the first time, gentlemen. If either of you moves, I cut your balls off. Got it?"

The two men sprawled at Lani Kail's feet—and the end of her Bowie diving knife—gave instant silent nods. *Hell*. Why did she have to have trespassers stumble onto her West Kaua`i beach tonight? And why did they have to be a pair of the most beautiful males she'd ever laid eyes on?

Trepidation gripped her again. Maybe they hadn't stumbled at all. They were breathtaking, the kind of hunks a resort developer bully like Gunter Benson liked on his support team. The first of them, though clearly between three and thirteen sheets to the wind, was a mesmerizing mix of rugged and beautiful. His blazing amber eyes were framed by a messy head of hair in a slightly darker shade. The other filled out the yin to that yang, his silky gray gaze and spiky dark hair no less arresting. They were both built like the walls of Waimea Canyon, huge and hard and covered in taut bronze skin. Their open shirts, thrown over wrinkled khaki shorts, made it sinfully easy to confirm the conclusion.

Throwing them into a comparison with her island's stunning tourist attraction brought a warning pulled straight from the canyon's hiking brochures. *Distracted by the scenery? Prepare to fall to your death.*

She gulped, tightened her grip on the knife, and re-firmed her face. No sense in letting the hulks think their presence here was a shock, despite the fact that it was. Since the main highway ended a mile away, the sunset-seeking tourists kept mostly to the beaches south of the Barking Sands base, and thrill-seekers on their way to Na Pali usually only made breakfast stops here. So where had these two come from, and why had she found them in the middle of a fight that looked like a failed audition for a UFC slot?

There was only one answer that made sense. They had to be part of Gunter's goon squad, sent out here in preparation for the "casual meeting" their boss had requested for tonight up at the ranch's main house. And this move just screamed *casual*, didn't it?

She glowered harder, though she thanked the gods she'd discovered the intruders now, thanks to being paranoid enough to conduct a preliminary property sweep. The only thing she regretted about the decision was not thinking out her wardrobe better. With her mind consumed by anxiety about the appointment, she'd walked out of the house without thinking, still dressed in nothing but her bikini and thigh sheath—a factor clearly noticed by her detainees.

Damn it.

The gray-eyed stranger tried playing chief negotiator. He raised a placating hand, as if her knife was nothing but a quill pen. "We got the message loud and clear, sweetheart. So why don't you just lower—"

"I'm not your sweetheart." She flicked the knife, making sure the blade reflected the light back into his face. But that meant she had to meet his gaze once more. *Why* did the man have to possess such mesmerizing eyes?

He lowered the hand. "Fair enough. Maybe you have a real name I can use?"

"Nice try." Like he didn't know her name already. The man's persistent sociability, even with her Bowie at his nose, answered that well enough. What the hell was Benson's game this time? Why had he sent in a pair of his "cabin boys" to act like drunk frat brothers on the beach like this? Did he think she wouldn't see through this game? That she wouldn't see him trying to "survey" the beach that wasn't even his yet?

She winced at her mental default.

His *yet*?

No. *No.* This battle was far from over, no matter what Benson believed or connived to make *her* believe. There was nothing on this ranch—*her* ranch—that belonged to Benstock Development, including this sand. And, she vowed with renewed determination, no grain of it would. She knew what the man and his company did to the lands they gobbled, to the people they took from their homes in the pretty and *not* so pretty ways.

Right now, Benson was making a run for the "pretty" angle. Shallow, devious coward.

"All right," she snapped. "Stand up. Both of you. Slowly. Hands visible. No funny shit. I can gut a bluefin in two minutes with this thing, and your testicles won't be half the challenge." She rolled her eyes as Golden Eyes mangled his obedience, staggering more than straightening. "Okay, the act's going to get old real fast, pretty boy."

"Huh?" It was the first thing she'd heard out of the guy since she'd found the pair wrestling out here, pretending they were out for each other's blood, even hurling booze bottles into her garden during the performance. But she knew better.

"The *soused and stupid* act?" she countered. "It's all right to cut it now. I know what's really going on here, okay?"

9

"Oh?" He managed a sarcastic grin that looked lopsided due to a slightly crooked canine tooth. "Hmmm. Maybe you can fill me in, dreamgirl, 'cause I'm a little lost."

He leaned over, forcing her to deny better sense and steady his gait with a hand to his waist. He really was as solid as a granite cliff. Thanks to the wind, she confirmed he really had hundred-proof vodka breath too. *Aue.* She didn't know whether to slap him or laugh at him. Normally, guys who did "drunk with a twist of cute" were more tempting to her than chocolate, but right now, she was much more ready for a Godiva than *any* of Benson's brutes. Still, a new resolve took root. She'd have to keep her guard up with *both* these bozos.

"A 'little lost,' huh?" She shoved him away and pulled up on her stance again. "And I'm the goddess Hina, newly awakened for my nighttime adventures."

"That explains a few things." Mr. Intense Eyes and Dark Hair—and, she observed now, Endless Legs—surrendered that in a tone of a thousand nuances. She dared a glance at his face, to find his stare still fixed on her, looking like he deliberated the pieces of an intricate jigsaw puzzle.

She looked away before the man evoked the pull of a god in his own right. Just as fast, she added an angry huff. *God?* He barely should've gotten the courtesy of "man." Both of these hulks were on Benstock's payroll, which placed them somewhere between banana slugs and heroin dealers in the evolution chain.

"I'm taking you both back to the house," she declared. "Sorry to cut your romp out here a little short, but since our friend arrives in less than fifteen minutes, you've given me no choice."

"We're goin' to your place?" Golden Eyes cracked a woozy

grin. "Suh-weet."

To her surprise, McDark-And-Dreamy was just as ready with his hospitality. "Like *I* said before, we're not here to cause trouble. And I'm sure any friend of yours will be a friend of—"

"Save it." She hardened her posture, still baffled by the angle these guys were playing. Usually Benson selected his groupies for the clean-and-cute image so he could be the alpha dog with his fitted suits and expensive charm. These two apes didn't fit an inch of that MO. But Gunter had never sent any of his men to play real-estate recon on her beach before, either. The bastard was busting out an arsenal of new tactics, which only made her queasier about his agenda for the upcoming meeting itself. "Let's go." She pulled Gray Eyes forward by fitting the knife's tip into one of his shirt's button holes. "You're taking lead, Yin-man."

Confused crinkles appeared at the corners of his eyes. "Huh?"

"Yin and yang. It fits you two, in a demented way."

He smiled. The look wasn't a copy of his cheeky smirks so far. It grew from the middle of his mouth and then moved outward in an ocean-like undulation...wreaking strange havoc on her stomach in the process. "Yeah. It probably does."

His voice was different now too. A little more serious. A lot more velvety.

Guard up, Hokulani!

"The path to the house starts there," she ordered, "between the two papaya trees. Look for the bamboo planks. Got it?"

"Had it scoped about five minutes back, sweetheart." He turned and trudged toward the trees, flexing calves the size of hams. For once, Lani was thankful for his strange cockiness. It made her consider the logistics of her order. *Damn.* The path

was only wide enough for single-file travel, meaning there was
no way to police both the men at once.

Or was there?

"Stop." Her slam on the syllable was sufficient to freeze
them both.

Yang swiveled his amber gaze back at her. "Dear Christ, I
like the way she says that."

"Down, T-Bomb," cautioned Yin.

"Well, don't *you*?"

Gray Eyes didn't say anything—until he looked again
to Lani. Though his lips remained motionless, his answer
slammed through every inch of her body like a tidal wave of
fire. *Gods*. The man wanted her. To be honest, that part would
be easy to handle, if this was just a case of a jerk letting his
dick control the guidebook. But the way he took her in, as if
he'd never seen a woman before and marveled over everything
about her, was something she'd never experienced from a man
before. From another *person* before.

What the *hell* was he doing this for? He didn't relent,
freezing her in place, binding her—terrifying her.

And elevating her next command to the stratosphere of
crazy.

"Give me your pants."

Golden Eyes slid out another smirk. "I like the way you
say *that* even better."

Gray Eyes glowered. "What the fuck?"

"You heard me." Lani jerked her chin, making sure to keep
the Bowie directly in his view. "Benson sent you down here
ahead of the meeting for a reason. I don't know what that is
yet, and I'm not going to risk finding out when one of you runs
ahead to warn the man. Your shorts are my insurance against

that. Hand them over."

Golden Eyes, having already shucked his khakis, finished tearing off his shirt, as well. His new outfit, nothing but his black briefs, left no doubt in her mind that every part of him was as mighty as a boulder. He extended both with another crooked grin. "Do I qualify for extra credit?"

Hell. How the man could make her want to scowl and smile in the same reaction was a mystery she didn't have time to untangle. She diverted her attention by turning to his friend, who still shifted uneasily on the sand.

"You sure about this?" Gray Eyes finally charged. "You already have his. Do you really need both—"

"Take them off or I'll cut them off. Your choice."

The tension continued in his face for another two seconds. When it suddenly disappeared, she wondered why a thread of uneasiness dragged through *her* nerves now—thickening to straight-up alarm as he drawled, "Your mandate, sweetheart."

Hell. He justified her anxiety the next moment—in hard, huge, and damn near erect detail. And the man, with that sensual smirk again sliding across his lips, just let her stare as he dropped the shorts, blatantly revealing he was a commando kind of guy.

CHAPTER TWO

You should be gloating. Standing on the beach wearing nothing but a doofus gawk does not qualify as gloating.

The reproach jabbed at Kellan Rush's brain. Correction: it pounded at him with more ruthless demand than the blood blasting in his cock, stirring confusion into his mental mix.

He'd finally trumped the woman, at least for a second. Normal protocols, Sergeant Rush style, dictated that his next step be a well-earned wallow in glory. So why the hell was he stalling?

Because "normal" didn't exist in the same world with this woman.

And it was freaking him the hell out.

In the last fifteen minutes, she'd knocked him flat on his back, reduced him to speechlessness and, for the first time in his life, made him wonder if lightning strikes from fate weren't metaphysical bullshit. One second, he'd been ready to pummel some sense into the buddy who'd decided to give up on life by backstroking through a vodka bottle. The next, he was paralyzed by this beauty with the magic of blue silver in her eyes, the grace of mist in her steps, and a goddess's strength in every curve of her body.

Dear fucking God, her body.

What the hell was wrong with him? As a member of the US Army's First Special Forces Group, he'd seen physical beauty like hers in every corner of the globe. But this insane draw to her...it wasn't understandable, let alone controllable. Wasn't as though he could blame this sexy fuckery on anything substantial, either. He didn't know her *name*, let alone anything else about her.

He only knew she'd had the moves to topple him and Tait, two experts of unconventional battle, like they'd simply been pieces of driftwood.

He also knew she'd been ready to put a knife through their balls if they so much as sneezed on her beach.

Most importantly, he knew that behind all her She-Ra posturing, her grip on that knife faltered when referring to some asswipe named Benson. Her fear of the guy had her so spazzed, she'd instantly lumped Tait and him in with the guy and his goons. Kell thanked fate that Tait, even with half a bottle of Grey Goose in his system, was alert enough to throw a look indicating he'd hopped on Kell's page about revealing their true identities. The mutual gung ho? They weren't. Not yet. When a guy's work suit was often the cloak of subterfuge, he became best friends with anonymity. With whatever shit was about to go down with Benson, they might help her best if they lay low for now.

At the moment, that was easier said than done. With his personal "tiki god" stiffening by the moment simply from her stare, his body was mighty stingy with the secrecy. In this case, that wasn't a bad thing. Kell reveled in watching her eyes on his cock. And her breasts, so full and perfect, pushing against her bikini's halter top with the new air pumping into her lungs. He fixated on the strawberry tint of her lips as she parted them, as if her body had gotten the direct download on *his* fantasy. Damn, he could even picture it. Her bow-shaped mouth sucking on him shyly at first but soon pulling as much of his erection down her throat as she could. Moaning around him. Devouring him...

"Shit."

Her gasp was husky—the perfect envelope for a hard-on. Kell cleared his throat and glanced at the pole jutting from his crotch. Fat fucking chance of a stand-down now. After looking back up, he gave her a fast shrug. "I tried to warn you."

"Shut up," she snapped. "And don't you dare think of getting back into those things before I say." Her glare referred to the tentative step he took back toward his shorts. "Kick the khakis over here, point man. Then get moving." A trace of mirth seemed to flicker through her crystalline eyes. "Guess you're uniquely qualified for the position."

Kellan dared a wink. "Just want to serve to the best of my abilities, ma'am."

The humor vanished from her gaze. "Your *service* isn't important to me, Yin-man. Your silence is. Lock the mouth. Then walk the feet." She nodded at Tait. "You're right behind him, Stolichnaya."

Tait wobbled a finger through the air. "Technically, it was Grey Goose."

"Technically, I don't give a damn." She flicked her Bowie toward the path. "I wasn't sure what I saw flying through the air a few minutes ago. Now that I realize it was your bottle of hooch, you'll have the honor of picking it out of my roses once we get to the garden, anyhow."

"Not a problem, dreamgirl."

Tait's vodka-inspired flirt confirmed a suspicion to Kell. His friend was as captivated by the goddess as he. No surprise there, given how her long ebony hair had picked up the sunset's lavender streaks when she first came upon them, but he hoped—fuck, he prayed—that once T sobered up, he'd see that "dreamgirl" was nothing like Luna Lawrence. Nor could she be expected to live up to the memory of the woman who still tortured Tait's soul.

But as they entered the shadows of the forest path, the irony of the whole situation didn't escape him. He and Tait had been ordered here by John Franzen, their battalion CO, in order to pull T's brain out of its mire of grief over Luna, a "special agent" for the FBI team they'd assisted on a case in LA almost a year ago. The battalion's history with Luna dipped back further than the case, but those two weeks had been the turning point in Tait's relationship with the woman. Best as Kell could piece together, they'd plunged so deep they had everything but the rings—right before Luna ended the mission in a coma that eventually killed her.

The aftermath was an epic mess, validating Kellan's own life rule about women in all its practical perfection. Fun? Yes. Sex? Definitely yes. But when a guy had a job that prevented him from owning even a dog, leaping over the relationship cliff was asking for disaster—the same kind of shitshow that had taken over Tait's soul and psyche and now threatened to decimate his military career.

The guy had paid his dues on the psychotherapist's couch for months before brass finally cleared him for active duty again—but on his first mission back, T proved he'd lost his edge, unable to shove his emotions into the proper boxes. As a result, he miscalculated a shot so badly they almost lost an ally soldier to a blue-on-blue shot—a friendly fire bullet from Kellan's rifle—and the real criminal had gone free. Less than three hours later, Franzen ordered the two of them to take mandated R&R in his family's place, located a quarter mile down the beach from here.

Banishment in paradise. It sounded like a brooding emo fan fiction website, but with a few choice expletives thrown in, the words perfectly matched the title Kell slapped on the assignment when they got here a day and a half ago. Yet despite his bitter bitch party, he hoped their CO was nailing it right with the call. Before Luna, Tait had been more than his sniper team partner. They'd been best friends. Bunkmates. Drinking buddies. Able to communicate complete paragraphs by using only three words. Before Luna, they'd been—

Yin and Yang.

Crazy. Ironic, even. The title might've been something Luna herself concocted and was invoked by a woman who bore more than a subtle resemblance to the woman. But damn it, this Bowie-bearing goddess was more than that. A *more* that demanded to be seen for its own beauty and unique fire, not just a beautiful substitution for a ghost. He'd take Tait to the mat to pound it into the guy's brain if necessary.

Astonishment almost halted him in the middle of the bamboo-planked walkway. Was he, the most happily unattached guy on the team, admitting to putting a woman on his priority list?

He snorted and kept walking. She wasn't on the *top* of the damn thing, for fuck's sake. And it didn't mean he was turning heel on Tait or the goal they'd been sent here to accomplish. If Tait didn't leave this rock in two weeks with his head tighter than a newly calibrated rifle, Kell was officially under consideration for having his own ass yanked off missions for a while, if not permanently. Franz had made that much clear, apparently following some mysterious commanding officer wisdom—or insanity. As if it mattered. Tait's mental fitness was the priority here, and he wasn't about to muck up the op.

But for one second, it felt good to simply forget all that pressure. For right here and now, it felt incredible to let his dick fly in the wind for something other than a mission or a mate.

It was crazy. So what if it could only be temporary? Maybe a little temporary insanity would give him a better window into helping Tait. Besides, if "crazy" kept him in the vicinity of this goddess awhile longer, then crazy looked just fucking perfect.

CHAPTER THREE

An acidic laugh tumbled off Tait's lips. He didn't think his brain would argue much with his feuding feelings, considering that he stood in the middle of a garden in the dark, in nothing but his briefs, doing battle with the thorns of a nasty-ass rosebush in order to retrieve the vodka bottle *Kellan* had thrown here.

His head spun as he bent over, fishing for the elusive Grey Goose. His ears rang. How much of that shit had he downed before Kell found him and hurled the bottle away? More than he remembered, obviously. Sufficient to put him in a stupor that had him comparing the damn clouds in the sky to Luna's hair, but not enough to render him numb to her memory. Not half enough.

That was before heaven had dropped her twin on the beach in front of him.

Okay, officially, *she'd* dropped *him* first. One second, Kellan had stormed across the beach and all but torn him a new asshole for indulging in the bender; the next, they were both tripped, flipped, and stunned, flat on their backs in the sand. When he'd pried his eyes open and received a horizon filled with that ebony hair and those incredible eyes, his senses had screamed with the first logical conclusion. *Hallucination.* There. Handled. Clean and simple.

But when his vision cleared and she was still there, especially after Kell started talking to her, he'd known he was in true trouble. This creature, with her exotic beauty and take-no-shit spirit, was real. The comprehension had been the universe's biggest embrace and coldcock in one. The dilemma that followed was no easier to wade through. Did he drag her into his arms, thanking fate for reminding him that the strength he'd adored in Luna still lived on so incredibly in the world? Or did he grab his shorts and run like hell before he dirtied her life with the taint of his? He had to stop the carnage somewhere, right? He'd just turned twenty-seven. Maybe seventeen years was long enough to maintain the ridiculous fantasy that his life would make a difference to someone, that his love wasn't the courier of their ruin.

Or their death.

More laughter peppered the air. This time it sure as hell wasn't his. There was a distinct hitch at the end of the bursts, Kellan's brand of "adorable yet awkward." The guy had perfected that laugh a long time ago, and Tait had watched him use it to snag women from Tacoma to Tangier.

Was the player trying to use it on...*her*? Now? Standing there on the path with his schlong flapping in the breeze between them?

Tait growled as he found the bottle and snatched it from the bush. He ran into a shitload of thorns along the way, creating a few bloody tracks along his arm, which went unnoticed beneath his immediate case of *what the fuck*.

Common sense jabbed its way past the booze and his ire. The woman, whoever she was, obviously had a brain beneath that sleek hair. She was smart enough to see through a fuckpuppy like Kell. If not, Slash-Man would learn what *she* was all about real quick. A woman like that would demand the best of a man. She was bold and strong and unique, Waterford crystal meant for filling with champagne. In Kellan's world, relationships were plastic party cups.

The guy would wrap his head around that disparity any minute now. Just in case he didn't, Tait hustled back, bearing the Grey Goose with a gamely grin. "I've beat aside the rosebush dragon and retrieved your treasure, my lady."

When he extended the bottle, his damsel tucked in her chin while arching both brows, a move full of serious sass. It was also the first that didn't remind him in some tiny way of Luna. That came as a welcome relief to his tormented senses— only his cock didn't read the memo. The woman was a torch on him, her bronze curves and fiery spirit igniting parts of his body that had been doused since last June. A lot of those sparks were familiar friends, but a bunch of new flames sneaked in, too, burning in strange and scary ways. The fire licked up his staff and nipped at its tip in a blaze that was thoroughly unique to this island goddess.

Who the hell was she? Where had she come from? And why did she look like she hadn't given herself permission to smile in months?

"I'm no more your lady than his sweetheart. Got it?" For a moment, she seemed years younger, indulging a teenager's eye roll. "What the hell? Did Benson let you all watch 'Shakespeare Your Way Into Her Panties' online? Tell him he wasted his money."

He glanced at Kellan. The tension in his friend's shoulders surely mirrored his own. That name was back again. *Benson.* The dickface—yeah, by now he felt safe going there—had caused one too many shadows across the woman's face to make their ruse acceptable anymore. Time to separate themselves, especially in her perception, from the bastard's posse. He gave Kell a quick nod to communicate as much. Kell didn't need any more encouragement. He stepped over, took the bottle from her, and curled a hand around her elbow. "So about this Benson—"

"Perfect." She interrupted him as the glare of headlights swung through the night, showing that they stood in an expansive garden of flowers and fruit trees that led to a sprawling two-story home with lots of windows and a wraparound lanai. "I'll just tell him myself."

Fortunately, she remembered to return their shorts as she turned up the walkway at a determined march. After setting the vodka on a worktable, Kellan slammed back into his in less than fifteen seconds. It took Tait that long just to figure out where the leg holes were. He fell over trying to get his second leg in, officially verifying he'd had too much to drink. Or maybe not enough. Sanction for that came from the bottle itself, now at his eye level, shockingly not empty after its end-over-end flight into the roses. "Fuck it." He wiped off the opening and chugged another shot.

The warmth in his blood and the fuzz in his head did their duty as liquid courage. He sprang to his feet with a surge of surprising grace, if the toppled bucket of papayas didn't count.

After dodging the rolling fruit, he ran to catch up with Kell, who'd trailed the goddess up to the house's lanai. They followed her to the front end of the porch and shouldered against each other as truck doors made foreboding *thunks* against what had been peaceful air.

He blinked hard and focused. Though the hooch dulled his senses, old instincts and hardcore training beat through his blood like a favorite song, impossible to forget. "Three Escalades, six henchmen," he murmured to Kell without moving his lips. "But only the two flanking Mr. Big are carrying heat. They're the only ones in jackets."

Kellan answered by softly clearing his throat. Though the sound confirmed he'd heard every word of the assessment, the guy's lips flattened, also disclosing that he smelled the fresh shot on Tait's breath. *Whatever, tight-ass. I'm the only choice you've got for backup, so deal with it.*

But the cavalier viewpoint fled as he joined his friend in glancing to the woman who'd prevented them from tearing each other up on the beach—who clutched at his gut as she hoisted her quivering chin. With her hand still clenched on the Bowie and her shoulders thrown back, she was desperate to convey whatever shred of strength she could to these invaders of her world.

Invaders? After fast assessment of the men, Tait decided it wasn't a stretch. *Shit.* These pretty boys belonged in this rustic setting as much as kittens on a battlefield. Every one of them looked like they'd stepped off the pages of some fancy men's magazine after a three-hour burn in the gym. He bet they'd all had manicures today too. Gag.

Whatever irritation he'd logged for the lot was eclipsed by the disdain on the goddess's face as the main pretty boy strolled forward. In white shorts and a light blue polo with a precision cut to his salon-streaked blond hair, the guy was one Botox treatment away from having his testosterone card revoked for good. But Tait had to hand it to the man for sincerity points. The dude was good, damn good. He owned that sheep's fleece over his wolf's pelt with the commitment of a religious zealot minus the Jesus sandals.

"Miss Hokulani Kail. My, my, my, you are stunning this evening." He tilted his head, giving her a once-over that turned Tait's nerves to barbed wire. Kellan's growl betrayed his friend's agreement. The only good thing about the exchange so far was that they finally learned her name. *Hokulani.* He imagined some rock band writing a song about it, the kind requiring everyone in the stadium to wave glow sticks in time to its ethereal chant.

She stepped forward, chin still level. "I'd invite you in for some wine and arsenic, Gunter, but hadn't planned on all the boy toys being along." She glanced back at Tait and Kellan. "You didn't tell me the whole gang was coming. You planning a slumber party for later? Going to sit around and swap tips on cuticle care and after-the-bender eye bags?"

Benson chuckled. "We're all about the *aloha* spirit at Benstock, Lani. You know that."

"*Aloha* is about giving, Gunter, not getting. It has nothing to do with your brand of greed."

Pretty boy's face went tight. "Damn, I'm troubled to hear you say that."

Tait took his turn to stifle a snort. If Benson was really "troubled," he and Kell were Princes William and Harry.

Hokulani was a little more delicate about expressing her disgust, letting out a delicate sniff. "My opinions trouble you less than your sock odor, Benson. So cut the bullshit and tell me why you bothered to drive all the way out here with your backup dancers."

The man's face relaxed again. Another laugh played at his mouth. "Or what? You're going to *cut us* with that nasty blade of yours, darling?"

She stomped forward again. "What the *hell* are you here for, Gunter?"

The two closest goons to Benson stomped up, reaching for the pistols Tait had detected. Their boss restrained them with a raised hand. "No need for wasted tempers, people." He directed a slick smile up the steps. "We're just here for a simple property walk-through, Lani. You can even stay in the house if you want. All I need is a stroll on the beach and the orchard and a quick peek at that beautiful lookout point."

She bypassed the sniff in favor of a full snort. "The beach, huh? Well, that does explain the watch dogs."

Benson frowned. "Excuse me?"

Tait joined Kellan in moving up a little. Giving up the jig was past due, and they'd already missed the first opportunity, so—

"*Bah*," Lani bit out. "Innocence, especially feigned, just makes you a bad drag queen, Gunter. Take one more step, and I'll add trespasser to that."

The man spread his arms. "Darling, as I've clearly stated, we're just here for a friendly visit."

"And in what universe will I let you do that without a shred of justifiable paperwork? You're a fine piece of work, thinking I'll let you tromp all over my land, scheming how you're going to ruin it in the name of timeshares and condominiums just because you threw the word *aloha* into the mix."

He lowered his arms on a heavy sigh. "I thought we'd been through this. We want to enrich the beauty of Hale Anelas, not strip it. We *are* maintaining a natural preserve, remember?"

"Three acres is barely a park, let alone a reserve."

"What about the land we're setting aside for the horses?"

"You mean the corral for the fifteen heads you plan to keep out of the fifty-four I have now? The ones you'll save to tote fat tourists up and down the beach?"

After a moment of steady silence, Benson slipped his hands into his pockets. He took a couple of steps, the movements measured and fluid, another indication of the pure oil flowing in his veins.

"If you want to keep doing this the hard way, Hokulani, that's fine by me." He made an attempt at elegance with his emphasizing nod but evoked a drunk lizard, instead. "But you need to accept how this is going to play out. The money you're making from selling the fruits and desserts is barely paying for your groceries, utilities, and private academy for Leo. You're six months overdue on the property mortgage itself."

"Because Benstock has blocked every application I've submitted to reopen the B and B." Tears tinged her retaliation, gashing Tait's chest open as if she'd turned on him with the knife. "You're a maggot, Benson. You kill things in order to feed off of them, and you love it!"

Pretty boy shook his head as if dealing with a small child. "Red tape troubles shouldn't be an excuse to call people names. What would Leo say if he were here?"

"How do you know he's not? Or was it you who *conveniently* had the fencing team practice moved to tonight, as well?"

Benson let the lizard nod have an encore. "I'm not the monster you keep assuming, Hokulani."

She swallowed so hard that Tait heard it this time. "No? There are three other properties for sale in this area, Gunter, but you've targeted Hale Anelas for your new resort. My family home. My only livelihood. The only thing I have left of my parents."

"And don't you think that your parents would want you to be happy? To not have to worry about this place all the time? To provide for Leo and have a simpler life for yourself?" With every question, the man shifted closer to the bottom of the lanai steps though kept his stare fixed on Lani's position at the top. He gave a small nod to his two henchmen, who motioned the others forward too. "Just let us look around, darling."

"I'm *not* your damn darling."

"*Hoaloha makamae*—"

"She's not that either, asshole." Whatever it was. Tait didn't need a translation app to comprehend the general tone of the endearment, one the guy took as seriously as the stinking feet Lani had mentioned. He'd had enough of Benson trying to turn his silver tongue into a dagger through her heart, which was clearly tied to the land onto which this fuck-wazzle wanted. Vitalized by a mix of fury and hooch, he stepped past Lani to brace one foot on the landing next to her, the other on the top stair. "And she's made her point for tonight. So it's time for you to leave, *GQ*-la-roo."

"What the hell?" Lani flashed a spectacular you've-grown-another-head stare. "What—what's going on?"

Benson's plucked brows cinched together. "Shockingly, Miss Kail and I agree on something. What *is* going on?"

Lani swung her frown at the man. "They don't work for you?" Her answer came before she was done. Benson's shrug said it all. "Then who the hell—"

"Do you need assistance throwing them out?" Pretty boy didn't waste time jumping on that golden opportunity. More accurately, motioning his minions to do so.

"No." Lani's protest sliced the air, desperate and harsh. "No, damn it. You're not getting onto the property in *any* way, Gunter. Wave your dogs off or I'm calling the police!"

Benson's boys reacted like that was the best punch line of the week. With matching chortles, they barely broke their strides toward the stairs. Tait didn't waste energy on an answering laugh but indulged himself inwardly.

Bring it on, fashion plates.

As soon as the first henchman dared a boot on the bottom stair, he stepped down. "The woman's made herself clear, dude. Back off." He kept his tone conversational. No need to let these tarts think they were worth anything more.

Kellan moved down to flank Tait on the step. All Gunter's minions tensed. After taking half a second to fully size Kell up, the henchman in front of him made the first move. Though the guy wasn't packing a gun, his chest was as wide as a C-130, his neck as big as the plane's loading bay. Kell was smart enough to recognize a lucky break. As soon as the guy cleared two steps, Kell shoved the heel of his palm into that broad target of an Adam's apple.

The C-130 crumpled so quietly that Kell had time to roll his eyes at Tait before the blow was noticed—and Benson ordered the rest of his posse forward with a snarl.

Tait grinned. The boy on his side of the stairs now raced up higher, enraged by watching his friend get toppled by Kellan. "Come and get some candy, sweet thing."

The boy turned up the speed. Tait smiled wider. The faster the velocity, the better the punch. Sure enough, the guy ran into his fist hard enough to cause an audible *crack* of flesh to bone—until the guy's wail drowned it. He stumbled back, clutching his bloody nose.

"What the hell?" Benson screeched it like they'd taken out his whole pack of Twinkies instead of the two. "Who do you two meatheads think you are?"

Tait snickered. It had to be the vodka at play, but he couldn't help himself. "Meatheads. That's a new one. I kind of like it."

"Says the flank steak," Kellan drawled while centering

himself on the steps with a wide stance, now directly guarding Lani. Tait had to hand it to the guy. Looking that daunting in nothing but khakis and an open beach shirt required significant balls. "Sergeant Kellan Rush at your service, Mr. Benson," he stated. "This is my brother-in-arms, Sergeant Tait Bommer. We're honored to be assisting Miss Kail tonight on behalf of the US Army."

"Oh, my God," Lani whispered. "Are you a couple of Franz's guys?"

"Would that be a bad thing?" Tait murmured.

She didn't take her stare off Benson. "I'm not sure yet."

"Nice to meet you, Sergeant." The new information didn't shake Benson. The man folded his arms and advanced by another smug step. "Under different circumstances, I'd offer to take you boys out for a beer to thank you for your service. But as they say, this situation is what it is—and I'm sure that my friends at PACOM would be interested to learn how a couple of their boys pulled my men into this dustup without provocation or—"

This time Kellan joined Tait in his laugh, sharp enough to cut off the bastard. "First, I don't see a spec of 'dust,' man—though that can be arranged if you're disappointed. Secondly, go right ahead and call your fancy mucks in Honolulu. I'm sure they'll also be eager to know how the local *businessmen* of their islands are showing up at private residences where they're not wanted and demanding entrance anyway."

Benson was still unfazed. Tait snorted and shook his head. Some idiots didn't get the message. Times like these were when it came in handy to let the vodka fairies fly away with a guy's inhibitions.

"Hey, Slash? You're being nice, aren't you?" He stepped

down to the same level as Kellan and backhanded his partner's chest. "This is strange. He's not usually the nice one. But that means we can't have fun, because *I* don't feel like being so pleasant right now. Not when a beautiful new friend of mine has been barged in on like this, slapped with threats thinner than rubbers from a truck stop bathroom, and then told she might as well not fight the asswads who made them, because it's *for her own good*." As he lowered his hand, he cracked his knuckles. "Shit like that makes my blood hot, especially when I've been drinking. And fuuuck, have I been drinking."

Kellan emitted a tight groan. "Goddamnit, T-Bomb. You that determined to live up to the call sign tonight?"

Near the bottom of the steps, there was a man giggle. Tait glanced over to watch the jeer spilling from one of Benson's goon boys. The dude had a lanky build, eyes like a rat, and a layer of stubble of which he was clearly proud, complete with styling product worked into the scruff.

C'mon, Benson. Let this pup off his leash. Let them all *off.* The itch to rumble with these posers was a fire in Tait's blood. Okay, so it was displaced fire. He wasn't so drunk that he didn't recognize that truth. What his body really craved was friction of a different kind, learning every incredible curve of his beach goddess's body. Yeeaahh, that was happening sometime... never. The woman already protected her *land* like a wrathful divinity, which made her person a no-fly zone. And studying her bikini—for pure recon purposes of course—made him note a snug custom fit along with snap-lock closures instead of string ties. The garment was made for utility, not intimacy. Not that he couldn't get her out of it in less than a minute, with the proper invitation...

Goddamnit, he needed to pummel something.

"Casey." Benson's clipped command didn't bode well for that cause. "Don't waste your time on the nice soldiers. They're likely getting ready for a trip to Lihue, hoping they'll be able to buy some *entertainment* for the night. It's sad, but some people need to do that."

"And some just name theirs *Casey* and keep it on a pretty leash."

All really wasn't lost. The crack did the trick. Casey's lips curled before he pounded up the steps toward Tait. Adrenaline rushed Tait's blood, mixing with the alcohol, sending him into a weird kind of high. Yeah, this was good. The euphoria he'd been seeking for six months. The nirvana of not giving a fuck whether he lived or died. *Finally*.

When the kid reached him, Tait stayed open long enough to let the boy land a solid fist to his gut. To any outsider, the blow became Tait's justification for retaliation. He took the punch with pleasure, curling his arm under and thrusting up with a satisfied grunt. The pup had washboard abs, but they were conditioned by weight machines, not battle drills. *Damn.* That meant the kid would only last one or two more whacks before slinking off in tears like his friend. Where were some serious warriors when a guy needed to taste blood?

Luckily, Casey's buddies surged up, eager to help answer that question. Tait eyed them with a feral grin. "Let's have some fun, boys. I love playing with puppies."

"Holy fuck." Kellan's mutter was lined with anger.

"Oh, my God!" Lani's gasp was filled with fear.

His reaction to both was a smile he felt from ear to ear—just before he was tackled, rolled over, and pinned to the steps with his arms spread wide. Casey's victory scream filled his ears, piercing his I-don't-give-a-shit bliss, before he looked up—into the kid's fist.

Make it good, Fido.

He vaguely remembered the words actually tumbling past his lips before the blow descended. Pain exploded through his head. Then at last, a bottomless blackness sucked him into its thick perfection.

CHAPTER FOUR

"*Hupos o na hupos.*" Lani spat it for the hundredth time in the last half hour. For the sake of emphasizing how high her fury soared, she repeated it for Sergeant Rush in words he could understand. "Morons. All of you damn men. You're half-brained morons."

She pushed harder on the ice pack against Bommer's face. The man groaned from where he lay on the chaise upon which Rush had dumped him. A second later, he flung out a drunken arm. "Garrhh! Unnnggh! Stop!" His arm went lax as his fingers found her thigh. "Mmmm. Ahhh. *Don't* stop."

"Shit." She shoved his hand away. Well, tried to. "Yep. Morons."

From his position under the doorframe, Rush rolled his shoulders a little. In a less formidable man, the motion probably resembled a squirm. "I think you've got the win on this one, sweetheart."

The man needed another glare hurled his direction for the slip on the endearment, but damn it, the words soothed her nerves in at least ten ways. Still she seethed, "What the hell possessed him to goad Gunter's pack like that? What would he have done if you weren't there to peel them away and convince pansy-man to call them back? Does your friend have a damn death wish?"

"It's beginning to look that way."

The dismal certainty of his statement caused her to stare

back to Bommer. She tried to ease up on the pack, but the unconscious man reached up, clutching her wrist like his torch in an abyss. "Don't go. Please don't let go of me, Luna."

Her breath clutched. The plea wasn't like his other ramblings. Every syllable of it was clear, pronounced—and desperate. She stretched a finger out from the edge of the ice pack, trailed it across his forehead. With every inch she covered, his tension ebbed a little more. Was he relieved? Grateful? Lost to a dream? If so, of whom? Or what? She suddenly burned for the answers as if she'd been awaiting them for months instead of minutes—and from the looks of things, she'd be waiting longer. Bommer began pulling in longer breaths, forcing her to call on an old friend called patience.

"I think he's sleeping."

Her gentle tone caused visible surprise in Sergeant Rush. She shared his curiosity. How had her anger turned to tenderness so fast?

Don't go there, Hokulani. Don't even start.

But she'd already done so, hadn't she? It didn't take thousands in psychotherapy bills to figure out why. She'd felt out of control for so long. She'd *been* out of control. She was not and never would be a victim, but Gunter's scheming with Hales Anelas was becoming harder to fight. Now, blood had been spilled because of her resistance to the man. Gods be thanked that nobody's injuries were lethal, but in those moments after Gunter's men had swarmed over Bommer like a pack of pissed-off apes, she hadn't been so certain. Her screams had been shrill with real terror.

But this moment gave her some empowerment again. This stranger, so impossibly foolish and lost, gave her a moment of importance. Even if he was obliterated and had her confused for someone named Luna, she'd finally done something productive in this world again.

"I think you're right." The soft concurrence came from the gray-eyed man in the doorway. Correction: gray-eyed hunk. *Aue ka nani*. Such beauty. Sergeant Kellan Rush really was a magnificently made man. His shoulders, chest, and torso gleamed like wild honey spread over a marble statue. The shorts did little to hide the matching muscles of his long legs, which were dusted with more of his dark hair. He affected her in raw, animal kinds of ways. Her skin tingled, her heartbeat sped...and her sex thrummed in demand. She swallowed to hide her reaction, lucking out on the timing. Rush sighed heavily at the same time. "Sleeping is good," he stated. "That'll make it easier to hump him back over to Franz's place."

"What? The hell you will." She balanced the ice so it would stay on Bommer's forehead before rising to square off against Rush. "We'll put him in the back seat of my jeep, and I'll drive you two back over. It may be a bit bumpy, but I don't think he'll notice."

"Out of the question." He folded his beautifully muscled arms. "That'd leave you to drive back here on that two-lane thing that barely calls itself a road. I wouldn't put it past Gunter to be parked somewhere nearby, figuring we'll have exactly this conversation, waiting for you to cruise back here by yourself. With his boys already whiffing blood, the man won't toss aside that kind of an opportunity."

No matter how deeply the words seared into her as the terrifying truth, Lani defaulted to her usual reaction: completely faked defiance. "He wouldn't try anything with Leo around."

Once more, the man barely moved, though his pewter

gaze drilled into her. "Yes. Leo. The one who's expecting to find you here in one piece when he returns from fencing practice."

She sprinkled the bravado with sarcasm. "You *were* listening in class, Sergeant."

"That's my job, Miss Kail." He intensified his scrutiny, almost sending a vibe of discomfort, but Lani wrote off her perception as silly. These guys worked for Johnny Franzen, who barely suffered fools in his civilian life, let alone what he demanded of his Spec Ops team. Despite how Bommer had pulled the jackass move of the decade, Franz wouldn't have turned over the keys to his place to any half-brained joes. Not that Rush helped correct her perception, with his semistammered follow-up. "So...Leo? He's...errmm...your son?"

"My brother." She smiled, not seeing any point in prolonging the man's stress. "I was my parents' college surprise, and he was their ten-year anniversary gift." She pressed her lips a little tighter to keep the smile fixed, despite the hit of sorrow that came—as it always did. "The age spread turned out to be a good thing, though. Mom and Dad died together two years ago, but I was twenty-three, old enough to file for legal guardianship of Leo. He's fifteen now and surpassed me on height about four months back. But inside, he's still processing the loss in a shitload of ways."

He tilted his head a little. "And you're not?"

"In my own way, each and every day," she countered. "Only I'm not doing it with a teenage boy's hormones screaming through my veins."

"You get the win on that one too."

She joined him in his good-natured chuckle but cut hers short when she sensed he had more to say. "What?" she prodded.

The man stunned her by shifting from his position in the doorway. She wasn't sure whether to be unnerved or thrilled by the way he moved toward her across the wood floor, every step quiet but deliberate, until he stood only two feet away.

Lani's breath snagged. She lifted her gaze to meet his. In this softer light, his gray eyes resembled sea-foam in a storm. Apt comparison, considering what his nearness did to every vital organ in her body.

He took a step closer. "What happened?" His voice was a murmur between them alone. "To your parents?"

His interest, issued with somber sincerity, touched her. "My mom and dad did a lot of volunteer guidance work with at-risk teens on the island. One of the kids they'd been working with sneaked away for a Saturday night rave in Honolulu with some college boys and got himself arrested for possession. My parents insisted on flying over to post his bail. There was a pilot with a bird parked on this side of the island—"

"At the strip at the Barking Sands missile base?" he interjected.

Lani nodded. "He'd just dropped a couple of guys at the base as a favor to the base's CO. There was a storm coming in pretty hard and fast, but my parents begged him for the ride. The kid in Honolulu had anger issues, to the point that he took meds to keep it all in check. He'd been off the meds for nearly twenty-four hours, and—"

A rock of grief stopped her from speaking for a moment. The next moment, she gulped it down. "They finally got clearance to take off, and...the pilot lost control." She tilted her head the direction of the shore. "We heard the bird go down from here. By the time Leo and I got to the beach, all we could see was wreckage. That's all they found, as well."

"Fuck." His mutter was vicious but oddly comforting. He finished it by lifting a hand to her arm, wrapping firm, long fingers just above her elbow. Though he gripped her lightly, instant heat spread through her from the contact... and something more. So much more. A release yet a tension. A surrender yet a power. A piercing consciousness of all this man's strength yet every shred of his vulnerability. "That's rough." Coming from him, the words weren't empty. His empathy was thick in every syllable. "I'm sorry."

"Thanks."

She curved a little smile, trying to convey she meant it too. The look froze on her face as her gaze tangled with his again. His fingers tightened on her skin.

Gods, she was in trouble.

His fingers spread over her arm in a boggling mix of pressure. Sweet concern...curious question...sensual searching. Every corner of her body responded to all of it, especially her most tender core. If her clit had just been dropping hints before, it clicked to full demand mode now. She wondered if he'd use the hold to pull her closer—and knew if he did, she wouldn't resist. It had been a long, *long* time since male body contact meant anything besides Leo and his bear hugs. The abstinence took its revenge on her body now in hot, ravenous ways...

Suddenly, Rush pulled back like she really had caught fire. At the same time, a hard shell clamped back over his features. She recognized the expression all too well, having seen it on Franz's face before. A soldier clicking into protective mode. She turned and straightened pillows on the easy chairs in an effort to loosen the tension squeezing the air. But damn it, the man didn't help. The weight of his stare, following every move she made, assured that every nerve ending in her system remained on high alert.

"So what about the dickwad?" he finally asked.

She froze, gripping a pillow. "Excuse me?"

"Benson."

"Oh." She dropped the pillow and laughed. "*That* dickwad."

He returned to propping up a doorway, this time the portal that connected the living and dining rooms. "I take it he's a developer of some kind. But you said several other properties are openly up for sale. Why does he want this place so badly for his project?"

Like Franz, the guy didn't miss much. "He's not disclosed that for certain." She let half a smile play at her lips. "But I have a few theories."

"Like?"

She let another thick moment pass by. Rush kept his features neutral, careful. Maybe he thought she'd brandish the Bowie at him again. The thought made her chuckle, to which he reacted with a curious smirk. The moonlight sifted in through the dining room's big window, highlighting his mouth. He had such fascinating lips. The top one was nearly bisected by the deep dip in its center. The lower was an elegant sweep of flesh, set against his nearly square jaw. *Aue.* Mouths like that belonged on pirates, rakes, and highwaymen, the kind of men who dragged women off to the bushes so nobody could hear them being ravaged and pleasured...

Which should have been the thought that lowered her hand instead of raising it back toward Rush.

Which should have stopped her from stepping over and curling her fingers around his.

Which should have cut out her tongue before she could return his smile and say, "It's best shown instead of told."

Rush dipped his head toward her. "Why does that sound like a challenge?"

"Why do you sound excited that it might be?"

"I'm the long-range shooting specialist for our team, Miss Kail. Just the word 'challenge' gives me a hard"—he choked and delivered a grimace pulled from the nice-going-you-dumbshit file—"umm...a hard time saying no."

She giggled as she slid into her light running jacket and then nodded toward the couch. "How long do you think the lion will sleep tonight?"

He shrugged. "Tough to say. Up until a month ago, back-to-back deployments kept me from seeing him for a while. He was on extended leave, riding a desk job back at our base in Tacoma—but I have a feeling he was riding the hooch pretty hard too." His face clouded over, making it clear he didn't want to share further details. "He'll be out for a while, but I don't want to leave him alone for too long." He cocked a quizzing brow. "How far away *is* this 'challenge,' lady?"

Thank the gods he injected the humor again. That made it simpler to mask how he captivated her more as the minutes passed. The man already had the muster and character to be a part of John's battalion. He was also fierce with the fight club moves when it mattered, listened with compassion, and openly cared about his shitfaced teammate. If he knew how to select good chocolate and could navigate a toolbox, as well, she might be a goner. And that was *not* good.

"It's not far," she clarified. "But it's nighttime and we're both barefoot, so I'll guide you slowly."

"Deal." As he tagged a grin to the agreement, deep

dimples appeared against his jaw. *Damn it.* Even if he wasn't into chocolate and tools, she might be lost.

He followed her through the kitchen and the den. When they hit the back lanai, she grabbed a flashlight and handed him one too. Once they stepped outside, she led him past the work shed where Leo's surfboard collection hung, where he gave the requisite male reaction of bugged eyes, plummeted jaw, and invisible drool. She took advantage of his distraction to open the gate on the other side, which led to the bottom of the stone steps that went nearly vertical up the hillside beyond. There were exactly a hundred and fifty-three of them, and Lani had been climbing them since she could walk. With the confidence stemming from that knowledge, she called, "Last one up mucks the barn tomorrow, soldier."

"Huh? What barn?"

She only answered with a gloating cackle, hitting her stride at step fifteen before she heard him land on number one. Another witchy-poo laugh trailed out. She *so* had this.

Or so she thought.

Things changed once she neared the hundred-step point.

She still had plenty of juice to get to the top, but as soon as they crossed the point where the end of the climb was in sight, she fast learned that Rush had more stamina left to burn. *A lot* more. After five more steps, his flashlight beam hit her ankles. After another ten, he passed like she'd simply stopped. Lani poured on her best effort, only to watch his gorgeous thighs and ass disappear into the darkness. At the same time, he serenaded her with "Carry On." Loudly. And on key.

"Show-off," she muttered, vowing to keep the glower on her face as she reached the top, no matter how rousing his song—which the adorable dork continued as she trudged her final steps.

"If you're lost and alone, or you're sinking like a stone, carry o-o-o-on—"

"Shut. Up."

"May your past be the sound, of your feet upon the ground, carry—"

She clapped a hand over his mouth. "Come and 'carry on' this way, Sergeant."

His snicker warmed her hand before she pulled away and led him up another small knoll. He stopped singing in favor of a soft exclamation. "Whoa."

She took her turn to wield a cocky smirk. His reaction wasn't new. Most visitors said something in that vein when they realized a hundred and fifty-three steps had just transported them from a tropical paradise to a landscape that belonged in the middle of a Celtic moor. The marketing gurus for the island liked to tell people there was a "terrain for everyone" here, and it wasn't an empty line. There had been a lot of rain this year, as well, so the grass was a cool cushion as she led him farther out on the cliff. She couldn't wait to hear his reaction once she got him to the perfect spot...

"Holy. Fuck."

Right on cue.

Lani remained quiet as he took it in. The experience of seeing her island through a visitor's eyes never got old, but this occasion felt more special than the others. Maybe because he wasn't any usual visitor.

The man's profile, as beautiful as an etching on a Roman coin, entranced her as he took in the panorama. The mansion, slightly to their left, seemed as tiny as a doll's abode in the moonlight. She was pleased with how she'd trained the hibiscus to grow up the lanai supports; in another week, the pink and yellow blooms would be spectacular. Past the small fountain beneath the hala and banana trees at the rear of the house were the rose garden and orchard, which were separated from the meadows by the barn and two small riding rings. At this time of night, a few horses cantered across the grass, but most grazed leisurely beneath the banyan trees, enjoying the cool air. Forest bordered the two long sides of the meadow. The trees on the far side extended all the way to the Franzen's property line. The bamboo and palms situated more closely were part of the covering for the walkway she'd marched Bommer and him on at knifepoint.

A flush burned across her face. Thank the gods for the darkness so he couldn't witness her mortification at remembering how she'd treated the two of them like criminals. She betrayed herself the next moment anyway, softly chuffing at herself.

Rush flung his stare back at her. "Yeah, yeah, go ahead and laugh. Guess you showed up my nervy ass."

"No. That's not—" She interrupted herself with a sharper snort. "I just thought about my unique *welcome* to you and Sergeant Bommer. And was being just a little mortified by it."

He laughed and swept a hand around them. "I'll count this as a really great way of making up. Besides, if I had someone trying to squeeze me out from all of this, I'd be a tad territorial, as well."

She peeked back up at him and couldn't help but giggle once more. She knew what he wanted to convey, but somewhere during his statement, his gaze drifted back to her—and locked there. She wasn't sure she wanted that to change, either. She'd never been the center of a man's attention quite like this. Unblinking. Intense. Heated.

And very, *very* "territorial."

Her legs started threats of turning to mush, so she turned and found a soft patch of grass to sit on. As Rush lowered next to her, she expounded, "Gunter wants to transform the house into the resort's lobby, as well as offices for his entire company. The garden and orchard would stay, though they'll take out part of them for a property spa. Where we're sitting will be a concrete slab, so they can install a wedding garden." She extended a hand to back up her explanation by pointing at the various landmarks. "Surprisingly, Benstock wants to keep the zip line to the beach. They think it's a cool idea to have brides and grooms take a *ride to the sand* after they say their vows."

He dipped his head and smirked. "Appropriate symbolism." After enduring her rib jab of chastisement, he jerked his chin toward the barn and stables. "What about all of that?"

"They'll be gutted and transformed into a five-star restaurant. A newer stable will be built on the far side of the property, for tending the horses they do plan on keeping."

"The fifteen who are strong enough to carry fat tourists."

She almost poked him in the ribs again but opted for a smiling shoulder bump. "There's my good listener."

He returned the nudge. The move, while friendly, sent tingles down the entire left side of her body. She was almost thankful for the distraction of his reply, which was tight with tension. "I assume the dickwad is selling the other horses off to make all that land available for building a swagalicious hotel?"

"Close. Swagalicious timeshare condos. Except for the biggest unit, which he's already claimed for himself."

A violent sound rumbled from deep inside his chest. He

still clutched his flashlight with his far hand, now glowering like he wanted to bash in a skull with it. Lani endured a little tremble. The comparison wasn't an empty one when applied to a six-foot-plus Special Forces warrior. The realization made her a little scared...and a lot aroused. The man didn't help things one bit by starting up his stare, the entrancing and territorial version, once more.

"Amazing," he finally murmured into their long silence.

"What is?" she queried back.

"I can see the stars in your eyes."

She let herself give in to a full laugh. "Oh, you're good. That's nice. How many times has that one worked for you, Sergeant?"

He dropped his jaw and spread his arms. "I'm not kidding! Hold still. It's so cool. I want to see it again!"

She giggled and squeezed her eyes shut. He tossed his flashlight to free up his hands in an attempt to grab her shoulders. When she whacked on his in return, he relented and pulled back, also laughing. Lani opened her eyes, only to have her heartbeat seized again. The mirth had made him a different person. All the darkness of his face gave way to dancing eyes, naughty eyebrow wiggles, and a devilish smile that made her long for a serious taste of sin.

It was time to change the subject. Fast.

"So...how long have you been in Franz's battalion?"

"Since the day I made Special Forces, six years ago. He'd taken a bullet to his leg in Afghanistan and led some team training during his rehab. I was one of the lucky fuckers he got really attached to." His tone was bone dry, but a thread of fondness was woven into it too. "There were days when I didn't know whether to be grateful or pissed about that, but serving under the man has been the best experience of my life."

Lani nodded. Her response was filled with equal affection. "Yes. He's awesome. I really love him."

"Oh." He straightened, seeming genuinely surprised. "Uh, I hadn't realized..."

Understanding hit her. A new laugh followed. "Oh, gods! Not like *that*. Ew. He's like my brother!"

"Oh." He drew the word out a little. The smile in his voice tugged her gaze back over to his face. The moonlight played over his noble features and thick hair in mesmerizing ways. "Well, okay," he murmured, seeming bashful beneath her scrutiny. "Umm, that's good. Brothers are good."

Lani pulled up her knees and then rested her chin on them, keeping up the stare. She knew this was ruthless, considering how she'd been throwing the man off-balance since the second they met, but she'd also witnessed him at the height of his game, a slick combination of ninja badass and focused soldier. The fluctuation in his composure was fascinating to witness. "How many do you have?" she finally asked.

"How many what?"

He seemed distracted. And once more, she loved that it seemed to be by...her. "Brothers," she clarified.

"Only Tait," he supplied.

"You're brothers? But your last names—"

"Are different. And our parents. And our upbringings." He returned her stare with steady conviction. "Doesn't matter. He's my brother. We've shed enough blood and tears together to make it true in the eyes of any god you throw in the mix."

She absorbed that statement in silence, choosing to convey her acceptance of it by mirroring his quiet strength. A couple of minutes went by, filled with the velvety crashes of the waves and the soft song of the wind, before she spoke again. "Who's Luna?" When he didn't answer right away, she added, "Does she have anything to do with why Franz let you two stay at his place?"

He funneled all his focus on her before replying. "That's not a typical thing for him, is it? Letting people stay there, let alone a couple of guys from his team?"

"Not typical," she echoed. "Yeah, you could say that. As in never."

"*Never?*"

"It's not a vacation rental for him, Sergeant. It's where he grew up, his heritage. Like all of this is for me."

"So no wonder you thought T and I had rolled in with Benson." There was a smile in his voice. It grew as he muttered, "Sorry. I didn't mean to embarrass you."

How had he seen her new flush? The moon was nearly full tonight, but both their flashlights were off. *He's also the guy in charge of shooting things from hundreds of yards away. He can probably spot a ladybug on the hibiscus from here.*

She tried to laugh off her discomfort. "You didn't exactly come calling in your Mess Dress, bearing apple pie and a meat loaf."

"Would've made it much harder for you to get me naked."

So much for the laugh. She groaned and ducked her head. "Gods. I *am* sorry."

"Don't be. I make shitty apple pie. My meat loaf, on the other hand, has been called *the mighty beast cake of Odin* by its fans." All too quickly, he sobered, as well. "Too bad I was busy trying to talk my friend out of turning his bloodstream into the Grey Goose river."

"And that woman—Luna—has something to do with all of

it?"

He didn't reply before taking a deep breath and releasing it with slow care. "Luna Lawrence was a special agent on an FBI team we worked with on a mission in Los Angeles last year. She and T-Bomb went full throttle on the bonding-in-the-face-of-danger ride."

"So they were involved?"

He ticktocked his head, once right, once left. "That's the tactful way of putting it."

"What's the not-so-tactful way?"

His lips compressed. "Not everyone on the team approved of Luna working on the op. Her...situation...was a little complicated. She'd had some trouble with the law and was 'on loan' to us from the Washington state penal system."

"Wow."

"Wow is pretty accurate. Wasn't exactly orthodox, but sometimes you do what it takes and hire who you must to get the job done. As you can guess, there was friction. But Tait's always had a thing about sticking up for the little guy. In this case, it was the misunderstood little girl."

Lani let her eyebrows drop as her confusion rose. His baritone kept the needle pinned right down the middle lane of neutrality. "Well, was she?" she asked.

"Was she what?"

"Misunderstood?"

His chin rose as he clearly gave his reply some thought. "Yeah. I think she was. Of course, that only fed into T's Prince Charming complex. Anything to be the guy who saved the day."

A memory flashed at her. The moment Bommer had trotted up to her in the garden in his briefs, panting like the happiest puppy on earth. *I've beat aside the rosebush dragon...*

my lady. Though he'd been half obliterated, he'd also been pretty cute. Sensing Rush didn't share her sympathy for Bommer's gallant streak, at least not now, she kept her thoughts to herself and pushed on.

"You're referring to her in the past tense." She let her voice dip to a murmur. "Does that mean what I think it does?"

"Probably." He raised his head and gazed out over the ocean. "The mission ended with President Nichols having to have his hand sewn back on and an explosion in Hollywood that rocked the Richter scale."

Her mouth popped open. "*Kahaha.*"

"Huh?"

"Holy shit."

"Oh."

"That was *you* guys?"

"Franzen didn't tell you?"

"He doesn't like to talk work when he's home." She let out a huff. "He's mostly out surfing with Leo and bugging me about why I haven't found a nice guy to settle down with."

He grunted, sounding eerily like Franz in the doing, though she couldn't figure if he issued the expression in approval or discomfort. Confusion hit harder about why she even cared.

"So you know the public details," he went on. "But the follow-up story is grim."

Her heart squeezed. Her mind returned to the moment in the living room when Bommer clutched her in tight desperation. No. Not desperation. It had been...grief. "The blast killed Luna?"

"Not right away." Kellan's jaw turned the texture of the rocks beneath them. "She was thrown by the shock wave. It fucked her up enough to put her in a coma for six months."

"Oh, my God."

"She finally woke up, but only long enough to—"

"To what?"

"To say goodbye to Tait." The words left his lips as if they'd come straight from his gut. They were full of deep pain for his friend, which led Lani to curl her hand around his shoulder. "Fuck. I never got it...until now."

"Never got what?"

He pulled in a long breath. "Tait always told me...well, he said that Luna had been his *flare*. You see, we use these sticks—flares—out in the field, if we need to alert exfil planes to where we're at or we need light really quick. They burn like a ball that fell off the sun, but it's fast and furious, then it's over." The corners of his mouth twinged. "I never faulted the guy for the comparison, though I came up with a hundred ways to call him out as an idiot for it. But T always answered by shaking his head, calling *me* the fool. He'd say borrowed minutes were some of the best we can have in life, a lesson *Luna* taught him. He also said that light is often at its most perfect before the darkness comes again and that those moments are worth risking everything for...worth mourning for." He shook his head as his face crunched into a beautiful contortion. "At which point, I usually called him a bigger fool. And at which point, we usually got into disgusting fights."

"I know." She infused it with the warmth of comprehension. When she'd first seen them on the beach, they'd been after each other like bears. Now, she recognized the brawl for what it was. Rush had been trying to beat some sense into his friend—literally.

"Yeah." A bleak laugh tumbled from him. "You do, don't

you?" He shook his head. "He's been an idiot, but I've been one too. I just didn't get it. I told him he was a fool to have sunk so much of himself into something that never could be, even if Luna had lived. She was on loan to the FBI from the Washington state penal system. Yeah, the *history* I mentioned even landed her a prison term for a few years.

"I thought they'd have something fleeting at best and that nothing like that was worth throwing himself off a goddamn emotional bridge. But T wouldn't listen. He said he'd found something real. I was a prick to him about that too. Told him there was no fucking way he could've found 'something real' after being with the woman for a total of a few hours, that connection didn't simply happen that way." He closed his eyes as if condemning himself for all of that. Clouds slipped across the moon, turning the night's silver glow into shadows that matched his compunction—and made him even more beautiful. Lani's throat constricted. As he even spoke the word "connection," she longed for more of it with him, if only for tonight. She was seconds away from tugging him into a hug when he slid a hand up to cover hers and raised his dark gaze to capture hers. "Hell. I was really wrong, wasn't I?"

She surrendered to a tight gulp. His touch tightened on her. His stare enveloped her. His body was so close and powerful and strong...and his presence permeated her spirit in all the same ways. It had been so long since she'd allowed herself anything like this. With *anyone* like this. Feeling her heart stop...in all the right ways. Letting her control go...in all the best ways.

A flare in the darkness. Magic for just a moment.

It wouldn't be forever. But that was the most perfect part. In a few days, Kellan would be gone, called to his duty across the world, and she'd be committed to nothing except some amazing memories to make the minutes with her vibrator *much* more interesting.

Stolen beats. Borrowed time. If only for now...

"Wrong...about what?" The words left her in tentative spurts, but somehow, he managed to hear.

Kellan dipped closer. He delved a hand into her hair and spread his fingers across the back of her head. Damn, he felt good. Huge, commanding, a warm refuge in the gathering storm.

"About this," he told her, mingling his breath with hers. "About exactly this."

His lips fitted over hers, taking her hunger and turning it to fire. He kissed her deeper, parting her wide so he could invade her mouth with his tongue. And he took again, transforming her high sigh into pure, sensual surrender.

With a groan, Lani readily gave it to him. And prayed he'd take so much more.

CHAPTER FIVE

Kellan's head spun. His senses careened. If the island's tsunami sirens suddenly blared, he wouldn't be surprised. Surely the earthquake that started the wave would have its epicenter here, in the strata of this cliff where a single kiss rocked the axis of his being.

He didn't do shit like this. He didn't *feel* shit like this. Miracles were for hipsters who believed in wheatgrass for breakfast. Life-changing kisses were for saps who didn't know better. That made him, here and now, the butt of the universe's biggest joke. Enthralled with how readily she opened for him. Moved by how beautifully she moaned. And harder than the rocks beneath them as he lay back and pulled her with him, savoring how she curved her thigh around his waist.

When he wrested his lips away from hers, his breathing came in harsh bursts. His fingers trembled. *Holy fuck.* He hadn't been a wobbling colt like this since Stacy Weebler pulled out a box of condoms after the ninth-grade dance with a shy smile. But Stacy had been a girl. Lani was a woman, aware of what she wanted, alive with what she needed, and telling him both with every magical silver light in her gaze.

She smiled and teethed a piece of her bottom lip. At the same time, she arched her leg to run her toes beneath his shirt and up his spine. The contact sent bolts of heat through his body. He groaned deep and then raked a hand along the gorgeous, generous curve of her thigh. When she hitched out a sigh in response, the sound was a pure beguilement.

As the woman herself would say, *dear gods*. What the hell was she doing to him? He'd always been the guy rooted in reality. Ruthless with the facts, steadiest with the trigger finger. But as he breathed her in, filling his senses with her ocean-and-jasmine scent, he barely remembered that man. His skin burned. His muscles clenched. And his cock was well on its way to being a swollen rod of torture. He hadn't lusted for a woman like this in a very long time.

Which was why his next words, as well as the conviction behind them, surprised him as much as they did her.

"I think we need to stop, sweetheart."

She swallowed like he'd just killed her puppy. "You just not feeling it, huh?"

A laugh shot out of him. "Are you kidding?" Knowing he tempted fate with the move, he shifted so she was completely beneath him, his crotch lodged against hers. "This is me *not* feeling it." Using the excuse of "clarification," he thrust a little, pushing his length against the sweet warmth of her cleft.

"Oh...mmmm...okay." Her high-pitched rasp was beyond adorable. "So...*why* are you stopping?" Suddenly, her muscles tensed. "Crap. You're seeing someone, aren't—"

"No." He stopped her from surging up by grabbing both her thighs. "*No*. There's nobody, I swear it. Nobody who's done *this* to me."

Her muscles went lax. The feeling of her acquiescence was...amazing. The woman's physical strength matched the conviction of her character. To feel her giving that up for him, softening for him, sent a sluice of raw arousal to his cock.

Kell grimaced. *Fuck*. Years of fighting and training with T-Bomb had caused his friend's kinky tendencies to start rubbing off on him. Not good. He didn't get major wood on the domination thing like Tait and a lot of the other guys did. At least not until now. As he envisioned lashing Lani's naked body down to these rocks and then watching the ocean mist drench her spread limbs and pleading mouth, his cock went as solid as a Sequoia.

Goddamn. The woman was turning him into someone he barely recognized. He should be horrified. Afraid. The trouble was, he liked that someone.

As if Lani had a window into his mind, she lifted a hand to his jaw and murmured, "I like it, Sergeant. I like feeling what I do to you,...and how you look when I do it."

He glided his hands from her hips to her waist. As he pushed them up under her jacket, a surge of energy, primal and powerful, slammed him. "Kellan," he growled, stopping short of making it a full command.

"What?"

Screw it. Maybe a little of that domination shit could be fun. "Kellan," he repeated. "That's my name, not 'Sergeant.'" He leaned over her, matching the angle of his face to hers so he could see every curve and angle of her features. "Say it," he ordered. "I want to hear it on your lips, your beautiful voice wrapped around it."

Her lips opened. But for a long moment, nothing came out. She held the expression, mouth parted and eyes longing, giving him her veneration in this exquisite visual form first. Her beauty impacted him just like the storm that approached: bold, magnificent, cleansing.

As he blinked from the blast, she smiled and whispered, "Kellan."

He gripped her tighter and returned her smile with the

stunned force of his own. "Thank you, Lani."

"Hokulani." Her hand, lifted to his face with sweet emphasis, relayed how she offered it as another symbol of her trust in him. He remembered how she'd stiffened when Benson used it and realized it wasn't a privilege she allowed from everyone. "It's *my* real name. Dad used to tell me it was a sacred gift. Right before Mom went into labor, they were on the beach and watched a star fall over the ocean. They saw it as the gods sending me down to be with them. Hokulani means heavenly star." She let out an adorably awkward laugh. "Kind of corny, I know, but..."

Kellan didn't want her to finish. With a rush of inexplicable feelings, he lowered his lips to hers again. He resolved to savor her slowly this time, trying to put important brakes on their passion, but as her mouth responded to him, her tongue tempting him in tender little sweeps, he abandoned the cause. After tasting her for a long, moist tangle, he pulled back for the privilege of uttering the single, meaningful word.

"Hokulani."

Her grateful hum welcomed him back to her lips, gaining resonance as he demanded deeper entrance. The weight of her second leg settled against his back, coaxing his resistance toward a valley of no return.

"Hokulani." He repeated it between heavy breaths as he finally dragged away, hoping it would invoke a spell of angel-strength composure. No such luck. "Damn...Hokulani." It became an invocation of need, drawing him into a heated trance that began and ended with the curves of her body, the desire in her eyes, the wet bliss of her kiss.

"Kellan." She extended his name with husky inflection, driving him as crazy as her fingers on his skin, flicking over his nipples before she reached for his head and scored his scalp with her nails. "Kellan. *Kellan.*"

The shower of her reverence crashed harder over him just as real raindrops descended around them, smacking the ground at a quickening pace. *Damn it.* Like he needed yet another reason to kick his self-control over the cliff. His fantasies of her nudity had definitely involved moisture...lots and lots of moisture. Now he had plenty of it to help him out in reality. The rain intensified, soaking them both inside a minute.

With an eager sigh, she shifted her hands from his head to pull at his shirt in feverish tugs, fighting the rain that glued it to his back. When she reacted to his bared torso like a starving woman given a slab of chocolate cake, his restraint waned further. When she pulled at the back of his neck and slammed their mouths together again, he didn't raise an inch of resistance.

Their groans mingled and reverberated through his body. She undulated beneath him in all the *very* right ways. The damn minx knew he was sporting commando status under his shorts too. She had to realize what her little lifts and grinds were doing to him. His dick pounded so hard for release, he was certain the horses below could stage a dance party to its rhythm.

"Hokulani." He issued it as half a plea this time. Okay, she was giving him all the high signs on this, and they were both grown adults, but two hours ago, she'd had a Bowie knife at his balls. Just because they'd changed altitude and body positions didn't mean she had alternative plans for his nuts. He pulled an important page from the battalion playbook. *Crazy times call for clarity and communication.* "Sweetheart, if we don't stop..."

His aroused snarl drowned the end of that as she ran both hands down his back and then beneath his shorts.

"Tell me." She rose a little, going for his neck with her strawberry-dark lips. The second she made contact, he shook from the power of her warm caress on his soaked skin. He had to consciously focus on gently forcing her back down.

"Listen to me." He growled it, which only seemed to spur her arousal, pumping *his* in a classic domino effect. "If we don't stop now, I *won't* stop. There's a condom in my wallet. I'll get it out before taking off my shorts for you again. Then I'm going to get you naked, and I'm going to spread you wide—yeah, right here in the rain—and I'm going to fulfill the fantasy I've had since first laying eyes on you. I'm going to ram my cock into your wet pussy and hit every spot in your sweet body that'll make you scream until you can't anymore. That'll be the moment that you come for me, sweetheart. You'll fall apart for me in a thousand different pieces, and I'll love it as I watch every second."

Mentally, it felt damn good to say it. Physically, he was a throbbing mess. He took a long moment before drawing back from her, steeling himself for any number of reactions. His blunt pillow talk had driven away more than a few fine women even after three dates, let alone two hours. But nothing less than his truth would do with this creature, so bold and fierce and passionate, who'd upended his senses from the moment she'd flipped over his body on the beach. Lying to her would be an insult to her, and that was *not* okay.

The rain fell harder as he swept his gaze up.

"Up" being a subjective term at the moment.

Like a man—or many women, for that matter—would condemn him for halting his eyes once they beheld her chest.

Her fully nude, damn spectacular chest, now exposed past the jacket she unzipped and the bathing suit she unlatched.

When he ripped his stare away to find her face again, he found a smile waiting for him there. She'd become half mischievous elf, half knowing goddess...and a hundred percent breathtaking woman.

"You may have beat me up those stairs, mister, but I've been three steps ahead of you ever since." Her eyes, brilliant as diamonds, fell to the front of his shorts. "Where did you say that condom was?"

CHAPTER SIX

Lani couldn't help but laugh as she watched Kellan's reaction. Though his gaze was heavy from desire, his mouth quavered like a kid who'd just scored his first Little League home run and couldn't believe it. But that was the only "little" thing about the man. She had trouble holding back an eager lip lick herself, trailing her stare over his rain-slicked chest, arms, and abdomen. Even his muscles seemed piled on top of muscles. In comparison, her ample curves felt soft and light.

And free.

Gods, how good it felt to be free. For this moment, life was joyously far away, tucked below. Benson and his schemes, Leo and his struggles, and the property with its bills were cares that belonged to tomorrow, worries for a woman who wasn't her right now. In the morning, she could return to responsibility. Kellan would too. But in this stolen sliver of the night, they only belonged to the wind, the rain...and the wild, wonderful force of their passion.

"Fuck." His serrated growl added to his illicit allure. Without lowering his head, he pulled out his wallet. She caught a glance of his military ID, his photo revealing him with a cute scowl beneath his regulation high-and-tight, before retrieving the foil packet that gleamed with wicked promise. "Next time, I may let you win that climb, sweetheart."

Knowing there would be no "next time" allowed her to delight in his humor. As she giggled, she started to wiggle off

WET

her bikini bottoms, but Kellan stopped her with another rough sound.

"*I'm* doing those honors." He already had his fingers hooked around the sides of the suit. Lani didn't argue. His fingers grazed her skin with steady purpose. His touch was like hot oil slicked over the cool rain as he pulled down the fabric. But once done, he didn't let go. His hands traveled back to her hips, hoisting her sex high, spreading her pussy open so the rain began to seep into sensitive crevices.

"Oh!" she cried. The sky's tiny kisses tapped on her flesh, coaxing her deeper desires from their warm folds. The contrast of the cool rain and her hot desire made her gasp, stunned and captivated. Her legs shook as she went up on tiptoe, needing more...*more*...

"Relax." Kellan gave the direction as he hoisted her legs off their moorings, hooking her knees over his shoulders. "Relax. I've got you, my sweet Starshine."

"Ohhhhh!"

He had her, all right. But how the hell did he expect her to "relax" when he slid his hot tongue over the tender tissues at her core? Lani cried out again as he nibbled his way deeper, seeking the knot of nerves that ached the most for his touch. When he found that special spot, she screamed and arched back, grabbing for solid purchase. How had she justified for so long that her vibrator was just as good as this?

Kellan moaned in satisfaction as he taunted her clit. When he ceased the torment, it was only to kiss her mound with slow reverence. "I think I've found my island ambrosia..."

With that wicked intent darkening his tone, he dipped his head to suck at her pussy once more. The rain fell even harder, a metronome for the thrumming need in her body. He pulled and licked at her engorged clit, turning her into a writhing ball of need, the rocks at her back be damned. The pressure swirled higher in her thighs, her ass, her sex. Deep inside her body, her womb pulsed in readiness. She whimpered in a mix of agony and ecstasy. He trailed his tongue through her pussy like he had a damn map to the most illicit parts of it, but every notch of arousal made her realize how empty her body really was... how she needed a completing flame inside it.

Finally, through the haze of her excitement, she heard the zipper slide on his shorts. She pried her gaze open to witness him tear open the condom with violent speed. Similar ferocity defined his face as he looked down at her, gritting his teeth as he palmed his steely erection.

"*Aiwaiwa.*" She swallowed hard. And stared harder. "Kellan, you're..."

Huge. Glorious. Perfectly made.

"Ready to be inside you, sweetheart." He hissed as he rolled the condom over his penis, which didn't relent a fraction of its stiffness. "Ready to fuck you deep."

The soldier kept his word. He lowered her legs to an angle where they wrapped around his waist before leaning forward so he could kiss her again. As he plunged his tongue into her mouth, he worked his shaft into the first inch of her body. When he shoved in a little deeper, Lani gasped into his mouth.

"Sorry," she explained, trying to smile past her pain. "It's... it's been a while for me."

His gaze darkened. "Yeah. For me too."

His confession made every inch of her vagina cream. She clung to his shoulders, feeling the strain of his muscles as he tried to slow the pace. "No," she protested. "God, Kellan. Deeper. Please!"

He clenched his jaw. "I don't want to hurt you."

"I *want* you to." If she was heaving caution aside, then why not have the aching legs tomorrow as a sweet memory? "I... need you to... I...just need you. Filling me. Fucking me. Hurting me. Please! Oh, pl—"

She cut herself off with her own scream. As Kellan drove his cock all the way into her, she didn't think she'd ever felt so stretched, so raw...so complete. Yes, it hurt. Yes, it was invasive. Yes, it blocked out everything for a long moment except for the certainty of his body, massive and rigid, inside hers. But even the pain was perfect for what she needed from tonight—and what she sensed he needed too. His features, now intense and feral, channeled the untamed force of the downpour itself. As the wind whipped higher, he seized her hips, syncing their pace with his fevered thrusts. The rain pounded faster as if to drive him on, ramming into her, emitting loud *thwops* as their soaked bodies collided again and again.

Lani thought she screamed but couldn't be sure. Her blood roared in her ears. Rain ran down her body. The grass burned her back as Kellan drove harder, faster, deeper...

Until he stilled.

Lani dragged her eyes open to have her gaze filled with the burnished beauty of his face, hovering inches over her again. As their breaths tangled, he lowered her ass to the ground. While the grass cooled her thighs, his cock pulsed against her walls. His gaze never left her face. Lani shivered and battled to break the contact. It was too much, this stare of his. Giving her too much. Asking too much in return. This was just supposed to be sex. That was all it ever could be.

But her inner war surged on, turning into torment as he used his hands to inflame her body all over again.

With his gaze still locked in hers, he circled one hand beneath her body. With the other, he found her clit again.

"Kellan!" She shuddered as he pressed a finger against that perfect, tiny button.

"No." His countermand was quiet but firm. "Not yet." He circled his hips, creating a new friction between them. The rain pummeled. The wind pushed. The storm in her sex was sweet and perfect and unbearable. Dear God, she needed to come.

"Kellan, please!"

"Not. Yet." He shifted the hand beneath her. Slowly, he probed the edge of her back entrance with a rain-soaked finger.

"Kellan!"

He slid in a second finger.

As he intensified the pressure on her swollen, needy clit.

As he taunted her with the slow rolls of his hips and the thudding girth of his cock.

As he took her to the brink of ecstasy but refused to yank her over.

She was in hell.

"Now, sweetheart." He pushed hard on the center of her pleasure as he plunged deep with the length of his cock. "*Now.*"

She was in heaven.

Nirvana crashed over her with blinding force, searing her senses, scalding her sex, blinding her mind. Her shriek gained harmony from Kellan's groan, long and violent against her neck as she felt his balls harden, blasting come up his shaft. As he climaxed, he ground harder against her, igniting her passion all over again. The second orgasm shot her out of nirvana and into another dimension. Her eyes went wide, staring in awe as the moon gleamed through the storm, turning the raindrops into stars and the clouds into satyrs.

All except for the one who continued to rock inside her, nuzzling her shoulder with a dark growl. Only when he bit a little harder did she turn her head and realize he was watching her.

"That smile looks damn gorgeous on you, Starshine." He rose over her again, fingering wet strands from her face. "I hope this means you won't toss me out of bed right away."

Though they laughed together, solemnity lingered in his gaze, bringing the feeling that the question wasn't entirely a gibe. It was a little unnerving. A touch confusing. But brought a few tingly butterflies too.

And...she was being a ridiculous female, making more out of all this than she should.

He was a soldier—a well-hung, gasp-worthy one, at that—and no doubt had a woman for every forward base he frequented. Well, she had no problem being his "Kaua☒i cutie." The fringe benefits were nice. Really nice. If she had nothing but a body full of interesting aches and a head full of hot memories when he left for duty again, that would be just fine.

"Tell you what," she murmured, trailing a fingertip over the alluring hills of his top lip. "Why don't we consider getting into a bed first?"

He rumbled through a chuckle. "It's a novelty, but I might be persuaded to try it."

Once more, his sarcasm was laced with a strange erudition, like the words were humorous versions of the truth.

And again, she mentally slapped herself for caring. Like she could afford to "care" for anyone right now—not while being both parents to Leo and battling Benson at every step he made to claim Hale Anelas. But more profoundly, not in the way she'd always dreamed of caring for someone. Not with the devotion she'd witnessed every day growing up, the *mau loa* love that bound Mother and Father every day they were alive and surely united them even tonight.

Mau loa. Forever love. She would settle for nothing less.

But there was more to that truth. She simply wanted too much. She was the first to admit it. Love like that didn't just "happen by chance," despite what the movies propagated. And it certainly didn't tumble onto a woman's beach one night, dressed in nothing but khakis, a wrinkled shirt, and a shit-eating grin.

Even if that grin turned into kisses she'd never forget and two mind-gouging orgasms.

They made their way back to the house dressed in nothing but their laughter, clutching their drenched, muddy clothes. Lani stopped Kellan on the back lanai, listening for a long moment in case Leo had skipped the fencing team's typical postpractice trip to Puka Dog. If that was the case, her brother would still be in the kitchen, having come in the back in his haste for food. All was silent. Seemed the lure of a lava sausage with papaya relish had snared her brother again, so they were in the clear.

Once they were upstairs, she headed straight for her bathroom and turned the shower to a pleasant temperature. Kellan watched her, wrapped in strange silence, as she grabbed two towels from the linen closet. "I give up," she finally admitted. "What's going on in that head of yours, Sergeant?"

He stood in the middle of her vanity area, all her things looking tiny and fragile compared to his imposing nudity, especially as he rammed hands to the ridges of his obliques. "A moment ago, the answer was I'd control myself from getting inside you again, considering we've expended my sole condom on hand. But looking at you like this may force me to get creative."

Thank heavens she'd moved to stand at the counter. Though the towels fell out of her grip, it appeared like she'd purposely plopped them there. "Cr-Creative? Why?"

He pivoted toward her, pulling the bathroom door back open as he did. With another step, he was braced totally behind her, twining her gaze with his in the mirror. Those dark gray depths were right at home against the steely set of his features, which tightened further as he leaned forward. With a low, feral growl, he slid his jaw against hers.

"Spread your legs," he ordered in a whisper. Like she had a choice. He used his feet to nudge hers apart, instantly filling the crevice between her thighs with an erection that had gone from half-mast to full-sail in three seconds. Lani gasped as his cock pushed through the V at the bottom of her ass cheeks and past her intimate entrance, letting his broad tip part her pussy from behind. She watched him do all of it in their reflection, making everything feel more surreal...and sinful.

"Oh, my God," she rasped.

He wrapped an arm around her waist. "You're wet, sweetheart. But so am I." With his other hand, he snared hers and pushed it down. "Feel me. Squeeze my cock. Wipe off my juice with your finger then suck it off."

Holy shit. He really was a satyr. A half-demon warrior sent here from some fantasyland to tempt her down the path of completely nasty acts and wanton ways...because he knew she'd willingly follow.

The thought sang through what was left of her mind as she caressed the knob of his shaft. She whimpered as she found the slit that leaked hot milk at her touch. After collecting the juice as he demanded, she thrust her finger deep into her mouth, prompting a guttural groan of encouragement from behind.

"Good. So damn good, Starshine."

He shoved harder, and she whimpered at watching his swollen red crown surge from the valley of her legs. She reached down and grabbed him again, stroking his throbbing tip. At the same time, he swept up his other hand and pinched one of her nipples. A high yelp burst from her. Kellan quickened his thrusts.

"Look at me again."

She quickly obeyed, filling her vision with his face in the mirror, so dark and intense, twisted in erotic agony. In response, her body shook and wept, engulfed by lust, on fire with need.

"Now touch yourself," he directed. "Do it, Lani. Rub your hard little clit for me."

She obeyed him—with a twist. Instead of using her fingers, she kept her hold on his shaft and rammed it against the ridge of her arousal as a flesh-and-blood vibrator. He gave an approving grunt while his massive thighs quaked against hers. With his eyes still on her in the mirror, he openly bit into her neck. She yelped as her sex came alive, pinged by a million more jolts of awakening. Her vagina clenched. Her pussy pulsed.

"Kellan!" She struggled to keep it from turning into a scream, all too aware they weren't exactly alone.

He answered with another possessive bite, this time on her ear. "My name on your lips turns my cock to stone, sweetheart."

They weren't empty words. His erection was a wand of pure heat against the stiff ridge of her need, coaxing it into higher peaks until there was no way to go but into the hottest fire her body could generate. She gasped and started thrusting back against him. *"Ke 'ale ne ke kai.* Kellan, I'm— I'm going to—"

He took the hand at her breast and swiped it to her forehead, keeping her cheek pinned to his jaw, burning his glorious scruff into her skin. "And I'm going to watch, Starshine. No closing your eyes. Let me see. All of it."

As the waves of euphoria slammed her and pulled her under, a breathtaking smile took over his face. A second later, the look turned into a passionate growl. His teeth clenched as he lifted her a little, high enough for him to release thick white streams of his seed into the sink.

For a long second, their stares held in the mirror while their bodies heaved in unison. For an extended moment, Lani still didn't move. She didn't want to. Her limbs and gaze were tethered in place, locked to him in that steam-clouded make-believe of the mirror. She was bound by the intensity of him. Riveted by the effortless strength of him. Spellbound by the burnished beauty of his form...and the fathoms of feeling in his eyes...

What the hell are you doing? "Fathoms of feeling?" What kind of poetic garbage is that? You don't have time for poetry. Or intensity. Or thinking of this as anything beyond what it is: a pleasant distraction for you both. End of story, Hokulani.

If only he wouldn't keep staring at her like they'd suddenly turned into the last two people on earth.

"I...I need to get into the shower. I still have some work to do tonight."

It wasn't a lie. Before she'd patrolled the beach and found him and Bommer playing the sand flea hustle, she'd sequestered herself in the office trying to determine how to get the bust in the north fence fixed, pay for Leo's next semester at school, and refile the permits to reopen the B and B. She'd been pondering a hitch over to Honolulu with Jean-Paul on the sea plane. Maybe the authorities there weren't in Gunter's back pocket, and she'd be able to bypass the mess that the man had created for her with the hospitality-permits office here. Dear God, she hoped so...

But that meant jerking herself away from stupid mirrors and the beautiful satyrs in them and forcing herself back to real life again.

Luckily—perhaps eerily—Kellan seemed to understand that. "You got coffee around? I'll be looking after T, so it'll be a long night for both of us. I can brew a pot."

"Thanks." She smiled in lieu of kissing him again. Gods only knew where that would lead. Being around the man was starting to translate into a deep need to touch him—and more.

Dangerous thoughts. Tendencies she couldn't germinate for another second.

Yep. Time for office sequestration again. A dose of reality would do her good, at least until the next time she could let Kellan carry her off into a perfect pretense of happiness for another treasured hour or two.

CHAPTER SEVEN

Tait groaned. It hurt. Well, no shit. When one's mouth had been turned into the Sahara, vocal action of any kind was doomed to be torture. That didn't excuse the camel who'd decided to stomp on his head. To make things feel better, he fantasized about pulling out a rifle and blowing the animal's head off. Which would do nothing, because camels were malicious sons of bitches who would survive the nuclear holocaust along with cockroaches and reality-TV stars.

A sound seeped into his senses, flipping his daydreams like card tables. A voice...feminine yet a little feral...throaty and sultry threaded into a music he longed to hear better. He'd recognized it, didn't he? How? From where?

The woman laughed. More sexy-husky. Lots more. *Fuck*. He *had* heard that sound before.

You going soft on me, Weasley? Seriously?

His eyes flew open. Sunshine blinded him. His chest imploded on itself.

"Luna." Why was it just a scrape on the air? He swallowed, struggling for moisture to blurt it louder, but his jaw and mouth *really* hurt. Everything hurt. God*damn*, that light was bright. Maybe it wasn't the sun at all. Maybe he'd finally succeeded at drinking himself to death and was now locked in some weird ether between heaven and hell. Maybe his crazy little woman was taunting him, just to get him moving again. And damn it, she was right.

You're asking for one hell of a red ass, aren't you, beautiful? Believe me, it'll be my pleasure to deliver, once I catch you again...

The woman, beyond the pale blue walls that met his gaze, had the nerve to laugh louder. She was instantly shushed. The silence police had a man's timbre. "Slash?" He forced his head up. Damn it, someone needed to turn off the room's spin cycle. Hardwood floors, potted plants, and wicker furniture mashed together in his vision. "Fuuuck..."

"T?" Kellan appeared, though he was sideways. Tait blinked, fighting to keep focus as his friend crouched down. "Welcome back to the land of the living."

"Yeah. Thanks." He lowered his head, realizing that it sank against a pillow that smelled like verbena and coconut. Some compassionate soul had draped him in a blanket that smelled the same. Kell would do a lot of things for him, but the tuck-tuck action with the great-smelling linens? Not a chance.

"Where am I? This isn't Franz's place."

Kellan chuckled. "Were you that obliterated last night?"

He managed to wobble his head, hoping it passed for a shake. "Just hurts to think." After a coarse grunt, he muttered, "We were on the beach. You threw my bottle away. And then we wrestled and—"

Fuck.

The memory gutted his voice. Filled his mind. Drowned him in desire. The cascade of black hair kissed by lavender lights. The wildcat-bright eyes. The body a man would commit major crimes for. But more than anything, the flame of inner spirit *his* soul recognized at once...a fire he hadn't experienced since one intense week in LA, during one of the most life-changing missions of his career...

A spark that flickered, hesitant but bright, deep inside him once more...

Especially as she walked into the room.

Tait swallowed hard against a mix of anguish and exhilaration. *She isn't Luna, you hungover dickbrain.* His mind rammed it as a command, and his gut finally, reluctantly obeyed. He'd scattered Luna's ashes over Puget Sound himself, for fuck's sake. Nothing—*nobody*—was going to magically nullify that fact.

Hokulani. His mind made it past the haze of last night to recall her name. He'd fiddled around with enough of the South Pacific dialects during language training to realize the last half of it meant "heavenly." Though that little tidbit had escaped him last night, he still remembered thinking how he'd stared at her with dreamy fixation, considering the word perfect for her.

Bommer, you're a fucking cheese bag.

Funny, how much fortitude a man could get from booze in one moment—and how much regret a few hours later.

Okay, maybe more than a few hours.

He glanced out the window next to the couch. The palms and banyans swayed in a gentle breeze. Cotton ball clouds lazed in the sky. The squalls of yesterday had given way to golden sunshine, though the shadows indicated it was somewhere between sunrise and noon.

"Shit," he mumbled. "How long was I out?"

"About thirteen hours," Kellan supplied.

"What the hell?" He shoved to an upright position. The room played shake, rattle, and roll again, but that didn't stop him from whacking Kell's shoulder. "Why the hell didn't you wake me up, asswipe?"

"Because I wouldn't let him."

The assertion came from the woman who now stood at the other end of the couch, arms folded and lips pursed. Her hair was piled into a cute bun with chopstick thingies poking from it, and she wore a flowery sundress with a built-in bra that pushed her breasts into better position than her damn bikini had. T tried not to fixate on how those incredible mounds were positioned in the scoop of the dress, so perfect for someone to just reach in and coax them into erection, before pinching hard and delighting in her squeal...

He dropped his line of vision to her knees, but even those were beautiful. Though the dress covered her to midthigh, he saw more than enough to remind him of the cocoa cream curves beneath...especially if a guy could envision those gorgeous legs wrapped high around his waist, encouraging him to go deeper as he sank his dick deep and—

Think of something else.

He'd be fine in a second, as long as she didn't start tapping one of those adorable feet with the turquoise toe polish adorned with little white flowers. The toe-tapping was always Luna's thing. If the goddess started it, too, he really wouldn't be responsible for his headspace anymore.

"I wouldn't let him because clearly you needed some sleep." No toe taps. Thank fuck. But hell, the way she shifted from one foot to the other, ending with a confident hip pop, might have been just as unbalancing. "And I'm the boss of the house."

Kellan flashed a glance that teetered on an eye roll. "Yep. She's the boss."

"Hey." She made the word a reprimand while jamming her toe into Kell's thigh, toppling him over. Tait watched in wordless wonder while his friend snickered up at her. He turned his stare back at Hokulani.

Who are you and what have you done with the tight-ass I call a partner? He looks a lot like this bozo here...?

"So I crashed on your couch all night?" he asked instead.

"Wasn't like it was an inconvenience," she murmured with a small smile. "Especially after the way you threw yourself at Gunter's gang for me."

A confused frown hunkered his brows. In weird chunks, the rest of last night's events flashed back to him. The Escalades. The pretty pouts. The shitloads of hair product. All Benson and his goons had been missing was their fashion ramp. It had been a funny joke at the time—until he'd goaded them all on.

"Damn," he muttered. It all returned to him now. The pretty boy's name had been Casey. He'd goaded the kid into punching him first, and had made sure Casey would go home by way of the ER, before the rest of the pack descended on him. He didn't remember too much more after that, likely a good thing. "Guess that'll teach me to pull the Rambo act."

Hokulani laughed and took his hand. "Rambo's a guy in a movie with five stunt doubles, Sergeant. What you did was real-life bravery, and I'm grateful."

Before he could think of how to react, the strange flicker of an expression on Kell's face distracted him—but it disappeared quickly as it came. His friend stood again. "You hungry, man? Lani made this killer scramble shit with eggs, Spam, bacon, and pineapple. Good stuff. There's still a lot left."

Lani?

"Yeah." He scowled again, feeling like he'd been thrust into the middle of an ongoing op without proper intel. His senses, trained to gather every speck of data they could, started firing on all cylinders again, but his mind didn't have any grid to process anything on. "Yeah, uhhh, that sounds good. Thanks."

"Cool." Lani beamed like she'd just been asked to serve her Spam eggs to the president. "I'll be right back."

Kellan smiled at her. "I can help, sweets."

Sweets?

Kell barely tolerated foreplay. What the hell was he doing, tossing around a word like *sweets*?

Despite how the room spun again, making the rocks in his head tumble into new piles of pain, he swung his legs out and then stood. He barely suppressed a groan while fighting the urge to sink back to the couch. But he'd learned a thousand new forms of fortitude in the last six months, and those lessons came in handy now. He had to keep an eye on Kell. He loved the man as equally as he loved his biological brother, but he also knew Kell as well as Shay—in a few ways, perhaps better. What was the guy's game here, and why was he running it on a jewel like Hokulani Kail? She wasn't his type. Correction: she was out of his league.

He moved across the living and dining rooms as quietly as he could, drawn closer to the kitchen door by the cadence of a warm conversation. Kellan's distinct timbre was balanced by the velvet of Hokulani's tone, sprinkled with the soft rasps of her laughter. He stopped for a second, just listening to the sound. *Damn.* A laugh like that could keep a man going in a shitty gun battle, inspire him to survive torture, keep his ass moving under horrendous mission conditions. It was a sound made for pillow talk and private jokes—

And for prefacing the kind of kiss that Kellan placed on her neck now.

Tait pushed open the kitchen door to observe them in profile, with Kell pressing himself against Lani's back as she scooped eggs from a skillet. He pressed both hands against the fronts of her thighs, using the grip to fit both gorgeous globes of her ass against his crotch. His head dipped against her neck, and he'd apparently gone in for teeth action on the nuzzle, since she gave a protesting squeal before giggling again. Kellan mumbled something to her, though Tait didn't hear it past the sudden, raging thunder in his ears.

He shoved on the door. It slammed against the wall with a *whap*. The pair at the stove snapped their heads up like a pair of new boot camp nuggets caught sleeping in, eyes wide and mouths open.

"T-Bomb. You okay?"

Was the man expecting an honest answer to that? When all Tait wanted to do was haul his skanky ass from the woman and send him flying across the breakfast bar?

"You fucked her."

Hokulani set the plate down with a clatter. "Excuse me?"

Kellan stroked her back gently. The action spoke volumes. Significant ones. The fury thickened at the corners of Tait's vision. In so many ways, he realized this didn't make sense. In so many more, it made all the sense in the world.

"I'm going to echo that," Kell stated. "Tait, what're you so—"

"You fucked her." He bellowed it this time. "On the first goddamn night you met her, you fucked her. Yes or no, Slash the magical man slut?"

Kell's jaw turned to steel. His eyes darkened to the same color. "That was uncalled for, man. I'm being nothing short of brutally honest here, with Lani *and* myself. Even so, I don't see what happened last night, while you were in an alcoholic stupor, has to do with—"

"It has to do with *everything*, you moron. With a woman like her"—he forced his gaze to lock on Kellan, certain he'd be searching for Hokulani's Bowie knife again if he even glimpsed her right now—"you don't get to be 'brutally honest.' You *don't* get to compartmentalize!" *Shit.* He was pissed enough to get physical. The hard teak of the nearest cabinet door sent a nice slice of pain through the fist he pounded into it. "You don't put her in a box like the rest of your crotch bunnies!"

"Crotch bunnies?" Hokulani huffed hard. "Okay, hold on—"

"Can't you fucking see that?" He wheeled back toward Kell with locked teeth. "Can't you see that she—"

"Is standing right here?" The shout came with her brutal shove into the middle of his chest. "And *she* can think and speak for herself?" She kept on going, flattening him against the cabinet he'd just punched.

Kellan didn't miss the chance to level a gratified grunt from across the kitchen, making Tait pitch forward again. "You disgusting pussy player! You'll run any game to make sure your sausage gets extra juice, huh?"

Hokulani dug her palm harder into his sternum. "Back off, Sergeant. Now!"

That order apparently didn't apply to Kellan. The guy John Wayne'd it across the room, shoulders back and hands splayed. "You know, T, I want to laugh at that. I have nothing to hide from anyone here about the sincerity of my motives, but are you going to even listen?" He tossed a head-to-toe stare over Tait. "Consider who the fuck is talking here—just who the fuck is throwing down about the cock leading the walk."

"Shut your hole. You have no clue what you're talking about!"

"Except that I was the guy who almost shot a soldier on *our* side, because you freaked about saving a woman who only *looked* like Luna." Finally halted by Hokulani's other hand, Kell released something that was half gloating chuckle, half derisive grunt. "You lost your grip in Indonesia, Bommer. It's the whole goddamn reason we're here."

"Hmm." Hokulani's interjection came with a purposeful stare swung toward Kellan, her brows arched in sensual intent. "Then maybe I need to be thanking him for the breakdown."

"I'm not broken," Tait snarled. He tore from beneath her hold. "And *he's* not someone you want to be gushing over like that."

Kellan bristled. "In case you weren't listening, the woman can think for herself."

"Fuck you, Slash-aroni."

"Damn it." Kell restarted the cowboy swagger. "That's it!"

"Stop!" The woman between them—literally and figuratively—rammed the guy back against the refrigerator. Tait backpedaled into the dining room, and Hokulani's stance straddled the doorway between the two rooms. "Okay, look. Your concern is appreciated, Sergeant Bommer. But the last time I checked, I was a grown woman with a mind of my own. And you weren't my father *or* my brother."

Kell snorted. "Want that ass served in a cup or cone, man?"

"Shut up," she countered. "You're not off the hook, mister."

"But—"

"Shut. Up."

It was too damn easy for Tait to cut loose a snide snort too. "What was that, dude? About 'ass'? You are, after all, the king of nailing it in every city we hit."

The woman in front of him pulled up on her posture. Just like that, she was every inch the imposing goddess who'd first had him gaping in awe last night on the beach. "Your welcome in my home has expired, Sergeant Bommer." She raised her gaze, sucking him straight in with the amazing blue silver of her irises—the same eyes that openly condemned him now. "While I'm grateful for what you did for me last night, I won't be labeled a piece of ass beneath my own roof."

Heat detonated across his face. "Shit. I didn't mean— It had nothing to do with you!"

"So if you'd come in and not found Kellan and me together, you'd still be singing his praises as the magical man slut?"

The image she brought up, of her and Kell pulling the goo-goo-mushy at the stove, brought a fresh mix of inexplicable rage. "Goddamnit, Hokulani. You deserve better than what he—"

Kell's roar cut him off. "Bommer, for fuck's sake, let it go!"

He ripped out a fresh glower at the man. "Are you capable of staying out of this conversation for two seconds?"

"Stop." It was a tight utterance from Hokulani, which Kell easily ignored.

"Are *you* capable of keeping your head straight and seeing her without your fantasies wound in?"

"Fantasies?" He pushed forward again. "I *buried* Luna, you asshat. My 'fantasies' got dissolved when I watched the waves swallow her ashes. I don't get the luxury of fantasies anymore!"

"All right," Lani charged again, "*stop*."

"Is that so?" Kell cocked his head. "So what do I have to blame for the shitty shot you called in Indonesia, huh? Simple dumbass-ery? Did you watch the waves swallow your brain, too?"

"Damn it!" Her voice now broke the air on a scream. "I said stop!"

Tait was one move ahead of her. He turned and let his head drop, unconcerned if his "buddy" witnessed the defeat in the move. Like Kell would care. The guy had a caustic streak; Tait had always known that, though never imagined he'd be on the receiving end of it. But Rebel Stafford, the team's resident southern boy philosopher, had a favorite expression. *If the chair's too comfy, wait five minutes.*

Who knew it applied to friendships, too?

He should be grateful for what life *had* given him with Kell. Tait had joined the army to justify his existence, to find the purpose Dad always said he never had. Getting one of the closest buddies of his life had been an added bonus of the journey, one he'd never expected to keep this long. He wasn't the kind of person people stuck around for. Dad had been tenacious about *that* lesson too.

Behind him, Hokulani's hisses peppered the air. Since he'd stomped his way back to the living room, he couldn't discern what she said. Kell's comeback was a clear crack, though.

"What? *He* started it, damn it."

Tait clamped down the urge to bellow a retort. He turned the indignation inward instead—and muttered the words during his march toward the front door.

"Fine, asshole. I started it. And you can deal with me ending it too."

★ ★ ★ ★ ★

After he slammed out of the house, it'd been painfully

ANGEL PAYNE

apparent that he had no fucking clue about his bearings. He
didn't want to calm down long enough to think much about it,
either. Flashbacks from last night gave up images of a bamboo
walkway and some rosebushes, neither of which were visible
from the front of the house. That left him with a choice between
a long paved driveway to the main road or a packed dirt truck
trail that bordered a huge paddock containing several dozen
horses lazing their way through the July day.

In his state of mind, animal therapy felt like the right
way to go. Besides, the trail was drenched in shade as the sun
rapidly neared its high point. The decision was a good one; the
pastoral peace buffed out the edges of his rage within a few
minutes. A few times, the horses daring to meet his gaze were
rewarded with a small smile.

It didn't take him long to start understanding Hokulani's
fierce devotion to this place. With the small mountain that
cushioned one side and the thick forest along the other, the
property was a self-contained paradise where the grass grew
thick, the flowers scented the air, and the wind blew warm.
What had she called it? *Hale Anelas*. Again accessing distant
knowledge from language training, he knew that meant the
home of something. His money was on something like fairies,
gods, or angels—creatures that turned this land into something
truly magical and serene.

Though whoever gashed the air with their angry bellow
might have an argument about that.

Tait heard the shout as he cleared the corner of the
pasture and planned on returning to the beach through the
grove of banana, mango, and breadfruit trees ahead. Instead,
his attention was tugged to the right, where he caught sight
of more fencing, this time the border of a small riding corral.

The sound of rapid hoof beats preceded the spirited swish of a dark-tan horse's tail, which brushed the fence once before disappearing.

More cantering. A heavy thud, like something hitting the ground hard. Another violent yell was followed by a youth's voice spewing the F-word. Then again.

The situation suddenly earned itself a little recon.

Tait walked along the edge of the barn until he could see the whole corral. When he did, his curious frown grew to a full scowl.

He would have attached a laugh to the look if not for his concern about the agitated Palomino filly skittering around the enclosure. Following the filly—correction, *chasing* the animal—with a lead rope and training pole was a lanky teenager who shared Hokulani's striking eyes and full mouth. The boy also had thick black hair in a spiky short cut that showed off his strong neck and jaw.

Tait sheltered no doubt that the kid was related in some way to the goddess back at the house. It was just a shame that he didn't share Hokulani's smarts.

"Fuck!" the kid spat again. "Damn it, I'm trying to help your ass here!"

"Do you kiss your mama with that mouth, boy?"

The kid lurched to his feet and flung a dagger of a glare. "My mother's dead, asshole, so back off."

Since they were skipping down the path of childhood traumas, Tait let his own act as advisor for a reaction. He envisioned Uncle Jonah appearing and scratching his cheek with that aw-shucks smile before issuing advice along the lines of getting a pissy 'coon to come around faster with a muffin than a stick. Damn what he wouldn't give for just one day with the man again.

"My mom's gone, too," he said softly. *And I'd give a row of teeth to find her again.* "So I get it."

The kid straightened the pole and rope, preparing to make another try for the horse's obedience. "You don't get shit, Sergeant Bommer, so don't try your army Jedi mind tricks on me. I'm not some dumbshit foreign hostile."

He held back another laugh—barely. "Could've fooled me," he mumbled through a smirk.

"*What* the hell'd you say?" the kid accused.

A verbal muffin was in order. "How do you know who I am?" The casual simulation came easy, since he and Kell had used it on Benson's boys last night.

The kid rolled his eyes. "You think I came home to find one guy krunked-up in my living room and the other napping on the office couch with my sister and not find out who the fuckers are?"

That brought a confused pause. Kellan likely had a wallet in tow last night, but the only things *he'd* carried from Franz's place were his shirt, shorts, and the flock of geese on his vodka bottle. "By reading my 'krunked-up' mind?" he finally challenged.

"By using my sober one." The kid didn't take his eyes off the filly. Thank God he got *that* part of the process right. "Rush's ID gave me a clue about both of you. For you, I snapped a shot on my phone and texted it to Franz for a positive check. He was very helpful with the positive scope...and a few backup details too."

Tait's gut clenched by the way the boy emphasized the last of that. "Wonderful," he mumbled, just as the kid took advantage of a break in the horse's attention to try to slip the lead rope around her neck again. Not a chance. The filly bucked at him, causing him to take another textbook ass plant. Tait couldn't hold back his chuckle any longer. "Franz may have given you some dirt on me, kid, but in the filth department, I'd say we're even."

"Fuck you!"

"Strike that. You officially take the scum crown now." He cocked a brutally placid stare back through the corral slats. "It's Leo, right? Aren't you supposed to be going to some fancy academy? They let you spew filthy language like that at your special school, Leo?"

"They let you turn into a pussy like *that* in Spec Ops, Sergeant? Aren't you used to much worse than this?"

Considering the morning he'd already endured, the kid's Prince Snotty act should've made him leave and let the idiot earn a hoof—or four—in the face. The sooner he left this place behind, with all memories of the blood-heating, soul-stirring woman back at the house, the better. But because of her, he turned toward the barn instead. He remembered Benson taunting Lani by invoking the legacy of both her parents, so Leo was the only family she had. If he left the kid to tame the filly and Leo wound up with a serious brain injury because of his stupidity, Tait would never excuse himself. And the list of unforgivable shit in his life was too damn long already.

As he'd hoped, he found some sets of extra boots sitting in the corner near the barn door. Barbecue bonus: several pairs of jeans hanging on some pegs on the wall. That made sense, considering the island's humid weather didn't make it tolerable to drag down one's legs in denim for hours.

He found some boots in his size and a pair of jeans that were close. Though the pants fit low on his hips, they'd get the job done.

After changing his shorts for the jeans, he walked back out to the corral. Leo didn't miss his cue to let out a mocking grunt. "You trying out for a romance novel photo shoot in those jeans?"

He moved on without pausing, stepping up on the fence and then swinging a leg over. "And do *you* want to get this horse in a bridle today or not?"

Leo's eyes went wide. Well gee fucking whillikers, the boy actually seemed surprised—and humbled. "Yeah," he stammered. "Yeah, I do."

"Then shut up and listen."

A huge slice of the kid's attitude slid away as he stepped back. "Her name is Isis."

He allowed a smile to slip free. "One of the most important goddesses of all time."

Leo rolled his eyes again, though the action came with humor more than attitude. "Well, it fits. And she knows it." As he extended the pole to Tait, a full crack appeared in his veneer. Beyond it was a core of pure tenderness. "I've been trying to get this around her neck for weeks. She doesn't get the pressure that's on. If she isn't fully saddle-trained by the time Benson gets his claws into this place, he'll sell her to the glue factory along with the others."

He didn't waste time on challenging the kid's assumption. Even if the literal translation of the statement wasn't accurate, real fear underlined Leo's words. After a few minutes with Gunter Benson last night, Tait couldn't blame the kid. The man carried a "concern" for the land only as far as it served him. If Isis wasn't pulling her weight—or slogging it up and down the beach in use to the resort—she *would* be sold, perhaps to a fate worse than a glue factory.

"You hang on to that," he said, indicating the pole. "You're going to be just as much a part of this, if you want the lesson to stick."

Leo nodded eagerly. "Good plan. So maybe you'll distract her while I sneak up and—"

He smacked the kid on the side of his well-groomed head. "Did you look up how to do this on YouTube or something?" He chuffed when the deep blush on Leo's face supplied that answer. "Did you research how to date girls on there, too?"

"Fuck no!"

"Then what made you think you could learn to win *this* girl like that?"

He let Leo stew about that while he walked around so Isis could see him. He took gentle, slow steps. The horse snorted, stamped a hoof, and backed away. He followed her with his head bent low, hands at his sides. When Isis stopped, he dropped to a knee, letting her sniff the air to get used to his presence.

"What the hell are you doing?" Leo charged.

Tait turned his head up, letting the filly watch his soft movements. He picked his reply to the boy with care. He had no idea what Franz had disclosed about him, though he doubted that his captain, who was a fellow and regular Dominant at their favorite BDSM dungeon back home, would've disclosed that morsel about Tait's personality. Nevertheless, many of the tenets of this situation could be culled directly from the beginning stages of a loving and honest D/s relationship. Not that he'd possessed any desire to exercise those principles lately.

"Tell me something," he began. "When you're going in for

the major impression on a girl, like wanting her to beg you for the goodnight kiss in a few hours, what are the most important steps to consider?"

"Well, you gotta have swagger," the boy asserted. "Impress her with your moves, your mojo."

Tait exercised his turn for the eye roll now. He leaned over and let the idiot have the full, dismayed impact of it. "Seriously?"

"Uh...yeah. What the hell's wrong with—"

"Dude, if *you* were a girl and saw Leo Kail sauntering into the room with that 'tude, would *you* be dreaming of some lip action?" He let the teen mull that over as he swiveled to face Isis again. Gently, he reached up to stroke the animal's muzzle with the backs of his knuckles. "Before a guy locks you in a harness, you just want to know you can trust him, don't you, girl?" He kept his voice low, his touch respectful. "You want to be sure he's going to treat you right. That your obedience gets you a nice reward."

He pulled his hand away. Stretched into half a crouch and stepped back a little.

Isis trailed him by a slow step, dipping her head and pushing at him for more.

"Fuck," Leo uttered. "That's...amazing."

Tait chuckled and shook his head. "That's just showing our girl how valuable her compliance is." He turned his hand over, rubbing her with the flat of his palm. "You *want* to be good, don't you, baby? You simply need to feel safe when you are."

Just as quietly, Leo walked back over. An amazed smile curved the kid's lips, and he ran a reverent hand down the horse's neck. "Wow. You did that in, like, five minutes."

Tait gave the kid a friendly shoulder clap. "Couldn't have without the foundation you clearly built. You just needed a few pointers on closing the deal." As Isis emitted a fluttering sigh, he instructed, "I'm going to step back again. Try the lead line now."

He made good on his word. Though Isis gave a little protesting nicker, she only jerked at the lead line a few times. Leo soothed her with soft tongue clicks and praising murmurs. "Good girl. That's my beauty."

"Nice," Tait complimented. "You're doing great, man."

His chest warmed with a duality of sensation when Leo sent a grin of thanks. It was incredible to connect with the boy, to watch him accomplish an important goal because he got smart and listened. But "torture session" got a cruel new meaning with every glance at Leo's smile and noticing every stunning similarity it shared with his sister. The deep dimples. The slight lift higher on the left side of his mouth, lending a mischievous air. The compassion in those silvery-bright eyes that spoke volumes about what the kid had already been through in life. Yeah, that one, especially. He and Shay shared a similar glint in their gazes.

Damn. *Damn.*

Had he been sent to this island and plopped next door to the woman as a blessing or a curse? Was Hokulani a sign to him or a punishment for him? And what good did it do to agonize over the answers? He wouldn't be seeing the woman anymore. He couldn't stand by and watch Slash slick her up with his Romeo act when the guy planned on carrying the whole plot through to its crap-fest of an end, figurative as it would be, in two weeks. *Here's to my love! O, true apothecary; thy drugs are quick! Thus with a kiss I die...*

Gag.

"Bommer!"

Leo's eager whisper drew him back. He was glad to do so. They both held their breaths as Isis, remaining remarkably still, allowed the kid to fit the simple rope head-collar on. "Fucking awesome," he stated. "Good job, Leo."

"Aha." The kid chuckled as he rewarded the filly with ample caresses. "I knew you had at least one decent F-bomb in there somewhere."

Tait huffed. "I've been known to indulge from time to time."

"So...uhhh...speaking of indulging..."

"Yeah?" He didn't hide his suspicious tone, though he allowed Leo to see the teasing smirk he attached.

"Does this psychobabble shit really work on girls, too?"

CHAPTER EIGHT

This wasn't right.

Lani was as sure of that truth as she was of the air in her lungs, the beat of her heart—and the tension that hadn't left Kellan's eyes in the last three days. Seventy-two hours in which he'd chosen to remain at Hale Anelas instead of going back to Franz's place to smooth things out with Tait. The brief trip he'd taken yesterday for some fresh clothes hadn't counted, especially because he deliberately took it after Leo announced he was meeting Tait for a horse ride up the coast, ensuring an "all clear" status for Kellan's trip.

The whole situation troubled her. Even more upsetting was when logic stepped in, telling her it shouldn't. The guys had only a little over a week left here, and then it would be a miracle if either of them returned to the island. Why should it matter to her if their friendship was bashed beyond repair and they chose to torpedo it *and* their careers in the names of pride and pigheadedness?

But even after her brief time with the men together, she knew the answer to that too.

They were better than this.

They were *worth* more than this.

Franzen had known it when he'd moved the army's version of heaven and earth, then tossed in the keys to his family home, to give them this opportunity at repair. If their captain knew what was really happening instead, what would he do?

She'd tried posing that question to Kellan last night at dinner but received his version of a shutdown—which was to drop beneath the table, spread her legs, tear her panties free, and declare he was in the mood for a different kind of "tasty meal." After his tongue had taken her body apart in a million orgasmic pieces, he'd dragged her to the floor, growling how he intended to make her scream for dessert. She'd done just that—three more times. *Shit, shit, shit.* If the man insisted on having the maturity of a fourteen-year-old, was it necessary that he possess the sex drive of one, too?

Because the mind-blowing sex didn't confuse things enough, their physical chemistry wasn't the only perk of having the man around all the time. Crazy, what happened when a girl owned a house with fifteen rooms and had the Energizer bunny hanging around, ready to screw her in all of them. With every new space they visited in his sexy version of a property tour, Kellan was also swift to notice everything that needed repairing there. Within the next hour, she'd hear him hammering, power drilling, tinkering, or even cursing his way through the fix. If she came in to see what was happening, he'd simply flash that stomach-flipping grin and give her a cocky wink before throwing his focus back into the work.

She'd left him doing exactly that to a ceiling fan in one of the upstairs guest rooms, tripling her guilt about lying to him when she left. It hadn't been a total fib; she really did run to the bank and the grocery store. Could she help it if Franz's place was on the way home and she had an extra bag of groceries thanks to some good sales? Could she also help it if Kellan hadn't been here since his ride over a day ago, nudging her a tad over the "reasonably worried" line about Tait? The guy *had* been riding with Leo a few times, but they had to skip the outing today due to Leo's fencing match. That left a lot of hours open for Tait to drink himself into another stupor—a potentially dangerous one, judging from Kell's assessment of how frequently the guy had been hitting the juice lately.

She rang the doorbell and knocked.

Three times each.

Damn. Either Tait wasn't here or really was shitfaced again. Both theories compelled her to fish out her own key to the place. Since she and Leo came over often to check on things for Franz, she could let herself in with one easy turn.

As she crossed the living room, she peered around in wonder. Though Tait had been the only guy actually living here, she expected the place to resemble the wake of a hurricane. Every day, Leo demonstrated the housekeeping nightmare even one male could create.

A deeper frown took over. While the minimal mess was a pleasant change, her perusal didn't include a Sergeant Bommer sighting, either. The three bedrooms and den, all reflecting the Franzen family's taste in comfortable island décor, were also empty.

She moved into the kitchen to put away the groceries. Still no sign of the man.

Checking her phone confirmed the time, four o'clock, which meant she'd been gone nearly an hour. She estimated she had another fifteen to twenty minutes before Kellan started his protective freak-out, so that was how long she'd wait too.

Or...maybe not. What were her intentions if Tait showed up? She couldn't shoot the breeze about the weather, which had been eighty and unchanged since the storm three nights ago. If she started to meddle, would the men appreciate it or resent it? Was she plowing her nose somewhere it didn't belong?

Just when she'd decided on a *yes* in answer to that question, car tires crunched on gravel outside. As the engine cut, Lani pulled in a breath with the intent of calming herself, but her choppy exhalation accomplished the opposite.

She stood in the middle of the living room, attention on the front door. And waited for what felt like an eternity.

"Hokulani?"

"Ahhh!"

Her yelp filled the room. Though his inquiry was quiet, its issuance from three feet *behind* her was as startling as a scorpion.

"Are you okay?"

"I will be after my heart climbs out of my throat." She stepped back before she could help herself. The shock of his ninja-style entrance from the lanai was only half the cause. His utter resplendence formed the other half. Even in board shorts that fit him way too well and a blue V-neck tee that hugged his body even better, the man seemed like a half-god sent from another realm. His gaze matched the late afternoon sun for depth. His hair, a little better combed today, still made her fingers tingle to touch it. And his mouth, luscious and smiling... *Ohhhh no. Too dangerous. Don't go there.* No use studying the strong column of his neck, either. Or how the masses of his biceps pushed from the short sleeves of his shirt. Or how those shorts defined things so perfectly from his waist down...

Thank God *he* wasn't at a sudden loss for words.

"Sorry." He gave up an awkward laugh, betraying how much he meant it. "When I saw the unfamiliar car outside, I had no idea who was here."

"So you decided to get the badass warrior jump on them."

Teasing him brought back a welcome wave of control.

He grinned. "Something like that."

A longer-than-comfortable silence descended. She glanced up, only to see that his stare was just as fixed on her as before. So much for regaining composure. "So." She twisted her lips. "Are you okay?"

"You're stealing my lines, dreamgirl."

Oh God. He hadn't forgotten his drunken nickname for her. And just her luck, it sounded much better when he was sober. Dangerously better. Low and silken and...intimate.

How the hell could the man be amazed that his partner had gotten horizontal with her inside a couple of hours? Kellan probably learned the technique from *him*. It was all she could do not to fantasize about letting him croon that word again, down the length of her neck. In her ear. Against her lips...her breasts...her abdomen...and lower...

You are going to hell, Hokulani. And your panties are going to be soaked when you get there, thanks to your wicked yearnings for two men at the same time.

She needed to refocus. Fast. Needed to think of boring things like...paying the bills. Cleaning out the storm gutters. Picking snails off the rosebushes. Going to the bank and fending off Dexter Greene's skeevy invitations for dinner. Grocery shopping.

"Groceries!" she blurted.

"Excuse me?" Tait exposed his crooked canine in a curious half smile.

"That's...errrm...why I—" While nodding toward the kitchen, she nervously twisted the ends of her summer scarf. "I just had some extra groceries and stopped by to share."

"You had 'extra groceries'? With a kid like Leo in the

house?"

She winced. "All right, you got me. Maybe I was checking in on you. Just a little."

Only when he chuckled again did she realize she was tensing for a different reaction. Based on what she knew of Franz, these Special Forces men were stubborn, prideful, and secretive. The traits weren't character flaws; they were job essentials. By coming here, she'd pushed at the first two and shattered the third with Tait. But the man actually smiled wider before replying to her.

"Guess I can't blame you, after the sloppy first impression I gave."

"Or the fight you had with your best friend the morning after?" she countered. "Because of me?"

His smile dissolved. "You think *you* caused this?" He shook his head. "Stop it. Right now. This is a bigger mess than what you see, Hokulani. It started before we got here. *Way* before."

She let a meaningful pause go by. "It started with Luna?"

His jaw went granite hard. "He told you about her?"

"Only because I asked." She caught him by the forearm as he wheeled toward the lanai. "You called me by her name," she blurted, "when you were still blotto on my couch. But you sounded so tormented, so I had to know."

"Now you do." He grabbed her fingers with his free hand and pushed them away. "Happy?"

She let him escape to the porch. After he'd stood out there a long minute, his posture so proud but his profile tautening by the second, she walked out to join him. "What is it about me," she finally asked with soft care, "that brings her back for you?"

He snapped his head at her. Grief, desperation, and

confusion flashed out from his gaze. "Nice follow-up, lady. Was Slash not so inclined to answer it, or did you want to save it for this special occasion?"

She let his words fall into another long silence. At last she asserted, "You're off the clock here, Sergeant. There's no answer required. I never asked Kellan to answer that, nor are you required to."

He pulled in an unsteady breath. "So...how'd you even know to ask it? Is there some cool mind-reading algorithm out there these days? Maybe a magical quiz in *Cosmo*, Just How Fucked Up *is* the Guy Next Door?"

She attempted an empathic smile while moving out to the railing. It faded as she neared him. His bitterness was a thin front for the loneliness that palpably rolled off of him, jerking hard at the center of her chest. Too bad he wouldn't be on the island long enough to know that "magic" wasn't a word one tossed around so casually on Kaua`i—in the good *and* bad ways. She'd experienced enough of both to know.

"When my parents were still alive and the B and B was running, we'd sometimes have movie stars who came to stay." She relayed it while gazing over the Franzens' little garden, with the gate to the beach path decorated with hand-painted pictures from the kids through the years. The flagstone trail led between two dunes to the ocean, full of azure tranquility today. "You look at me like Leo used to gawk at the celebrities. Like I'm not real. It gets worse when I stand a certain way. It gets *really* bad when I yell at you."

He stunned her by setting a laugh free. "Yeah. That makes sense." The next moment, he grimaced again. The look hardened before he stalked away a couple of steps. "My beauty always loved yelling at me."

Lani chose respectful silence once more, though the restraint was agonizing. The sight of his spine, so stiff in his inner struggle, made her long to run and press herself there, wrapping as much of her comfort around him as she could. She yearned to pull his grief out of him if only for a little while...

When she teetered on giving into the impulse, he turned around. He'd pulled out his phone and swiped the screen as he walked back over. Without a word, he set it down on the table, exposing the home picture.

Lani gasped.

With the exception of the dyed streaks in her hair and the enviable figure with the lithe legs, the woman could be her sister. The photo's smiling subject even had luminous, near-silver eyes.

"Sorry," he murmured. "Guess I haven't been subtle with the oh-god-a-ghost gawks, though maybe you understand now."

"Just a little." She didn't pull back on the sarcasm. "This is...a little weird."

"You think?" His matching irony brought a surprising dose of comfort. "I hope this also explains why I went all John McClane on Kell the other morning."

She slanted him a wry smirk. "While Kellan *is* as hot as Alan Rickman, it's understandable."

He blinked at her. "You know I have to officially fall down and worship you now. You actually got the *Die Hard* reference."

"Duh. I live with a sixteen-year-old male. Besides"—she lifted her brows expectantly—"at the risk of being dork fangirl at large, that movie has *Alan Rickman.*"

He grimaced again, this time in a way that made her giggle. "Really? He was always the bad guy."

"Watch it! Snape was *not* the bad guy."

Their moment of humored relief was just that, a moment. His mien descended back into grim territory before he muttered, "And you're a Hogwarts fan too. Figures."

Change of subject, take two.

She hitched herself up onto the lanai rail, straddled it, and leaned against the support post. She'd worn a full ankle-length skirt for her errands, so the fabric made it possible to reclaim her regular spot from the days she used to hang out here to watch the sunset with the Franzen kids. "All right, you've got the four-one-one on where I just was. Where were *you* today, Sergeant Bommer?"

He kept up the scowl, though his eyes began to smile again. "We've traded McClane and Potter references, Hokulani. I'm just Tait from now on, okay?"

"Fair enough." She let a little smile sneak across her lips too. "But you still haven't answered my question."

He dipped his head in a semiknightly bow. "I was at the esteemed Kekaha Boys Academy."

The smile dissolved. She nearly fell off the railing. "Leo's school? Why?"

"There was a fencing match today."

"I know. The match he ordered me not to attend, to the point of threatening to fake malaria if I did."

He shrugged. "Don't take it personally. He was having heebs about the match. The only reason I got an invite was because of the strategy we discussed during yesterday's ride. He went up against some Dursley who's been antagonizing him."

"Parker Smythe," she supplied. "Though Dursley *would* be a great surname for the kid." She wished his tribute to the boy wizard's world, even the scheming bully from it, made her feel better about referencing Leo's nemesis.

"Yeah, him." A full smile finally took over the man's face. At the same time, the sun broke into the lanai, highlighting every mesmerizing curve of his mouth. "The strategy worked, by the way. Leo won. You know, he's really good."

"So his coach tells me." She tossed a perturbed glance. "But as mentioned, the brat threatens to disown me if I show up at any of his matches."

He slipped a roguish quirk over his grin. As if he needed any help making those lips more enticing. "That's because Kalea is usually there too."

"Kalea? His little friend from the rec center social nights? Ohhhh, how nice. She's so sweet and— What?" She fired the question in response to the way he scratched his temple and pursed his lips, holding in a laugh. "*What?*"

"Errrmm...she's not such a *sweet little friend* anymore."

She jolted to an upright position—though wasn't sure she was ready to fire her next words. "What do you mean?"

He folded his arms with unnerving calm. "I mean that after we got off the horses yesterday, the kid wanted to talk about condom choices."

She fell back against the pole. "Oh, my God."

"Chill out; it's okay. It was handled."

She widened her eyes again. "Handled? The *condoms*?"

"No. The talk."

"So you just *talked* to him about condoms?"

"Well, yeah...among other things. I gave him a bunch of pretty heavy shit to think about. Manhood. Accountability. The responsibility of being a girl's first lover."

"Ohhhh, God." She planted her head in her hand. He did

not help her tension by laughing again.

"Lani. *It's okay*. He's a bright kid. He got the message. I'm fairly sure you won't be encountering a stampede of Trojans in his drawer for a few more years to come."

She swung her gaze out toward the water. Though the sunset wouldn't be in full bloom for several hours, the rays on the water, brilliant orange and amber upon the cobalt waves, were a welcome soother for her whirling thoughts. "*Mahalo*," she finally murmured. "Thank you...for being there for him." She threw over another sarcastic smile. "Can't say I appreciate the image of finding condoms in my little brother's room, but I'm still really grateful."

He lowered his arms and braced his hands on the back of a patio chair. "I'm probably the one who should be thanking you, missy."

"Huh?"

He hitched a fast shrug. "I wasn't the most lined-up guy when we first got here. But Leo's been good medicine." His features grew reflective as the wind kicked up, tugging at the edges of his hair. "Actually, with the exception of the night I barely remember and that crap-fest of a hangover, the last five days have been great therapy."

Warmth surged through her chest, even gathering a little behind her eyes. She climbed off the rail, rushed over, and pulled Tait into a hug before she could talk herself out of it. "I'm glad," she rasped into his shoulder, which smelled so clean and masculine, like cedar-infused soap.

"Me too." She felt the words, equally sincere, vibrate through him. To her ongoing surprise, he returned her embrace, swathing her in strength that was so like Kellan's but heat that was different too. Kellan was a volcano explosion, searing and intense; Tait was like magma, forceful and fierce... and demanding permanency. And making it so tempting to accept.

She was in trouble. Her heart fast-forwarded by at least ten beats. Her muscles softened against him. And other places in her body, those intimate and secret places, puddled with hot, enlivened need.

Stupid move, Hokulani. Stupid, stupid, stupid.

So why did it continue to feel like one of the best things she'd done in her life?

He finally pulled away, though kept his head dipped so she met his gaze through the fringe of his sinfully long lashes. Could this ordeal get any harder?

"For the record, what's going down between you and Kell is solely between you two. It's none of my business—never should have been. You can thank Leo for that too. He's got a damn good head on his shoulders. If even half that sense comes from you, then I'm going to trust that you're okay with your Slash-olate chip cookie."

She gave him her first gut reaction, an incredulous giggle. "My what?"

The ends of his lips curled up. "Come on. You know what a Slash-olate chip cookie is. A tasty nibble for a while, but no way in hell will he stick around to be the whole meal."

Her mirth faded. The crack should have pissed her off. Yeah, she wanted to be angry, not struggling against the sadness that filled her heart, instead. "Who says I have room for a 'meal,' Sergeant?"

His eyes darkened to dark bronze as she called him by rank again. The rest of his face went taut too. He'd gotten her firm message, which should've made her feel better but dipped her deeper into frustration. Nothing she could do now; the damage was delivered. She steeled herself for the "T-Bomb" he'd pull out of his personality missile silo in retaliation.

His actual reaction was more devastating.

His heavy sigh delivered the first shock. It did nothing to prepare her for what she confronted in his stare, fixed on her with unalterable focus.

A sadness as profound as her own.

"You deserve the whole meal, Lani." He brushed a strand of hair off her face, tucking it behind her ear. His murmur was as musical as the waves against the sand. "And yeah, I know what I'm talking about. Leo and I haven't only been discussing horses, swords, and condoms."

"*Aue.*" The mutter left her on a shaky rasp. It did nothing to allay the frantic thunder of her heartbeat at the base of her throat. "What the hell has he said?"

"Nothing that didn't stem out of his love." He let his fingers slip down, trailing rich warmth on her skin, until they rested in the dip between her throat and collarbone. "And nothing I don't agree with. You've had to be so strong for so long. Don't you see? Someone should be serving you steak and lobster every day, making you smile every minute."

Ohhhhh, hell.

Her senses swirled. Her body swayed. She steadied herself by grabbing his free hand. His fingers, long and steady beneath hers, were the anchor she needed to form her reply.

"I know you mean that. I can even feel how you do." She squeezed him tighter. "But steak and lobster isn't as easy as that. If it was, it wouldn't be special." She let her lips lift a little. "I was lucky to see that version of special until the day my parents died. They were smart enough to enjoy every bite of their steak and lobster. And the truth is, watching them all those years, seeing how happy they made each other, made me vow I wouldn't accept anything less for my life."

The corners of his eyes tightened in curiosity. "Even after the plane went down?"

"Especially then." Surprise jolted her again. "Leo even told you about *that*?"

"The kid's a real Chatty Cathy when he wants to be. But I'll deny it if you tell him I gave up his game."

"Your secret's safe. But I'm still perplexed. Leo's always been so shut off about all that. It hurts him to talk about it."

He skimmed his hand back up to her nape, releasing her to bracket the other side too. "You sure about that?"

She twisted her lips. "What does that mean?"

"Okay, rephrase. You sure it hurts *him* to talk about it?"

He didn't back down from the statement, sweeping his strong thumbs to her cheeks, cranking up the force of his gaze. His eyes became a gold-drenched x-ray on her soul, exposing her truths like hairline fractures, only with more pain. It hurt. Too much.

She yanked away from him and stalked back into the house. "Weren't you in the middle of telling me how you're going to mind your own business from now on?"

"Something like that." He followed her at a leisurely stroll, goading her annoyance all over again. "Back before you talked about yearning for steak and lobster but are okay settling for cookie crumbs."

She spun a glare at him. "Says the guy who's become the booze industry's patron saint over the last six months."

"And fooled most of the world while doing it." His gaze didn't flinch. "Which makes me a unique expert in the ways people cover up their pain and loneliness."

She tucked in her chin and cocked her brows. "I'm not lonely, Tait. I'm *busy*. There's a heartless bastard who wants to buy my childhood home out from under me. At the same time, I'm trying to keep the place running while playing mother, father, and big sister to a teenager who loves me one day then hates me the next." She jabbed both her thumbs backward at her shoulders. "In case you haven't noticed, the space up here is packed these days."

At first, all he did was pull in one slow breath and let it out with equal measure. Damn it, the man's serenity tapped its bottomless source as he made his way back to her with deliberate steps. Or maybe he was siphoning his self-control off hers. As he came closer on those endless legs, looming larger by the second, she couldn't feel anything but the nettles that had been her nerves and the thunderstorm that had been her heartbeat.

Both sensations worsened as he raised his hands and framed her face again. Gods, it felt more wonderful than before. His torrid lava touch infused every inch of her limbs. Her lungs began to ache from holding her breath, working in concert with the soul that never wanted this moment to end. Just when she thought they'd burst from the effort, he slid his hold down, across the tops of her shoulders, until he grasped her by the crests of both arms.

"So that load feels pretty good, hmm?"

Yeah. It was official. He was leeching his composure straight off hers. "Wh-What the hell does that mean?" she managed. "Were you listening to anything I just said? You think I *like* all this pressure?"

He turned his hands over to brush her skin with his

knuckles. "I haven't known you long enough to even guess at everything you 'like,' dreamgirl. But my job requires observing a lot about people in a very little amount of time, and I know what the stiffness in these shoulders tells me." He raised his gaze, amping it to x-ray intensity again. "I know what the shadows at the back of your eyes tell me."

"Oh?" She cocked her head, making a stab at an open challenge. "Enlighten me, Mr. Peabody."

He tilted his own head, matching her angle so their stares met again. "I think the weight has become so normal for you that giving it up would be strange...even terrifying. It's like the big silver dome on your food tray, keeping everything and everyone out, because it's safer that way. Nothing to feel, nothing to get rotten...nothing to get hurt."

His hands never left her shoulders, but it felt like he'd punched her in the gut. "Stop it," she whispered.

Her protest went unnoticed. "But when nothing gets in, nothing gets out, either. Underneath the dome, you're wilting, aren't you? You're needing, wanting, begging for something more."

Okay, *now* she needed to get furious. The ignition for the rage was there; she felt it burning through her chest and the base of her throat—only when the heat rose, it turned to liquid. She glared at him through the tears. "You have no right," she rasped. "I'm not Luna, and you have no right!"

He didn't drop his hands. But his head flinched as if she'd thrown a physical blow. The sun, dipping lower, filtered its way in to flow across his face, so classic, carved, strong...

So wanting.

Don't. Don't *want me. Please.*

"Yeah," he finally uttered. "You're right." He pulled away

slowly and gave an apologetic shrug. "Guess I overstepped again."

"It's all right."

"I know. And thanks. But before you turn and stomp your sweet ass out of here, let me set something straight. Even if God had cloned you after fucking Orphan Annie, I'd have said exactly what I did. The fact that you've got those eyes and that hair and that body—yeah, it's damn nice—but that's where *Luna* stops and *you* begin. And I'm sorry if the other night, and the grey geese soaring in my head, led you to think that I'm not wise enough to know the difference."

She folded her arms and threw out a shrug of her own. "You're not an idiot, Tait, nor did I ever think you were. You're serving under Franzen, and he's a picky *koa* when it comes to the guys on his team."

Like a morning swell on the waves, an answering smile rolled beneath his lips. "Damn. You're one of a kind, woman. And yeah, if Luna were alive today, I'm sure she'd like you too."

She blushed and punched his shoulder in retaliation for it. "You still barely know me."

He pointed a couple of fingers back at his chest. "The guy who has to add people up fast for a living, remember? Also the guy who's spent a shitload of time with a brother who can't stop talking about you and will be eating something besides chips and salsa tonight because of you."

She narrowed her eyes at him in blatant skepticism, though the three bags of tortilla chips on the kitchen counter declared his statement more true than she'd like.

Tait leaned against the back of the couch before continuing on, with warmth suffusing his face, "I know you two would've been good friends. You'd balance out her pragmatism with your spirituality. You'd show her a woman can be just as powerful in flip-flops as stilettos. She loved creating art to make the world more beautiful, but you see the world as art already." He paused, cocking his head once more to deeply study her. "Yet in many ways, you're exactly like her. And for seeing all of that, I can't and won't apologize."

Lani shifted again. *Don't ask it. Don't ask it.* "In many ways...like what?"

He straightened his gaze, sure and steady about it. "In your soul," he answered. "In the fire of it, the unfaltering conviction of it. The way you'll fight for what it knows to be right, no matter how dangerous the fallout is for you. The beauty it gives to your complete bravery."

It was suddenly very hot in the room.

Lani coughed, jabbing a toe at the floor.

"Sorry," he mumbled. "*Again.* 'Overstep' seems to be my new call sign today."

"It's okay," she blurted. "I asked, right?" The words depleted her air. Damn it, she'd remember to breathe again in a second...hopefully.

Aue! Was this what a girl got when she simply wanted to make sure a guy wasn't starving to death? She'd come here bearing groceries and was leaving with a mind that had been torn open, a soul requiring a hazmat sign from being irradiated so much...and a body that was sinking fast into a quicksand of need, inspired by a man who'd barely touched her.

The best friend of the man she *was* sleeping with.

Ohhhh, yeah. Hell's travel agency was giddy and booking her trip this second. One way. No refund.

She needed to get out of here. Now.

Easier said than done. Because doing it meant looking

toward Tait once more. His proud stance. His piercing gaze. His set jaw. His decadent lips...now silent and still. Thank the gods.

They had to keep it that way. Feelings had to stay silent now. Safe now. Not just for Kellan's sake, but for *her* sake—and, most importantly, for Tait's sake. She had to keep telling herself that, because the intensity on his face, dizzying her with desire all over again, already made the resolve a bitch to keep.

She finally summoned fortitude to speak. "I...I don't think I'll be able to come back here again."

"I understand."

She shifted her weight, feeling even more ridiculous. "So... don't starve, okay?"

Where was the damn door?

A girl had to be careful about letting her attention wander in the same room as a man who'd studied ninja tactics for job training. When she lifted her head again, he stood less than a foot in front of her. And when she opened her mouth to gasp, he invaded it with his own.

He gave her no choice about protesting the kiss—and she didn't want one. With a whimper, she gave herself to every demanding sweep of his tongue, every crushing mash of his lips. Her ears rang. Her knees buckled. She gripped him for purchase, sighing at the feel of his rippled shoulders beneath her hands.

All too fast, the explosion was over. An anguished cry spilled from her. The same sentiment seemed to grip every breathtaking angle of his face as the sun turned his hair into a dark gold halo.

With silent strength, he stepped away. A bittersweet smile took over his entrancing lips. "I won't starve. I promise."

The words, soft and sad, were a relentless echo in her head during the drive home, through the early evening chores, and into dinner preparation. They finally diffused when Kellan came barging in, hot and sweaty from replacing a bunch of rusty pipes in the water pump. He was accompanied by Randy and Roger, the married couple from next door who'd been invaluable in helping her keep Hale Anelas running. As a reward for the guys' hard work, she made a pizza with hand-rolled dough, topped with fresh mango and tomatoes from the garden, along with caramelized onions and barbecued pineapple. Baked chicken wings and a salad, tossed with more fresh fruit, completed the meal.

As the men relaxed with postmeal beers on the lanai, it was impossible to ignore fresh thoughts of Tait. He would've filled out the conversation so perfectly with his sarcasm and smirks.

She beat back her melancholy with a sharp mental stick. *Gods!* The stubborn shits had done this to themselves! Since when had it become any of her concern? Why the hell did she care about playing peacemaker for two grown, muleheaded men?

Since you realized that every inch of your body craves both of them. Every *inch...*

She had to get a handle on this nonsense.

A dunk in a bunch of cold water should do the trick.

After changing quickly into her swimsuit and grabbing her towel, she made her way back out to the lanai.

"Grrrr," Roger teased in greeting. "Hel-lo, Honey Rider. You going my way, Bond girl?"

"You wish." She giggled as she sidled onto the arm of the chair filled by Kellan. His gaze slid over her in open appreciation.

"I'm beginning to crave a martini and a tuxedo myself," he drawled, "and I hate that dress-up-like-a-monkey shit." He trailed an appreciative knuckle down her thigh. "What's up, hot stuff?"

She gave him a smile and a warm kiss. "I need a swim. Feeling a little tense. Be back soon. Promise."

The tide was low and the waves were calm, allowing her to concentrate on nothing but the flow of her body as she swam. She left the cares from the shore back *on* the shore, wishing for a brief escape from the conflict in her body and the increasing divide in her heart, made worse by the events of this afternoon. Made damn near impossible from the moment Tait had kissed her...

It's done. Gone. In the past. Which is where it will stay.

The resolve powered her steps back onto shore. Even made it possible for her to issue a hard nod to herself in encouragement while she walked to the rock where she'd draped her towel.

But it didn't prepare her to turn around and be stunned by the man who appeared out of nowhere. Tait was clearly not the only one who'd taken stealth training.

"Gods," she blurted. "Kellan, I think you scared my toe polish off."

He dipped his head with a knowing glint in his eyes— another move eerily similar to what Tait would do. "Maybe that's a good thing."

"Really? Sneaking up on your lover to the point she has to book a fresh pedicure tomorrow? That's a good thing with you Spec Ops boys these days?"

"Can be." He leveled his gaze with the same steady

omniscience. "If we think it'll get her to talk to us."

She was glad to already have her towel in hand. Averting her gaze seemed natural instead of purposeful as she began drying herself off—and breathing down her quickened pulse. "Well, here I am, talking to you."

"That's not what I mean, and you know it."

She slid the towel along her arms. "What are you getting at? How many beers have you—"

"One." He took the towel, twisted it to form a thick rope, then whipped it over her head in order to trap her by the shoulders. "Come here." Though his grip was ruthless, his tone was beseeching. "Look at me, Lani."

Despite his plea, she spluttered with aggravation. "What the—"

"Look at me," he countered. "You barely ate at dinner, which means something's eating *you*. So out with it, woman. Talk. *Now*."

CHAPTER NINE

Kellan was grateful that Randy and Roger had noticed Lani's strange behavior as soon as he did. Right after she took off, they both confirmed their suspicions to him. They shared that even though the woman could be private at times, she seemed extra burdened by something tonight. Sharing his concern in duplicate, the couple insisted on leaving shortly after she disappeared for the beach, encouraging him to go after her. That was all it took to send him jogging down the bamboo planks.

Now that he'd locked her in his embrace, all their suspicions were substantiated. In every inch of her twisted lips and tensioned neck, he saw the evidence of her anxiety—and wasn't going to let her get away with it any longer. Not that the woman didn't clearly have other plans.

"I picked at my dinner, so you think something's bothering me?" she snapped. "*Pupule kela*. This is crazy."

"Nice try." He let the coiled towel fall to her waist. Yanked on it to haul her against him. "Go ahead and fling all the caca you want, Starshine. It wasn't just your nonexistent appetite that has us here—where we're going to stay until you spill." He gave a taunting sigh. "I could easily stand here for a few more hours. How about you? The air feels good, the stars are bright and incredible—"

He was stopped by the dual fist thumps she gave to his chest. He grunted but didn't budge. Shit, the woman could pack a punch when she wanted.

"Damn *pa`akiki*," she spat.

He grinned. She was pretty adorable like this. "Why, thank you."

"It means stubborn ass."

"Then thank you very much."

"Fine." Just like that, her rebellion dissolved into obvious insecurity. She turned her head in a longing look toward the path back home, which Kell decided to allow. "There...was more to my afternoon than just the bank and the store."

Though he'd expected the answer, a weight pressed his chest. "I'd figured as much."

She gaped. "You had?"

"Of course." Despite his tension, he lifted her chin in order to give her a soft kiss. "You've been strung tighter than a greenie about to blast your first cherry in airborne."

She winced. "Good heavens." Her horror made him laugh, until he felt the tension still gripping every inch of her body. "I'm sorry," she murmured. "I really am. I guess I didn't think it was that big of a deal, and I didn't want you to be upset, so—"

"Lani." He gripped her chin a little tighter. "Out with it already. If I'm pissed, it's certainly not going to be with *you*."

Her lips twisted. "Huh?"

"Just tell me. Where did Benson find you? At the bank? Or was he catching up on his gossip mag scoops at the grocery store? And what kind of crap did he try to pull?" Though he was certain his ire wouldn't dim even if the asshole had given her a simple wave from his fancy-ass Escalade.

She shook her head. "No, no. Shockingly, Gunter doesn't have anything to do with this."

He firmed his stance, though now her discomfort crawled

through him too. "Okay." He did his best to keep his tone encouraging.

"I stopped at Franz's house."

A long moment ticked by. She still bit her lip like she'd sold state secrets to terrorists.

"Ummm...okay?" he repeated.

"I was worried." She gave him a tentative glance. "About Tait."

He did his best to respect her solemnity, but a chuckle slipped out. "And you thought I'd be upset about that?" Her answering scowl, radiating confusion, grabbed his heart and squeezed. "Starshine," he whispered, sprawling fingers across her jaw to ensure she kept looking at him, "the depths of your heart blow me away."

He meant every damn word, an admission that scared him a little. Perhaps more than a little. But tonight, that fear felt...good. Really good. He wanted this fear if it meant having the woman who came with it.

"You're really not mad?" Though the tension in her frame began to ease, her face still carried a crunch of bewilderment.

"Holy fuck." He laughed again. "No." After sliding another kiss across her lips, he went on. "Lani, he's my best friend. My *brother*, remember? We may be going through a strange patch right now—a *really* strange patch—but I love the guy." He brought up his other hand to caress her nape. "Your compassion for him doesn't upset me. It moves me."

She turned to kiss his palm. "You're pretty incredible, Kellan Rush."

Her admiration, especially over something so simple, made him feel higher than the moon. Giddy. And bold enough to break out a deep scowl at her, filled with his real vexation.

"What *does* piss me off is the fact that you kept all this from me in the first place. I'm not your teenage brother, sweetheart. I'm a grown man, capable of processing things like one."

A grin—of sorts—quirked her lips. "And the man wonders why I was worried."

He dipped a hand to playfully bat her ass. Lani giggled and squirmed against his hold. The action, combined with the fact that she still stood here in nothing but her damp bikini, flared his irritation into a different kind of fire. He lowered his lips to hers once more but took them with harder emphasis. After dragging away, he growled, "I really *should* spank your ass for that, naughty one."

Her eyes went wide. The blue-silver depths had picked up brilliant flecks, instantly betraying the woman's excitement at the idea. One side of her mouth kicked up. "You wouldn't dare."

"No?" He spun her around and then locked her back against him, wrapping arms around her shoulders and waist. "I could and I would," he growled into her ear. "And maybe I still will. It'd be a first for us both, but I guarantee you one thing: Tait's shown me enough techniques that I'd know just how and where to redden your beautiful ass."

She let out a little moan that hardened his cock and softened his hold. He slid both hands down to her thighs, caressing them from the inside juncture and out, setting his goal for the sweet swells that she rubbed straight up the shaft beneath his khakis...

Just before she bolted from him at a full run.

Her laughter rocketed through the air in her wake. "Spank me?" she teased over her shoulder. "We'll see about that—if you catch me."

He let out an answering growl, finishing it with a laugh.

Lani squealed and quickened her sprint into the forest. Between the black ropes of her wet hair, the black lines of her swimsuit, and the shadows cast by the moonlight through the trees, it was natural for him to click into hunter mode, tracking his elusive she-panther through the jungle.

Tracking—but not catching.

After several minutes, the scenario hit him as a plausible, if incredible, possibility. "Damn," he muttered, pausing in a clearing that was a little over halfway to Franz's place. He'd been wrong to think he had the advantage here. He navigated terrain like this for the day job, but she'd been doing the same since she could walk.

Just when he considered finding a hiding place and waiting her out, Lani's laugh rang out, reeling him forward once more. His senses sharpened, zeroing in on her location. He veered right, smiling.

She was getting cocky. And careless.

He answered her giggle with a snarl, playing up its frustrated edge. The tactic worked. Her next laugh shot through the trees, directing him back toward the left. As the sound of her footfall sliced through the trees, he altered his own, adopting the careful tread that his battalion mate, Ethan Archer, affectionately referred to as "snaky steps." Going silent was infinitely easier without a rifle in his arms and a hundred-pound ruck on his back.

He sneaked through the trees until he spotted her again, fifteen feet away. So close...damn near within pouncing distance. And close enough to hear what she muttered to herself.

"Shit, shit, shit. Where'd he go?"

Her moment of hesitation was his instant of opportunity.

He sprinted, catching her unaware. Lani shrieked, laughed, and dodged but made the move too late. He scooped a foot beneath hers, forcing her to topple toward a bed of moss. Before she took a full header, he caught her by the waist, controlling her descent. That was a good thing, since he went down with her. In seconds, they were surrounded by the lush knee-high plants, with the cool, thick grass as a makeshift bed. And goddamnit, what the combination of this woman and *any* bed did to the shackles of his sexual control. This time, it was even better. She was pinned against him once more, her ass slammed to his crotch, her skin damp and gleaming, and her body shuddering with the force of her breaths.

He leaned in, scraping his teeth along her carotid. She shivered harder, lurching against him. He tightened his hold and let out a low rumble. Their struggle turned him way the hell on—not a confession he'd normally be proud of, except that her throat was right under his mouth, enabling him to feel the needy mewl that vibrated up the silken column.

A question filled his mind. He wondered, with every new beat of blood to his cock, how she'd react to it. "Did I scare you?"

"A little," she finally rasped. "Y-Yes."

He dropped his teeth to her shoulder. She writhed and pushed back at him again. He widened his knees and held on harder, digging his fingers into her pliant curves. This push-and-pull between them, an erotic wrestling match, was something he'd never attempted with a woman before, something he'd never even dreamed of trying.

Because he'd never met a woman like her before. Lani, who matched him strength for strength. Lani, who'd almost outrun him in a jungle chase. Lani, his perfect island goddess—

now his gorgeous, vigorous captive.

"Are you still scared?"

She swallowed hard before arching her spine, trying to struggle with him again. She was either really alarmed or really aroused. Kell guessed a little of both. "Do...I have something to be scared of, Sergeant Rush?"

He switched up his tactic. Instead of yanking her back against him, he pushed her onto the ground, pinning her there, both his hands over her wrists. "Maybe you do, Miss Kail."

"Are you...still going to...spank me?"

"Hmmm. Good question," he drawled. "Though I wonder why you raised it." After drawing up his knees to make his body hover inches over hers, he slid a hand down to the perfect hills of her backside. "Could it be that you *want* to be spanked?"

Lani whined softly but didn't shift position. Kellan studied her a moment longer. Was the sound a legitimate protest or just a whimper of confusion?

"There's nothing wrong with wanting it, sweetheart," he murmured. "A lot of women like it, you know. Even crave it. Endorphins are a nice high."

"Oh, God!" The high little cry verified her standing. She was conflicted. And scared too. Most of all, of herself. During the few times Kell had accompanied Tait to the Bastille club as an observer, he'd seen this more than enough to recognize it. Thinking about one's kinky side was one thing. Acting on it was another.

Time to drag this she-panther back to territory she knew.

"Perhaps I'll make you wait for that spanking, little girl." He skidded his fingers under her bikini bottom, rolling her soft flesh between his fingers before giving her a sensual pinch. Lani squealed against the ground as he repeated the nip on her other buttock. "After all," he continued, dipping his hand between her cheeks in order to tease the rim of her vagina, "anticipation can be just as excruciating as execution."

A gasp burst from her. "Kellan!"

"Hmmm?"

"Ohhhh...Kellan...yesssss..."

The sight of her like this, shivering and squirming beneath him, was fucking exquisite. His cock pulsed a thousand times harder than during their impromptu WWE show. Damn, he loved doing this to her...controlling her very breaths with the subtle movements of his fingers. The mental rush was just as powerful as considering his hand smacking her ass.

You made the right call on that, man. She wasn't ready for the spanking.

He'd just been preparing to start a finger fuck Lani would never forget but stilled his hand. If a freight train slammed the forest that very second, it wouldn't have equaled the jolt from the voice crashing into his senses.

You made the right call.

Inside seconds, he knew why the affirmation had felt so strong. He and Lani weren't the only ones out here. His nerve endings sizzled with the certainty of it, exactly how they did when he was about to squeeze the trigger on a dead-perfect shot. He raised his head and peered through the trees, needing to know if his intuition was on the mark...terrified that it would be. Wondering if he'd really find the one person on this earth with whom he shared a connection so strong, it bordered on a psychic mind meld at times.

Times like this.

When his gaze locked onto the eyes, deep and gold and more familiar than his own, he swallowed. And wondered if there was still a way to summon the freight train instead.

Logic stomped on his alarm. If Tait were going to mess this up for Lani and him, the guy would have done so already. Instinct as sure as his heartbeat assured him of that, the same way he knew Tait had his six on the decision to hold off on spanking Lani. He tossed a thankful smirk at Tait. His buddy returned the look, his way of not only apologizing for the asshat behavior of the other morning but also submitting his approval about fulfilling the goddess in any and every way she needed.

While he watched from where he was.

Ohhhh yeah. That assurance was written across Tait's face too. Kellan saw it in the rigid set of T's jaw, the brightened glints in his gaze. He wondered exactly what had gone down when Lani visited the guy this afternoon. The two of them hadn't screwed; the stark longing on T's face wouldn't be so pronounced otherwise. Whatever *had* gone down, it turned Tait into tonight's eager voyeur, staring at Lani like a forest butterfly who'd lead them to a plant that cured cancer. The heights of her journey were the key to his happiness. Tait gave a slow but firm nod confirming that fact, openly encouraging Kellan to go on.

Kellan gave his buddy a sardonic salute. If T was up for this, he sure as hell was.

There was just one more approval box to have checked off here. The most important one.

"My Starshine." He made it a verbal caress to go with his gliding knuckles down her spine. He kept his other hand between her legs, gently stroking the moist petals there.

"Mmmm?" she queried, trembling from head to toe again.

"So, no spanking. What *am* I going to do with you, sweetheart?"

She gave him a coquettish peek over her shoulder. "You could just chase me again."

He responded with a low growl, slipping both hands back to her waist again. She broke into a yelp as he tugged back hard, raising her ass to the level of his cock. Holy hell, did his body get on board with that geometry lesson. His dick pushed against his fly, clamoring for the fastest way to angle its way straight inside her. With gritted teeth, he sent his balls to detention.

Get out the chalk and start writing, guys. "I will not think of fucking her this soon... I will not think of fucking her this soon... I will not—"

"Nope. No more chasing, sweetheart. I think I just want to fuck you."

He was never good at detention.

"Ohhhh." Her answering moan was tinged with a little bit of lingering fear and a lot of burgeoning arousal. "That... sounds like an interesting plan."

"Interesting is only half of it."

"Oh?" She let the end of that trail into a meaningful sigh, staring over her shoulder as he tore off his shirt and tossed it into the ferns. He couldn't resist slamming his chest to her spine once more and then dropping a hungry bite into her shoulder. A savage hiss exploded off her lips. She reared against him, inciting his cock with her ass again. When she started rolling her hips with sensual abandon, desire tore at his control.

"Fuck," he rasped. It seemed their hunter-and-prey adventure turned her on more than he'd thought. Sure enough, when he slipped his grip inside her bikini top, her nipple stabbed his fingers, so beautifully stiff. It hardened more as he adored it with reverent squeezes. Lani stilled as he teased her there, erupting in another high, needful sigh.

"Mmmm. Your tits tell me you like the idea of *interesting*, sweetheart. Of letting me take you here in the middle of the jungle...of fucking you like an animal on the ground."

"Yes." Her acquiescence was a rough sough on the air. The raw need in it thickened every drop of his blood, especially the stuff pounding harder in his dick. "Yes," she echoed, renewing her sexy hip rolls, making him pound even harder. "Take me like this, Kellan. Fill me. Fuck me!"

Holy shit, the woman talked nasty like nobody he'd ever met. Her dirty pleas made him bring his other hand around so he could unhook her swimsuit and set her breasts free. The swells burst into his hands, stuffing them full. Her erect nipples felt fucking incredible against his palms. He rolled and tugged on the hard stems until she bucked harder. Her passion drove his head down, diving at her neck, suckling until he found his way to her ear again.

"What was that?" he teased. "You want me to fuck you? Rut hard on you right here?"

"Yes. Dear gods, yes!"

"Even if that means other creatures may be watching us?"

"Other...creatures?" She practically panted the words. "Like the animals?"

He skimmed one hand down toward her pussy again. "No, sweetheart. Like...another man."

She went still for a long moment. Her head raised a little. He watched the silver swirls of her gaze as she darted it through the ferns—but he'd bet his left nut that she wouldn't see a thing. The art of subterfuge was as natural as walking to a Special Forces soldier. Tait had already blended himself with the forest.

"He's here, Starshine," he finally murmured. "You can't see him, but you can feel him, just as I can, right?"

"Wh-Who?"

"You already know the answer to that."

He leaned in again, trailing his mouth along the elegant line of her jaw while once more dipping his fingers between her thighs. Her face rumpled, caught in a battle between astonishment and arousal. "Shit," she whimpered. "Oh, shit!"

Maybe she needed a little help with her vacillation. Who was he to leave a damsel in distress, especially this one? But genteel wasn't the proper tactic for this moment. She had to be shown how the night would proceed, if she was going to give her consent about things moving on from here.

Without preamble, he wrapped her hair around a fist and pulled her head to one side. She gasped in deeper surprise, and he had to admit to shocking himself a little with the action. While he'd always liked dancing at the edge of his inner Dom, he'd never fully pulled on the boots and let himself stomp to the primal beat of that commanding force—until tonight.

It was kind of...incredible.

Maybe more than incredible.

All right, it was fucking awesome.

But he wasn't an idiot. His sexual high was possible only because of the woman in his arms, answering his aggression with breathtaking fire. Her nipples beaded even harder. Her eyelids drooped in arousal. Her lips parted, gleaming like strawberries, inviting him to taste as deeply as he desired.

He hesitated about two seconds before succumbing to that temptation.

She tasted amazing. Even better than the first time he'd ever claimed her lips, during that magical night in the rain. This moment was drenched in so much more meaning, sweetened by the nectar of her surrender, perfected by the comprehension that Tait watched it all. He heard every needy cry that escaped her throat...smelled the tangy musk of her spiraling need...saw every gleam of the moonlight on her nearly naked body, so bronze and beautiful and ready to be fucked. And he shared every second of torture that Kellan endured in holding back from doing so.

He let out a hard groan. His pants felt like a goddamn iron cage, every movement taunting his cock. The denim was already damp from his precome, which seemed to have tapped a bottomless pool somewhere in his balls. *Dandy.*

"You know why he's here, right, Starshine?" He saw that she did, smiling a little when her breathing audibly hitched. "He wants to watch me fuck you. He wants to watch me drive my cock into your cunt like an unthinking beast. And sweetheart, that's what I'll become if we go any further." He kissed her softly. "The choice is yours. I think you can guess where my vote goes."

She attempted a trickling laugh at that but was drowned by her obvious torment. Kell didn't blame her for the indecision. He even understood it. That didn't mean he could wait on it a lot longer. If he wasn't inside her soon, then the alternative was a long, cold dunk in the ocean. Either alternative had to happen fast.

Maybe he could help her reach this verdict too.

He'd been resting a hand inside the top edge of her bikini bottoms. Now he dipped it lower, parting the trimmed curls at her apex, seeking the warmth of the hot grotto beyond. Lani moaned as the tip of his middle finger found the sensitive ring at her core.

"Holy fuck, Starshine. You're soaking wet just from the idea of all this."

"Oh," she squeaked in return. "Ohhhh gods, that's..."

"What?" He teased her vagina as he spoke over her harsh gasp. "What is it, Lani? Are you speaking for the pussy that wants to be fucked here or the body that wants to be carried home and fucked in bed?" He rolled his finger, spreading her entrance wider, pushing in a second finger. Her body clamped on him in welcome, making him roll his eyes toward the trees in silent exigency at the friend he could still feel out there. Oh, yeah. T was still here. He heard his partner's snicker on the breeze, a sound discernible only to him since Lani was oblivious, judging by the sexy bucks of her hips and the urgent trembles of her shoulders.

"*Kahaha.*" Her voice bumped all over the entreaty. "Kellan, please!"

He kissed her spine between her shoulder blades and murmured, "I'm here, sweetheart. Right here. You just need to tell me what you need and when you want it. What's it going to be?"

CHAPTER TEN

Lani had never taken funny drugs in her life—though she wondered if the herbal tea she'd iced down for dinner had been laced with some extra "limbo leaves" from one of the island's "special" gardens. Her blood hummed in her ears and zinged through her clit. Her heart sprinted against her ribs. Her whole body felt transported, lost in a world where all she wanted was more of the dark-eyed man who commanded every beat of her blood...and the golden-eyed man who watched him doing it.

Reality? Oh yeah, that. She stormed her mind for it, even scrabbled her hands at the ground, hoping the cool moss would help her get a grip on her mind again. No damn chance. She was helpless, a willing pawn of Kellan's hands and voice and kisses. Powerless against needing his body, so huge and magnificent, looming against her. Defenseless against the thoughts, so carnal and naughty, of Tait witnessing everything they were doing.

"Ohhhh, gods." And she'd thought the events of this afternoon were her direct ticket to hell? At this point, the demons had drilled a hole straight down and planned on throwing her in.

"What is it, Starshine?" Kellan's lips were at her nape again. His hand tightened in her hair. He pumped his fingers deeper into her sex. "Talk to me, Lani. Tell me. Talk to me."

"I'm— I'm afraid."

"Of what?" He pressed closer, surrounding her in his

warmth. He glided his mouth down her right shoulder. "Of this? Of us?"

"N-No." *Crap.* She sounded so small and unsure. This was insane. *Small?* The boobs and hips she inherited from Mom ensured she didn't do *small.* And she sure as *hell* didn't do unsure. But here she was, stammering out, "I'm afraid of... of— Oh, shit!"

Her electrified gasp was a reaction to his teeth on the back of her arm—and the third finger he fitted into her vagina. God help her, the man had learned all of her sexual weak spots in just three days.

"Afraid of what?" His murmur was shaded in a teasing tone. Smug bastard.

"I'm afraid of what you'll think of me...if I want this. If I... if I like it." She cried out in pleasure as he thrust his fingers farther in. "Ohhh, damn you!"

His wicked chuckle thickened the air. "If you like it? Starshine, I think you're past the point of *liking it.* Your pussy is dripping for me...coating me." He scooped them around her tunnel in a tight circle, as if needing to swipe every drop. "You may even need this."

"Damn it!" Her breath escaped on a quivering thread. "But I— I can't—"

"What?" he countered. "Need it? Want it? Like it? Why?" He felt amazing. All of him. His hand in her sex. His thighs framing hers. His mouth traveling the valley between her shoulder blades so he could tantalize the skin of her other arm. "Because it doesn't make you a *good girl?*" He growled in answer to her desperate cry. "There's where you're wrong, sweetheart. You *are* good, Lani. So beautiful, amazing, sexy... and so damn good for me. And now, even good for Tait too." He whipped her hair over, yanking her head to the other side before slamming his lips to her ear again. "Help me bring my friend back to life, Lani." His rasp was a beautiful blend of command and appeal. "If we show T how life is celebrated, in the most perfect and primal way there is...if we help him remember how good it can be to feel like this...maybe he'll wake up this time."

She cut him off with a sob and a laugh mixed, with the same crazy mix of emotions as the source. His words were like a spell on her soul, though his fingers were still a thrumming taunt to her body. The combination ignited her, illuminating so much, setting her free. Her senses. Her soul. Her inhibitions.

"Yes." She smiled as the word left her lips. "Yes...yes!"

Hell. Maybe that tea *was* spiked with giggle grass. None of this made sense. She should be running. Racing away and telling these men to go back to their own house. This woman, who was letting Kellan slide off both halves of her swimsuit, wasn't her. This creature, cognizant of the man who now stepped through the bushes to get a better view of them, wasn't her, either. But most of all, she didn't recognize the woman's heart that beat in time to both men's harsh breaths, filled with the yearning to please them both, aching with the desire to serve them both.

She shouldn't want this. She *couldn't* want it.

It's just sex.

The refrain echoed in her head with perfect timing.

Of course. She'd overthought everything. Why blow it so far out of proportion? This was just an episode of naughty fun. A fling to fulfill fantasies. All she had to do was keep words like *heart, soul,* and *needs* out of the equation. And damn, if she was going to punch the voyeur box on her sexy fun card, why not indulge with a pair of the most magnificent men fate had ever dropped on this island?

She sighed high and deep as Kellan guided her to roll over, stretching her flat to her bed in the moss. Gods, what an upgrade. The new position enabled her to watch him unzip his fly. A quick scan of the underbrush still didn't reveal any sign of Tait, but she heard him breathing, perhaps from behind her, in heavier huffs. As Kellan shoved his pants down to his hips, the rasp of Tait's zipper sliced the air too.

Before Kellan got completely naked, he reached into his back pocket and slipped out the square that had turned him into the condom makers' favorite guy this week. She giggled as he dropped it to the ground next to her but fell silent when he arched a brow. Maybe this was just sex, but he was definitely taking their performance as a responsibility.

Well, then. Yes, sir.

Her silent crack had a sarcastic edge for about a second... before it was silenced by wonderment.

As he knelt there for a long moment, simply looking at her, only one word in any language came to her mind.

Wow.

He was her dark satyr now more than ever: beautiful, dark, and intense. Streams of moonlight played across his head, weaving silver strands into the spikes of his hair and mystery across his noble face. Years of being in Special Forces had turned his arms into collections of defined muscle, which he positioned at his sides in a commanding pose. They made a perfect frame for the perfect abs that laddered his abdomen. At their base was a pair of toned ridges that guided her gaze right...

There.

She gulped.

His nest of dark pubic hair supported a breathtaking erection. His cock was already thick and dark with the force of his arousal, its crown agleam with the milk that attested to how much he wanted her. Kellan groaned beneath the weight of her stare, lifting a hand to share his precome with the rest of his taut length. Lani shifted restlessly, a whimper escaping before she could help it.

"You like this, Starshine?" he asked from gritted teeth. "You enjoy seeing what you do to me, how badly my dick wants to bury itself in your pretty cunt?" When she nodded and mewled again, his jaw took on even more rigid lines. "No," he charged, "tell me. In words. Look at my face and say it."

Technically, the feat required her gaze to shift a few more inches. They might as well have been a cliff of Waimea. His stare gutted her heart like titanium—and kept going until it reached her sex. "I..." Her throat went dry. She took a deep breath and started again. "I like it," she said. "I...I love it. I love looking at your cock. You're beautiful, Kellan. So perfectly formed. I want you inside me."

There was a rustle from the foliage behind her again. And a single, low groan. She recognized its timbre at once. Tait was there. She definitely felt him now. Staring at her nudity. Listening to her words. Watching her about to be fucked by another man...and from what she could discern by his voice, loving every second of it.

"Show me." Kellan's mandate swung her attention back to him. He pumped his penis with his whole hand, expanding the girth he was going to pound into her soon. God, she *hoped* it would be soon. "Show me," he repeated, "how much your body wants me. Spread your legs. That's good. Wider. Yes, sweetheart. Perfect."

She smiled as he stepped into the wide V she'd created, close enough for her to see the engorged veins in his shaft. "It feels good to please you," she whispered.

He rewarded her with a gentle smile. "I know. I really do. But there's someone else you've got to please tonight, remember?"

She flashed a saucy smirk. "Oh, I haven't forgotten."

"Good." When his lips took on an audacious angle of their own, alarm skittered down her spine...and through her pussy. "Because I know for a fact that our 'guest' has special cravings from time to time."

"Cravings?" She gulped. "For what?"

Kellan lowered to his knees. Just watching his quads do the work on that made her sex pulse all over again, not that she'd openly disclose that tidbit. Her gaze was drawn back to his face all too fast anyhow. His intense study was a little unnerving. "He likes the sight of a woman receiving all the pleasure she can."

She grinned and wiggled her hips. "Sounds good to me."

"He likes to make sure of that by tying her down."

Her lips fell. "Excuse me?"

He stuck out his lower lip in contemplation. "No movement, no temptation to get in the way of the pleasure. It does make poetic sense."

"I'm not a big fan of poetry."

Kellan chuckled. "Not asking you to be." He lowered a kiss that was soft at first but grew in sexy intent as he teased her tongue with the tip of his own. "Why don't we just pretend?"

"I don't understand."

Keeping his face just inches from hers, he reached to secure both her wrists in his hands. His lips stayed sinful and intentional as he stretched her arms straight out, making her feel like a splatted butterfly. "Keep them there," he directed, "as long as you can." He brought his own arms back in by trailing his fingertips along the inner flesh of her wrists and elbows and then across the sides of her breasts. As he slid his thumbs over her nipples, making her shiver and gasp, he murmured, "I have to admit, maybe T is on to something. You're pretty damn sexy like this, my captive island goddess."

She prepped a sarcastic comeback, but it faded as he dipped his head, capturing one breast and then the other in lingering kisses. Gods, how this man knew how to touch her, to make her quiver as he added his teeth to that treatment, tugging her nipples with insistence, teasing to the point where she wanted just a little more pain to stoke the fire deep in her pussy...

She brought her arms up to seize his head, trying to urge him on.

Kellan grabbed her wrists again. Lowered both of them again. "They call it *play bondage* for a reason, sweetheart. Is that really all you could take?"

The tender claws of his fingers made her gasp. "Was that really your idea of *playing*?"

He pinned her mouth beneath his in a merciless kiss, finally pulling up to trickle a wicked laugh along her cheek. "Welcome to my jungle gym."

She moaned low and long. The rough cuffs of his hands on her wrists...the stubbled needles of his jaw on her face... the consuming hulk of his body... If this was the big kids' playground, she knew why no one ever wanted to leave.

Kell kissed her again, harder and deeper. She opened willingly for him, letting him jam her mouth wide, possess her completely with his tongue. Less than a minute of contact, but oh, how it flipped a strange, permanent, amazing switch in her psyche. Fighting this was no longer an option she needed—or wanted. The realization stunned her. He was going to use her. Fuck her. Excite her. Satisfy her. Offer her, along with himself, as a gift to his friend, helping Tait build a bridge back to himself. And she was going to let him. Trust him. Expose herself to both of them in a surrender she'd never allowed a man before, by letting herself be completely helpless.

Just the knowledge of it set her free.

"Oh." Her voice resounded in her ears, full and vibrant in its new amazement. As Kellan slipped his grip off her wrists again, she kept them locked down without effort.

"Good girl," he uttered, pushing the hair from her face and kissing her forehead. "You *are* my good girl, Lani. So beautiful for me. So open...for us."

"Yes," she whispered. She wanted to say more, but the words clogged in her throat. If they came out now, she'd mean them too much. Care about them too much. *This is just sex. Just an erotic dream coming true.* The increased huffs from the bushes behind them, accompanied by the rhythmic sounds of a hand pumping against flesh, embedded that affirmation deeper. She sighed in response, lifting her hips toward Kellan. Without taking his eyes from her, he seized the packet from the ground and freed the condom with one rip. His breaths quickened as he rolled it over his rigid red stalk.

"You can hear him, too, can't you, Starshine? He needs to see me fuck you. Take you hard. Bury myself to my balls in you. Kind of like—*this.*"

With his hands clawing her hips, he pulled her body forward as he thrust hard, invading her fully in one plunge.

"Ahhh!" Lani arched her back and screamed it to the sky, hating him and loving him in the same surreal moment. She kept her arms stretched out because honestly, there was no other choice. She had no strength. All the energy in her body flowed toward the cave that was captive to Kellan's thick, hot cock.

"Holy fuck," he rasped. "You're taking me so deep, Lani. It's so good. So damn..."

He cut himself off with a groan. The air was filled with the violent sound of his balls against her ass. Lani bit back her scream, using the violent energy to clamp her body tighter around his shaft. His cock grew in its demand for release; her clit throbbed in its lust for completion. She curled her hands into the moss, borrowing the strength of Mother Earth to keep from losing control. It was hard, so damn hard not to let his lunges stimulate her to orgasm, especially as he pumped even harder. His thrusts coincided with the increase in Tait's frantic cadence. Both men growled in the throes of their primal need.

"My sweet Starshine. You have no idea how beautiful you look right now. Neither of us can keep our eyes off you. Such perfect tits, bouncing every time I fuck into you. Such an obedient body, spread wide in surrender. Such a gleaming, wet pussy, clamping me so tight..."

"Kellan," she managed to whimper. "Oh gods, Kellan!"

"You want to come, don't you, sweetheart? You're so close..."

"Yes. Ohhhh, yes!"

"But you won't, will you? Not until I'm ready. Until *we're* ready. Say it for me, sweetheart. Focus on me and say it."

"I...I won't come until you're both ready."

"That's our girl. Our good, sweet girl."

A strong wind suddenly kicked up, sending untamed energy through the forest. Lani breathed in deeply, smelling hibiscus, papaya, and pineapple...and salt, sweat, and sex. She moaned, joining the symphony of harsh male grunts that consumed the clearing. Screw the ganja; this was a high that couldn't be paralleled: the beautiful, feral energy of two warriors with cocks that needed to explode...because of her. She still couldn't see Tait, but she guessed his body and face were a lot like Kellan's now: taut with passion, focused on release, eyes fixed on her open nudity with unbridled lust. Just thinking of it made her vagina clench with wet, wild need.

"Kellan! Please!"

Like a miracle, a snarl erupted from the bushes, seeming to concur with her urgency. *Thank you, Tait!*

Kellan gave her a tight nod. *Finally.* "Yeah. Surrender to it, Starshine. Scream for us, baby. Come hard for us."

As if she needed it, he slicked a thumb over her distended clit. The single contact, along with Tait's long groan, sent her spinning into a vortex of pure bliss. Her entire pussy convulsed, consuming her with blistering joy. The euphoria increased upon hearing Tait groan in the throes of his own climax.

"Damn," Kellan growled a moment later. "Damn, sweetheart. You're going to make me blow like—" His roar practically shook the fruit out of the trees. "God*damn*it, Lani. Yessss."

She exulted in how his cock expanded against her walls, stretching her even tighter before his come left him in a long climax. Lani wrapped her legs around his waist before succumbing to the urge—too intense now—to touch him again. He groaned his approval, dropping his head in order to claim her in a deep kiss that made her wish for the power to freeze time.

Fulfillment rushed through her like a tsunami, lifting out all the garbage of her life, making it feel like floating pieces of nothing. For the first time in a long time, her mind was actually free. Without a care. Without a decision that extended beyond what part of his back she wanted to explore next with her "unshackled" hands.

For the first time in a long time, she was...happy.

Any second, she expected the inevitable. Her brain was going to echo with the screech of mental brakes. Loud ones. There'd be a cogent explanation for them. This was all just postorgasm endorphins at work, combined with the extra electricity generated from the wind. She could once more tell herself this had been solely about sex—hell, she wondered how much longer Tait was even going to continue hanging out—but why? She refused to acknowledge logic again right now. The bastard needed to go take a long break.

She needed to just...be. To keep feeling the soul-drenching, bone-deep satisfaction that had come with Kellan's soft words. *Good, sweet girl.* Her eyes closed as she let the perfection of that moment drench her again. Though Tait hadn't said a word, she'd felt his deep approval. She smiled, sorely tempted to toss a glance at the foliage where she still felt his presence and fling a saucy zinger. *How was* that *for lifting the dome off my platter, Sergeant?* But that would entail an explanation to Kellan about their conversation from this afternoon, leading to her memory of the kiss that followed and the furious blush she'd try to hide after that. True to form, she'd ride the massive fail whale on that front. Unacceptable.

The irony of it didn't escape her. Was she actually squirming at the thought of Kellan learning Tait had kissed her, after the jungle fever the three of them had just shared?

Maybe the shit under her emotional dome really was a casserole of crazy.

Or maybe that kiss meant more than you're giving it credit for.

She didn't realize she'd given volume to her scoffing laugh, until Kellan shot an inquisitive glance over his shoulder while pulling his khakis back on. Since he only had the pants halfway up his ass, she thanked herself for the timing. Was there any part of the man that wasn't muscled perfection?

"A half-moon for your thoughts?" he quipped.

"Just enjoying the view." At least it wasn't a lie.

"Once we're back at the house, you can 'view' a lot more if you want."

She giggled, acknowledging stomach tingles she hadn't felt since seventh grade. "You're insatiable."

"When it comes to you, I am." A curious grimace crossed his face, as if the admission surprised him. He banished it by quickly shaking his head and pulling up his pants, and then offered a hand to help her up. Once she stood, he pulled her in for a long, hot, tongue-tangling kiss. Lani let him take over, melting into his strength with a sigh. What a damn good thing he wouldn't be here long. She could get dangerously addicted to kisses like this...

Even when thoughts of Tait made her pull back from them. More accurately, the emptiness in the air that he left behind. How could it be that she felt his presence, and lack of it, like some strange light switch got flipped in her soul?

"He's gone, isn't he?" she asked Kellan quietly.

He nodded. "Likely bugged for Franzen's again."

"Will he be okay?"

Another contemplative frown crossed his face. "I may have to finagle a reason to stick around here if you don't watch it, woman."

Damn it. There went her stomach, trying out for a tumbling act again. "Why?"

"Because that enormous heart of yours is going to get you into trouble one day, and someone needs to be here for the rescuing part." He chuckled when she socked him in the chest. "Don't worry about T, okay? I'll go over and see him tomorrow. He likely needs some time to process." He rolled his eyes. "At least that's what he calls it, after all the shrinking his big lid's been through. If you ask me, they've all been poking around in the wrong place. It's his fucking heart that needs the work. It was long before Luna, too."

She took a turn to frown now. "What do you mean?"

He sighed. "T-Bomb is...special. He's more than a good soldier. He's a good *man*. He has a Super Bowl-sized heart. It deserves—"

"Cheerleaders and foam fingers?"

He laughed with her. "Damn close. Celebration. And joy. God knows, life's shown him more than enough agony and sacrifice."

Lani wanted to press for more details, but Kellan gave himself another dismissive head shake and tugged her hand into his, effectively closing the conversation. She tucked her head against his shoulder, telling herself that was for the best. Deeper discoveries about either of these men would only make their departure harder—and she'd already started steeling for a bumpy goodbye.

No.

She crammed the thought away while snuggling tighter

to Kellan as they made their way toward home. If logic was banished for the night, so was melancholy.

The wind hit a strong speed as they crossed the garden and half-jogged to the house. It brought the smell of a strong rainstorm with it, making her hope Coach Price had called an early end to Leo's fencing practice. To her relief, they entered the kitchen to find her little brother hunched over the pizza pan, inhaling the leftover contents in his practice sweats.

"Hey, *kaikaina*," she greeted. "Are you *still* hungry? I thought you already grabbed some dinner with the guys from the team."

Leo grunted. "That was a half hour ago."

"Oh, yeah." She stepped next to him and bumped shoulders, though her shoulder now hit him a few inches above his elbow. "Forgive me for overlooking *that* pertinent detail."

She moved a hand up to squeeze his neck in affection, but Leo shrugged her off, ducking deeper over the pizza. She rolled her eyes toward Kellan. He held up his hands with a smirk. "Your sister makes good pizza, yeah?"

"Uh-huh."

"Hey," she chastised. "Manners?"

Leo let out the universal teen boy chuff of irritation. "Yes, Sergeant Rush. My sister makes excellent pizza."

"Thanks for the support," she gibed.

Leo only grunted again.

"How was practice?" Kellan queried. "You're on the fencing team, right?"

"Yeah. It was fine."

Lani succumbed to a wave of alarm. Yes, Leo's communication style was largely chat-speak shorthand, but her brother had also been fond of inserting his new nickname for Kellan into every interaction he could. When "Slash-gasm" was officially a no-show for the conversation, she looked at Leo with heightened concern before glancing back to Kellan. She was a little vindicated to see a concerned frown on his features, too.

"Just 'fine'?" she prodded her brother.

Leo sighed. "It wasn't brain surgery. It was practice, okay?" After grabbing a soda from the refrigerator, he pivoted for the back stairs, back still hunched and hoodie still up.

"Hey!" Lani rushed after him. "We're not the enemy, *kaikaina*."

"I have homework."

"Yeah?" She grabbed the back of his jacket and yanked, toppling his hood. "Well first, you have an apology to—"

Her breath clutched in her throat. She felt her jaw working to find words, but she was shock's speechless bitch thanks to the black-and-blue welt that swelled up Leo's left eye and cheek. A gasp finally escaped as she stumbled back.

"Whoa." Thank the gods for Kellan, who'd obviously dealt with sights like this more than she. "If this was 'just practice,' dude, I'd love to see what you do in competition."

Maybe her thanks for the man was premature. She whipped her stare between the two males. "Are you two *laughing* about this?"

Kellan shrugged. "You have a better suggestion?"

"Are you serious, Sergeant?"

"Are *you*?"

"Look at him!" Despite her dictate, it was torture for her to do the same. Since she'd decided to toss logic out the window for the night, she had to fumble to find it again, to dissect her rage. She was angry—make that enraged—with whoever had done this to him, not the kid himself. But Leo was the one standing here. And like it or not, she had to consider that damage like this wasn't usually one-sided.

"Oh, I'm looking," Kellan replied in a tone that sounded like they were still taking their postcoital stroll through the garden. To Leo, he murmured, "Just assure me the other guy is worse off."

Leo raised a sideways fist. "You know it."

As Kellan lifted a fist to meet the bump, she snapped, "You are *not* helping." The grin he turned back to her, deepening his dimples, only worsened her frustration. How the hell did he make her want to slap him and jump him in the same damn moment? "And you"—she pivoted back at Leo—"are grounded. One week."

"What?" Her brother winced as his face retaliated for the effort of trying to return her glare. "Why?"

She arched her brows when he pulled his fist back from Kellan and drove it against the fridge. "You want to go for two?"

"You suck!"

"Better stop while you're ahead, ace," Kellan murmured.

Leo curled his upper lip. "Figures you'd take her side."

Kellan grimaced and shook his head. "There's no 'sides' here, man. Your sister cares enough about you to throw out some discipline. Be grateful."

Lani folded her arms. "Amen."

She'd no sooner gotten out the quip than the man sucked away all her composure once more, pivoting to face her again, crossing his arms too. His bigger, harder, beautifully tapered arms. "That doesn't let you off the hook, Miss Kail."

She felt her jaw open and then shut. Then again. Who *was* this man? The one she'd gotten to know over the last four days had intensity sewn into his DNA by the angels, but it had always been accessorized by charm and sensuality. This person who loomed over her now was the unadorned Kellan Rush, stripped to a steely core, unflappable. This was a glimpse—maybe a little more—at the soldier with the call sign Slash. *Just* Slash. The guy who got the job done with one stab... or one bullet.

Who was making her pussy throb for him like it never had before.

"I—" she stammered. "I—"

"Haven't given your brother a chance to explain?" He nodded. "Yeah, that sounds like a damn good answer."

Hell. And...*wow.*

"Okay," she finally spat. "Yes, sir."

She felt better then, at least enough to dare a glance at him. She was glad she did. Though he was still all hard-jawed GI Joe, his eyes remained full of silky gray affection. His stance was still badass commander, but he gave her a nod of complete respect.

She was stunned to feel her lips returning that smile. Damn his luscious hide.

Her brother's snigger was a spike ball in the middle of the moment. "Yes, sir?" Leo cracked. "Oh-em-gee. Sistah-girl lies down and whimpers for Slash-gasm. Mark this day on the calendar."

Kellan backhanded Leo's shoulder. "You really want to push your game at this point, kid?"

"No, sir."

"Then muffle it."

"Yes, sir."

"And now spill it."

Leo shuffled and slumped against the wall. "Not much to spill."

One look at her brother told Lani it was the truth. She also discerned why. There was a specific kind of defeat etched into his face—at least the side that hadn't been turned into a touchscreen of bruises. "It was Parker Smythe, wasn't it?"

Leo attempted another grimace. "He's such a tampon. Just because I finally kicked his ass in a match, he fabricated some loser excuse about how I purposely spilled water on his gym bag, and escalated shit from there. I tried to laugh it off, but he gave me lip about how the bag cost a grand and how I intended to ruin it, and—" He shook his head and twisted his lips. "If he spent a thousand dollars on the thing, why was it on the floor and not in his fucking locker?"

Lani slapped his shoulder. "*Language.*"

"What*ever*," Leo rebutted.

Kellan snorted. "Maybe it was like his man purse or something."

"And his lip gloss was stored inside."

"You couldn't help it if he got bitchy about the whole thing."

"Right?"

Lani rekindled her battle stance at the soldier. "Okay, what the hell?"

Kellan returned her scrutiny with equal conviction. "He didn't start the scuffle, okay?"

"Scuffle?" she snapped. "That's what you're calling it?"

He pinched the bridge of his nose. "Compared to the conflicts I've seen in my time, Starshine—yeah, that's what I'm calling it. And from where I stand, Leo's shown some behavior you can be proud of. You Kails are a proud bunch. He served the family name well by refusing to let a dickwad roll him over and paid the price with his face."

"No shit," Leo muttered.

"Language!"

Kellan shot her a look of forced patience. After a long moment, his eyes flicked over to Leo. "You want some ice for that wreckage, man?"

"Yeah. Thanks."

"And a beer?"

"Hell yeah!"

"No!" Lani went at Kellan's shoulder with her fist this time. It felt like punching a brick wall. "You are *really* not helping!"

Leo's laugh warmed the top of her head. "Don't believe her, Slash-gasm. You're helping a lot." There was a meaningful pause as her brother locked gazes with her soldier. "For the record, I'm glad you're here...you *and* T-Bomb."

As Kellan flashed a warm smile at Leo, a surge of emotions slammed Lani—and built up in the heat behind her eyes. She stared hard at Leo, forcing herself to see him as Kellan did: not as the kid he once was but the man he was growing to be. It wasn't the first time today that she'd arrived at this awareness, either. Tait's words of this afternoon had started opening the cracks on those thoughts.

How had these two men brought so many changes in just a few days?

And how the hell was she going to wave goodbye to them in a week...making sure that list didn't include *her*?

She couldn't think about that right now. She refused to think about it.

Instead, embracing the perfect joy of *now*, she wrapped

her arms around Kellan's waist and squeezed hard. "For the record," she whispered, "I'm glad too."

CHAPTER ELEVEN

For the first time in over a year, Tait voluntarily rose with the sun. He added to that stunner by jamming his feet into running shoes and setting off down the road with loud guitars in his ears—and mental clarity as his goal.

He planned for a very long run.

The events of yesterday, and all the sensations they'd brought, collided on top of each other with every step he took. The cartwheels in his gut when he first saw Lani in the house. The rockets in his soul when he'd kissed her. The lurch in his cock when he'd been out for a night walk and came across Kell and her instead. Then the surreal dream of watching Kell fuck her...and knowing she was aware of his own presence through every second of it. That maybe she was wetter because of it. That her pussy squeezed Kellan harder...

The memory of it forced him to seek a cold shower when he'd gotten back to the house, but even the freezing jets hadn't helped. He'd played the scene over again in his mind, including every gasp she'd made and scream she'd released, and pumped himself to completion once more. Finally exhausted enough to sleep, he'd fallen into bed still clad in his shower towel and didn't wake up until the sunrise filtered through the blinds.

It was the first time, in nearly two hundred nights, that a vision of Luna hadn't pulled him to consciousness in a pool of his tears and sweat.

The realization made him run faster. His lungs started

to burn, and his legs declared him a Class-A motherfucker. Wasn't any worse than what he'd been calling himself since swigging his vitamins on an empty stomach and welcoming the wave of please-induce-me-to-vomit-now that followed. And oh yeah, there was that other temptation, too—the one that pulled him toward the bar, taunting that a drunken coma was the best place for a guy like him. A guy who'd easily scooted aside memories of the love of his life after simply watching his buddy screw someone else. Who had to watch happiness from the bushes, unable to figure it out for himself anymore.

He pounded harder into the run, switching to his screaming punk rock track. His body flooded with sweat. He sucked in the ocean wind, enduring the light-headedness of his anaerobic zone.

When he got back to Franzen's place in a heaving mess, the guilt only ripped harder at him. After tearing the earbuds out, he beat feet for the shower once more. This time, he cranked the water to a scalding temperature. With one hand, he braced the tiles. With the other, he palmed his balls.

In his mind, he summoned Luna.

Hi, beautiful...

She was giving him sass in that Los Angeles bar again, in those painted-on red jeans hugging every inch of her supple hips. Then he was bending her over the chopping block in the bar's back room, commanding her to take the pants off, telling her how he was going to hurt her, fuck her, pleasure her.

He groaned and gripped the base of his cock.

She was standing with him in the condo they'd turned into a safe house during the mission, all of LA sprawled beneath them, kissing him and begging him to take her. Then she was beneath him, sucking his penis harder with every twist he gave her nipples, rubbing herself to a climax as he thrust deeper into her mouth.

He started stroking himself. Brutally. Precome surged and disappeared, washed away by the hot streams beating on him.

In his mind, Luna came hard. Screamed from her hot explosion, over and over again...

Suddenly, the cries took on a huskier edge. A deep urgency, swirling with a night breeze that smelled like paradise. There were words, too...pleadings in a musical island accent. *Kellan. Oh, gods, please!*

He gritted his teeth and beat the wall, fighting the invasion of it. Of her. Satin hair fanned on the ground. Arms spread out, making her look like a bronze forest goddess.

"No. *No.*"

Round, perfect breasts. Pink, moist clit. Legs spread, ready to be taken.

Stop. Stop!

He pumped harder. Faster. Fire roared up his shaft. Come built in his balls.

Surrendered nudity. Open and willing.

He needs to see me fuck you, Starshine. To bury myself to the balls in you. Like this...

He fell to his knees as his ass clenched, his sac drew tight, and the orgasm blasted through his body. He forced his eyes open even as the shock waves kept up, blinking against the water to watch the thick milk from his body swirl down the drain.

Wasted seed. Useless sewer sludge. Like so many other attempts to make his life count for something. To prove Dad wrong.

Damn it! Can't you kids keep this place clean for one day?
Damn it! Can't you kids stay quiet for just one hour?
Damn it! Can't you kids do anything right?
It's no fucking wonder your mother left.

Though he'd just poured himself out—literally—in the last fifteen minutes, a frantic energy whorled in his gut, up his throat, through his head. He wasn't freaked by the assault. He knew this shit well. It was his old friend self-hatred, come for a visit in his soul for the day.

He pushed his forehead against the knob to turn the water off, closing his eyes for another moment. The fury swelled up once more, burning and disgusting, finally exploding from him in a long, terrible roar. In the thick silence after it, there was a distinct *click*. He'd shaken the shower door open. As the glass panel slid out with a slow creak, he let out a bitter laugh then a grateful snort. Without the distraction, he would've likely sent a fist into the wall. Retiling Franz's shower would've been an interesting way of staying busy for the next week.

He stumbled out of the stall and into the bedroom, managing to find a clean pair of shorts and a T-shirt that didn't smell like half-baked ass. Then he walked out to the living room.

Where his gaze zeroed in on the bar.

Where a full bottle of Grey Goose beckoned, a beacon of flawless liquid therapy.

"Yessss."

He pretended he didn't see the clock on the microwave, revealing it had just turned ten a.m., as he U-turned into the kitchen to grab a glass. If he was going to be a roasted lush for the day, he'd do it with some manners this time, in the privacy of the lanai. Not doing the soused-hobo-on-the-beach thing.

Correction: Lani's beach. *Not cool to share the dirty laundry with the neighbors, man—even if you* did *share orgasms with them last night.* He had boundaries, after all. He just had to remember where he put them.

In the meantime, he'd get tanked the civilized way, with a glass in his hand and a cushion under his ass. Then he'd pass out more normally, too: silent, angry, and alone. Like father, like son, right?

A rumble chewed its way up his throat. "No," he spat. He *wasn't* like Dad, at least not in the most critical way. He hadn't totally fucked up the self-worth of a couple of kids before drinking his life into the toilet.

After securing a glass, he swiped up the vodka, headed out to the lanai, and found a comfortable chair that allowed him to prop his feet on the rail. After the short rain shower that had blown through last night, the sun rose on another postcard-perfect day in paradise. Before opening the vodka, he paused to enjoy the tropical panorama. No better time than now, since he wasn't going to be conscious by the time sunset fell.

Yeah...about that...

A funny thing happened on the way to the great Grey Goose wasteland.

It started after he poured his first drink. He was three gulps in on the hooch, still grappling for a mental off-ramp from Memory Lane with Dad, when a different vision replaced the bastard in his imagination.

His stare drifted over to the lanai railing. Where once more, Lani appeared.

She was fuzzy at the edges but just as breathtaking. Just like yesterday, she sat with legs straddling the rail, turquoise-polished toes peeking from beneath her sundress. The breeze sifted through the dark ribbons of her hair, and the sun glinted off the silver swirls in her eyes.

Suddenly, his mental skirmish in the shower felt like a lame training exercise.

"Leave me alone," he growled.

She just lifted a serene smile and swung her feet in leisure. *Don't think so.*

"Damn it." With shaking hands, he dumped more vodka into the glass. Chugged the whole thing. Familiar lethargy sank into his blood. He let his head fall back. The buzz couldn't come fast enough. And after that, the blessed numbness...

After soaking for several minutes in the vodka bath, he pried open his eyes again. The horizon swam a little. It was nowhere near how blasted he wanted to be but a good start. He'd finally be alone. Once he got to this point, his mind was too busy racing for the Shitfaced Speedway finish line to bother with memories.

He jerked in his chair as Lani's laugh tinkled on the air again.

He glared to his right. There she was, still smiling at him. Still tilting her head with that inquisitiveness that was too damn cute for her own good. And certainly not for his.

"Fuck. Me."

The hallucination folded her arms and narrowed her eyes. *Are you serious?*

"Yes," he snarled. "Go the *hell* away."

So everything you spouted at me yesterday is just bullshit? All that crap about giving up the dome *on my pain, believing I can have life's whole meal, taking off the masks even though it's scary... All that's okay for me but not you? I'm supposed to try a change, but you aren't?*

Guess that makes you a hypocrite and *a lush.*

He grimaced and bared his teeth as the lanai converted to a torture room. Somewhere in his soul, he'd tap into the right combination of rage and pain and profanity to hurl back at her. Why was it such a problem to find it all when it crawled right under the surface of his skin every fucking day? He tore through the muck of his senses, but the booze had dropped a fog on everything, making it impossible to see or touch anything.

A roar tore from his gut and ravaged his throat.

He seized the bottle and flung it into the dunes.

A second later, he pitched the glass in its wake.

The silence, perforated only by the *shoosh* of the waves and the music of the lanai wind chimes, was worse than her spiritual laughter. "Feel better?" he finally sneered at her. "Because I sure as hell don't."

He knew the drill on this scene now. With the booze gone, he'd have to face the pain. Walk himself through the same shitty, stinking emotional labyrinth he'd progressed a thousand times with the shrinks back at base. Couldn't someone just pull up his file and read it this time? *Mother left the family when subject was ten years old. Raised primarily by father, who died of alcohol poisoning when subject was seventeen. Subject has unresolved issues of guilt, accountability, and—*

"Generally being fucked up."

Hey. That was pretty funny. He snickered while rolling his head back again. The sun washed across his face, imparting a little physical warmth while the ice floes of his psyche kept ramming each other. He let his eyes drift shut. Fate decided to smile, sending the sandman to tempt his mind back into the rescue of sleep. As his mind crossed from consciousness to slumber, he felt himself smile as distant voices echoed in his head.

Why do you let him hurt you, Mama? I don't understand.

I don't expect you to, Tait. Sometimes...loving people just hurts.

Do you love him, Mama?

Yeah, Tait. I love him a lot.

Well, I don't care what you say. It shouldn't have to hurt. He's not ever gonna do that to you again. I'm gonna protect you.

Ohhh...my big T man. You'll always be my hero.

I love you, Mama.

And I love you too, Tait. No matter what happens, remember that...

"Hey, Rumple-shit-skin. What the hell else do I need to do here?"

The crack, which he vaguely attributed to Kell, was punctuated by an icy stab in his thigh. Then his neck. "Mmmfff? Whaaa?"

"Whoa," his friend sneered. "It lives."

Two more ice pelts, this time direct hits on his crotch. He jerked upright to observe his friend sitting about six feet away, a bowl of ice cubes on the small table next to him. Revision: only half the bowl was full. The rest of the cubes were strewn on the deck around Tait.

He lowered his feet, which knocked the pair of cubes down from his zipper. "Having fun, asshole?"

Kellan smirked. "It was either this or dump Tabasco down your maw. You were sawing logs hard enough to give me real easy access."

"Guess you want me to thank you for choosing the frost attack, instead?"

After a moment of contemplation, his friend cocked a

brow. Gone was the hot-and-horny lover boy Kell had morphed into last night in the forest. Sergeant Rush was back in all his carefully reined glory. "Someone's in a rough mood."

"Yeah, well..." He shrugged, hoping the strange telepathy of their friendship, which had spasmed back to life a little during their time with Lani last night, would activate and convey his words as the apology he intended.

"You look like crap too."

"Thanks, honey. But is my butt fat in this dress?"

There was a significant pause. "You been hitting the sauce?"

He let another moment stretch before replying. "Tried to. *Wanted* to."

Kellan actually gave half a smile. "But you didn't."

Tait surged to his feet. "Don't go striking up the goddamn violins."

"Fair enough." Kell held up both hands but lowered them the next moment, bracing his elbows to both knees. "But since your head is all here, maybe we should talk about—"

"What time is it?" There was no way in hell he was letting the guy bring up last night. It happened; it was over. He wasn't about to spill how he'd longed to be the one slapping bodies with Lani last night or how the woman had taken over his five-knuckle-shuffle in the shower this morning.

"Half past one," Kellan answered.

"Damn. I slept a long time."

"You want to go get some lunch? Lani keeps telling me we have to hit the restaurant at the Kilohana Plantation during our stay. Guess it's famous, and the food's supposed to be decent. Waitress service, even."

He sent the guy a broad smile, again hoping it conveyed

more than what he put to words. "That sounds cool. Unless we have to wear ties."

"Dude, when was the last time you saw me in a tie?"

"Hawk's wedding?" he conjectured. "Well, the first one. Second time around, we all got to make like Ren Faire peasants."

"Sure made it easier to scratch the nuts. Discreetly, of course."

He tossed half a grin as they walked out to the rental car. "I assume nut scratching is frowned on at this plantation thing, huh?"

Kell chuckled. "Probably."

"So we're on the needle between Windsor knots and open testicle attention. Sounds do-able."

★ ★ ★ ★ ★

A little over two hours later, Tait polished off a perfectly cooked piece of halibut, while Kell had gone for the restaurant's massive Reuben sandwich. They'd split a plate of fries, too, and scarfed on the last of the potatoes while waiting for the waitress to process the check.

After the fries were demolished, Kellan tossed his napkin onto the table and swung a steady gaze at Tait. "There *is* something I need to talk to you about, T."

Tait took a swig on his water in temporary evasion. How the fuck was he going to deflect the house visit from uncomfortable this time? "Look, man, I don't really think we—"

"It's about Gunter Benson."

"Oh." He disguised his surprise—and relief—by taking

another swig. Both feelings were overshadowed by the ire that came with thinking about Benson and his fashion plate posse. "What about the asshat?"

Kell's jaw stiffened. "I don't think he's got straight-up intentions about Hale Anelas."

Tait almost laughed. "'Intentions'? You going all protective papa on me about an estate that's not even yours, dude?"

"Like you'd blame me? You've spent enough time at the stables and the beach with Leo to know why the words mean *home of the angels.*"

Or maybe one angel in particular?

It took one fast glance with his buddy to confirm Kell "heard" the thought, loud and clear. He felt a flash of guilt for causing the tight lines at the corner of the guy's eyes, but trying to reroute the very neurons of his brain was going to be impossible. Kellan had to realize, from the second they'd first seen Lani, that it'd be impossible for Tait to douse *some* kind of attraction for her—and after last night, that little campfire in his psyche had combusted into a full pyre of lust. But they didn't have to dissect the issue, either—nor had he been concerned about Kell pushing for such a debrief. In the history of their friendship, the sharing-is-caring sessions had always been Bommer-sponsored endeavors. If he was officially back-burnering last night's events, he counted on Kell to do the same.

"Okay. Giving you the gold star on that one," he conceded. "But I still don't follow your tack on Benson."

Kell scooted in tighter, sliding his trigger finger up and down along the tablecloth, indicating the rapid spin of his thoughts. "The guy's hotter for Lani's land than a dog for peanut butter, right?"

"Nice work, Sherlock. But I still bet you can't name my last deployment by eyeing my tan lines."

"Your tan lines do *not* interest me, dick brain. But Benson and his motives? That's another story."

Tait scowled. "Motives?"

Kell pulled in a breath and changed his finger pattern to a full circle. "I don't think he wants the place to build a resort."

This time, Tait leaned forward. "You're right. That's way more interesting than tan lines, even mine."

"Something hasn't added up about the guy for me, ever since we met him and the pretty boy crew that first night. I kept wondering why he didn't want to survey the mansion, the gardens, or the pasture. He only asked to see the orchard, the beach, and"—Kell's voice hitched for a weird moment—"the lookout point."

"Interesting observation. But I'm not the guy to be asking about accurate memories from that night."

Kellan cracked only a slight smirk at that. He took back his napkin and started folding the thing with more precision than he gave his airborne harness pack, so Tait knew the guy was entering serious deliberation mode now. "Something just hit me wrong about the whole thing, so I started poking around online. Personally, there wasn't much to discover about Benson. He's made a religion out of his privacy. Has a permanent residence—actually, a small fiefdom—in Beverly Hills. He exclusively dates indie film actresses but drops them if they make it into big commercial releases or start bitching about commitment. He's got a thing about publicity and relationship strings."

"What about the company? Benstock?"

"Also privately held. He started it with trust fund money but has worked his ass off to make it into the multibillion-dollar monster we all know and love. There's a partner, too. That's the source of the last half of the company name. But he's more reclusive than Benson. I didn't hit on anything other than his credentials are stellar, ensuring the company has excellent markers on its bets."

"He...or she."

Kell stabbed an affirming finger. "Good point."

Tait tapped the salt and pepper shakers together to keep his own hands busy. "None of this reveals anything crazy." So the guy owned an estate in the 90210, was in bed with some deep pockets, dated girls who gave him street cred in Hollywood, and was a condescending dickwad to women like Lani, who were the real deal. He studied Kell with expectancy. Where was the ricin on the guy's envelope?

"So on the surface, Benstock's main game is real-estate purchase and repurposing, primarily for five-star hotels and resorts."

"Still not dropping my jaw."

"Hold on to your panties. I'm getting to the juicy stuff." The guy rolled his shoulders then settled his elbows back to the table. "Hotels are only the start of Benstock's client list," he asserted. "Close to home, they have a division that secures high-end properties for filmings and special events for the entertainment industry. There's another subsidiary that brokers extended-stay property rentals for offshore investors, those needing 'ultimate attention to luxury *and* privacy.'"

Tait felt his teeth grinding. "In other words, oil sheikhs wanting to bang American virgins."

Kellan's face tautened. "That's just the tip of the iceberg."

"*What?*"

His friend nodded tightly. "Benstock has another subsidiary, not listed on their website and deeply hidden on most others. It's called Forte. Clicking on links for it always leads to a screen requiring a password. Nothing came up when I tried cross-searches, either. I even did a mind-fuck on myself and pretended *I* was an oil sheikh seeking the 'services' of the company."

Tait hunkered his brows. "And still nothing?" When Kell affirmed with another head dip, he probed, "So then what?" His senses started sizzling in commiseration with the frustration his friend must've felt at hitting those dead ends. But he also knew that in true Spec Ops style, Kell hadn't given up there.

"I bought a burner phone, then used it to call Benstock's corporate headquarters in California. I faked an accent for the call, something between early Vin Diesel and vintage Omar Sharif."

Tait chuckled. "And I don't get a sample?"

Kell pursed his lips with sarcasm. "You'll thank me for sparing you. Good news is, it worked on the first five layers of gatekeepers that I spoke to at Benstock."

"*Five?* Damn. Who do they let you talk to on level six? The Pope?"

"Not sure. But get this: the dude I spoke to on level five was strange enough to make me hang up as soon as he put me on hold, on my way to level six." The color drained from Kell's face. The sight was weirdly fascinating, mostly because Tait had never experienced it before. "I'm only going to admit this to you, T. The fucker scared me."

Tait scooted in again. "Damn. You're serious, aren't you?"

"Wish I wasn't." Kell's face, still too pale for Tait's comfort, gave up that answer. "I could've dealt with a typical henchman act, you know? The whole battery acid crossed with tacks kind of voice? But this bastard was smooth, like a shiv dunked in butter—that had attended Oxford."

"An Alan Rickman vibe?"

If it was possible, Kell's glare narrowed again. "Damn it. Lani hit you with the swoony-over-Rickman thing too, eh?" Though they shared a couple of snickers at that, the guy's humor faded fast. "Strangely, the weirdo's accent wasn't what made me eventually hang up."

"Then what was?"

"After I went through the drill of asking about the Forte project and indicated I had *substantial* funds to invest, he got even oozier on the demeanor. Then he told me, as if he were some servant just checking my martini order, that he noticed I was calling from a location on Kaua`i"—he stopped to let Tait bark the F-word at that—"and assumed I was on the island to take a look at their *unique opportunity* here. He assured me that the *asset* was *days away* from being secured and accessible." Like a character from a bad spy movie, Kell hunched his shoulders and leaned deeper over the table. "Then he asked which delegation I was representing: Pyongyang or Tehran."

A two-by-four of shock knocked Tait back in his chair. "Are you fucking with me?" He took another hard gulp of his water. "Don't answer that. Of course you're not."

Kellan worked his jaw back and forth. "Now you know why I hung up."

"No shit." He swallowed hard. "Rephrase. *Holy* shit."

"I've been running all kinds of nutso scenarios in my head since then," his friend supplied. "Like maybe the words are just some sick inside joke among the Benstock crowd. Maybe

ANGEL PAYNE

they're using them to stand in for something else, to make the *poseur* investors run when hearing them."

Tait shot him a hard stare. "You really going to play ball with that hunch? Kell, crazy men print the president's likeness on toilet paper in both those cities for the fun of wiping their asses on his face. This intel is too insane not to—"

"Okay, back that pony up. Like I said, we're not even sure it *is* intel."

Thanks to his time with Leo the last few days, Tait had perfected the art of eye rolls. He threw a good one at his friend before charging, "Whoever the hell you called, he was able to drop a locator pin on your *burner* phone. And if you were calling from a car—"

"Fuck," Kell cut in. "Yeah. I was in Lani's jeep."

"Then the reason why the guy got sappy on you was due to stalling. He was likely repositioning some private satellites with the intent of photographically feeling you up."

"Shit."

"You tossed the phone after you hung up, right?"

"Straight into an eco-collection bin."

"Good." Nevertheless, the breath he released was harsh and heavy. "Dude, we've got to call Franz. There's a good chance he can pull in his buddy from the spooks and give us guidance on what needs to happen next."

Kellan's relief blared across his face. "Dan Colton, right? He still with the CIA in South America?" At Tait's nod, he continued, "Good man. That's a sound plan."

Tait consciously schooled his features as he managed a nod of agreement. Truth was, he'd never forget Dan. The guy had been a key support during the six months of Luna's coma and, more importantly, the six months since she'd gone to sleep

163

forever. At least once a week, Dan had called from wherever he was in the world for regular check-ins. While Tait was sure the guy was motivated by misplaced guilt—Dan wasn't even with the same agency that had "borrowed" Luna for the mission— he was still grateful that somebody remembered Luna's sacrifice. Her actions had prevented a domino effect of bombs that would have put everything west of the Rockies beneath a radioactive cloud for decades to follow.

He gave himself a mental wrench. Right now, there was no room for sticking even a toe into grief's swimming pool. Much bigger issues were at hand.

"Let's get the hell out of here," he asserted while tossing down his napkin. "I'd rather call Franz from the house, where we can't be overheard. And I think your protective fleas have jumped to my hide. I don't like the idea of Lani and Leo being alone back at the estate, so the sooner you get back to them, the better." When Kellan didn't match his haste, a thread of discomfort snaked back through his stomach. "Come on," he prodded to cover for it. "Let's bug, bro."

"Tait." His friend's voice sounded like a bucket of dry lava rocks. "About Lani..."

He thrust to his feet. "Not going there, man."

"I think we need to."

"Well, *I* think you're wrong." He grimaced. "Since when are *you* such a fan of the emotional slice-and-dice anyway?"

"Did I say I was a fan?" He thrust up his jaw. "Some people are just worth getting uncomfortable for. Like it or not, dickhead, both of you fall into that category for me."

Hell. Ignoring the shitball now really would make him a dickhead. "Okay, fine. We'll talk about it, just not here. First things first. Let's get back to Franz's place, grab the guy on the horn, and make sure your discovery is disseminated to the right people. After that, I promise we can sit down, brew up some herbal tea, and have a long, cozy chitty-chat, if that's what you want."

"Chitty-chat?" Kellan glowered as he pushed to his feet. "You're pushing it, T-Bomb."

"But I'm worth it." He batted his eyelashes in an open taunt. "Remember?"

★ ★ ★ ★ ★

Thanks to a huge accident on the 50, their drive time back to Franzen's was prolonged by an hour. A stroke of luck helped Tait in veering Kell away from approaching the subject of Lani again. He gave himself a mental high-five for thinking to load the full Timbaland music library on his phone. After plugging it into the rental car's USB, he was able to keep Kell more occupied than a two-year-old with his mama's key ring.

When they got back to Franzen's house, the sun had disappeared, leaving the sky a brilliant blend of purple, crimson, and gold. Lani's jeep was still in the driveway, as they'd expected, but it was joined by a black pickup. Since the wheel wells were splattered in fresh mud and dust, Tait drew the conclusion that the second vehicle had come from Hale Anelas, as well. He peered at the house in curiosity. The living room and lanai lights were aglow.

"Somebody's here," he stated. "I didn't think we'd be gone that long, so I didn't leave the lights on."

"Shit," Kell spat. "You think we need to be worried?"

"That's not what my gut's saying," he replied. "But who the hell is—"

He was plunged into silence by a figure bursting from the house and racing across the packed earth. His breath was kept captive by the sight of luscious hips encased in snug jeans, incredible cleavage in a flowered camisole, and a flowing mane of thick black hair—

Flying around a goddess's face, flooded with terror.

"Starshine?" Kellan followed it with a rough grunt as Lani launched herself at him. She sobbed hard into his shoulder, revealing she'd been waiting a while to do so. "Hey, hey," Kellan crooned. "Sweetheart, what's wrong?"

Now Tait's gut began its alarms. "Is it Benson?" he charged. "Has he fucked with you again? Where is the bastard?"

As he fired the demands, someone else emerged from the house. Ike, one of Hale Anelas's ranch hands, appeared in the twilight. The man's face, normally ruddy and smiling, was redrawn by lines of worry. "It's not Benson," he explained. "It's Leo."

"Leo?" Screw the alarms. His stomach clenched into a full fist of dread. "What's wrong with Leo? What's happened?"

Kellan held out a surprisingly steady hand. "Whoa. Wait. This isn't undue drama, is it? Ike, we already know about the shiner."

"The *shiner*?" Tait growled. "When the hell did that happen?"

Ike shook his head. "No. This is more, I'm afraid."

Kellan scowled. "More...how?"

"He's gone." Lani's confession spilled from trembling lips. Tears were so thick in her eyes, they resembled iridescent glass.

"Gone?" Tait echoed. "What the fuck does *that* mean?"

Ike shifted forward again. "We didn't notice anything

screwy until it was time for dinner. Most of us were down at the barn all afternoon, and Hokulani was working in the rose garden. Everyone thought Leo had gotten home and was in his room, doing homework. We didn't realize the room was empty until we called him down for dinner with no response."

Lani sucked in a shaky breath. "Th-That's when I checked my texts and emails."

She held out her phone for both of them to view.

Lani,

I love you, but I can't do all this anymore. I was so proud of myself for standing up to Parker yesterday, but I should have seen what the prick was up to. He only backed down because he had a better plan in mind than bashing my face in. Kalea is with him now, and my heart is ruined instead.

What's the good of continuing to try, when shit like this keeps happening? Mom and Dad are gone. Soon our home will be too. And having to see my greatest love with my worst enemy... It all sucks bigger bones than what I can handle.

I want to be alone. Forever.

Tait read the note over one more time and returned the phone to Lani. Yeah, the message dripped in teenage melodrama, which should've had him snickering a little by now. But that was the guy he was a year ago. A guy who'd been through a year of pain a lot like Leo's closing line.

A guy who also had a CO and a best friend who hadn't given up on him.

The thought gripped him so deeply, he didn't notice Lani pull away from Kellan and approach him. When she twisted both her hands into his, he started a little—then went completely still. Within seconds, the woman wrapped his soul and senses again. Seized by the desperation in her clasp. Eviscerated by the sorrow on her face.

"You've spent the most time with him in the last week, Tait. If you have an idea where he might've gone...what he might be thinking... God, anything..." Another cry burst from her, filled with distraught need. "He's the only thing I have left. Help me...please!"

CHAPTER TWELVE

Lani had been through a lot of fear in her life. Hiding in a cave from Hurricane Iniki when she was four. The night they'd come to tell her about Mom and Dad's plane crash. Anytime Gunter and his gang came calling.

None of it came close to this new terror.

Her throat was clamped shut. Her veins ran with ice water. "He...he doesn't pull stunts like this," she explained, trying to breathe but getting ragged results at best. She peered frantically between Tait and Kellan. "He *knows* better than this. We are Kails. We don't just run away from our issues. What the hell is he thinking?"

As if her thoughts had a conduit to the elements, the sky over the ocean snarled. They all looked to see massive thunderheads, rolling in fast.

"Well, isn't that special." In true *Kama`aina* style, Ike gave the situation a softly sardonic commentary.

"Shit!" Lani spat.

Tait and Kellan's reaction, nearly the same wide stance with hands to their hips, gave her an odd, immediate surge of confidence. Without turning his assessment from the horizon, Tait asked Ike, "How long do you reckon before that shit hits?"

"Depends," Ike supplied. "If the wind stays low, four to five hours. If it starts to blow hard, we could be under showers in an hour."

Kellan turned to them. "Apologies for sounding like a guy

who grew up just outside Spokane, but it's still eighty degrees. A little rain won't give the kid frostbite, right?"

Lani paced away from them then, unable to listen as Ike explained what a downpour did to some of the rocky cliffs along their side of the island. Hearing the phrases "slick as Vaseline" and "love-sick teenager with three seconds of patience" wasn't doing a thing for her agitation level.

After the men deliberated for what felt like days, they moved into action at the same time. She jogged back over in time to watch Ike transfer the first aid kit and a blanket out of his truck and into her jeep. At Tait's order to do so, he also peeled back the jeep's convertible roof.

"That's good," Tait remarked as he emerged from the house with a coil of rope and some bottles of water. He'd changed into heavy khaki pants and a windbreaker. "We'll have better sight lines without the lid."

"What's going on?" she asked.

Tait stopped to give her a tight hug. "I've got a pretty good idea of where he is," he stated. "We're taking the jeep because we can get it onto the sand."

"I can drive," Ike offered. "I grew up on this shore."

Tait nodded tightly. "Good."

Lani squared her shoulders. "I'm going with you."

His features tightened. "Lani—"

"I grew up on this shore, too, *hupo*."

He curled a hand around her nape to keep her gaze bolted with his, lowering his head to help the effort too. "You'll be calling *yourself* an idiot if he comes back here, finds no one around, and decides to fly again."

A unique yet familiar scent came from behind her. Kellan's bergamot-and-musk essence instilled her with much-needed resilience. She was tempted to kiss him for it as he injected, "I'll stay here, T. She needs to go."

Tait looked up. The two men held each other's stare for another thirty seconds, in which Lani could've sworn she was witness to a conversation that didn't have its volume knob turned up. Tait actually nodded at the end of it, like Kellan had made a final point with which to concur. "Got a jacket with you, dreamgirl?" he issued. "It's likely going to get a little breezy."

She shrugged, not about to let her wardrobe be his next excuse for deterring her. "I'll be fine. Come on; let's go."

Tait turned from her without a word and disappeared into the house. A few seconds later, he strode back out with a sweatshirt in hand, passing it to her on his way to the jeep. "*Now* you're fine. Put it on and hop in. We're racing the sky."

She tugged the sweatshirt over her head, feeling tiny in the large garment. As she started rolling up the sleeves, it was impossible to avoid the intensity of Kellan's stare—on her chest.

"I've always loved being in the army, but Starshine, you give the word new meaning." He playfully traced the "R" that was pushed out by her right breast as he pulled her in for a kiss. Lani didn't resist the fervent press of his lips. She wrapped both arms around his broad shoulders, gripping him just as eagerly in return. When they pulled apart, she moved one hand up to his stubbled, sexy jaw.

"I'm so glad you're here," she confessed, meaning the words a thousand times more than she had in the kitchen last night. She hoped he saw the thankfulness in her eyes. His answering smile conveyed that he did.

All too soon, she had to step back. Kellan squeezed her hand one last time before he let her go. She pressed it into the center of her chest, hoping his strength seeped into the one place where she needed it most right now. Her heart.

★ ★ ★ ★ ★

"Pull in here."

Tait's shout prompted Ike to jerk the jeep's steering wheel, directing it across the sand and toward the deep alcove in the cliffs to which he'd pointed. Lani fought to stay upright in the back seat as they bounced over the rockier ground of the shore. The moment Ike cut the engine, she glanced frantically to the clouds over the water before jumping out and joining the men, who tested flashlights and coiled rope for inclusion in the backpacks at their feet.

"Are you sure about this?" she questioned Tait.

He checked the attachments on a supersized utility knife. "Of course I'm not sure. But he's a sixteen-year-old on a pretty small island who doesn't have many options for a stunt like this. Besides that, he was gung ho about showing off this 'discovery' to me just two days ago. If this was *Final Jeopardy*, I'd write it in and bet everything but a buck."

"But we're over three miles from home. How could he have gotten this far, over the rocks, since school got out?"

Tait flashed her a rugged soldier's version of his crooked grin. "Because he didn't come from home." He tapped the phone that had become a permanent fixture in her hand, a symbol of the hope that Leo would simply call and say he was just kidding and was back at Hale Anelas. "Timestamp on the email. Twelve thirty. I'm going to go out on a limb and bet he tossed in the towel on school after that."

"And just phoned the bus driver for personal car service?"

she countered.

"I wouldn't put it past the kid, but not likely in this case."

"So how did he get out here?"

His stare widened with speculation as he slipped on his backpack. "You really itching to know my theory on that one, too?"

Lani gulped. "Would the wise answer to that be no?"

"Probably."

As the weight in her chest tripled, she gestured toward the cliff, giving him clearance to lead the way. As Tait stepped past her, he slipped a hand around hers and held on firmly. She accepted the support with greedy gratitude. Like his best friend, the man had figured out she talked a good game when it came to I-Am-Woman-Hear-Me-Roar, but having them confirm her strength by borrowing a bit of their own, through their simple physical reassurances, was what kept her putting one foot in front of the other right now.

The cave was wider than she originally thought, since a big portion was hidden by a secondary rock outcropping. The natural disguise also cloaked a path: a narrow dirt ingress that was wedged between the steep bluffs like a secret note between two books. Tait led them straight toward it. "Here's where we'll need the flashlights," he instructed.

Unbelievably, the path tightened. Lani felt like the mountain was swallowing them, though she could still hear the surf on the shore—and the thunder in the sky, crawling closer. She coupled those observations with the packed dirt beneath her feet and summed up the courage to voice her conclusion. "The tide's rising with the storm. We're screwed if we're not out of here in an hour."

Tait didn't break stride. "I like to save the word 'screwed' for different connotations, dreamgirl. I've cross-trained with enough SEALs to keep us alive and afloat in here if needed."

The hoo-rah bravado didn't fool her. The undercurrent in his tone was gooier than the moans of the wind through the tunnel. "But if we don't reach Leo—"

"We're going to reach Leo."

No darkness this time. Only determination that wasn't accepting any hints at failure. Lani gladly supported that initiative.

They climbed deeper, then higher, then back down, until natural light once more poured in from above. The passageway widened into a cavern about the size of the front living room at home. Replacing the picture window was an opening in the rocks that gave a breath-stealing ocean view—and a direct drop of a hundred feet. Where the rug usually rested, there was a big puddle of water. Sitting next to that puddle, which looked deep enough to drown in, sat her little brother.

"Oh," she rasped past tears. "Oh, thank God! Leo!"

She took only one step before Tait yanked her back. Leaning close, he murmured, "The thorn's still in his paw, mama bear. Let's do this carefully."

She gave him a concurring nod and backed off, letting him approach Leo instead. Though the man lowered quietly, Leo jumped as if Tait had turned into a giant scorpion. The tear streaks on his face ripped at her heart. She knew all this was only typical teen boy dramatics, but at that moment, she wouldn't have thought twice about selling her soul for the chance to teleport Parker Smythe here and bash his face in.

"Dude," Tait chastised, grabbing Leo's arm, "Chill. It's only me."

Leo slanted a glare back at Ike and her. "You've got serious problems with bending the truth, T-Boner."

Despite her stress, maybe because of it, Lani had to stifle a little laugh. Leo had a nickname for Tait as well as Kellan. Her heart warmed. Judging by Tait's smirk, it did the same for him.

"Your sister cares about you, man. She's been a wreck. I think she said something about how you were all she has left."

Leo snorted. "That's bullshit. She has Slash-gasm now."

Tait's chuckle echoed off the walls. "Slash-gasm. Damn, why didn't I think of that?" He sobered as he shook his head. "Despite the cool hashtag, you're missing something key there. Kellan, like me, will be out of here in another week. And like it or not, the man's hard drive doesn't recognize the phrase *long-term relationship*."

"Yeah? I call bullshit again."

The hearth in her heart was swept by a gust of shock. She hadn't missed the growing length in Kellan's stares or the lingering tenderness in his touch but until now had written all of it off to the enchantment of the island, not her. Hawaii turned a lot of people into swooning idiots, even gritty Special Ops soldiers. But the surety of her brother's statement couldn't be denied. And the resulting confusion in her heart couldn't be ignored.

"You wanna tell me your head's in the same sand, man?" Leo pressed closer to Tait to murmur it, but the cave's acoustics made his effort useless. "You see how he looks at her, right?"

For a long pause, Tait didn't say anything. Lani told herself she was relieved, though the man's profile, looking out to the sea as if he yearned to fly into the thick of the storm, yanked the feeling from her. The next moment, the expression was gone. He turned back toward her brother and uttered, "Look...Leo..."

"Fuck!"

Lani hissed. She got ready with a finger-snapping follow-up to condemn Leo's language, a reaction as instinctual as teeth brushing and room cleaning reminders, but Tait stopped her with a firm glare. It felt odd and insane, but also natural and perfect, to step back in deference. This situation was beyond harrowing, and Tait's lead on it was amazing—for which she'd be forever grateful. If he wasn't here, it'd be her sitting next to Leo. Talk about the blind leading the blind—a holy-shit scenario to consider even when there wasn't a sheer cliff drop just a few feet away.

"Going to let you have that one, kid," Tait finally said. "The situation sucks, period."

Leo's shoulders fell even more. "Parker's probably mooning over Kalea right now, and vice versa. That piss-sucking fuckwad!"

Lani prepared to snap her fingers again. Tait reined her back with another glower. This command was as daunting as the first, but his face contained a new element now—a tension that showed her every drop of freak-out in his mental frying pan after Leo's comments about Kellan's not-so-hidden feelings.

Damn.

She'd fix it all soon enough. After all this was through, she'd sit Tait down and clarify things. She'd explain that no matter what the flight plan of Kellan's heart, she had no intention of rerouting hers to match. More than anyone, she was aware of the depths in her soul and the passion in her spirit and what they'd require from a man long-term. Too much. Kellan Rush was too good a guy to be drained by her outrageous needs. Once she explained that to Tait, maybe she'd even have an ally to help out with her goodbye to Kellan next week.

Right now, they had a more daunting task. Getting Leo to say farewell to this damn cave before they had to breaststroke their way out at the bottom while watching the jeep get carried out to sea. Shockingly, Tait didn't appear to share her urgency. The man smirked at Leo as if they were just kicking it at Waikiki, cruising the sand for babes.

"Nice face paint," he finally said, pointing to Leo's bruises. "Though I may need a four-one-one on what you're going for. I've narrowed it down to marble table on crack or zombie apocalypse wannabe."

Lani rolled her eyes, only to watch Leo guffaw at the joke. "Really?" she whispered to Ike, who was laughing as well. *Men.*

"Just tell me you smacked the same into Smythe," Tait went on.

Leo snickered again. "You and Slash sharing hard drives again?"

Tait cocked a grin. "He said the same thing?" At Leo's nod, he chuffed. "Figures. Assmunch steals all my best lines."

Leo slammed his chin atop his knees again. From Lani's corner, she watched his face contort again. "Feeling you, man. Only the assmunch in my world makes off with other guys' women too."

His head dropped again. Tait wrapped an arm across his quaking shoulders. "Leo—"

"He even ripped off my words, T. All that stuff I practiced with you, speaking from my heart and shit? Kalea loved it. All of it." His shoulders shook harder. "That choad took it all and retooled it to sound like his own. Everything about his game is a pathetic reboot."

"I know," Tait said softly. "And I'm sorry. But—"

"Don't you dare give me some lecture now about losing

shit and setting it free, then sitting back and watching if it's *meant to be* while smiling like an idiot in the rain."

"Sitting on a pink fluffy unicorn?"

"Right."

Tait curled his hand up to Leo's head and ruffled his hair. "Unicorns are good for target practice and not much else. Having your heart broken in the billions of ways this douchenozzle of a universe can dream up for us? That's another story. It sucks, plain and simple. I can't teach you how to talk this one into a bridle or tell you it's going to get better tomorrow, because it probably won't."

Leo tilted up a quizzical glare. "You sure you came to *help*?"

Lani released a small huff of triumph. She couldn't have said it better herself.

Tait yanked on his ear. "Listen to *everything*, you dork. I said it wouldn't get better tomorrow. But it will get better... eventually. You're an awesome guy, Leo. Another Kalea is going to come along who sees that."

Leo shrugged him off and howled. "No! There won't ever be another Kalea. Not for me."

"Yeah, dude; there *will* be. And she'll be amazing. I guarantee it."

Her brother straightened. Stared Tait nearly directly in the eye, as if examining him, before issuing what was clearly an open challenge. "Just like you believe there'll be another Luna for you, huh?"

Lani's breath caught. She dropped the gloating stance she'd been throwing Tait's way, now wincing in sympathy for the man—and feeling weirdly responsible for Leo's knee-jerk words. But the man bore the blow with dignity, returning her brother's scrutiny with carefully considered words.

"Tell you what. I promise to work on my pain if you promise to work on yours."

Leo took a second to ponder that. "It'd be a hell of a lot easier to die up here, thinking of how much Kalea's day will suck when I do."

Ike snickered softly. Lani elbowed him. Tait barely moved before volleying, "No, it wouldn't." He finished it by lifting his gaze to her. The look only lasted a moment, but it tackled her with a million sensations at once as he reassured her, supported her, and adored her, all between one blink and the next. "The only one you're going to devastate here is your sister. You really want to do that to a woman as incredible as her, who's going to support you through everything and anything?"

Leo shot him a grimace full of sixteen-year-old disgust. "Dude, she's cool, but I'm not going as far as 'incredible,' okay?"

"*Mahalo* to you, too, twerp." Lani threw him a smile full of loving sarcasm. When her stare scooted back to Tait, she softened her lips into a thankful smile. The man was right, of course. If she'd lost Leo tonight, much of her world would end. In the twinkle of his eyes, she still had a little of Mom. Through his broad and easy smile, Dad reached out and brightened each of her days.

There wasn't anything she wouldn't do for the kid, though lately his needs were getting more complicated. A plate of cookies and half a pizza often weren't enough to help Leo anymore. Why didn't life come with a guidebook? Just like the island maps carried by the stores in Lihue, she needed a set of directions for what curves were coming ahead. If she knew what to do, she'd do anything short of resculpting the Na Pali Coast for him. Maybe that too.

She just wished, so desperately, that she could do something to help Tait Bommer in the same way.

CHAPTER THIRTEEN

Kellan wondered how many times he'd have to pace Franz's lanai before the boards wore out beneath him. The estimate didn't stop him from walking the same line as before, shooting a worried gaze up the driveway and then back toward the empty beach—and the looming storm.

"Fuck." The sky looked like a page out of an Edgar Allan Poe story, dark as slate being chewed by demons. He cursed again, pivoted, and hoped the wind would hold the storm off a little longer.

As he finished the thought, the first plops of rain hit the dunes.

A second later, headlights from a jeep blared across the beach.

"Shitheads did that on purpose," he muttered sarcastically. The vehicle bounced over the berm, barreled down the access road, and circled around to park next to the house. He observed Ike at the wheel. Tait was his wingman in the front passenger position. Lani was in the back—with Leo.

The air left his lungs in a thankful whoosh while watching Tait leap out and then open the door for Lani. Leo came around and yanked both of them into the same hug before turning to throw a hearty wave toward Kellan. He raised his hand in return. With the other, he rubbed at the ache that persisted in his chest, despite his relief.

What the hell?

WET

The thought hit him more as confusion than complaint. The pressure was actually...good. Just unexpected. It usually hit him on occasions like Christmas, when first dropping his pack in Mom and Dad's foyer. Or when he looked out the window of a transport and saw the summit of Mount Rainier. Or when his phone rang and the window lit up with Kadie's face along with the title she'd given herself in the device: *Goddess Sister, ruler of your universe. Pick up at once.*

Belonging. Home. Family.

After Leo released Tait and Lani, the kid swung back into the jeep. Ike backed the vehicle away. Kell frowned in deeper perplexity. He redirected the look at Lani as she bounded up the steps, not that she noticed. The woman was too busy launching herself into his arms and then clinging with zealous strength.

"It's over." She released a sigh into his neck that sounded both happy and tired. "Tait's instincts were right. He led us right to Leo. The *hupo* was playing lone-man-dipshit-of-despair in a cave in the cliffs."

He countered by pulling her perfect curves tight and close. So this was how it felt to hold a live flame. "Wish I could tell you this'll be the last dumbass move he makes, but sweetheart, he's a guy."

"Yeah, yeah." She pulled back to peel wet hair off her face, emitting another sound that bordered on a sob. "But for now, thank the gods, he's safe and it's over."

He helped her with the hair-clearing effort, sifting his fingers through her soft tendrils. "Then where the hell is he going?"

"Kid's pretty dirty and hungry," Tait explained. "We were only halfway here when he put in a request with Ike for a ride home, a shower, and some chow."

Lani gave that an open pout. "I still don't understand why he didn't want me along. I had at least the chow covered."

Tait flicked a teasing glance. "No offense, Sister Kail, but tonight, you're the wrong gender in his book."

As Lani tossed back a huff, it sealed the deal on an impression that had only been a guess to Kellan before now. There was a new energy in the air between those two, a bond undoubtedly forged by the ordeal they'd just weathered together...though his senses registered something more. An unnamed "more" for now, but if so, then what? He couldn't figure it out yet. He *did* know that he hadn't seen Tait banter with a woman like this since...

Fuck.

Since the night Luna had met the team at that seedy bar in Los Angeles, declaring herself their newest mission member. On a wet and windy night, after a crazy adventure of a day...

Fuck.

Paranoia came in a lot of fun new flavors these days, didn't it?

Wait. Was that what he really felt? Signing on for Special Forces meant he'd nearly agreed to have "Paranoia" embossed on his dog tags as a new middle name. He knew the burning, thumping tension he should be enduring, and this didn't qualify. This shit skewed more toward deep curiosity, amplified by the profound affection he had for both these people. And it all still burned so deep in his gut, it could've easily been indigestion.

Enough of this crap. It was time move on. To celebrate.

With a casual smirk, he gave Lani's nose a quick kiss. "Hate to say this, sweetheart. T's probably right this time."

Tait pumped a fist. "Score."

"Don't get cocky, asshat. I said *this* time."

Lani tossed the guy another mocking glare. "He's been doing too much of that 'being right' shit lately." She was answered with Tait's chuckle and retaliated by poking her tongue at him.

That officially ruled out indigestion for the strange gut twinges. The conclusion was confirmed by a ruthless squeeze in Kell's chest, tighter than the broadside of two minutes ago. But that wasn't what caused him to suddenly stiffen. The credit for *that* shock belonged to his developing hard-on.

What the hell?

He couldn't deny it. There was something about watching these two and their growing connection...something captivating, nerve-zapping...

His body instantly surged with the need to join the party. The private, illicit version of the event.

Damn. The universe was wreaking its karmic revenge over their sinful forest romp right now—on his dick.

You were mission leader on that episode, asswipe. Heavy is the head that wears the crown.

He covered his surprise by clearing his throat. His johnson had the growing rainstorm to thank for its camouflage, distracting Tait and Lani with a new boom of thunder. He was more than happy to help the effort along. After grabbing Lani's hand, he opened the door to the house and guided her through. "Time for shelter, Starshine."

The living room, which had glowed so bright when he and T returned from lunch, felt dim with the gloom of the storm all around. But when Tait hastened to activate more lamps, Lani held up a hand. "Can we leave them off? It's more relaxing. And gods, I could use a little of that." As lightning flashed, turning the edges of the clouds into celestial mountains for a moment, she grinned. "See? Lono himself is helping us. No need for the lamps."

Tait spread his arms. "No argument from this corner."

"Lono." Kellan repeated it on purpose, psyched about getting to impress her with the Hawaiian culture research he'd sneaked in. "He's the god of storms, right?"

Lani slanted an impish grin at him. "And fertility."

Damn. "Walked into that one," he muttered, enduring the laugh shared by her and Tait.

Fortunately, his buddy came to the rescue. "Awkward moment fixer, coming right up." Tait jabbed a thumb toward the kitchen. "Anyone hungry? I think I know where to find a fully stocked refrigerator. I can manage a few BLTs."

Lani planted hands to her hips, looking as if he'd just asked to serve them arsenic brownies. "Are you really offering to make sandwiches, Sergeant Bommer? After what you did today?"

Tait let his thumb descend. "Uhhh..."

"Shut up and hump your ass over here."

Tait's face widened with incredulity—while he moved to obey her order.

Kellan threw back his head on a loud chuckle. "Well, here's a first."

"Shut it," Tait snapped.

"What?" Lani asked.

"Sweetheart, don't you remember what I've told you about T's...umm...fondness for being the one in charge? Why *he* likes to be the one telling *me* where to shoot the bad guys?"

"Hmm." She shrugged on her way to meeting Tait in the middle of the room. "No bad guys here."

Kell snickered a little harder. Even as they neared each other, she was totally oblivious to his buddy's textbook case of awkward, including shuffled feet, dropped head, and a slack jaw of watchfulness. *Welcome to the Stupid-Over-Lani-Kail Club, dude.*

She stepped closer. Tait visibly tensed, but Kellan didn't flinch. His fascination—and his cock—swelled by the moment.

As Lani hauled him into a crushing hug, Tait's breath left him on an audible grunt. The collision was perfect fodder for another good laugh, but Kell matched his buddy's burst with a hard gulp, falling into silence instead.

They looked so damn perfect like that. And as he looked on, all he could feel was one overwhelming sensation. Gratitude.

He wasn't the only one. Lani affirmed it as she fervently whispered her thanks into Tait's shoulder. "*Mahalo.*" She twisted her head, tucking it against his chest. "Thank you for helping to find him. For talking to him. For caring. For... everything."

For an instant, Tait bent his head toward the top of hers. One of his hands clenched tight against her back.

In that simple action, Kellan observed the thankfulness had reached full circle. Lani would never know how many needs she'd just met for Tait, but Kell did. Tait would spend the rest of his life trying to compensate for what he'd never been able to do for his mother—living for moments like this, where he *could* make things okay. Thanks to Lani, sharing her joy with him so openly, Tait soared as close to heaven as he could without dying.

When they pulled back from each other and Lani sealed her gratitude by giving T a sincere little kiss, Kellan wasn't

ANGEL PAYNE

surprised—or hurt. The moment simply felt like another
sublime gift from fate. And the instant tent that popped in his
friend's crotch? Wasn't a stunner, either.

Nevertheless, he watched the exchange in more silence...
and deeper curiosity. He waited for the "raging jealousy" part
of the equation to rush in, but it never came. A lot of other
sensations were more than happy to step up. Camaraderie.
More erotic demand. But most of all...completion. To watch
the two people closest to him right now, perhaps closest to him
ever, sharing the same bonds he felt to them both... It really
was a gift.

No. It was more.

A blessing.

The only things that didn't fit were the scarlet flags across
Lani's cheeks and the guilty twist of her lips. Huh? Why was
she looking at him like that?

Okay, he understood the conventional answer to that—
but when the hell had "conventional" applied to them in the
last six days? Plain and simple, this was a moment for triumph
and joy, not shame and embarrassment. How the hell could he
yank her out of the societal straitjacket to see that?

The sky flashed again but didn't equal the burst of his
mental clarity. The answer was easy. Were intense ops ever
attempted alone? The truth was perfect as it was plain. He
and Tait would be in this together, working together on the
best mission of their lives: bringing this woman to the ultimate
heights of her passion. The best thing? It wasn't just what Lani
needed. It was what *Tait* needed. And if the pressure in Kell's
cock could talk, it was sure as *hell* what he needed.

Lani was in the process of stepping back from Tait—and
looking pretty reluctant about it—when Kell made his way to

her side in three forceful steps. "Stop."

Lani flashed a confused stare. "Excuse me?"

He nodded toward Tait. "You need to thank him again."

"Uhhh...she really doesn't," Tait rebutted. "Dude, we're good."

"No, you're not." He didn't waver his tone, more sure of this than aiming a tranq dart at an elephant's ass on a windless day. With the same confidence, he guided Lani's fingers back up to Tait's neck. The air clutched audibly in Tait's throat. "Guess that proves my point already."

"About what?" Tait growled.

He ignored that. Balancing the command of his words with the tenderness of his touch, he smoothed back Lani's hair. "You're not done yet. Thank him again, Starshine. Like you mean it this time. I'm going to watch every second. I want to be sure you don't skimp on the effort."

"Kell." Tait's comeback was a helix of shock and disbelief. "What the hell are you—"

"With all due respect, shut up. You want this, too, meathead. Every square inch of your body is clamoring for it." He swiveled back to Lani, lifting a soft smile. "And sweetheart, every inch of *yours* is too."

As she snorted at him, the color intensified on her face. *Goddamn.* A little pissed-off turned the woman into a lot of enticing. "That has nothing to do with this."

"That has everything to do with this." He bit back a chuckle as they both fumed. "I care about you. And God help me, I care about this asshat too. So what's wrong with wanting to see you two share some joy after the ordeal of today?"

"What's wrong with it?" Lani snapped. "Kellan, you can't go ordering me to simply make out with your best friend, like—"

"Even if you want to? Even if *I* want you to?"

She swiveled her sneer to Tait, obviously in a bid for his support. "Is he always this much of a *pa`akiki*?"

Tait's gaze narrowed. "Yeah. Pretty much."

Kell punched his shoulder. "Like you understood that."

"I know *bossy asshat* when I hear it in any language."

Lani arched her brows in victory. "And he agrees with me."

"Perfect. That's another thing you can thank him for."

She bared her teeth, threatening to actually snarl. When Kellan didn't alter his own certainty, her eyes joined the fight. "Fine," she snipped, irises swirling with blue-and-silver heat. "You really want this?"

She didn't wait for him to answer. Without any more hesitation, she grabbed both sides of Tait's head and pulled his mouth to hers again.

Kellan's cock surged with new blood. He'd be stunned if Tait's didn't too. The pure anger in which Lani first seized him coalesced into a passion that ignited the air and amped their connection. In a nutshell, it was fucking hot. If T wasn't on board with that message with the first smash of her lips, he signed up for the program fast after that. A crease formed in his friend's jaw as T shoved open Lani's mouth with his own. The guy growled while stabbing his tongue down, ruthlessly invading her. Lani responded with a decadent moan, sweeping her arms around Tait's shoulders.

More thunder growled overhead. Like it mattered. The energy shooting off the two of them was a storm in its own right, whipping Kellan into its vortex. He gulped hard, one of his hands on the back of Lani's head, the other on Tait's shoulder. A glance down showed Tait's cock was definitely up to speed on the direction of this mission. As his buddy continued kissing

Lani, Tait cupped the generous swells of her ass, using the hold to slide her crotch hard against his.

"Damn," Kell grated. He smiled when Lani moaned. "Sounds like you're enjoying that, Starshine."

"One of us sure as fuck is," Tait declared between harsh breaths when he pulled from her a little.

"Count me in as the next vote," Kell drawled.

T flashed an intense stare. "Are you serious?"

"Hell yeah." Kellan stepped in to tug at Lani, redirecting her toward him. "Let me show you what I mean."

Her eager sigh told him she supported that decision. It blended with Tait's growl as Kell drew her closer, fitting her curves to his body before slanting his lips over hers in relentless need. As she palmed his jaw in return, he felt Tait press in and squeeze her ass again, working at the flesh through her clothes. Kellan groaned and claimed her tongue harder with his own. Her taste was a heady assault of rain, desire, and the spicy edge that had come from Tait's kiss.

"Fuck." Tait blurted it on a harsh breath. "You're right, man. Watching's as much fun from this distance as it was from the damn bushes."

Lani lifted her face and looked at them both. "Not *more* fun?" Her eyes were as bright as a misbehaving fairy. Her lips trembled with a touch of fear...and *a lot* of lust.

To his credit, Tait breathed in and out, clearly thinking about his reply. Though Kellan was grateful for his buddy's consideration, he finally prompted, "Just say it, man."

"Say what?" Lani's voice had turned into a sexy rasp.

Tait gave Kellan a meaningful glance over her head while pressing behind her. He fitted his crotch against her ass and tucked his mouth into her ear. "Sometimes, it's not a good idea to let me slide too close, dreamgirl."

Lani's eyes drifted shut. Her thick lashes trembled against her cheeks. Goddamn, she was breathtaking. "Wh-Why?"

"Because when I'm this close, I'm tempted to...do things." He snaked his tongue along the rim of her ear. "Demanding things. Dominating things."

She shivered. Her hands slid from Kell's jaw to his shoulders, where she dug her grip in tight. "Like...what?"

The muscles in T's arms flexed again. When Lani let out a sharp yelp, Kell did the math. The guy had found a way to pinch her ass good and sharp, even with her pants on. T-Bomb could be a creative fucker when he wanted, a fact that didn't always make Kell happy. This occasion a huge exception.

"To start with," Tait went on, "I'd want to grab every inch of this fine, gorgeous ass."

"Errmmm, you mean like you are right now?" Her smirk was just as sarcastic as her gibe. Kell arched his brows in warning, though it was probably too late. The T-Bomb Dom had officially been awakened, meaning her sass would earn her at least a tiny swat.

Sure enough, the next sound out of her kiss-plumped lips was an enticing yelp, coinciding with the smack Tait delivered to her wriggling backside. The guy silenced *and* stilled her with his next move, pulling her hands off Kell to shackle them in a commanding grip over her head. With her wrists joined in his grip and her neck beneath his mouth, Tait growled low, openly enjoying the moment before spanking her a second time. "No," he murmured, emphasizing with a wolfish bite over her carotid, "it'd be a lot more like *that*."

Lani's face went through a fascinating transformation. Kell looked on as her eyes widened a little and her lips parted with new need. "Ohhhh," she rasped, letting her head fall back. "Gods, why is it so warm now?"

"What is?" Kellan stepped forward to take advantage of her new position, spreading his hands across both her breasts. The camisole she wore under his sweatshirt had minimal padding, thank fuck. "Talk to us, Starshine."

"My...my backside." Her forehead pursed as she clearly struggled for focus on the words—just the way he liked it. Her nipples jutted against his fingers. Her wrists writhed in Tait's sensual captivity. "It's hot. And tingling. It...feels...so... *aiwaiwa.*"

"Mmmm. Yeah. *Aiwaiwa.* My point exactly." Tait's arm flexed as he massaged the stunning curves of her ass again. "It's only the beginning of the treatment I'm fantasizing for these naughty buns of yours, girl."

Her captivation seemed conquered by confusion. "W-Wait. You want to spank me *more*? Like make me wear pigtails, call you Daddy, and beg you for my punishment?"

Kell thanked God that elite sniper work required the ability to stifle emotions. But even his skill at the feat almost crumbled against his laughter at her suggestion—especially when guessing Tait would drool a bucket if she appeared in a plaid mini, knee socks, and a knotted shirt over a red lace bra.

His buddy's reaction, not restrained nearly as well, confirmed that supposition. After letting out a long rumble, Tait slipped his grip from her wrists in order to shove both his hands beneath all her clothes. From the positions of the lumps beneath her clothing, Kell guessed he'd dug his fingers in hard to the sides of her waist.

"You have the begging part right, dreamgirl. But I wouldn't make you bend over for detention swats. Not your first time in

Sergeant Bommer's class."

Lani's tongue sneaked across her lips. She looked a little drunk, clearly trying to comprehend how she stood here, pressed so intimately between the two of them. "So...what's the purpose of class, then?"

Kellan watched as T worked one of his hands toward the front of her body. As he dipped lower, making her mouth drop in flagrant arousal, Kellan ground his teeth until his jaw ached. God knew, his cock was already there.

"Pleasure, Hokulani," Tait told her in a husky murmur. "That's what Sergeant Bommer's class is *always* about. Your pleasure...and ours."

He'd let a significant pause lead to his last two words. *And ours.* Kellan watched T carefully after that, rewarded for his diligence when his friend glanced up. They smiled together. The shorthand of their friendship was up to speed once more, letting them silently agree on the same significant message.

Let's give this goddess a night she'll never forget.

Of course, that was *their* plan. Securing Lani's buy-in on the concept was going to be a different challenge. As soon as she figured the intent of Tait's words—and she *would*—they'd learn just how high the wall of her resistance would be. In case they were dealing with a steel-lined fortress instead of a thatched fence, Kellan breathed down his erection a little. He noticed Tait doing the same as he extracted his hand from beneath her clothes.

Lani sure as hell didn't make their efforts at composure any easier. Tait's words had made her chest rise and fall with more urgency, and her gaze raced between the two of them like she sought permission to reach into Lucifer's candy jar. *Dear fuck, woman. If it's sweets you want, I have some hard treats right here.*

While his brain lingered in that torture chamber of a thought, she turned toward Tait. The result was a view Kellan would remember forever: her profile, soft and vulnerable in the lamp's glow yet so breathtakingly honest. And so thick with desire...

"I like the sound of this class," she whispered.

Tait looked as stunned as Kell felt. And elated. Fuck *yeah*, elated. "You're certain?"

Lani nodded, swiveling her magical gaze between them again. "I want to give you pleasure. Both of you."

Tait leaned closer. "You're *really* certain?"

Kellan shot his friend a glare. "Dude, don't you know how to quit when you're ahead?"

"And don't *you* remember how I play this fucking game?" He snorted before turning back to Lani. The woman returned his gaze with worlds of expectation in her eyes. Normally, that kind of blind trust would scare the crap out of Kellan. But this was Tait Bommer, the one person on the planet who wasn't going to abuse such a gift. Spending hours on rooftops with a guy didn't leave a lot of his life unexposed, ensuring Kell knew, better than anyone, about Tait's understanding of broken trust and its lasting pain.

That didn't mean T was going to be gentle about making his point to Lani. With another growl, deeper now, the guy used a ruthless grip in her hair to pull her back around to face him, latching her stare on to him. A gasp spilled from her lips. Her eyes dilated. Her chest pumped harder.

"Slash has told you I like a little control, right? Sometimes, that phrase changes to *a lot* of control." He lowered his head in order to skim his mouth along hers in a back-and-forth tease.

"Times like this one."

A tiny sigh echoed up Lani's throat. That, along with this incredible view of her unfolding passion, heated Kellan's blood to unbearable levels. With a grunt, he shifted in his shorts. Unable to resist, he reached and palmed her ass for himself.

"Wh-What do you mean by...'a lot'?" she whispered.

Tait prefaced his answer by capturing her top lip between his teeth. "I mean that nothing makes my cock swell more than the idea of ripping those pants off you, bending you over the back of the couch, and laying into your bare ass with my palm until it glows deep red. Nothing turns my brain to fire more than wondering how your screams will sound because of it. And nothing makes my balls pound harder than thinking of watching Kell rub out the sting of my spanking, just before he plunges his dick into your pussy from behind."

"Oh," she squeaked. "Ohhhh." It became a moan as T bit her bottom lip.

Kellan merged his groan to her arousal. "For the record, I'm really on board with that flight plan."

"For the record"—Lani's rasp came between the little bites she gave Tait's lips in return—"I am too."

Tait's face went through a transformation. Kellan had seen it happen before, on the few nights he'd gone to the Bastille dungeon to witness the guy in scenes with eager submissives. The change happened when Tait crossed his final mental bridge into Dom brain. His eyes gained hoods with their hot concentration. His cheeks sharpened. His mouth firmed. His very posture changed, tautening yet bending as he focused his power completely on his partner. T had attempted an explanation once. He called the process "being invited into her soul." At the time, Kellan had openly laughed at his friend, had even called it a pretty crowd of words when one would do fine. *Foreplay*. Now, he rammed a mental boot up his ass for the foolishness.

Without relenting his hold on her head, Tait scanned her whole face before demanding, "Do you absolutely want this, dreamgirl? You completely understand what you're asking for?"

Lani sent him a steady smile. "I may live on an island, Sergeant, but I read. And I dream. And I...fantasize." She let the implication of that sink in for a few seconds before going on. "I want you to make my fantasies come true...please. I know what I'm asking for."

T gazed hard at her once more. "Then you also know I'm not going to be gentle."

Lani trembled. Her nipples jabbed to full erection, discernible even through the layers of her clothes. "Yes," she replied. "I know."

"And you know that unless you scream 'red,' your safe word to stop everything about this night, I'm going to smack that luscious bottom until *I* think you've had enough?"

She processed that one a lot longer. The moment Kellan figured she'd performed a "Lani mind game" on herself and declared this "fantasy" too wild for her reality, she looked back up and declared, "Yes. I understand. *Red* is my safe word, and I only use it for a full stop."

Tait jerked half a smile at her in approval. "And the rest, too, babe. The part about my hand on your flesh..."

"Yes." Her voice was a breath this time. "I understand."

"And my will acting as proxy for your needs. That I'll do the thinking...and you'll do the feeling."

"Yes, Tait."

"Yes, *Sir*, will be just fine, dreamgirl."

Her face softened, her eyelids dipping with arousal. "Oh, yes, Sir."

"Ah. Very nice. Maybe you *have* been practicing this fantasy, Hokulani."

"Perhaps." She let her gaze shift to both of them in anticipation. "A little."

Tait slipped his hand from her scalp to her shoulders and then down the length of her body, kneading her curves with rough possession. With a nod, he motioned for Kellan to do the same. "Then you probably know what comes next, babe."

She swayed between them. Little sighs tumbled from her at every commanding sweep of their hands. "M-Maybe," she whispered. "Especially if it means more of this..."

"Oh, yeah," Tait assured. "So much more. But before we can feed our goddess's soul, we want to see her body...all of it. Let us see your naked beauty, Lani...all of it."

CHAPTER FOURTEEN

Unbelievable. She called this the fulfillment of her erotic dreams, but Tait couldn't remember ever having, let alone realizing, a fantasy this incredible. There was an upside there. Knowing his libido would never give his dreams permission for something like this confirmed the reality of it. *Thank fuck.*

That was only the beginning of his gratitude. It continued on to the woman who'd entrusted Kellan and him with her naughty secrets. As for Kellan himself? There were few times when Tait was totally wordless, but this was definitely one of them. He hoped his glance at the man, full of as much thanks as he could cram into a second and half, communicated how thoroughly his mind was blown. That by inviting him into the cocoon of their island passion for tonight, Kell actually made him look harder at the island into which his life had become. It wasn't a sight he enjoyed anymore.

Time to slip another board into his bridge back to humanity.

Kellan gave him a smirk in return, letting him know the message was received, before helping Lani unfasten her bra. The lace fell away and her breasts came free, fully bare for Tait's gaze at last.

Dear Christ, she was stunning.

"Dreamgirl." He ran reverent fingers over her nipples. "You make my knees weak."

"Mmmm." She licked her lips as he intensified his

caresses, circling his thumbs around areolas that tightened into mahogany ovals, centered by nipples now resembling sweet little cinnamon sticks. "That makes two of us, then."

Kellan reached around from the back to unhitch the latch on her pants. "She's still way overdressed, Bommer."

"Roger that. Big-time."

Lani huffed. "*I'm* overdressed? *Sir?*" She added the addendum only after he pinned her with a pointed glare. "I— I mean that maybe you two would be more comfortable in less, as well?"

Kellan groaned before fitting himself tighter behind her. "Smart women are so fucking sexy."

"Agreed once more." Tait tilted Lani's face up with a finger beneath her chin and then kissed her lightly. "We'll start shucking in a minute, impatient one. Right now, first things first." He made sure she understood his reference by finishing what Kell started, tugging at the waistband of her pants, dragging down her underwear along with it. Within three seconds, he had the clothes puddled at her feet, finally exposing all of her glorious nudity. "God*damn*," Tait growled, palming the luscious curve of her waist. "Just as beautiful at this distance as you were from the bushes, babe."

She sighed and let her head fall back again. "Does this mean 'first things' have been handled?"

He took a knee in front of her in a smooth sweep, flashing a wicked glance at Kell during the dip. "Dreamgirl, they've only begun."

Before the woman could conceive a comeback let alone issue it, he parted her dark curls with a couple of fingers and flicked out his tongue to taste the slick treat beyond.

"Ohhhh!" Lani's moan layered atop another timpani roll

from the sky. Both sounds vibrated through Tait, stirring the beast inside who thrived on taming this incredible creature beneath his tongue. With primal hunger, he licked at her folds again. With untamed passion, Lani shrieked and bucked. "*Aiwaiwa*. Tait— *Sir*— Ahhhh!"

"You're turning me way the fuck on with those screams, babe. Every time you let one out, your whole pussy trembles."

Kellan inserted a long growl into things. "And look at what it's doing to her tits. Mmmm...these nipples are perfect for biting."

"And clamping." He didn't miss the extra moisture that dotted her labia as soon as he said it.

"Gods!" Lani's keen was an aching, nearly pleading, sound. She added another scream when Tait pulled back to spread her intimate wings. Her folds shimmered and trembled for him.

"Damn," he exclaimed. "Her clit's so hard already. So moist. You have to see this, Slash."

Kellan slid around and crouched next to him. "Yeah... this has definitely become a favorite view." He pressed a finger along the crest of dark pink flesh that Tait had separated from the rest of her glimmering pussy.

"Is she always this responsive?"

Kellan chuffed. "Why do you think you haven't seen a lot of me?"

Tait joined him on the chuckle as he rose back to his feet but let his humor go for the chance to capture Lani's mouth in another tongue-twisting kiss. "You wearing my buddy out, dreamgirl?" he challenged. "Well, I don't tire as easily as this fuzzball."

Kell grunted. "I'm at striking distance to your wank noodle, Bommer. You gonna revise that?"

Tait grinned. Kell wasn't good for the threat, and they both knew it. *Yeah.* They did, didn't they? For the first time in a year, they stepped totally in sync with each other. The comprehension was jolting but amazing. He was at last fearless again. And confident as all fuck.

"You want a revision? Send an email to my editor." He congratulated himself on making Lani giggle. The action made her breasts jiggle in decadent ways, instantly dipping him back into one of the best preludes to Dom space he'd had in a very long time. "Personally, I vote for stripping as naked as this goddess."

"*Now* you're talking my language, man."

The new gleam in Lani's eyes proclaimed her own approval for that plan. If Tait's blood wasn't pumping so hard to start the swat party, he would've simply stared at her like an idiot for the next ten minutes. Would there ever be a moment when the woman didn't captivate him like this? "Don't worry. You get to watch, dreamgirl—from your position on that couch." He wheeled around to give her ass a commanding smack. "Knees spread on the seat cushions. Ass nice and high. And notch in a good grip on the back of that thing. You're going to need it."

With a shivery little sigh, she hastened around the couch but stopped to whimper when Tait and Kell pulled off their shirts together. Tait was impressed as fuck when Kellan beat him to the punch on slicing a reprimanding scowl at her. *Well, well, well.* He'd always respected Kell's clear preference for the vanilla side of sex—granted, it was boiling vanilla, if the screams of the guy's lovers through hotel walls bore any weight on the subject—but now he had to consider there may be an unrealized Dom inside Sergeant Rush after all.

That could all change once everyone was fully naked.

Yeah, yeah; it wasn't like Tait had never seen the Slash-master in his bare-assed glory before. But this, as the saying went, was a different ball of come. Four of them, if every nut sack in the room was being fully accounted for. The situation wasn't your typical third-wheel's-a-charm date. It was a gift, plain and simple, extended by a guy who took the term "brother" pretty damn seriously. That tagged Tait to return the integrity. Okay, his erection raged as hard as Kellan's—but that didn't mean he planned on putting it anywhere except his own palm tonight.

"Come on, man." He offered a warm grin while beckoning Kellan to follow him to the couch. "You can watch me melt this raindrop of ours. I'll turn her into the perfect puddle for you to fuck into oblivion."

As Kellan replied with an approving growl, Lani made a sweet little mewl. Tait expected she'd drop the kitten act any minute, though. The opportunity was too ripe for her to slide in at least one sarcastic zinger, if only to mask any lingering awkwardness she had. But the beauty stunned him by keeping her head bowed low and her hips raised high, even rolling them a little as he and Kellan came near.

He nearly froze in bewilderment. In-fucking-credible. There wasn't a shred of self-consciousness in how she presented herself, not an ion of discomfort in her atmosphere. He dropped a knee to the couch and leaned over, gently tilting her head so he could see her face. He smiled as she dragged her eyes open. Her irises had deepened to thick, burnished pewter. Her lashes swept her cheeks as she blinked with indolent arousal, entrancing him and igniting him with each languorous glide.

"Is she okay?" Concern underlined Kellan's query.

Tait nodded. "Ohhh, yeah." He held back from sharing his impression that the woman had slipped into a preliminary version of subspace without even knowing what the euphoria actually was. "Sweet woman," he murmured, "you really *have* entertained this fantasy before, haven't you?" He swept a kiss across her lips, taking his time, making sure she felt how much he'd heard her, truly saw her. "You need this to take the silver dome off, don't you? You need someone to show you the way, to make the choice for you."

After Lani blinked again, tear tracks streaked her cheeks. "Yes. Take me away...please."

Tait kept his mouth close to hers. "We're on our way, dreamgirl. Your trust has opened the gate on this path. Now let us handle the rest of the journey."

He reached and skimmed her spine in a long, praising stroke. A high sigh rolled out of her in direct proportion to his stroke, until he reached the end, raised his hand, and—

Smack.

"Ohhh!"

He grinned as her sweet cry pierced the air, and then he threw his smirk at Kell. "I love that sound almost as much as I love nailing the first swat."

His buddy nodded, swallowed, and shifted on his feet. Tait empathized with his buddy's hot-and-horny discomfort, having experienced it from the middle of a lantana bush last night. "Goddamn," Kellan finally uttered. "You turned her that red from one blow?"

"I did say I nailed it."

Kell stepped forward and reached out a hand toward their woman's backside, still raised at a perfect angle for their admiring gazes. "May I?" he asked. After Tait swept out a hand in gentlemanly invitation, the guy swirled his touch across his woman's backside in a figure-eight pattern, emitting a low whistle of sensual approval. "Hell, Starshine," he finally grated. "You're so fucking beautiful like this." He paused, savoring the seductive undulation she gave him in thanks, before straightening again. By this point, the guy grimaced like he could hang a lead counterweight off his dick. "I don't know who's going to be suffering more at the end of this, her or me."

Tait lifted one side of his mouth and shook his head. "Prepare for your ordeal, dude. The destination for this goddess is *not* the valley of suffering."

Though Kell smiled as well, something extra entered the guy's gaze. Complete curiosity. Tait almost pumped a fist in triumph. It was damn satisfying to see his friend's eyes opening about the Dominant/submissive dynamic and what it could do for a submissive. Yeah, Kell had accompanied him to Bastille plenty of times, but even after all those nights, the guy still didn't get it. Kell still thought the BDSM lifestyle was a one-sided advantage for the Doms, an objectification of women wrapped in flowery terms and Victorian manners to make it "romantic" for the subbies. But now, Kellan couldn't deny the reality that drenched every inch of Lani's face in satisfaction—and every inch of her pussy in glistening dew.

God, he couldn't wait to take her deeper into bliss.

"Hang on tight, sweet girl." He angled himself to lower a steadying hand to her waist. "Here comes more."

"Yes, Sir," she rasped. "Thank you, S—"

Smack.

"Ahhhh!"

Smack, smack.

"Ohhhh!"

Smack, smack, smack.

"*Kanapapiki!*"

"I sure hope that translates to *Thank you, Sir. May I have more?*"

She let out an adorable girl growl. "Not exactly."

"Hmm." He paused to massage the burn into her skin, making her writhe like a wet cat. "Too bad."

Smack.

"Ohhhh! *Aia!*"

Kellan came back over. He secured one knee on the couch in order to press his upper body atop hers. "Starshine, if you take your mind off the screaming and direct it toward the experiencing, maybe you'll get the program of what T-Bomb's trying to do here."

Bingo. The guy really did understand now. Tait dipped an appreciative nod at his buddy. "Good point, Slash-gasm. But I don't mind subbies with a little spirit. Makes it so much more fun when they tumble over for me."

"Tumble?" Lani snapped. "Tumble where? What are you—"

Smack, smack.

"Owww!"

Smack.

"*Kahaha!* Are you doing it *harder* now?"

"Maybe I wouldn't have to, babe, if I could hear myself working here."

Kellan chuckled. "What was that about liking a little spirit?"

"Shut up."

"Damn. Maybe I will. The view alone is worthy of silence." His friend dropped his gaze, transfixed on the new condition of Lani's gorgeous bottom. "Fuck me, Starshine. If you could see how breathtaking your ass is..."

Tait motioned him over with a jerk of his head. "Wait until you feel it."

"Shit." The word was a verbal form of Kellan's appreciative sweep across one half of the woman's ass. Tait took charge of the other half, reveling in the burn of her skin beneath his palm, greedily watching as the heat prowled her whole body. Her shoulders bunched. Her nipples beaded. Her breathing shallowed. "I had no idea... This is incredible," Kell uttered.

"Yeah," Tait replied, "it is." He smoothed his hand up from her bottom, over the gorgeous landscape of her hips, her waist, her back. Kellan wasted no time in following his lead on her other side. Beneath them, Lani had slipped into silence. That wasn't surprising.

"Is she still okay?"

He grinned at his friend. "Oh, she's fantastic."

"She sure as fuck is. Damn. Think anyone has a radioactive meter handy?"

"There's a reason it's called power exchange, my friend. She entrusted hers to me, and now we're returning it in a transformed state. Purified by her pain...but strengthened by her surrender."

"Wow."

"That's a good way of putting it."

"And what happens now?"

He let a grin spread. "The really good stuff."

In short, the best way he knew how to show her that she didn't have a monopoly on profound gratitude tonight.

CHAPTER FIFTEEN

Lani heard Kellan and Tait talking, but they could have been reciting regulation manuals for all she comprehended—or cared. Had it been minutes since Tait rained that sting storm on her ass or hours? She couldn't figure that part out, either, and still didn't care to. Right now, all that mattered was the heat. Covering her. Consuming her. Lifting off the shell of her control and pulling her senses into a haze where she was weightless yet anchored, soaring yet safe...free to simply feel.

And *aue*, did she feel. Every exquisite moment. Hands on her skin. Fingers in her hair. Knuckles rolling down her spine, over the tingling planes of her ass—

Then fingers again, spreading her...there.

Growls filled her ears. Appreciative versions of naughty words. She moaned as the fingers pulled apart her labia, seeking and finding her intimate entrance.

"*Kamaha`o*. Gods, yesss!"

There was another harsh groan. Not Kellan. She knew many of his sounds of passion by now. "God*damn*, her little Polynesian words are a turn-on."

"Roger that, brother. With the volume turned up."

One of the fingers slipped inside her. "Dear fuck. Her pussy is an inferno." A hand grazed her ass before drawing back and giving her another swat. The blow was fast but hard, tearing a sharp keen off her lips. "That's it, dreamgirl. Give me some more juice. Damn, Slash. This is going to be a good fuck for you, man."

Just above her, Kellan emitted a tight grunt. "I can't wait much longer. My balls are on fire."

"Mmmm," she managed while writhing against Tait's finger. When he curled another digit in, capturing her clit beneath, it escalated into a moan before she could help it. "Ohhhh!"

Tait laughed. "I think she'll be willing to help you with that blaze."

"Thank fuck." The audio backdrop for his declaration was the crackle of foil being opened, the wet sluice of latex against skin, and the louder tumult of the rain against the earth outside. Through it all, Tait sparked new flames through her body and mind, fanning her blissful ether, spinning her senses higher, reaching for a pinnacle that seemed so close yet so far...

Please...please...please...

"Ready to rock this, Slash-and-burn?"

Their large bodies shifted. The pressure on her clit was pulled away, along with Tait's fingers from her vagina. Lani whimpered in protest. "Ahhh!" she cried. "Please...I need..."

"What?" How Kellan could turn one word into a work of sensual art, she'd never fathom. He continued that satyr's growl while scooting her knees out with his own, spreading her wide to accommodate his muscled bulk. "Tell me what you need, Starshine. Don't hold it back any longer. What can I give you?"

"Fill me." She gasped when he teased her entrance with the tip of his cock. The heat of his desire was palpable even beneath the condom, the edges of her entrance trembling from the kiss of the tip, now filled with his precome. "Ohhhhh," she moaned. It was everything she'd yearned for, yet it wasn't. In an instant of clarity, she realized the illicit thrill she *did* crave. *Ohhh, shit. The express elevator to hell's basement is waiting on you now, Hokulani.* She licked her lips nervously. Then again. Did she dare say anything? They'd told her this was safe ground. Guided her to it themselves. Opened her senses to so many new horizons already. If there was ever any time to ask for this fantasy to come true, this was it. "Fill me," she repeated before biting her lip and blurting, "B-Both of you."

For a second, the only sound in the air was heaven's waterfall, pounding everything around and over them. More thunder snarled. The torrent intensified.

Exactly like the tension inside the house.

Tait's gritted voice was the first to crack the silence. "Dear Christ."

Lani had expected that. Waiting on Kellan's reaction was a harder ordeal—

Ending in a much greater surprise.

"That's our good girl." Once more, he sounded like the talking version of a Godiva bar. "Very good."

Tait's cough hammered the air. "Dude, do you understand what she's—"

"Of course I do. Maybe you don't. Say it again, Starshine, so T-Bomb has the full message. Let him hear what you need right now—from both of us."

She smiled at the new surge of warmth in her heart, this time as a gift from Kellan instead of Tait. Had this man really walked onto her beach a week ago by sheer chance? How could that be possible when he saw into her mind, knew all of her darkest and dirtiest desires, and shelved his own ego to help make them reality? Either she'd racked up a huge favor from the deities of luck and magic somehow or there was another power at work here.

Right now wasn't the time for figuring it out. This moment was simply about savoring the gift.

"I need to be filled." With the repeat, she dared a glance up at Tait. She discovered his stare already locked on her, his eyes burning with amber lust but his lips twisted in beautiful conflict. "By both of your cocks," she whispered. "Pleasing both of you...at once."

Kellan gave both her ass cheeks a reassuring squeeze. It burned in all the right ways, making her tremble with need for the hot stalk he still teased at her sex. "You heard the woman, my brother. You still all about meeting her needs or not?"

The torment deepened on Tait's face. Despite the need in her body, her heart ached with the appearance of every new crease around his eyes and along his jaw. She witnessed the battle being waged in *his* heart. Embracing this moment, this passion, meant stepping out from the shadows of his yesterday—and the six months of yesterdays before that. It meant being vulnerable again. Feeling something besides grief and anger again.

She knew the fear well.

Though he still didn't say a word, Tait reached down to her. He pulled in a stark breath. His fingers shook against her head, twisting her long hair in his grip. His hold tightened as he knelt on the couch again—and now there was no way she could avoid the view of his penis, swollen and crimson, sprouting from the nest of dark gold curls between his rock-hard thighs. He was inches away now. She breathed heavily in hopes she'd soon taste his thick, hot flesh...

"Look at me." Tait gave her the order from teeth that were bared. "So goddamn beautiful," he uttered when she did, coiling her hair tighter, forcing her face a little higher...aligning her mouth with the head of his cock.

"No more beautiful than you, Sir." Every word was true. Tait's physique was as drool-inducing as Kellan's. His chest, looming like a cliff above her, was his most striking feature. He had pecs, delts, traps, and biceps that should have had their own Facebook page, especially with how the lamp's glow turned them into a collection of copper artwork. She longed to reach up and explore every ridge and valley of his magnificent torso, but the man had decided on other plans for her. Thank the gods.

"Kiss my cock, dreamgirl."

As her spirit rejoiced, Lani eagerly obeyed. She opened her mouth and captured his crown, letting his tangy milk dot her lips. She wiped the liquid clean with the tip of her tongue.

Kellan emitted a sparse snarl. "Fuck, that's hot."

"Not arguing." Tait's reply was equally graveled.

Words eluded Lani as Kellan pressed the first inch of his erection into her channel. She let her high cry do the communicating. *Holy hell.* The man's voice may have been verbal chocolate, but his cock was solid, sinful meat, filling her body in all the best ways.

"Christ, man. Her cunt is even hotter. If I burn alive, what a way to go."

Tait curled a hand to the back of her head. With his other, he guided his tip to her lips again. "Make me hot, too, dreamgirl. Take me deep, Hokulani."

The heat in her senses, already so dense, consumed her fully. One word alone resounded through her mind.

Yes.

Yes...

As if Tait would give her any other choice. With one hand, he fed his stiff flesh into her mouth. The other, still locked on the back of her head, angled her to suck as much as she could. And then he was...everywhere. On her tongue. Stretching her lips. Flooding her with his taste, earth and salt tinged by the hint of cedar that was simply part of him. She moaned, drew in a deep breath through her nose, and hungrily took in even more. She wanted as much of his body as she could hold. As much of his power as she could drink.

"Damn." His ragged rasp filtered through her aroused haze, inspiring her to open her throat deeper. "*Damn.*"

Kellan hadn't moved much during that minute, though his clasp on her hips, kneading her skin with increasing force, communicated that he hadn't missed a moment of her exchange with Tait. "You like that, Starshine?" he asked in a rugged rasp.

She moaned again, the fire in her body turning it into a sound she barely recognized. That came as no surprise. Nothing about her body, her entire being, was familiar anymore, as if the fire of this night had morphed her into another creature entirely. She felt as untamed as the storm churning across the sky outside, a force of nature ruled only by her most primordial desires...to give as much pleasure as she was given.

Kellan made it even better by praising, "You're so breathtaking, sweetheart. So goddamn sexy. I've never seen lips that looked so perfect around a cock before."

"I've never *felt* lips this perfect before," Tait amended. "And that tongue... Damn, Lani, your tongue is a gift from every one of your gods."

Lani sighed from their veneration, but her pussy reacted more fiercely. Her vagina walls squeezed down, silently begging Kellan's cock for more. He groaned though stopped to spread her legs a little wider as he solidified his positioning. "I'm going to fill you up now too, sweetheart. So deep..."

Tait astonished her by emitting a wry chuckle, right before swinging over to sit on the back of the couch. The new arrangement ensured that his erection filled her throat from straight ahead and freed up his hands to lock her wrists against the cushions beside his hips. "Let me help you hang on tight, babe. Slash has that fire in his eyes. I think you're about to get shot to heaven."

The words were no sooner out of his mouth than Kellan brought the prediction to life—in screaming detail. His cock rammed her sex, huge and commanding. His balls slapped her pussy, hot and teasing. His hands, now at her waist, jerked her back against him, over and over, while his hoarse grunts kept her mind latched to the primitive pulse of his.

It was pleasure, total and complete, twined with the pain of Tait's clamps on her wrists and the continued invasion of his flesh in her mouth. He'd hardened to the texture of a battering ram, stabbing the succor of her throat with violent lunges of his hips. His hissing breaths mixed with Kellan's urgent effort. Lani added her greedy sighs to the mix, unable to fight the rising demands of her body anymore. Her skin throbbed in Kellan's hold. Her thighs ached. Her ass clenched. Her nipples tingled. She'd never been more aware of every sensation in her body before, had never felt all those impulses zinging together, pulling at her like lightning to thunder, a seagull to the wind... passion to its climax.

As the heavens collided overhead, those needs crashed in the core of her being. Her scream, muffled by Tait's flesh, exploded through her head. Rain fell harder somewhere, its deluge weaving with the chaos of her mind, the ecstasy of her body, the completion in her soul. She was drenched in its joy. Wet with its wonder. Ready, so ready, for her warriors to give her their floods too.

"Fuck. Even my balls felt that scream, dreamgirl."

"She's going over. Oh damn, T, she's squeezing me so tight. I'm going to blow. Any...second..."

"Our sweet girl. You're coming so good for us. We're right there with you. Take my come...deep in your throat...yessss..."

Kellan's bellow drowned out the rest of it as his penis swelled against her walls and then jerked from his orgasm. Seconds later, Tait's fluid filled her throat, torrid and thick and perfect.

And stinging...and tart?

No. What was happening? What the hell was the rest of this moisture?

The answer came from the massive fist in her chest and the sharp pricks behind her eyes.

In horror, she pulled away from him. She tried the same thing with Kellan, but judging from the trajectory of Tait's eyes when she looked up, the pair had already exchanged some message via their mysterious "Bat Signal" connection. Kell had already received his friend's silent alarm. "Whoa," he soothed, looping an arm around her waist. Nevertheless, she tried escaping again—not an easy feat when trapped by a hulking man who still had his most significant muscle buried inside her body. "*Whoa*, sweetheart. Ssshh; it's all right. It's—"

"Stop," she snapped. His tone, so strong yet soothing, made her composure nearly impossible to regain. "I know it's all right. I just...need a minute."

She pushed a hand to her face. Tait slid down so he sat

properly on the couch in front of her, tugging at her fingers on the way. "A minute to slam the silver dome back on?" He tightened his hold, a wordless command for her attention. "I don't think so, babe. No running, Lani. No hiding. Especially not here and now."

"Please," she whispered. "I...really need..."

That did it. The effort of forcing out even those words, and she was done. The wall of her composure, weakened so much by her sexual release, started caving to the rest of her emotions. The sobs detonated in her chest like clay skeet discs, the debris flying into every corner of her soul. As Kellan finally slid his cock out, she collapsed forward onto Tait, dumping her tears onto the chest that was so perfectly made for capturing them.

Poor Kellan, with his arm still caught between them, simply pressed against her back and kissed her nape. His tenderness made her cry harder. "T is right," he told her. "Keep the covers off, sweetheart. You're safe with us. You always will be."

If that wasn't enough reason to let the barriers fall more, Tait lifted his hands to frame her face, compelling her gaze to meet his. The smile in his eyes was the dark amber of an August sunrise. "Your tears are an extension of your surrender, babe. A beautiful one. Every one of them is another gift to us, Lani. We want all of them. We treasure all of them."

Kellan's gruff laugh spread warmth between her shoulder blades. "And they say *I'm* the one with the perfect words."

Tait scowled. "The fuck they do."

"You two are making it hard to lose my marbles here." Despite her watery giggle, more tears came. The wall buckled harder. Everything she'd dammed up for two years—the loss, the fear, the loneliness—gushed past her careful barriers, spilling out in huge sobs. She managed a tattered breath while battling for familiar mental footing, anything that felt familiar again. But their hands, Tait at her face and Kellan along her waist, continued turning her into a weeping mess.

"That's it," Kellan whispered into her ear. "Go ahead, sweetheart. We've got you. We're both here, and we've got you."

She grimaced. "I'm...I'm afraid."

Tait thumbed away her tears. "You don't have to be. Feel us here, around you, holding you. We can handle it. Let us take it from you. Let us have it all, sweetheart."

What choice did she have but to obey?

The last of the tears were the worst. They heaved out, violent and racking, in a soul-scrubbing both blissful and terrible. True to their word, Tait and Kellan were there for every moment, even after Kell pulled her back up and carried her to the comfort of the bedroom. Their voices and their touches surrounded her, cradled her—which only worsened the confusion that came in the stillness of the night afterward, as the two soldiers quietly snored.

Taking care not to wake them, she slipped out of bed and stood watching the world outside, still so drenched and wind-whipped. But in several places, the clouds had started to break apart, indicating the storm would be rolling away soon.

She stared at the two halves of a human storm sprawled in the bed. Thunder and lightning. Wind and rain. Eruption and magma.

Kellan and Tait.

Her incredible force of nature on four legs.

And soon, they'd be gone too.

Never to be really hers again.

She gulped hard, silencing the cry that begged for release

against the admission.

Feeling anything for these two, besides the given of raw lust, is a mistake. You knew it from the moment you first saw them on the beach, Hokulani. You still know it, as inescapable fact, in your spirit of spirits.

"Gods help me," she whispered. But the strength she expected, deep in that spirit core, never came. Her only answer was the lonely moan of the wind and the ravaging pound of the rain.

An aching sigh escaped as resolve gripped her anew.

She had to reclaim that spirit before it was too late.

She had to summon her heart back home before it left on a military transport in a week.

CHAPTER SIXTEEN

"Satan's flaming balls. How did trouble follow you asshats like a goddamn rain cloud to that island?"

Franzen always did have a way of hitting the thematic nail on the head.

Tait propped his elbows on his knees, now covered by a pair of light pants, and loosely laced his fingers. He caught Kell's eye roll before the guy leaned toward the cell phone resting on the lanai table. It was still soggy and cloudy out here, but the porch gave them the privacy needed for the call to their CO, along with good sight lines into the house, where they could see if Lani woke up and came searching for them.

Kellan scooted in a little more before responding, "With all due respect, Captain, it's not officially *our* trouble this time."

"Yeah, damn it. You're right." Franzen sounded like Grumpy the Dwarf crossed with Kaipo, his big Samoan friend from the convenience store down the road. Whether Franz had always possessed the slight accent, or it gained strength when he spoke to people on Kaua`i, Tait wasn't certain. Didn't matter at the moment. They had a bigger tuna on their plate to fry. "Look, I'm sorry," Franz muttered. "Lani and Leo are like family. I figured you'd meet them sooner or later during your stay, but now I'm glad it was sooner instead of later. This bullshit with Benstock... I didn't know it had gotten to the point of Benson harassing her like this."

Tait smirked. "Too bad you're not here to meet his little

band of merry men, Franz."

Kell palmed his forehead with a chuckle. "Damn. Can't believe I skipped that part."

"Slash-tonic's losing his touch. Seriously, Captain, you would've eaten those boys for breakfast." He cut his laugh short when Franz didn't hop on that one to issue a good bacon or Pop-Tarts joke. "Franz? You still there?"

"Yeah, yeah." There was a hint of bemusement in the man's reply. "I'd just forgotten what it sounded like to hear you laugh, T-Bomb." The man didn't let the awkward moment stretch for too long. "Band of merry men? I'll take your word for it, though I have some ideas based on the one time I had the pleasure of meeting Gunter."

Kell curled a smile at their captain's caustic tone. "'Pleasure,' eh?"

"*Psshh*. Our afternoon tea lasted for two minutes before I told him to go to hell. Bastard made an offer on *our* place so he could use it as a tennis club for the resort."

"You mean the resort that isn't going to be a resort?" Tait stated.

Franzen's huff filled the line. "Fuck," he muttered. "Slash, you're absolutely sure you heard the guy from Benstock say Pyongyang and Tehran?"

Tait traded a troubled glance with Kell. It wasn't like Franz to question their intel, even if it had come verbally. But this situation wasn't like any other. This mystery wasn't happening in some foreign land, to complete strangers. It was going down in the man's own backyard, directly involving people who were "like family" to him. A little hesitation, perhaps denial, could be understood.

For a few minutes.

They'd made this call, even risked Lani overhearing it, in order to enlist Franzen's help. That urgency was stamped on Kellan's face as he returned, "Those aren't words a guy has trouble understanding, Captain. And though I was on a cell, I made the call from downtown Lihue. The connection was good, no static or interference."

Franzen exhaled for a good ten to twenty seconds. "Okay, I believe you, man. It's quite a crazy story, but I've heard crazier."

"So what's our next move?" Tait asked.

"You two aren't doing anything except making sure Lani and Leo are safe, though that duty roster is subject to grow once I get the CIA's take on this. We'll likely have to interface with several of their field units, but I'm going to start with Colton to try to expedite things. You'll need to be patient. As of right now, I'm putting you both back on the time clock. Start keeping logs. You'll report in twice a day; I'll let you know ASAP whether that's to me or a CO with a team positioned closer to the island."

Kellan tilted his head, illustrating the depth of his thought. "And positioned *farther away* than you in other ways?"

"Yeah, yeah, Swami Slashie. You got me. Look, I won't gloss coat this for you boys. I care about the Kails—a lot. When their parents went down with that plane, it was like part of our family was gone too. Lani and Leo have been through ten years' worth of pain in the last two, and I promise serious pain to any and all scumbags who add to that."

He traded glances with Kellan again. *What if we're a couple of those pain-inducing scumbags?*

"Gentlemen? Are you still with me?"

It didn't escape Tait that they both drummed nervous

fingers on their thighs because of a voice in a box smaller than a SIG magazine. "Affirmative," he stated. "Here and acknowledging you, Dragon."

He purposely used Franz's call sign in hopes of shifting the man back toward a mission logistics mind-set. But fate wasn't in the mood for leg ups today.

"That's mighty good to hear, T-Bomb—especially from you."

"Especially from me why?"

"I sent you there to deal with your past. Hokulani Kail is more than a passing look-alike for a big piece of that past—in walking, talking, sass-slinging form."

And moaning, writhing, climaxing form. And screaming, too, if his cock hadn't been buried in her throat...

He gritted his jaw to force the image from his mind. "Uhhh, yeah. It didn't escape my attention, Captain."

"And yet you're still functioning."

Beneath his breath, Kellan cracked, "Guess you could call it that."

Tait kicked him in the shin. "Lani's an understanding person." *And insightful. Generous. Smart. Sweet. And passionate... Holy hell, is she passionate...* "Being around her and Leo has been...weirdly therapeutic."

"I know the feeling."

His reflective mood was replaced by a surge of alarm. And yeah—he went ahead and admitted it—jealousy. Had Franz and Lani been an item? Were they still? "Uhhh, you do?" He had no idea how he kept his tone so neutral.

"Absolutely. The vibe between those two is addicting. They're good kids. And Hale Anelas... Well, you've probably discovered that the place lives up to its name. There's something magical about that little valley."

They're good kids. Whew. So Franz looked at Lani like a little sister of sorts. Now he just hoped the "of sorts" part had casual connotations, not protective, testicle-stabbing ones.

"Agreed." Kellan jumped in, ensuring he didn't have to shoulder this part of the conversation alone. "We convinced Lani to let us help with a few repairs around the place. T's been great with the horses."

"Horses?"

"Believe it or not, my boyhood wasn't completely wasted," he answered to the amazement in Franz's voice. Uncle Jonah had made sure of that, thank God. "Been around a few flying hooves in my time and managed to avoid most of them."

"Outstanding." Their CO burst back into his hoo-rah GI Joe mien, accenting with a loud hand clap. "Sounds like you're making progress, then—which makes me even more grateful that you two are in the right place at the right time. *Mahalo,* Sergeants, from everyone in my *ohana.*"

From everyone in my family.

Tait purposely didn't look to Kellan now. He already knew what evidence he'd see on his friend's face. The same conflicted conscience that stabbed guilty needles into him.

"Captain, there's no need for that. I'm just glad to be doing my job again." At least every word of *that* was the truth.

Kellan helped guide the conversation deeper into the safety zone by cracking, "Oh, yeah? Tell that to my Remington, sitting in the closet here with nothing to do."

Tait rolled his eyes. "I still can't believe you brought that thing."

"The sniper rifle stays in the closet, Slash," Franz mandated. "With any luck, this is going to be a babysitter's club of a gig for you. Easy and fast. Make sure Benson doesn't go near the Kails *or* the ranch, and stay sharp on gathering more intel."

"Roger," they answered in tandem.

"Let's round the wagons up again in ten hours, at nineteen hundred hours. Call me at the same number unless I text otherwise."

"Roger," Tait repeated.

"Maybe by then we'll find something for me to shoot," Kell muttered.

"Dear Christ," Tait retorted.

"Sergeant Rush, keep your hands off the Remington. And Sergeant Bommer, keep your hands off Hokulani Kail. And both of you, try to keep the island intact for another day, would you? Dragon is peace outtie."

The line went ominously silent.

Tait still leaned and peered at the phone's window, making sure their CO had really hung up before falling back in his chair, slamming the butt of a fist against his forehead. "Fuck. Me."

"I'd rather not."

"*Now* he tells me to keep my hands off her?"

Kellan sank into a chair opposite him. "I think I feel shittier. He thinks I've been sitting around mooning over my rifle."

"He pinned half of it right. You *have* been mooning, in a sense."

"Ha fucking ha."

"True fucking true."

Kell's eyes bugged before he slammed them shut and shook his head. "Why do I feel like we just slept with the boss's sister?"

"Because we did." As crushing a weight that settled on his chest from that, his next admission took his lungs into the freshly crushed category. "But that's your issue to deal with now."

"What do you mean?"

He cocked his head. "I mean that you don't have to worry about me going gonko over everything that's recently...errr... transpired. I may have thrown out a few morose moons of my own over Luna, but I'm shooting way more straight with this situation." He leaned forward again, deliberately casual with the posture to balance his dip into serious intent. "What happened last night...was a gift. One I'll never forget. So thank you."

Kellan's dark perplexity wasn't on his list of expected reactions. "What the fuck are you talking about?" He spread his feet and cupped his knees with both hands. "Tait, I can't believe you don't see the gift *you* gave *me*, not to mention Lani." He snorted, seeming damn near amused. "The way she reacted to that spanking...the place where it took her...she looked so fulfilled. So peaceful. And holy shit, when she finally orgasmed..."

He laughed, watching his buddy's eyes roll back. "Pretty good, eh?"

"Thought I'd never get my cock back."

"Not necessarily a bad thing."

"Not at all." Kell cleared his throat and joined in on the laugh. But a second later, he sobered again. "I had no idea," he murmured. "I had *no* concept at all about what this D/s stuff could really be like."

Tait smiled. "I'd always sensed there was a Sir Kellan

buried under that thick skull somewhere. You kept coming back to Bastille with me, so I knew you remained curious." He shrugged, another attempt to diffuse the impact of his words. "But you're not the first one who's been scared off by witnessing that kind of an intense connection."

Despite softening the statement, he braced himself for Kell's backlash. The man never let anyone past tab one or two on his well-ordered emotional file, where there was never anything out of place or needing to be "examined." His parents were still together, sent him cards for every holiday imaginable, and doted equally on Kadian, his younger sister. He'd come from the heart of baseball-and-apple-pie USA, meaning there couldn't possibly be anything missing in his head or his life. In this friendship, Tait was the fucked-up one needing advice— and Kellan never forgot it.

Until, apparently, today.

His buddy lifted a smile that actually touched on self-deprecating before answering, "Connection. Shit. Yeah...that's what it is, isn't it?"

"There's no way you can give a subbie what she needs without it," Tait offered. He let his smile grow reflective as he went on. "To watch her skin shiver then form little drops of perspiration...to feel the pulse beneath her wrists and neck... even to hear her every breath and know that you can heighten all of it with the power of your domination... Hell yeah, connection is key. It's everything."

"It's amazing."

His friend's confession came on a guttural grate. To Tait, it was also the most meaningful thing his friend had ever said. "Amazing is also a damn good way of putting it," he replied.

"But for her, too, right?" Kell lifted a stare that was darker than usual. "For the submissive. She's just as connected back to you, isn't she?"

He nodded. "Her freedom to let go and fly comes from your strength as the Dom."

"Which was what you gave to Lani last night." Kellan let his hand go flat on the table. "And exactly what she needed. So who's the one thanking who for *gifts* around here?"

Tait turned his gaze out toward the sea. The turquoise and azure depths still swished with whitecaps, clinging to the violence from last night's storm. His psyche felt the same way. Part of him craved to be back on that couch, lost in the sensual symmetry of what the three of them had shared; another part already accepted the fleeting fantasy of it...perhaps the stupidity of it.

Because now, life felt even emptier than before.

Which made his next statement even harder to form.

"Yeah, well...from now on, you'll be the one giving her what she needs, man."

Kellan let out a heavy breath. "Fuck. You...you really think?"

"Hell yes. Take it in little bites—or in this case, gentle swats. You and Lani have the most important element already. Open, considerate communication. Talk to her. Ask her what feels good and what doesn't. She's very good at expressing herself."

I need to please both of you...at once...

Dear fuck was the woman good at self-expression.

"Okay. I can do that." The statement was Cool Hand Luke, but Kellan's fists, now twisting with each other atop the table, were complete Joan-Crawford-with-a-pile-of-wire-hangers.

Despite the throb in his groin, another grin was

surprisingly easy to produce. "Hey, it's all right to be a little scared."

"A little?"

"*Breathe,* Slash-aroni." He chuckled. Kellan didn't.

"T...I have to say something. I'm not sure I've ever felt this way for a woman before." His gaze flew across the floor as he worked his jaw back and forth. "I don't know what this shit is. And I don't know whether I even *like* it."

"But imagining your life without it is impossible?"

Kell gawked like he'd just revealed the secret formula for time travel. "Exactly!"

"Imagining your life without what?"

The interruption came from the doorway to the house—and the woman standing there, a little sleepy, a little disheveled—and a lot of too fucking sexy. Tait adjusted his position to try hiding his hard-on, already given a kick-start from the flashbacks of last night. Lani wasn't helping things a goddamn bit with her girlish stance and robe-covered body. The garment, clearly borrowed from a female's closet somewhere in the house, was a pale pink contrast to her hair, which she'd tugged into a loose side braid. He wondered if she was still naked under the thing. Part of him prayed yes. Part of him bellowed no. If Kell decided it was time to start "communicating" with her right now about their newfound discovery of kink, it was going to be time for a long, *long* torture session of a run for him. Or maybe he'd just go out to Waimea Canyon and wear himself out on a ball-breaker of a wilderness trail. Or five.

"Well, good morning, Starshine."

Thank fuck one of them was still able to function. Besides, it made more sense for Kell to go greet her, rise, and pull her close with a tender kiss on her lips, which were still plump as ripe strawberries from all the attention they'd gotten last night.

Stop staring at her goddamn lips. Stop thinking about anything they did with you last night. Or to you.

Tait rose as well but headed as far down the lanai as he could without seeming a reclusive douche. Lani peeked around Kell and gave him a mock scowl anyway. "What, no 'good morning, dreamgirl' from the T-Boner?"

What was that word Franzen used for her? "Sass-slinging?" Yep, that was about right. Every muscle in his body longed to stalk back to the woman, hike up that pretty kitty robe until he saw pussy of another kind, and make her sling sounds of a different kind until she apologized for letting that snark fly.

Instead, after tossing a shit-eating smirk of his own, he swept a low, teasing bow. "You twinkle above us, babe, and we twinkle below."

She giggled.

His pulse raced.

Yes, his fucking heartbeat *raced*, like a line from a bad pop song by a guy with good hair.

Shit, shit, shit. Time to lie low—translation, cut the hell out of—this bantering with her. It was playful and innocent yesterday. It was outright flirtation today. All three of them knew it.

Thankfully, Lani let the moment slide, as well. She wasn't benevolent enough to give him mercy from her sweet smile, swinging it to both him and Kellan. "Thanks for letting me sleep in. Guess I needed it."

Tait studied her. "Guess you did, considering all the times you got up to pace."

A glance from Kellan indicated Tait had stolen the words out of his mouth. So his buddy had noticed her nocturnal ramblings too. Kell hooked a gentle hand to her elbow when Lani turned, presumably to gaze over the ocean. "You were up at least three times, sweetheart."

"Four," Tait corrected.

"Wasn't counting her stop at the head." Kell said it without breaking his attention on Lani. "Care to share what's going on in that beautiful mind, sweetheart?"

The pause before her reply was long enough to notch up Tait's apprehension, as well. "I'm fine," she finally asserted. "Really. Just fine." Her averted eyes, gleaming bright as the foam topping the waves, said otherwise.

"And I'm Tinkerbell." Tait strode back with slow but purposeful steps. "You want to try that one again? Keep in mind that your audience is a couple of guys who've been trained to tell someone's lying in less than a minute."

"I—" She gave a little huff. Pursed her lips. She was clearly going for frustrated, but Tait was so entranced by her effort, he hoped she never got there. "I just have a lot on my mind, okay?" In a surprise turnabout, she dropped the insecurity for a new, saucy smile. "Besides, it was fun watching the two of you sleep."

"Oh, how sparkly vampire of you."

Hell. How long had he lasted on the ban to the bantering? A minute? But the gibe was too good to pass up. Lani's impish grin said she agreed. *Damn.* He could get addicted to that smirk of hers...to the warmth it spread through his senses, pleased as hell with himself for lightening her day. But that was the problem with addiction. The words itself had synonyms like *dependence* and *enslavement.* And somewhere in that mess, there was guilt, leading him back to the throne in his soul reserved for the one woman who'd ever dared occupy it.

Luna.

She was still there, all right. He felt her, reclining in her serene feline glory—but why the hell was she only smiling, giving him cute little golf claps of approval?

Why are you playing with me like this, woman? Where the fuck is my slam of remorse, my gut punch of grief?

They were gone.

And he was confused.

Thank God for Kellan and his disgusted scowl. "Sparkly vampire? Did you really just go there?"

Lani laughed louder. Another box added on the addiction list. "He totally did. And it was cute."

Tait narrowed his eyes. "I don't do cute."

"Yes, you do."

Kellan joined her on the comeback. His friend sobered fast after that, running his touch up to her shoulder. The guy's features went gooey in a way Tait had never seen before. "You want me to take you back to the ranch?" he queried. "I'm sure you want to see Leo."

Lani returned the Valentine's card stare, running a thumb across the stubble on Kell's jaw. "He's up and off to school by now. At least he'd *better* be."

During her statement, the phone on the table *bing*ed with an incoming text. Tait knew that because the phone was his. "I can confirm the school arrival," he said, reading the window. "Killer K says he's going to first period, sends his love to sis and Slash-gasm, and promises there won't be any cave explorations on his behalf again today."

Lani's face relaxed. At the same time, she slanted him a

curious glance. "Killer K?"

"The kid doesn't have a monopoly on creating dumb nicknames."

She smiled at that, but the look was a more subdued version of her norm. Once more, Tait observed that Kellan shared his insight. There was a deeper issue on the woman's mind, and a rocket-science degree wasn't necessary for figuring it out. "Tait's made some coffee," Kell offered. "Let's all go grab some and then sit down for a talk."

Tait wasn't surprised to watch Lani's posture stiffen. Fuck. He knew the feeling. So much to say. So few ways to say it without everyone signing up for Camp Uncomfortable. Forget wanting to spank her. Now he just wanted to pull her close one more time, inhale the jasmine of her hair, and tell her everything was going to be all right. *Everything.* They were going to protect her land from Benson, and he was going to save her spirit from conflict.

What she and Kellan had forged together already was clearly awesome. He refused to be the dickwad to stomp all over that, no matter how incredible things had been over the last forty-eight hours. All he had to do was say that, right? A cup of coffee, a few lines of speaking the truth, and they could all shelve the last couple of nights into the closet of damn good memories. Best plan for everyone. Safer for all. Especially Lani.

"I don't want to talk."

Except if the woman herself dropped a grenade on the plan.

Kellan slid his hand from her shoulder to her nape. "Sweetheart, I think we need to. I can speak with confidence for Tait in this case. We've both come to care about you—a lot.

And while the last two nights have been...errmmm...enjoyable for everyone—"

"Enjoyable?" Tait shoved out a snort. "Step down, Poindexter. You aren't talking for me anymore. They were fucking awesome."

"All right," Kell muttered. "What he said."

Lani's gaze shined at sun-bright power once more. "I couldn't agree more." Her smile, though tinged by sadness at the edges, was no less dazzling. "Which is why I don't want to talk."

He fell into silence along with Kellan. *Damn.* This was an unexpected impasse. As his buddy jammed hands into his pockets and shuffled in confusion, Tait let his stare fall on Lani. He really studied her now. Tension still gripped her stance, but that celestial calm continued to rule her gaze. In short, she revealed nothing.

"Shit," he finally muttered. "Lima-Lima-Mike-Foxtrot."

"Copy you loud and clear, brother."

"Huh?" Lani queried.

"Lost like motherfuckers," Tait explained. When she returned a puzzled grimace, he charged, "Why don't you want to talk? Girls always want to talk."

Her whole face darkened. "You don't always get to peer under the dome, okay?"

He hated admitting it, but she was right. She wasn't his submissive. She wasn't even his girl. From now on, it was probably best that she wasn't even his friend. She was his stunning mission asset, and nothing more.

"Fair enough." He took a measured step back. He wondered why her face fell like he'd shot one of her horses at the same time, but maintained his new position. That plan didn't earn a thumbs-up from the woman, either. Her eyes squeezed as if she were about to open the waterworks again. Kellan stepped over and grabbed her shoulders again, shooting him a what-the-hell-happened glare, and Tait spread his arms in a wide shrug. This was the most bizarre "morning after" he'd ever experienced.

The next second, it twisted even weirder.

With a tight cry, Lani shoved away from Kellan too. In an instant, Tait realized why his buddy had just been glowering at him. Seeing her upset in the arms of another guy, even his best friend who'd done nothing, made his very marrow scream with the need to yank her away and hold her.

"Starshine? You sure you don't want to—"

"I don't need a talk." As she cut him off, she also spun back toward the house. "I need a drive," she called from the living room. "We *all* do."

Kellan didn't look back to Tait until she'd crossed the living room and disappeared toward the bedroom. His friend blinked a bunch of times, as if trying to reconcile his perception with reality, before muttering, "I guess we're going for a drive."

Tait rocked back on his heels. A black laugh tempted his lips, "Appears so."

Kell paced to the edge of the lanai, turned, and came back. "You think Leo will be all right if she totes our asses to the opposite side of the island?"

He nodded. "Ike adores that kid like the son he never had, so I can text him to be diligent. Besides, Gunter doesn't know we're digging in his secret underwear drawer...yet."

"Good point."

Tait glanced down at his feet. "Think we should put on shoes?"

"Hmm. Probably."

"Do you have any idea where we're going?"

As he issued the question, Lani walked back through the living room, pink robe replaced by a dress apparently borrowed from the same closet. From the photos in the house, Tait knew Franz had a couple of biological sisters. Thank fuck they were similar in size and coloring to Lani. The dress was stunning on her. It was pink, too, but in a darker shade, pulling out the gorgeous glow in her cheeks and the color in her lips. Her hair hung free now, brushed to a sheen so smooth it reminded him of black latex.

Fuck. Yeah.

Pink was nice, but black latex? The best invention since shoelaces. And Christ, would that woman's curves look amazing in a corset formed of the stuff, cinching and exposing her in all the right places...

Shelve it, Bommer. High up and far, far *away.*

"Uhhhh...what'd you say?" Kellan finally blurted.

He swallowed before answering. "Just...errr...asked if you knew where we're going."

Kellan chuffed. "Does it matter?"

"Very good point."

★ ★ ★ ★ ★

He was damn glad they'd decided to put on shoes. That didn't stop him from feeling five kinds of underdressed and unsanitary from the second they'd exited the car at their final destination. As they walked down a pretty stone pathway shrouded by thick tropical trees, he still kept jabbing both hands through his hair, hoping the thick strands would, for once, behave.

Kellan walked up and punched him in the shoulder. "You want to relax, Benson groupie wannabe?"

"Huh? What the hell?"

"You're coming off like a pretentious ass from a hair product commercial. Worse, you're missing all this beauty. Look at this place! It's like the freaking *Jungle Book*." The guy scooted in close enough to murmur, "You know, this'd be an awesome spot for a nudist colony."

He seized the chance to land a counterpunch into Kell's arm. "It's a *church*, you bozo. Show some respect."

"Right. Because look where all your forced time in Sunday School got *you*."

"At least I'm not a heathen, walking around here with nudity on my mind."

"Why is it even called that? Sunday School needs a new name. Maybe even a new image."

"Are you really skipping down that yellow brick road?"

Lani slipped between them from behind, looping her arms beneath both their elbows. "You're both right—and wrong." Though she pulled them along, her pace was slower, reverent. Her voice matched. "Though the Saiva Siddhanta Church *is* located here, the complex is about much more than that. It's a spiritual sanctuary for over twenty swamis, yogis, and sadhakas from all over the world, furthering the Hindu principles of humanity's unity and divinity through harmony, generosity, and love. It's also a center of learning for pilgrims from all over the world. Besides all that, it's amazing."

With every word she spoke, Tait felt a smile growing and his stress liquefying. He watched the same effect taking hold of Kellan. At face value, the syntax of Lani's words were normally hippie-talk hooey he blew off faster than incense ash, but the peace on her face, joined with the music of her voice, worked a strange magic on him. As he lifted his head and peered around, the feeling grew. The place really was amazing. Though there wasn't a square foot of this island that wasn't breathtaking, the sanctuary grounds were like Kaua`i in ultra-high-def, with towering banyans, eucalyptus, and palms overlooking bushes that were covered in lush vines that sprang from carpets of ferns. The air was better than any florist shop on the planet, a bouquet of plumeria, hibiscus, sandalwood, lilies, and even a little cinnamon and curry. As they climbed a gentle slope, he glimpsed a sparkling river that was fed by postcard-perfect waterfalls.

Kellan tugged at Lani. Though he kept his voice down as well, there was no missing the tease to it. "So how am *I* right and wrong?"

Her smile quirked with her unique style of mischief. "Let's just say you're not the first one in this party to think about 'doing the naked' in this neighborhood." As Kell smirked and preened, she hurriedly added, "Which means that unlike Tait, we *both* need more Sunday School."

"Pffft."

"Do me a favor and elbow him," Tait quipped. After Lani obliged by giving Kell a good-natured nudge, she added a smile that rivaled even the scenery for radiance. Tait couldn't take his eyes off her. She'd always been double-take beautiful, but something about this place and this mountain added layers to the pull she had on him. In every part of his mind...and body.

Hell. The natural-and-naked fantasy party had a brand-new member.

He needed to steer the topic elsewhere. *Now.* Thankfully, the feat wouldn't be difficult. Clearly, Lani loved this place.

He'd simply enroll her as their tour guide. Maybe that would haul his mind from the scene that unfurled in his head, of stretching her out on one of the grassy riverbanks, stripping her nude, and worshipping her as a newly inducted goddess of this place...

Tait Gabriel Bommer, you're in church! Straighten up and pay attention, or there will be no cookies at hospitality for you.

Wonderful. Like his senses needed any more havoc today.

"Okay, Mom," he murmured, holding on to the sweetness of the memory for a tiny moment longer. If he closed his eyes and concentrated hard enough, he could almost smell the Juicy Fruit gum she'd always kept in her purse...and her floral shampoo...and the cracked leather of her Bible...

"Okay who?"

Lani's soft inquisition made him cough hard before shoving Melody McKay-Bommer to the back of his soul again. "Nobody." He locked down his smile. "Nothing important."

"You sure?" Her gaze flicked over his face. A breeze sifted through the trees, blowing her hair at him. It smelled like flowers...

This whole place smells like flowers, you dumbshit.

"Yeah, I'm sure." Since her hand was still curled under his elbow, he pressed his opposite hand atop it while continuing to walk toward what appeared to be the temple itself, a modest stone building with a pedestal in front that supported a large carved black bull. "Tell me about all this," he appealed.

Kellan looked on, also interested. On his friend's face, Tait recognized the visual form of everything *he* felt: wonderment, gratitude, peace. And as sunlight broke through the trees, comprehension pierced his senses. Being here with the two of them, even after what they'd shared last night, didn't seem weird or wrong. It was a perfect completion to the magic they'd created. Did Lani know that when she insisted on driving across the island to get here? He received a big chunk of that answer in the meaningful glance she lifted before fulfilling his request.

"The tourist guide answer for that is that the church and monastery have been here since the mid-nineteen seventies, and things have grown from there. People make pilgrimages from all over the world to come and experience this. I'm sure you can simply feel the reasons why. There's a special energy here. I wish I could explain it better than that."

She shook her head as if rebuking herself for telling a silly joke, but Kellan leaned over, securing her other hand beneath his. "Don't know if I could've said it any better, sweetheart."

Tait gazed up at a crew of colorful birds babbling happily to each other as they constructed a nest in one of the trees. "There are probably a lot of great memories for you here too. Did you come a lot with your parents and Leo?"

Her eyebrows bunched again, as if that perplexed her. "The first time I came here was a little over six months ago."

Tait almost stopped in the middle of the path. Her confession swiped a strange scythe of awareness through his gut. He forced his voice to stay on an even keel while replying slowly, "Six months ago?"

"Yeah." Lani's voice still resonated with bewilderment. "It's kind of weird, I guess. Mom and Dad raised Leo and me to have a deep grasp of our spirituality and how our energy contributed to the universe as a whole, just like the Hindu concept of karma. And the Polynesian gods are similar to the Hindu ones, with multiple deities that support one main creator through their unique powers and virtues. But we were always so busy keeping the ranch going, especially during the busy seasons for the B and B, that setting aside the time to come here just never happened."

He almost swallowed back his next question, but holding it in was a worse option. He simply had to tell himself that the answer would lead nowhere, which made him grateful for the stone bench they arrived at, atop of a scenic hill beneath a sprawling kapok tree.

He sat, planting both elbows to his knees and sucking down air with long, steady care. "So what changed your mind six months ago?"

Kellan sat down next to him. Lani chose to stand. That was so okay with him. As if put in place by a photographer wanting a shot of an exquisite island beauty, she stood in a shaft of sunlight that haloed her hair and bathed her features in deep gold. "I'm not sure," she admitted. "I hadn't planned on it, but I was in Lihue, wrestling again with the business-permits office about reopening the main house as a B and B. As you can guess, it didn't go well. I remember walking out of the office in a puddle of self-pity. But it was a few weeks before Christmas, and the rest of the world was prancing in tidings of comfort and joy." She folded her arms and poked a toe at the ground. "I tried opting for some retail therapy, but when I actually snarled at a Boy Scout for offering to open my car door for me, I knew something was wrong." She glanced up at them, lips twisting. "I sat in the jeep and lost it. Melted down. I felt so dead and defeated, like I'd never be happy again. It was like—"

She interrupted herself with a frustrated grunt. Tait clenched his fists to fight the assault of memory but racked up a massive fail on the effort. He saw it all over again. Luna, limp and lifeless in his arms. Her hand, still resting on his neck after using her last breath to kiss him. The candy canes and tinsel at the nurse's station, blurred by the haze of his tears.

"It was like what?" He managed it on a rasp.

Her face wavered like she prepared an apology instead of a confession. "It was like...I cried for more than just me." He watched the mental whack she gave herself. "Agghh. This sounds so stupid."

"Man purses are stupid, okay?" He latched eagerly on to the relief of the humor. "Flavored mayonnaise? Stupid. *You* are not stupid."

"You forgot Twitter accounts for dogs," Kellan added.

"She has the picture."

Lani beamed at them both. "Yes, she does." With a sigh, she spread her arms. "I'm not sure how else to express that moment, except that my tears felt...bigger. Heavier. I'm not one of those people who can read people's auras or 'sense' when some crazy world event is going to go down. But that moment, in the jeep, I had this feeling that something had happened beyond my understanding. *Something* tore into my heart and ripped it open."

Another breeze kicked across the hill. Clouds drifted. Leaves rustled. Birds sang. Squirrels scampered across the grass. Movement and life, in so many places...

Except Tait's heart.

When his chest slammed his lungs against his ribs again, he dropped his head. His vision was filled with the white-knuckled union of his hands while his soul and sanity grappled at each other.

Ask her.

Ask her!

ANGEL PAYNE

Are you kidding? You've started to look at the world with a jar full of whole cookies again. Forget this is happening. Stick to the plan. Hands off Hokulani Kail—and that includes her mind. Especially *her mind.*

"Was it a Wednesday?"

She didn't say anything right away. But Kellan did. "Fuck." He felt his friend swiveling a glare on him. "You had to, didn't you?"

"I like broken cookies."

"*What?* Good Christ, Tait, what the hell are you—"

"Yes." Lani cut him off with a whisper that exploded like a bomb. Tait jerked up his head, his heart clenching to a stop again, as he met her gaze. Another detonation. Her eyes, silvery and sunlit and boundless, spilled over with tears. Her lips trembled. "Yes," she repeated. "It was a Wednesday."

Tait surged to his feet. Jammed his hands across the top of his head. This time, he simply didn't know what the hell to do with them. He laced his fingers at the back of his skull and did a feverish lap around the bench. Another.

Thank fuck for Kellan. His buddy, also standing, held out both hands in a smoothing motion. "Okay, kids. Everyone's skewing a little too Andrew Lloyd Webber here, and the last time I checked, nobody packed a mask or a cat costume."

Tait shot him a sardonic glance. "That's because none of us are John Franzen."

The levity helped a little. Kellan walked over to Lani and gently tucked her head against his chest. "What'd you do after the meltdown?" he queried.

"She came here."

The interjection came from a new visitor to their knoll. The woman was hard to miss in her long Indian sari of bright

241

yellow and blue but would've snagged their attention without it due to the lyrical power of her voice. Though her headscarf didn't hide all her gray hair and her pace was more a shuffle than steps, she carried herself with such regal grace that Tait was prompted to rise a little and then bow to her. She patted his head and murmured something in Hindi, which he painstakingly translated to "you're a good boy," though he was rusty on everything from that region except Pashto and Farsi. Nevertheless, he looked up to give her a smile of gratitude— and only then realized the woman was blind.

"I'm sorry," Lani said, pushing from Kellan to approach the woman, "but how do you know that?"

"Because I saw you, my dear."

"You...what?"

"You think we've only been given eyes with which to see?" The woman slipped her hand into Lani's while shuffling toward the bench. Though Kellan stepped over to help her, she shooed him away before sitting, pulling Lani down next to her. Right away, she raised a hand to Lani's head, running fingers lightly over her hair and shoulders. "Ahhh! Your energy is different today. So different from that first day. Both beautiful sights, but *that* day"—she sighed, folding her hands back in her lap, Lani's still pressed between them—"imparted a memory I shall truly carry beyond the veils with me...and, if lucky, into my next existence, as well."

Tait leaned forward. "Why?" It blurted out as a demand before he could help it. The woman's wisdom and experience were imprinted in the lines on her face, yet she spoke of the first day she "saw" Lani as if it rivaled a journey to the summit of Everest. Her excitement injected his own blood with a crazy blend of awe and excitement compelling him closer to her.

Her next action shouldn't have stunned him but did. She lifted a hand, bidding him to crouch on the ground in front of her. When he did, she repeated the same exploration of his head that she had of Lani.

"Told you the Sunday School hair was worthless," Kell mumbled.

He let the comment pass. It was pretty damn easy. The woman's touch was like a rain shower of peace, pelting him with warmth, opening him without judging him. He swayed from the bliss of it, trying to steel himself for the loss and pain that was sure to follow. Women of quality, especially one able to bring him a feeling like this, didn't stick around for long after seeing his fucked-up soul.

"Ssshh." The woman pressed her fingertips into his scalp. "Be still. Let the fears rest."

"I know how to be still," he growled.

"No." Humor danced across her face. "You do not." She leveled her face with his, and for a long moment, her eyes widened as if a miracle had restored her sight. "Outside, you are a windless ocean, but inside, you keep running, fighting. You have declared war against your own beauty and the unique truth of this moment. Why? There was a time that you didn't fight destiny. That you believed in magic. The time has come for you to believe again, warrior. And you can. You are safe here."

He clenched his jaw until it ached. Battled to pull away from her. He had to escape before it was too late and she took him into canyons of his soul he'd vowed never to visit again.

You are safe.

No. That was something he guaranteed for others. A net he assured for submissives. It was a luxury he couldn't afford to indulge—and this encounter, now eerie and bizarre, was vivid proof.

"Damn." Kell's voice was gruff with new solemnity. "She really does see you, man."

"Shut up." His lungs pummeled the crap out of every breath he took. His mind sizzled and his pores awakened, sensations he hadn't felt since the morning they'd called from the hospital to tell him Luna had awakened from her coma. Three days later, every angel that had lifted him was all too eager to jump to the dark side, dragging him to a grieving hell.

He had to escape. Had to shake this woman's eyes and words and fingers. Why couldn't he move? She barely touched him, yet her face held an intensity that bewitched him, a tenderness that humbled him. He'd seen expressions like it before, on the faces of the wives and mothers who greeted the boys at the base, returning from their deployments. But when a guy worked Spec Ops, he often arrived home like he'd left: in subterfuge and silence. Didn't matter much in his case, anyhow. If they threw him a parade down the center of town and dumped five tons of confetti on it, Mom wasn't coming out of hiding, and Luna wasn't rising from the grave.

This is insane. Kellan was right. Where are the phantom mask and cat costume?

"So lost. So confused. So afraid." The creases in the woman's face deepened as she kept exploring him, though she released one of her hands to reach again to Lani. "This was exactly how *you* looked that day, my dear."

Lani followed her lead and lowered next to him. "I imagine I did," she murmured. "I thought I was going a little insane."

As if he wasn't in enough torment, Lani pressed one of her hands around his. Tait jerked, but she held fast. *Fucking great.*

Fate's torture chamber of an afternoon was more fun by the minute.

He gave up staying balanced on his haunches and dropped fully to his knees. They hit the ground hard, making the moisture from last night's rain seep through his pants. "I'm not insane," he snarled.

The old woman laughed. "But why not?" She persisted with her fingers against his head. "'Breaking down' is simply breaking free, my friend."

Lani laughed. Not just a giggle but a full and melodic laugh. As Tait gave her the only reaction he could summon, a stunned gawk, she declared, "Yes. That's it. That was what I felt that day. It was like a mountain had collapsed on top of me. I was trapped and had no idea how to move the damn thing. And then I arrived here..."

"And you walked down by the water," the woman filled in. She closed her eyes again, finally freeing Tait from the stare that saw nothing and everything.

Lani's laugh faded, though the enchantment on her face remained. "Yeah," she rasped, "I did."

"And what of the mountain on your soul?" the woman prompted.

Lani swallowed hard. She let her gaze trail toward the river, but that meant including Tait in its path. Before she spoke, she looked back to him. "It was lifted. Completely."

She spoke only four words. Followed them with the equally simple beauty of her stare. Then why did the moment feel like so much more? Why was there a downpour in Tait's spirit that started with the silver salvation of *her* tears? And why did his three words of response feel like opening a gate that would turn the torrent into a flood?

"Lifted by what?"

His answer came from the old woman. "Not what," she whispered. "*Who.*"

Lani blinked at her. Her face was a sunlit portrait of awe. Her fingers twisted harder against his. "Yes," she rasped. "You're right."

Kellan grunted. "I'm glad to hear that, sweetheart, because I'm in the wilderness without a compass here."

"Me too." Tait peered more intently at both women. If Lani had come here seeking answers that day and one of the monks or fellow worshippers had helped her, that was awesome—but certainly not a cause for acting like she'd been visited by an angel. "What are you trying to say? She's right about what?"

The woman dipped her head toward Lani. "Tell him, dear one. Tell him about the voice you heard. The voice that belonged to the energy that I saw."

As her voice again turned each word into poetry, it also transformed the hairs on his neck into spikes that could cut diamonds.

Visited...by an angel.

On a Wednesday.

Six months ago.

Suddenly, he longed to be anywhere but here. Just as suddenly, he knew if the whole hill caught on fire, he wasn't going anywhere.

CHAPTER SEVENTEEN

Lani slammed her eyes shut. Tears soaked her lashes and then tumbled down her cheeks. She heard Tait's breath freeze in his throat and was certain hers did the same thing. She'd never told anyone about those bizarre moments on the riverbank during that day filled with so much loss, anger, and confusion. It had been so easy to write the experience off to the power of her emotions, mingled with the transformative magic of the monastery.

This special woman, with her all-seeing soul, had shown her otherwise. Beseeched her otherwise. Called the truth out of her soul again.

She had to obey.

"I thought I was going crazy." Her voice was barely a crack on the air, though the wind held its breath in consideration. "At the same time, it was the most wonderful crazy in the world."

Tait squeezed her fingers again. "I understand," he whispered. "I do."

More tears stung her eyes, which were filled with gratitude for his thick, sincere words.

"I thought it was just a trick of the wind at first, that maybe I overheard somebody else's conversation. But—but she repeated herself until I listened."

She heard Tait's rough gulp. "A little husky?" he asked. "And a lot bossy?"

As she giggled, the salt of her tears tickled her lips. "Yes.

Exactly."

"Shit." The astounded blurt came from Kellan, who instantly ducked his head and cowed his voice. He mouthed his next words. *Holy. Fucking. Shit.*

Tait cupped his hand to the side of her face. "What did she say, Lani? It's okay. Please tell me."

She gave him a shaky nod. "'Don't give up, goddess.' That was all it was...at first." She smiled a little. "It took a few minutes to ditch the *tricky wind* excuse and buy into the *I'm officially going crazy* one. After that—"

Her mind chopped into her voice. Was she really about to do this? To say this? Suddenly, the bridge between remembering the moment and recounting it out loud was enormous and terrifying.

"Lani." Kellan appeared again. He dropped to his knees alongside Tait, taking her other hand in the unshaking strength of his own. "T's right. It's okay. We're both right here. Let it out, sweetheart."

She wound her fingers just as tightly through his. It didn't help her careening balance or erratic heartbeat, but she finally sucked up enough courage to give a what-the-fuck to her qualms. So what if the two of them wrote her off as a whacko after this? It wasn't like she had to worry about running into them at the grocery store or seeing them at *all* in another week.

"She told me that life wasn't always going to be so hard. That all the bullshit and the struggle were going to be worth it. That sometimes, walking through fire is good because it strips your spirit to be replanted with better things. Then she said—" Another stupid cry burst out. *Shit!* Why was she giving this such importance? It wasn't like they would, despite their comforting touches. "She said that those new things were coming soon. That they were both being prepared for me."

The guys went still, palpably considering her statement. Even lost in the whirl of her memory, she could discern how the words must be hitting them. *They were both being prepared for me. Crap.* Could it have sounded any more Biblical and pretentious? Yet neither of them snickered. Neither of them *moved.*

The silence stretched on. It was broken by the blind woman's prod. "And what did she say then? The last of her message?"

Lani looked up and winced. "You heard that part, too?" She returned the woman's nod with a shrug that edged on embarrassed. "I'm not sure that part was real. I mean, it sounded like a joke." Were stress-induced head voices from on high even allowed to have a sense of humor? "I think I just overheard it from other people walking in the garden."

The woman turned, undeterred. "Just tell them what she said, dear one."

Lani opened her eyes. She pulled her hands free in order to swipe at her cheeks, an effort to hide her nervous laugh. "It was...stupid. I muttered something about how I really must have been crazy, with voices in my head so clearly not my own. And then *she* said—"

"What?" The prompt came from Tait when she interrupted herself with another huff.

"At first, I could've sworn she giggled. And then she said 'Crazy is good, girlfriend. Don't you know that the craziest witches snag the hottest wizards?'"

★ ★ ★ ★ ★

Ten minutes later, honestly wondering if her arm was being yanked out of its socket, she stumbled across the monastery's parking lot in Tait's wake, rushing three steps for every one of his urgent strides. Kellan had been following as rear sweep but jogged forward to unlock the jeep before opening the back-seat door. She stifled an urge to laugh, undoubtedly to play cover for her dread. The two of them moved with military precision, meaning her confession about the "visit from the voice" had been an unknowing revelation of national security secrets, a hypnotic trigger to kill her, or solid proof for thinking her one almond away from the nuthouse.

No matter what, their goal was obvious. To get her out of here fast.

Had she really been awash in tranquility just a half hour ago, walking with them beneath the trees, feeling a little balanced about life again? Had she truly thought it a stroke of genius to come and let the magic of this place push destiny's reset button for the three of them?

Way to go, mastermind. Look how well her "brilliance" had paid off. Prophecies from voices out of thin air, random Potter references, and now this fire drill ending to their field trip... Yeah, some picture-perfect day.

The disaster's lead-in had been no less weird. As long as she lived, she'd never forget the moments immediately after her bizarre gut spill. She'd prewritten a script filled with nervousness and discomfort from both of them but instead received a pair of unblinking stares, filled with tangible intensity. After that, they'd taken a pair of long breaths, Kellan pushing his out while Tait pulled his in. They were in complete sync—about honestly believing her.

The icing on their astonishing cake was delivered by Tait, who raked her with a gaze that made her wonder if she'd sprouted horns or wings or both. Still, she hadn't been able to turn away. His eyes. *Gods, his eyes.* Their golden fires contained both hell and heaven, searing her to the core with their depths of pain but blazing to her soul with the strength of their hope.

Her confession had unraveled him. In return, he'd done the same to her.

She'd been so consumed by his gaze, she barely noticed when he pulled her back up and started dragging her back to the car. The realization was astounding, considering the pace he set. That was when her confusion hit, pounding harder with every step they took, until now. Lani planted her feet, hesitant to climb into her own damn car with the man.

"Hokulani." Though his eyes still tore into her like spiritual blowtorches, the rest of his face was locked in tension. "Get in the car."

Instinctively, she stepped back—only to collide with the brick wall of Kellan's chest. "It's all right, Starshine." His voice was steady, strong, and warm in her ear. "It's going to be okay. It's not our intent to freak you out any further—"

"I'm not freaked out!"

"You're shaking like a soaked kitten." His hands on her waist, as solid as his voice, proved his point with maddening clarity.

"Fine," she spat. "D-Do you blame me?"

"Blame you? Sweetheart, we *understand* you."

"Huh?" She jerked her gaze up at Tait, which deepened her confusion. He was wrapped in more layers of strain than before, his chest taut, his shoulders coiled, his legs braced.

"Okay," she snapped, frantically trying to blink back tears, "I'm glad someone *understands*, because I sure as hell still don't."

Damn it. How had things gone so sideways? Three hours ago, she swore to wean herself from these two. Now she was the filling in their hard-bodied soldier sandwich, wondering why she couldn't turn off her body's hot reaction to them, while her mind screamed orders to beat them away.

Kellan grunted. "I'm really fucking this up."

Tait rolled his eyes. "Because you think *feelings* and *talking* shouldn't be in the same sentence."

"Working on it, assmunch."

Surprisingly, Tait threw out a crooked smile. "I know, man." He turned the expression down to her. "Just like I've been digging up more of my own shit lately, too—and 'working on it.'" He raised his hands to her shoulders, pulling her a little closer with gentle command. "Amazing what a couple of stubborn dick-smacks will do when they have the proper motivation."

Heat rushed up her face. *Lovely.* Like she needed to feel like a sixteen-year-old being flirted out of her panties, on top of everything else her senses had been through today. "I just thought we could all come here for clarity," she admitted. "And now..." She dropped her head. "That's sure as hell not the case."

Tait ran a reassuring hand to her nape. "Clarity? About what?"

"What do you mean, about what?" She jerked her head up, including Kellan in the scope of her scowl, as well. "About this. Us. Whatever it is. About both of you—and making sure that I don't get attached to it." She couldn't hide a small wince. "To either of you."

Once again, their reaction didn't throw her for a loop. It

tossed her for two or three. Their chuckles came as a shock yet a reassurance. "Did you hear that, T? She doesn't want to get too attached."

Tait skimmed his fingers to the side of her face. His gaze, capturing hers in its direct beam again, was more molten and brilliant than it'd been in the garden. "Too late, dreamgirl," he whispered. "It's so completely too late. If you don't believe me, ask the crazy witch who visited your head."

His profession incited a wave of reactions. First, she laughed. He made everything sound so easy, so normal. After that, a sigh emerged. He did all that while channeling the beauty of an angel, the sun glinting in his hair and etching every bold line of his face. Finally, she swallowed on a throat thick with elation and gratitude before rasping, "Then you don't think my mind is grilled cheese?"

Tait's stare dipped across her face. A heavy, hungry intent defined his gaze. Lani held her breath, horrified he was about to kiss her right here...knowing she'd die if he didn't.

It was time to die.

He halted his lips less than an inch above hers. "Goddamn, could I go for some grilled cheese right now."

"Hmm." Kellan's voice brushed her ear at the same teasing proximity. "Isn't that a coincidence? Me too."

"Hop in the car, babe, and we'll show you how much."

It was suddenly the easiest feat in the world to follow Tait into the back seat of the jeep. And the hardest. As Kellan gunned the car's engine to life and sped them back toward Kuamo'o Road, effectively toppling her into Tait's lap, that internal skirmish worsened. As she'd hoped—and dreaded— the man didn't let her scramble back to her seat. With commanding sweeps of movement, he had her straddling his lap before Kellan made the left turn that marked their official exit from the monastery.

"Sergeant Bommer." It was a bitch to summon an incensed tone, especially as the man cupped both sides of her ass to seat her more fully against the apex of his body. As he did, she instantly felt his cock surging for her, pounding against his pants. "Listen to me! We have a seat belt law in this state, and if you think that just because we're out in the middle of—"

The fast *thwick* of the seat belt, yanked out by him then clicked into its holster, cut her short. She gasped as the belt retracted a little, locking into its new position—across her back. He'd belted both of them in. At once.

"There." He curled an utterly roguish grin. "Now we're law-abiding citizens."

Gods. She really felt like grilled cheese now. The warmth of his eyes, the slow burn of his smile, and now the hot ribbons of his fingers, up the center of her ass and along her spine, turned her into compliant goo in his arms. The scenery sped by in reverse as she spread her hands along his broad shoulders, desperately fighting for any logic she had left. "I guess you want me to thank you now?"

The sarcasm drifted from Tait's lips. He slowly shook his head. "No, dreamgirl. This is the part where *I* thank *you.*"

Logic, say buh-bye. The rest of the world joined the exodus from her senses as he wound a hand against the back of her head and dragged her mouth against his.

Lani sighed, joyous from the instant explosion of him. There was no melodrama about the comparison. He breached her with brutal passion, filling her at once with his tongue, his taste, his heat. His growl detonated through her body, a perfect companion to the wild, tangled jungle that sped past the windows. She returned his eruption with a high-pitched moan, though she heard the sound as if someone else made it, another creature camped out in her body, made of pure, wanton desire.

"Damn." Kellan's snarl was as rough as Tait's, coaxing the savage need deeper through her blood. "You two look fucking hot."

"It's because of her," Tait said against her lips.

"Well, it's not because of you, brother."

Lani giggled. Though Tait responded with a smile, his gaze remained solemn. "It really is because of you." He followed the murmur by bracketing her cheeks with his hands, forming a tunnel between his face and hers. "Your courage, back there in the garden...*aiwaiwa*, dreamgirl. *Mahalo*, Hokulani."

Fingers of emotion clutched the bottom of her throat as he raised his lips to hers once more. The offering of her native words, followed by his tender worship of a kiss, was like telling the creature in her blood to roll over and accept a long, luxurious caress. She returned his kiss with speechless wonder, finally seeing the depth of what she'd done for him in opening up about an experience she'd pushed off as a weird mind trick so many months ago. His adoration moved her. Humbled her.

"Stop," she finally chastised in a whisper. "Tait, I don't need or deserve what you're—"

He vetoed her protest with another mouth-meshing kiss. This embrace was deeper than before. Hotter. Glutted with more intense sweeps of his tongue, with a new grip of his hand on her head. When they dragged apart, Tait used that hold to tug her head back, making her gasp from the illicit sting through her scalp. He groaned while redirecting his mouth to her throat, scraping her skin with his teeth before openly licking the burn away.

"I'll be making the calls on what you deserve," he charged, "and, for that matter, on what you need." He gently bit into the valley where her jaw met her neck. "And on the gratitude we're both going to show you, once we get back to the house."

Kellan's groan was an open sanction on that. "Damn straight," he added.

Lani shook her head, an action of new desperation. She pried her eyes open, hoping he saw the root of her protest. The she-beast in her bloodstream was hot, hungry, and impatient. It twisted urgent heat into the tips of her breasts, slunk fevered fire through her belly and thighs, and danced a demanding beat through every inch of her pussy, still riding the massive ridge between Tait's thighs.

He said he'd know what she needed. Well, she needed them both. Here. Now. Before she recalled her promise to last night's midnight rain. Before reality reminded her of why she'd made the oath to fate, that giving in to her lust for their bodies and her need for their touches would only worsen the pain of saying goodbye to them next week. In exponential chunks.

Regrets for another time.

"Please," she rasped, making her way toward the middle of his mouth. Tait's gaze had been full of questions, but when she sneaked her tongue between his lips, touching the tip of her tongue to his, his vacillation ended on another impassioned hiss.

When they emitted tandem moans, Kellan slowed the car. "What's wrong?" he demanded.

Tait tilted his head to meet his buddy's eyes in the rearview mirror. "Do you have condoms on you?"

Kell chuffed. "Does a Boy Scout know how to start a campfire?"

"Thank fuck."

"Why?"

"Pull over."

"*What?*"

"She's not going to last. And frankly, neither am I."

There was a long, torturous pause. "Lani?" Kellan finally called out.

Tait groaned. She joined him though and laughed a little at the end. "Stop the damn car, Sergeant Rush. I need my yin—*and* my yang."

His husky laugh filled the air. "Willingly obeyed, goddess—but enjoy your time on the throne now. Once I get back there, you're at *my* mercy."

"*That's* my best friend talking," Tait approved. Lani laughed, until he tucked his head and recaptured her lips in a fierce, plunging of a kiss. She surrendered with a long sigh, guessing her mouth would be wonderfully bruised tomorrow—and hoping many other body parts would be in the same basket.

The second Kellan slowed the jeep and turned it off the road, Tait unclicked the seat belt too. He flung the restraint aside with a snarl then reset his voracious gaze on her. With his locked teeth showing between his parted lips, he jammed her skirt to her waist, clawed both hands to her hips, then thrust her body atop his with the raw strength in his long fingers. It was primal and brutal and wonderful, matched by the jeep's rocking force as Kellan guided them beneath a copse of thick trees. Lani grabbed the back of the seat with one hand and his neck with the other, a move that jammed her cleavage directly in his face. He reacted with a long, pleasured growl.

"Damn," he uttered. "Opportunity knocks, dreamgirl."

He punctuated that by suckling the side of her right breast, sending a thousand shards of heat across her sensitive skin. That was only his opener. He used his nose to tunnel beneath her dress, inching his mouth over her bra until he teethed her nipple through the lace. Lani let him feel the all-over shiver he incited from the nasty little stab, throwing back her head in carnal bliss. Her eyes slid shut as both her areolas puckered, shoving her erect nipples against her clothes, bringing on a harder tremble. "H-How do you kn-know exactly how to d-do that?"

"Ssshhh." He issued it while sliding his mouth to her other breast, dropping enticing nips on her skin along the way, until he sucked in her waiting flesh with a groan of sensual hunger.

"*Kamaha`o!*" Gods, the man had a talented tongue. He circled her nipple over and over, abrading her skin with the lace he'd soaked, turning the treatment into an exquisite lesson in how to make a woman wet even before her panties came off. Both her breasts pulsed and throbbed. So did every inch of her sex. Trickles of arousal continued permeating her deepest tunnel, preparing her for the full pleasure promised by Tait's mouth and hands. Her need became a deafening refrain when Kellan cut the engine and set the brake.

In her periphery, she caught the lithe flash of his body as he rolled out of the driver's door and then opened the one behind it, his moves as smooth as a hero from an action movie. Then he was there, filling the opening, dark and glorious and huge—and practically burning away her dress with the power of his thunder-gray eyes. Without veering his gaze by an inch, he fired, "Why is she still dressed?"

Though Tait afforded his friend a little glance, his head barely budged from the valley between her breasts. "Did you want me to have all the fun, dude?"

"Looks like you already were."

"No way." Tait rolled his hands under, fully encompassing both swells of her ass in order to spread her thighs a little wider. "We're just starting things. Aren't we, dreamgirl?"

She had no idea how she managed her answering nod, especially when Kellan interrupted it to lift her face for his own conquering kiss. As he explored her mouth with his commanding tongue, Tait peeled back her dress and unhooked the front clasp of her bra, spilling her naked breasts toward his greedy mouth. *Finally.* She whined in gratitude as his lips explored her aching nipples once more, making her fists curl and her blood ignite. But Kellan's mouth evoked the opposite effect, melting her muscles, reminding her it was okay to be soft and surrendering. They really were her yin and yang. The two halves of her desire. The accelerants of all her body's fires...and the only saviors from those flames. They touched her like they'd been rehearsing for it, each knowing what need the other's actions would instigate in her and then shifting to fill that need with a perfect kiss or touch.

As if they'd both been prepared for her.

She let out a stunned gasp. When her eyes flashed open, too, Tait was there, consuming her vision with his burnished beauty. He lifted a hand to her face, delving his gaze into hers. A smile spread across his lips. She was certain he'd not only read her thoughts but also understood them.

"Baby." His voice was thick with meaning. "It's okay. Turn off the thoughts and simply open the feelings."

She ducked her face away. "But it's...too much. So much."

Kellan was there too. His lips pressed the top of her head. "What is it, Starshine? What's wrong?"

Tait drew in a long breath. "It's all coming together for her.

Angel's voices are one thing. The reality of destiny fulfilling them is another."

She swallowed. How could he be so damn calm about saying something like that? "I...I don't know how to..." *Feel about this. Or how to process it. Or what to do about it.* Angel's voices? Destiny? What happened to this being just a fun fling with a couple of hot soldiers, both of whom she'd sworn off for good not more than twelve hours ago? Now she clung to them like life rings in the storm they'd brought. And hated them for it. And needed them for it.

"I know it's big and overwhelming." Kellan skimmed his mouth along her neck. "Do you trust us to make it better? To burn it away for you?"

She let her head fall to the side, weighted by her thoughts but freed by his light kisses. "I want nothing more," she confessed in a rasp.

Kellan raised his lips to her forehead. "Us, too, sweetheart. Us, too."

She dragged her eyes open a little, gazing up at him and then at Tait. "Don't take turns," she pleaded. "I want... I *need*..." A surge of embarrassment stopped her. Not that she had any other life experiences to draw on for comparison, but common sense dictated that calling the shots on a threesome with two men the size of trucks was *not* in the approved manual.

"What?" Kellan filled in her hesitant pause, which came as a surprise. "Look at me and tell me what you need, Lani." He hooked a finger to her jaw and used it as a rudder to guide her face, now widened by astonishment, back toward him. "Look at me and tell me. And why don't you call me 'Sir' when you do so, as well?"

Well, that solidified a suspicion. *He'd* taken up mind

reading, too—and Lani couldn't wait to satisfy his mandate. Following Tait's orders last night, being the sole subject of his attention and the object of his domination, had made her feel desired, valuable, and special—feelings that had been missing from her world for a very long time. While Kellan had brought her to a shattering climax after the spanking, she'd wondered what things would've been like had he accessed "Sir Kellan" and joined him to Tait's command. What would it be like to have both these beautiful hulks to direct her, use her, dominate her?

The consideration made her quiver from head to toe, but she managed to fumble past the discomfort. "I need to have you both...Sir," she stammered. "I want both of you, filling me at once." She flicked a shy glance up at them. "When you both take me at once, I'm overwhelmed. Transported. It's..." One more attempt at a smile. No use. A blush overwhelmed her instead. "It's amazing. Please, can we maybe...do what we did last night?"

Tait was the first to respond. He raised his head to brush her lips with his. "Liked that, did you?"

"Yes, Sir. Very much." The formal address flowed naturally. If they were going to have a replay of the scene from Franzen's living room, then why not? The man's smile, made even more roguish by his off-kilter canine, gave her more hope of that possibility.

All too soon, his expression sobered again. "First things first, dreamgirl," he dictated. "Off with the dress." With the hand he still had at her hip, he twisted the waistband of her panties and gave a brutal tug. "That takes care of that." Satisfaction toughened his tone. "Slash-man, pop the seat back on your side. I've got this one."

Sure enough, as soon as she'd peeled off her dress, she found herself naked and prone atop Tait, who flashed devilish gold from his eyes and raw sin from his lips. The man's face tightened as Kell tugged her bra all the way off, officially making her their nude, vulnerable play toy. The comprehension was a little scary but a lot more arousing. The guys only heightened the impression with their mutual growls, both filled with sensual expectation.

Kellan continued the sound while sliding fully behind her. He swept his huge, forceful hands along her thighs, around her hips, over her spread buttocks. As he skimmed a finger across the sensitive cleft of her rear hole, she gasped in new awareness, only to have her breath stolen by Tait, who pulled her down for another wanton kiss. As their tongues tangled, she began to writhe. She needed more of his hard sex against her aching pussy. She also needed more of Kellan's powerful hands on her flesh.

She just needed...more. Of everything.

"God*damn*," Tait grated when their mouths finally parted. "If we could bottle your passion, dreamgirl, we'd put nuclear pirates out of business."

"Hell yeah," Kellan added. "She's perfect, isn't she? Fuck. I have a new favorite view."

Tait laughed a little. "And we've only just begun. My dick's still trapped. And *not* happy with me about it."

"You think I care about your schlong?" Kellan countered. "It's this girl's ass I can't stop staring at." He dug his fingers in deep to the flesh of her moons, inciting a pained but delighted hiss from Lani's lips.

"Oh!" she cried out. "Again! Please, Sir? *Ahhhh!*" Her voice became a scream when he added harsh scrapes of his fingernails to the treatment, ending with more attention to the fissure between her buttocks. As he slowly slid a thumb into the opening, she winced. He groaned.

"That's so good, Starshine. You're doing great. Push back against my fingers like we've been practicing, and you'll help me get in a little deeper." She focused on his instructions, rewarded with his longer grunt of approval, followed by a drizzle of soothing liquid into the tight opening. "You're so fucking perfect, sweetheart. Guess it was a good move to add a bottle of lube to the emergency kit, as well."

"Damn." Tait emitted it on half a laugh. "Did you think you'd sneak some quick anal training while waiting for burgers in the drive-through?"

Kellan chuffed. "With this goddess, it helps to be ready for any kind of adventure."

"Kiss-ass. Last time I checked, there was no Boy Scout badge called the domination do-gooder."

"Bite me."

"No, thank you."

Despite her shaky senses, Lani felt a smile breaking free. She loved being surrounded by the warm timbre of their bantering. The affection they had for each other was a tangible weave on the air, forming a unique, secondary safety net for her trust. No matter what happened, the two of them were going to take care of her. They'd already logged years of experience doing it for each other.

Kellan punched out a rough grunt. "I'm going crazy here, T. You can't imagine how beautiful this woman's ass is."

Tait hissed, matching it to hers, as he thumbed both her nipples. "If it's half as good as her sweet strawberry tits, I'll bet I can."

"I don't know if I can resist taking the plunge, dude."

"Roger that, brother. And copying big-time."

Lani whimpered. She connected the euphemisms instantly because of the physical positions they were in. The second her mind made the link, so did her body. Her pussy tickled with its new infusion of moisture. Her pulse jumped to hyperdrive from the utterly carnal scene they suggested. *Aue*. Could they be serious?

Tait, observing the connection on her face, pulled her down for a reassuring kiss. "You know what we're talking about, don't you, dreamgirl?" When she managed a nod, he prompted, "Then tell me. I want to see the words on your lips, to know that you fully understand."

She hesitated. It wasn't that she didn't trust them or denied wanting the wicked experience...but saying it aloud? It represented a bridge her mind faltered to cross. A signal that she was ready to fully, willingly transfer her body into their control. "I...I don't know if I'm comfortable with that."

"Then are you calling a red light?" He ran gentle fingers over her shoulder. "It's all right if you do. We won't adore you any less."

"No. This is just new for me. And a little scary. I'm sorry."

"Sorry?" A scowl pleated the man's gorgeous features. "Why? Because you've been handling everything in your life and Leo's for so damn long that you've forgotten how to let someone else do it for a little while? Because *surrender* is a word that's always meant defeat and *soft* is a word that's always meant weak?" When she dropped her head, afraid to let him see how solidly he'd nailed her emotional target, he wrapped a hand to the side of her head and pulled her back up. "We've expected that, babe. And we celebrate it."

ANGEL PAYNE

She blinked at him. "You do?"

Kellan joined his friend in a chuckle before spreading his fingers across both sides of her ass again. "We're going to enhance your light, Starshine, not extinguish it." His hold intensified.

"Mmmm." It left her on a higher note than before. With every word, every touch, and every action, these incredible men pulled her closer to the clouds, physically and emotionally. While many called her stupid for standing up to Gunter, they deemed her brave. When most would label her a lunatic for listening to phantom voices in a garden, they were visibly moved. Now they wanted to give her more, a fantasy she'd only dreamed of. Best of all, it was the best gift she could give them in return.

"I'm not a rocket scientist, Kell, but I think that means she'd be okay with a little *skin conditioning*." Tait twisted his head to meet her gaze. She returned his grin, knowing what he saw in her eyes: open longing, lust, anticipation. Her heart indulged a girlish flip. How had she gotten so lucky to have *two* amazing guys wanting to satisfy her like this? And why had she been so hesitant to cross the bridge and surrender to them?

As her senses ran over the last of that bridge, she pushed her hips back into Kellan's grip and moaned again. "Yes, Sir," she pleaded. "Yes, that *is* what it means."

Kellan emitted an appreciative snarl. "Beautiful words, sweetheart. And this Sir loves every one of them. Now put them into action."

"Sir?" She gave him a questioning glance.

"I want to see more of your ass, Hokulani. Raise it up so I can spank it well."

Tait growled in endorsement. "Perfect idea, my friend."

He tugged at the backs of her knees. "Bring these forward a little, babe. Now angle your backside up. If I wasn't lying here, you'd have your forehead against the floor and your hands stretched over your head. Some Doms call this *presenting your ass* or *kissing the floor*. I like to call it an invitation to heaven."

She smirked a little as he pulled her arms over his head, mashing her chest to his and bringing their faces within inches of each other. "Heaven?" she quipped. "Yours or mine?"

Tait grinned and nipped at her lips. "Both, dreamgirl. Both."

He'd barely finished before Kellan landed his first smack to her raised bottom.

"Oh!" she yelped. "*Kahaha!*"

"Damn." Kellan's murmur was unnervingly soft. The touch he used to spread the burn was even more so.

Closer in, Tait raised his fingers to her face. "Everything okay?"

"Yeah," she whispered, drawing in a breath. "He's just"—she shrieked as Kellan's hand came down again—"*really* enjoying this."

"Oh yeah." Kellan swept his fingers to distribute the pain again. "He really is."

Smack.

The blow was even harder than the first two. Lani twisted her lips while flipping through her mental insults file. There had to be something good and filthy she'd heard from Franz at some point, a zinger this soldier wouldn't forget. It wouldn't be like throwing the safe word at them, just a clever nudge to make him back off on the impact a little...no matter how good her ass started to feel, suffused with heat that blended to the most tender tissues of her body...

Smack.

"Owwww!" She reared up. Well, attempted to. She bolted a nonplussed stare at Tait, who'd spread his arms as if lazing at the beach while keeping her wrists captive beneath his hands. His lips even curled in a laid-back surfer's grin. "Are you actually smirking at me?" she seethed.

"Everything okay there, T?"

"Couldn't be better. You may proceed. Throw some muscle into it, would you?"

"No!" Lani yelled. "N—"

Smack. Smack.

When she screamed this time, she let Tait have the full impact of the sound. His eyes lit up with the victory of gold medals. *Maha`oi.* The nervy bastard *wanted* her like this, squirming and seething, unable to think about anything except the fire whipping across her ass, the heat bubbling through her veins—

And the warmth suffusing her sex.

Okay, there *was* that.

Smack. Smack.

"Owwww! Damn it!" She slammed her eyes shut. "*Damn it!*"

Tait's breath washed over her lips. "Hokulani. Baby. Look at me."

"No!"

"Do you trust us?"

She grimaced. "Aggghh. *Yes.*"

"Then look at me." His face awaited her stare, stronger and more tender than she'd ever seen. "Then give it all over...to us." The afternoon sun filtered into the car, igniting the glints in his eyes, playing over the crinkles at his eyes and lips. "It's time to let the pain transform, dreamgirl. To let it heat you, soften you...so we can fill you."

Her breaths twined with his as he finally released her wrists. As he glided his knuckles back up her arms, she sighed from their wakes of luscious warmth. He widened his fingers as he continued around the curves of her shoulders and into the lengths of her hair, where he spread the strands with adoring strokes. Through every moment, she was exquisitely aware of every touch, breath, and caress. Every move he made was wrapped in a magical gauze of altered reality, soft yet tingling, alight yet shadowed. Her muscles liquesced. Her resistance waned. And the heat that began in her ass flowed everywhere in her body, making her a flame ready to be lighted by these two incredible males.

"Yes," she heard herself whisper. "Gods, yes. Please..."

Tait glided his lips along the bottom of her jaw. "Please what, Lani? Say the words for us now. Your Sirs need to hear the plea from your own lips."

She nodded, understanding him now, even in her heated haze. They'd be taking over her body in one of the most illicit acts of consummation, and they needed to hear that she wanted them in that sinful way.

"Please...fill me," she finally answered. "I want this. I want both of you. At once."

His eyes narrowed at the corners. "You've already had both of us, babe. How is this going to be different?"

He was really going to make her spell it out, wasn't he?

Sometimes, a girl just needed a volcano instead of magma. Kellan came through as that vital explosion, landing two sharp swats to her ass before demanding in an irrefutable growl, "Out with it, Starshine. No more shame, doubts, hiding, or fears."

The sizzle of his descending zipper ripped through the air. In seconds, she felt his throbbing penis against her hot backside. "Tell me where you want my cock. *Now*."

"Y-Yes, Sir!"

He laid another slap across her buttocks. "That wasn't an answer, sweetheart."

Lani swallowed. He'd left her no other option but the obvious. The core of her desire. The naughtiest of all her fantasies. "In...in my ass. Please, Kellan...Sir...I want you to slide your cock into my ass."

As the words tumbled out, so did a slew of her inhibitions. Locks fell free in her mind, accelerated by Kellan's approving growl and then Tait's praising kiss.

"Damn, that sounded nice," Tait murmured. He shifted a little underneath her, and she felt him opening his fly, as well. His face was captivating to watch, its open relief from the freedom followed by the fast clench of his jaw, holding himself back from the simple thrust he needed to be buried inside her. As it was, his cock's steely crown pushed against the heated folds at her core. At the same moment, Kellan dripped more lube into her back hole and used a finger to work it in. She gasped and shuddered from both illicit contacts.

"Now tell me where you want mine to go, dreamgirl. Say it sweetly, like you did with Slash."

With his sexy lips so close, a smile naturally bloomed on hers. "In my pussy. Please, Sir...will you give it to me deep?"

He answered her with a look that conveyed a multitude of things, most of them making her wonder if she'd just accidentally read him some sappy sonnet instead of asking him to join his best friend in taking her to the stars via Starship Kinky. In a thick murmur, he replied, "Thank you, babe. For everything you are and all you're entrusting us with. Thank you."

Kellan's grunt formed the ending dot on that sentence. "Mark me down as a ditto on everything he just said—but I swear, you'll be hearing it from a dying man if I don't fuck this beautiful ass soon."

He spread her cheeks, bringing cool air into the deepest valley of her backside before working more lube into her hole with a slick twist of two fingers. Then three. Lani gasped but immediately wondered why. The pain wasn't new. Kellan had been fascinated with her back hole for days and made no secret about wanting to sample it with his cock. But now, the burn carried erotic new meaning and a world of fresh arousal. This wasn't just training. In a few minutes, her body would accept his in a way that had only been a forbidden dream before now.

"On the same page, scoutmaster." Tait glanced up at his buddy. "Toss me a Trojan, and we can start worshipping this goddess the right way."

Unbelievably, Lani felt a blush heat her face. She might as well be a wanton sex slave positioned between two lusty gladiators, yet Tait talked like she'd become Aphrodite and they were *her* willing servants. She'd never felt more decadent, desired, or wholly on fire in her life. Her blood zinged with electricity. Her vagina vibrated with need. But most perfectly, her spirit soared with freedom...and her heart fell open with gratitude.

Again with timing that seemed practiced, the guys rolled on their condoms together. Lani joined her anticipating breath to theirs.

"Relax, sweetheart." Kellan's voice was rough but reassuring. "We're almost there. What a sweet rose you're giving me to fuck..."

"No different than these wet petals." Tait worked his penis between her tender tissues, stimulating all the best parts of her pussy before sliding his cock deep inside her. Lani cried out in joy and arousal. Gods, he felt good, his hard flesh cushioned by the wet tissues of her intimate passage, flaring heat through every inch of her sex. "Damn." He gave brutal, beautiful voice to their need, his head arching back from the force of it. "Damn, I had no idea."

Lani frowned. "About what?"

"About how sweet your cunt can grip a man's cock, baby."

"Things are about to get better, brother." Kellan intensified his assault on her ass. He prodded at her walls with all three fingers, expanding her wider. "*Much* better." The wolfish confidence in his tone was a gut-flipper of a turn-on. Still, Lani tensed when he withdrew his fingers from her entrance. Not more than a second later, he pressed the well-lubed knob of his erection there instead. As her membranes screamed, her mouth whimpered. "*Relax*, Starshine. The head's the hardest part."

"N-Now you tell me," she grumbled.

"Concentrate on me for now." Tait leveled his face in order to brush her lips with his. He increased the pressure as Kellan worked his dick into the first inch of her anus. Lani screamed into his mouth as Kellan began penetrating her with eye-popping pressure. "Breathe, baby. Push out then take a little more. *Breathe.* An inch at a time. You can do this."

"No," she whispered. "I can't."

"You already are," Kellan grated. "And fuck, is it good. Lani—goddess—my dick's never felt anything like this."

"Second that intel." Tait tunneled one hand into her hair

as he slid the other between their bodies, curling a couple of fingers along her clit. "You're so hot for us, dreamgirl. So hot and wet and ready to take both our cocks."

She let out a deep sigh, confirming every one of his words as true. Her sensitive nub responded to his fingers, trembling with the force of her need. Having them both inside her was a fulfillment beyond imagining, awakening her sex to a call of erotic fulfillment. Her breath spiraled and grew into a long, primal moan.

"Yessss." Kellan grabbed both her ass cheeks, squeezing them to bring back the burn of his spanking. "Almost there, sweetheart. You've got me so deep now. You're squeezing me so tight."

Tait growled as his dick expanded inside her. "Do you feel me too? Do you feel my dick sliding on that special spot in your pussy? Open your senses and feel it, Lani. Beautiful goddess... you deserve it. You deserve all of this, after everything you gave me today." He pulled his fingers back a little, which should have been a torment for her but wasn't. Without the stimulation on her clit, Lani focused on what he'd said. *Aue*, there *was* a different kind of feeling inside her now. Kellan's cock throbbed through her membranes, adding to the fullness of Tait's, bringing a sexual fire she'd never experienced before.

"Gods," she rasped. "What the hell is happening?"

"Clamp down." Tait's instruction was a rod of sensual steel. "Clench it all in, babe. Hold our cocks as hard as you can. Feel our dicks pulsing for you, every inch of them hard and thrusting. We both want only one thing: to feel you coming apart for us."

Kellan pushed once more to seat his cock completely in her ass. His long groan erased away her last bits of pain.

He pressed himself over her, suckling her nape as Tait again took her mouth. "You're so perfect, Starshine. So amazing. So brave."

Tait pulled back enough for her to see the golden iridescence in his gaze, focused solely on her. "You've given us so much today, baby. Let us give you this."

Kellan added to the wonderful burn in her ass by rolling his hips. "Come for us, beautiful girl," Kellan commanded. "We need to feel your orgasm around our cocks."

Denying them would have been telling her heart not to beat anymore. It halted anyway, succumbing to the burst of fire that started deep inside her sex and then exploded through her clit and pussy. She was a ball of silver-white flames, a sun captured, a comet turned into the willing plaything of these two demigods. She screamed, throwing her head back into Kellan's brutal kiss, her mouth consumed by his bellow as he rammed her even deeper and heated her back passage with his climax. A moment later, Tait groaned as he emptied his cock too.

In the immediate aftermath, she began to shake. Her muscles turned to rubber. Her mind suddenly felt like a schizophrenic pinball machine. Tait and Kellan, still both inside her, felt the strange change and hung on tighter—but their murmured reassurances only made the ordeal worse. Her soul needed to find the exit door again. She couldn't remain out in the emotional open like this. It was nice to take a little visit to vulnerability, but now it was time to make a dive for the bunker of reality again, and—

Too late.

A significant wind blew past the car.

And with it, a whisper of sound...in her mind.

Tears spilled. She shook her head.

It's okay, girlfriend. Please don't fight me. I'm only here to help. I just wanted to know if you'd convey a little message for me...

"Lani? Lani!"

"You think we should take her to a hospital, T?"

She peered up at the two of them from where she lay in the jeep's bed, flat on her back. She had no idea how much time had passed, though a guess said not much. She was still naked. Hell, the guys hadn't even zipped up, though their used condoms had been stowed—well, somewhere.

A strange giggle left her.

When the guys peered down in confusion, she laughed even harder.

What a difference eight days could make. Now *she* was the one in the prone position, feeling like she'd been sucking down half a bottle of vodka. Her mirth clearly didn't help their befuddlement.

"Dreamgirl?" Tait leaned forward. "You okay? You phased out on us."

Kellan snorted. "What he means to say is, you scared the living shit out of us."

"Yeah. That too."

"Can you sit up?"

They coordinated efforts to pull her upright. Once done, they both pulled off their shirts. Kell pushed the neck hole of his over her head. Tait tucked his into her lap. She took in both their rippled torsos and bit her lower lip. "Maybe I should phase out a lot more."

They both rolled their eyes. "Drink this." Kellan pushed a bottle of electrolyte drink into her grip. The Boy Scout struck again. She wanted to giggle again, but they kept staring like she'd turn into a ghost any second—which wasn't such a farfetched notion, considering what she was about to say.

"I'm fine, okay?" She set down the drink and brushed her knuckles across the stubbled edges of both their jaws. "I'm better than fine, actually."

Their eyebrows jumped in tandem. Tait found his voice again first. "Okaaay. Care to expound on that any further?"

She pushed her arms through the arm holes of Kellan's shirt, carefully folded her hands in her lap, and leaned against the jeep's back door, hoping it lent a little stability. Though she was grinning like an idiot again, filled with joy about getting to play messenger girl this time, the circumstances were still a little unconventional.

Maybe *a lot* unconventional.

"I need to relay some information," she finally stated.

Their mutual scowls didn't surprise her.

"What...kind of information?" Kellan queried. When she took a second to close her eyes, he lurched forward to grab her. "Sweetheart! Stay with us!"

"I'm right here, you big dodo." She chuckled. "It's your own damn fault. Concentrating is a little hard, given the scenery." While reopening her eyes, she murmured, "I think she agrees with me."

Tait cocked his head. "She who?"

A grin spread across her lips. "The one who says that you need to move on, Weasley. If not, she'll find some cosmically terrible way to kick your ass."

The man straightened his head. And his shoulders. And took in the scope of her words with a heavy nod—until the weight of their meaning crushed him, dragging down his head and hunching his shoulders.

Kellan was the first to grab one of those shoulders as Tait succumbed to the force of a release six months in the making. There was an unmistakable sheen in Kellan's deep gray eyes, so easy for Lani to recognize because the tears in her eyes matched. The three of them held each other, rocking a little, swallowing a lot, washing away pain in tears that were unfettered, unapologetic, unashamed.

How was she going to say goodbye to them?

It suddenly became the hardest *and* the easiest question in the world.

Undoubtedly, she'd never opened herself up to any man, let alone two at the same time, as she had with them. Nor was she likely to ever again. But in the gift of this moment, she also saw fate's sublime hand in bringing them to her life, here and now. They'd taught her how to feel again. To trust again. To once more believe that the impossible could be very real.

When Tait lifted his tear-salted lips and kissed her, she felt a thousand feet tall. When Kellan leaned over and added his passionate embrace, that figure was doubled. Though things were still a mess back at Hale Anelas, she was bolstered now about her ability to handle it. She'd take on a hundred Gunter Bensons if she had to—and win.

The resolve filled her with a burst of brilliant joy, matched only by the two walls of hard, heated soldier flesh pressing around her once more. As Kellan and Tait cajoled her into just a few more minutes of enjoying their jungle lust cocoon, she didn't forget to close her eyes and reach inward, tiptoeing into that special place in her soul once more, to let her heart whisper two words to the presence who waited for her there, somehow filling her mind with an image of high-heeled boots, lavender fingernails, and a divine Catwoman smile.

Thank you.

CHAPTER EIGHTEEN

Kellan trailed a couple of fingers down the side of his water bottle, watching as the last rays of the sunset filtered through Hale Anelas's orchard and rose garden, turning the condensation into liquid gold. His motions were as relaxed and lazy as the breeze sifting through the hibiscus blooms along the rails of the back lanai.

They were also a lie.

What a difference twenty-four hours could make.

When he and Tait returned from the monastery with Lani yesterday, he'd changed into a T-shirt he'd never worn before: a gag gift T had given him during the team's vacation to Los Angeles, before the trip wasn't a vacation anymore. There was a stick figure on the front of the thing, wearing a dork-ass smile and accompanied by the line Life is Good. He'd thrown a shit ton of sarcasm at the guy, telling him the shirt would be worn when the saying really held true. With that in mind, he'd expected to be using the thing as a car rag in a few years. Yet last night, he'd ripped off the tags and proudly pulled the fucker on.

The lip he'd expected from Tait about it? Nonexistent. The guy, clearly flying on their mutual high of camaraderie and connection, actually grinned and gave him a fist bump. They usually saved shit like that for special occasions like the opening night of a Vin Diesel film or drilling a kill shot through a terrorist's skull.

They'd made up an excuse about running to grab some dinner so they could sneak in their update call to Franzen. Trouble was, their CO had no news, except that Colton had passed their information to the proper CIA division and careful follow-up on their intel was in play.

The news had been a weird relief. In many ways, Kell desperately wanted his revelation to hit a dead-end so they could continue dealing with Benson as nothing more than the pretty boy lowlife developer they'd originally assumed. Buy-offs to the local permits officials were toddler games compared to what shit Benson could be in with heavy hitters from Pyongyang and Tehran.

Their good fortune continued when they returned to the house with their Chinese takeout feast, though it hadn't seemed that way at first. Lani was waiting for them in the living room, trays set up for the food and last night's episode of *Scandal* cued on the DVR. She made the torture worse by having changed clothes herself, flopping on the couch between them in a cute little tank top over shorts that hugged her ass and not much else. *Great.* It had been an hour of lukewarm chow mein, Olivia Pope melodrama, and a hard-on of unrelenting fury—a torment that he at least didn't have to endure alone, if he read Tait's pained glances correctly.

Unbelievably, the guy stood up as the show ended to make the noble though half-assed move to leave for Franz's place again. The moment had *awkward* spray-painted all over it, especially in light of everything that had happened during the afternoon. But before Kell could give him a proper what-the-fuck smack, Lani stood as well, converting to full minx mode. With a kitten's grin over her shoulder, the woman told T he could do what he wanted, but *she* was taking advantage of

Leo's late practice to take a long shower—and damn, it would be nice to have some help washing her back.

A half hour later, balls deep in the woman's pussy while she "soaped" his buddy's cock with a hand job from heaven, Kell knew it'd be a shower he'd never forget.

After they'd all toweled off, he'd let Tait collapse into bed with Lani, sensing they needed the extra time with each other. He supposed the decision should have been weird, but it wasn't. It had simply felt right.

Perhaps the knowledge that this "arrangement" was temporary, along with the healing she'd brought to T with the afternoon's revelations, had lent him the bold thought—but his gut started nagging at him with a different impression of things. A number of them, actually. He'd stuffed the thoughts right back down into their origin point, the valley in a soldier's soul that wasn't meant for the light of scrutiny. The place called vulnerability.

He'd kept his mind well out of the valley for the rest of the night, even saving Lani from Leo's scrutiny by falling asleep in front of the TV, before Tait shook him awake just before dawn so they could call Franzen again. Once again, their CO relayed that there was no news from the spooks. Kell's solace had gotten another hall pass.

Three hours ago, fate called in that chip.

They'd known it as soon as Franz came on the line, during the call that took place during their "afternoon jog" on the beach. The man's voice was tight, without a single line worthy of a movie marketing slogan. Instead, he went straight to confirming the two of them were alone and could speak freely. *Not* a good sign.

Kellan had unearthed a bigger information landmine

than anyone had dreamed. Intelligence agents in Iran and North Korea had confirmed mysterious "travel plans" for high-ranking generals in their countries, cross-referenced with flight plans from private jets that had landed at Lihue three days ago, having somehow skirted the customs process in Honolulu.

While the FBI had been tasked with discovering who had been paid off and where, the task for the CIA—and now, their two-man Spec Ops team—was far more immediate. After a day and a half of hard searching, the spooks had found their two needles in the five hundred and fifty-two square mile haystack of the island. Surprise, surprise; both generals were shacking up at the same off-the-map luxury retreat, making cell phone calls to the exact same number. There was no information available for the burner phone, which had been purchased with cash by a local kid who'd been paid off for the transaction, but they'd at least secured a GPS lock on the device.

Whoever the generals were talking to was sitting on the beach a quarter mile south of Hale Anelas.

Franzen had stirred the shit pot even thicker by informing them about the conversations overheard by the spooks. Both agents confirmed that a meeting was happening tonight in something called "the cave." All he and Tait had to do now was find that bad guy, approach him undetected, and then learn where this "cave" was located. And by the way, they didn't know what he looked like. And oh yeah, the spooks needed the information as soon as possible. And another thing: if their cover was blown, the army's official line would be that they were AWOL soldiers, acting without the government's knowledge or permission.

"Piece of fucking cake," Kell grumbled.

Lani's laugh, spilling out of the kitchen door like a string of bells, turned his mental disconnect into total hell. Tait was still inside with her, issuing reassurances that he and Kell would be fine while she accompanied Leo to college recruitment night at school. T always was better than he at feigning charming and jovial, though the second they hit the path toward the beach, he was back to being the epitome of don't-fuck-with-me steel. "You have your knife?" he queried in a terse mutter.

"Affirmative," Kell answered. The feel of the Bowie he'd "borrowed" from Lani, strapped to his calf, was added security he hoped *not* to use.

"Let's do this shit," T snarled. "If these assholes are behind *any* of Benson's monkey-fuckeries, I guarantee I'm gonna knock some douchebag heads."

Kell didn't know whether to celebrate or hassle that statement. The good news was T-Bomb was back in his full, furious, focused soldier glory. That was also the bad news.

They hit the beach but kept as close to the trees as they could. Kell rolled a silent prayer toward the emerging stars that Tait had opted for an easy silence instead of attempting one of his mind-whack heart-to-hearts. A little therapy, especially right after Luna died, had been a good thing for the guy. A lot of therapy had turned him into a psychobabble freak show.

"Kell...this is probably a good time to clear the air."

He flashed a glare at the sky. *This is what I get for the shout-out of gratitude?*

"Slash-tastic? You listening?"

"Actually, I'm trying not to."

"Fuck." Tait halted his pace for a telling moment. "I guess some things don't change."

Kellan stopped too. "What the hell's that supposed to

mean?"

Tait cocked his head. "I thought you cared about this woman. A lot."

A flare of ire hit his chest. "You usually come up with better bait than that."

"And you're usually better at avoiding the hook." He straightened his head. "Which means I'm right."

Just like that, the anger vanished. In its place, a strange curiosity spread. He took a turn at the Dr. Freud head tilt. "Nail on the head, buddy. You absolutely are right. Is that what you're after? Can we move on now?"

The answer to both questions was no, and he knew it. There was a good chance Tait did too. Kell just hoped his switch-up to honesty would satisfy the guy for a while.

Yeah. And a rainbow would burst out of the night sky and onto the beach, bringing jolly leprechauns that would form a magical ring of protection around Hale Anelas.

"So you'd really be happy with that?" Tait charged. "Just 'moving on' from here, like any other recon gig we've been on, like any other day we've been through?"

Kellan exhaled with deliberate slowness. Then counted to ten for patience. Then sucked the breath back in, again with steady purpose. "And how would *you* have us proceed, oh head shrinker on high?"

His dig didn't faze Tait. "We should start at the obvious."

"Such as?"

"Such as how you're feeling about the direction of things with Lani."

And there it was. The only F-word he always wished they'd drop from existence—at least before today. Right now, it only made him lift a grin at his friend. He'd always scoffed at Tait for putting things so balls-out in the emotional communication department, though it made perfect psychological sense when realizing the guy never received a sentence of meaningful communication from the bastard who'd sired him. But today, Kell was damn glad for the candidness. Let the scrotum revelations commence. "Maybe the better question here is how *you're* feeling, dude."

T's brow furrowed. "What the hell are you talking about?"

He pivoted to square his stance at the guy. "You want feelings, T? You want clarity?" Odd satisfaction came at watching his partner's gaze narrow with more astonishment before he continued. "Here's what I'm *clear* about, man. I'm clear that the guy standing in front of me isn't the same shell of humanity who got off the plane with me nine days ago, making me wonder if I'd ever see my best friend again. I'm clear about the fact that my buddy is back, full of the blaze and balls that've made him one of my biggest heroes, growling about turning bad guys into fertilizer again. And I'm *very* clear that Hokulani Kail was a big part of the force that made it happen. So what am I 'feeling' about all this?" He rocked back on his heels. "*You* want to take a stab at doing the math on that answer?"

They played visual chicken for a long second. "You're talking like all she's done is made me some cake and let me kick back in front of the TV with you two."

He was tempted to flip the cake comment into another snarkism, but this was too important for humor. After abandoning his cavalier pose, he stepped over and stabbed a finger into the middle of his buddy's chest. "I'm only going to say this once, so listen up, asswipe. The birth certificates may say I only have one sibling, and you know better than anyone how much I love Kadie, but God chose to give me one hell of an awesome bonus bucket. Bommer, you are my brother in every sense of the word, including the blood we've mixed in some of the world's craziest shitholes. So don't you dare insinuate that I don't know what I'm talking about here. Don't you *dare* tell me that I'm just discussing cake and TV night when you know that's not how I roll."

Tait let out a ragged exhalation. "I'm not trying to second-guess you, Kell. And I certainly haven't forgotten every wild ride we've ever had together. But let's face it, we've redefined the term *wild ride* this week."

"And you think I haven't thought about that? That I didn't consider it with a shitload of care the other night? That I just told her to kiss you another time because it turned my rocks hard, and that it 'happened' as some brilliant accident?"

"I don't know *what* to think, dude. It's why I'm asking."

He lifted his jaw and set it. "I told her to do that because I knew she wanted it—because I knew she wanted *you*—and because, God help me, I want to give that woman *everything* she wants. But it goes beyond that." He lifted his head higher. "She also needs Sir Tait. Don't get me wrong; it's been fucking awesome to let Sir Kellan out of his stuffy nut sack. But the way you control her...it's pretty damn amazing." He relaxed his stance, breaking into a smile. "Let's face it. She's an extraordinary woman, T. Her heart is as big as that ocean, and her soul is just as deep. To be honest, I'm not sure one man will ever be enough for her."

Tait turned his gaze toward the waves that Kellan just evoked. His face constricted in thought. "Damn. I didn't think about it that way."

"But there's a good chance I'm right."

"Yeah, you bastard. There's a good chance you're right."

"That's not even where my awesomeness of *right* stops."

As the guy looked back, he rolled his eyes. "Why doesn't *that* surprise me?"

"She also meets needs in *you,* dickwad. And it goes far beyond the miracle of her confession at the monastery." He flashed half a smile. "She's brought that fire back to your face. Ignited you in ways that I'd given up on witnessing again. You're laughing again. Driving like a maniac again. Damn it, you're even hogging all the fortune cookies in the takeout bag again. You may have a few extra pieces of luggage on board your brain train, but *you* are back—and for that, I'm not sure I can give the woman enough orgasms to express my gratitude."

"But maybe I can help you try."

Kell met his friend's uplifted fist with a countering bump. "Hell yeah, you can."

That was normally the spot where fate tried to cue up an imaginary soundtrack of sappy bromance music, extinguished by Tait regaling him with the newest Seahawks news. The team's championship had given the guy permission to convert from fanboy into freakboy, and there was always some new trivia Tait was gleaning about the team. Fate, in its mercy *and* cruelty, had other plans. They blended back into some fern and Ti plants together as a man approached from a bend in the beach, running a hand through his designer haircut as he spoke rapid Korean into a cell phone.

Kell tossed an expectant glance at Tait. His buddy had always been the better of them with foreign languages. His jaw tensed when T shook his head and grimaced. "Weird dialect," he whispered. "I'm only getting every third or fourth word. I think he's referencing a meeting and saying that a 'final bid' will be requested tonight. Either that or he's ordering kimchi for takeout."

The guy took a turn inland, down a narrow path cutting through some sizable boulders. Kellan stifled a groan upon realizing they'd have to hump over the rocks to keep following him unnoticed. Luckily, their target stopped for a long second, his voice rising in the middle of an argument, giving them time to find footholds on the boulders. Things weren't easier once they reached their goal, since haircut boy was on the move again. They had to step more carefully than he did. Boulders on the island were notoriously unpredictable due to the eroding effects of the weather, so they hustled as cautiously as possible.

"Where the fuck is he going?" Kellan finally muttered.

"Not sure." Tait's answer was grim. "But I'll bet he's not on his way to a friendly fuck in the woods, which means my hackles are up."

Kellan grunted his agreement. He didn't need to say more. T's statement addressed what they'd both noticed. The man was on a direct trajectory back toward Hale Anelas. *Shit.*

Abruptly, the boulder walls flared out as the ground dipped down by at least ten feet. They now overlooked a sizable, sunken clearing carpeted in beach sand and surrounded by the looming boulder walls. It was like the island's own version of Bruce Wayne's manor—

Complete with a bat cave at one end.

"Ker-ching," Tait murmured.

Kell nodded.

Haircut hunk made his way to a double-sided steel door that was clearly a recent addition to the scene. The portal had been custom-cut to fit the large opening in the rocks. As the guy ended his phone conversation with a couple of terse words and stuffed the thing into the back pocket of his jeans, Kell joined T in dropping belly-down against the nearest boulder. They watched him walk to a smaller rock near the door and stomp on the thing, revealing it as a trigger for the door. The portal retracted on itself, accordion style, to let the man inside the entrance.

"Fuck me," Tait murmured.

"All they're missing is the signal in the sky," Kell added.

"Something tells me they want to stay off Gotham's grid. And everyone else's."

Kell swept another stare through the surrounding boulders and foliage. "I don't see any suspicious red camera lights," he stated. "But that doesn't mean they're not here."

"Do we still follow him?"

Kellan could've punched the guy for putting that question on him. "Well, I know what Franz would advise."

Tait twisted his lips. "He'd want us to pull back and wait for the CIA to do their magic spy thing. Probably loop the feds in on it too."

"Which could take weeks."

"At least."

"Even though there's a meeting going down tonight."

"*Especially* because there's a meeting going down tonight."

Tait snorted hard before letting a significant pause go by. "How close do you think we are to the ranch now?"

"Maybe three hundred yards."

"In other words—"

"Too damn close."

Tait cocked his head so their stares met. They didn't exchange thousands of words with the look this time—because they didn't need it. They already shared the same conclusion about their action plan. The next second, Tait acted on it. With a soundless roll, he slid off the boulder, leading the way down to the cave's entrance.

It was simple to locate the same rock their predecessor had used for the entrance. Kell hoped whoever awaited the guy inside didn't have the thing rigged to any additional sensors. If they did, then he and Tait would have a very short visit here, Bowies or not.

The door opened with nothing more than a whisper of sound, forcing him to give Benson and his penchant for the high-end at least one approving check mark. Once inside, they found themselves in a passageway illuminated by top-of-the-line camp lanterns, though a maze of wires ran along the walls in indication there'd be an upgrade to electrical fixtures soon. That was the place's only nod to the modern world so far. Giant tufts of moss still hung from the ceilings, and the air was damp and musty. Kell would've given a kingdom for his mission vest right now, outfitted with all the tools they'd need to collect more evidence. In its place, he locked his mind into experiential memory mode, all five senses engaged to commit as much of this place to his mental recall as possible.

Tait held up a fist, ordering a full stop to their progress. The reason was clear. Voices penetrated the air from up ahead, where the lighting also amplified. Kell thanked fate upon finding an alcove big enough to squeeze into, with Tait snagging a matching nook a few feet ahead. They took up their vantage points and went into complete stealth mode: breathing shallow, ears open, senses alert.

"Mr. Tan. What a pleasure to meet you in person."

Before Kellan could get a view of the speaker, the shaving cream commercial voice gave him away. Benson, in all his I'm-better-than-you-because-of-the-suit glory.

"Forgive me for not dwelling on pleasantries, Gunter." The man who stood opposite Benson now, looking on as haircut boy melted back into the shadows, eschewed a full suit in favor of a crisp white button-front shirt and custom-tailored pants. He also had a better haircut than Benson, spoke in a London-educated accent, wore one of the nicest watches Kell had ever seen, and called Benson by his first name. He was definitely a heavy hitter for the Koreans—whatever the hell it was they were hitting at. "As you can well imagine, the general's time is valuable, so I am here on his behalf to act as final emissary for our country. He seems to think your setup here is impressive; I am here to support or deny that theory. We know how emotional generals can be."

The last sentence bugged out Kellan's eyes. *Generals* could be emotional?

"Of course," Benson responded, again smooth as Gillette foam. "We have, as you know, enjoyed enthusiastic patronage from the general over the years. He has...interesting tastes in his leisure pursuits."

"I'm not here to discuss where the man prefers to put his dick." Tan straightened and crossed his hands, again every inch the London gentleman. "I'm here to discuss where he can store his arsenal."

Kellan ground his knuckles into the stone wall, focusing on the pain in place of cutting loose a roar of outrage. This was worse shit than he'd ever suspected from Benson, even after his revelatory phone call to Forte.

"What would you like to review first?" Gunter asked Tan.

"You know the answer to that," the Korean returned. "My sources state that you have already met with the delegation from Tehran. How much have they offered?"

"Seventy million."

The man recrossed his hands. "Which means they've only offered sixty."

Kell took a chance on angling his head out far enough for a clear view at Benson, who stood deeper back in the cave. The guy was in his Armani finest, choosing a dark gray suit despite the humidity of the night, keeping his red tie knotted. His face was a mask of smooth impassivity, allowing it to crack in just the slightest smirk at Tan. "Why don't we return to that piece of the conversation after you've viewed all the details?" He stepped back and flipped a switch, turning on another sizable light over a wooden camp table. "For now, please step into my office." He motioned haircut boy over. "Chris, grab us some drinks. What's your pleasure, Tan?"

"Alacrity," the man snapped. "Get on with it."

Benson swept a diplomatic arm toward a table covered with giant sheets of paper that were weighed down with rocks. Kell stole enough of a glance to see that they were architectural blueprints and geological surveys. His eyes also adjusted to notice the extra people in the chamber, taking care to stick to its shadows. In addition to Chris and another pretty boy from Benson's team, Kell recognized Casey, the Abercrombie model wannabe who'd led the group sack on Tait's drunken ass last week. Tan had a henchman with him too—a giant who almost had to duck to fit inside the cavern. The big bastard had Kell more concerned than all three of Gunter's boys. Unlike the fashionistas, it wouldn't be pleasant to take him on.

Benson ran a finger down the middle of a map close to Tan. "Here's where you met Casey on the beach. As you have likely already learned, most of this side of the island has more rugged terrain, dominated by the half dozen state parks and the Na Pali range to the north."

"As well as the Pacific Missile Range Facility at Barking Sands to the south."

Kellan drilled his hand harder against the stone.

Benson lifted a smooth smile. "Yes, sir. There *is* that."

Tan braced both hands to the table. For the first time, he seemed to relax. "It *is* an ideal insertion position."

"Hmmm, yes. You must admit, it's a more discreet alternative to launching a full-bore assault on the West Coast of the U.S."

Tan chuffed. It was probably the closest thing the man came to a laugh. "We all recall how well *that* worked out."

"No one clearer than my partner."

Kellan was certain every hair on the back of his neck jabbed straight up. Before better sense could stop him, he looked over to Tait. His buddy glared back, clearly wrestling with the same gut-punching rage. Benstock's elusive silent partner was once again the burr under both their saddles—but this time, the guy was drawing blood.

Tan tapped a finger to his mouth, deep in thought. "Tell me again about the logistics of mobilizing transports on and off the beach."

Benson cocked another confident grin. "Disguise your vessels as night fishing fleets, use only the quiet skiffs, keep to the darkest hours of the night, and I guarantee you won't even encounter curious seagulls. The neighbors go to bed early."

"Including the army captain who lives to the immediate south?"

"My, my. You *are* thorough." Benson began a slow stroll around the cavern, forcing Kell and Tait to duck back into their alcoves. "Take John Franzen off your list of concerns. He is indeed with the army—in their Special Operations Forces."

"Ahhh." Tan's tone resonated with relief. "That means he's likely in my country more than yours."

"Beautifully phrased," Benson offered. "And if I may add to it, consider that most of the locals have trusted the Franzen family for generations. Very few will suspect that the nocturnal comings and goings of their 'new neighbors' are anything more than a corporation's eccentricities in building up their new island resort."

"Brilliant." Tan peered again at the big sheets with their intricate plans. "But do any of those 'loyal locals' know about this cave? And its connection to Hale Anelas?"

"The last time the family stepped foot in here was to wait out Hurricane Iniki, in nineteen ninety-two," Gunter explained. "Before that, the passage wasn't actively used for over a hundred years, since the days when pirates ran slaves, jewels, gold, and other illegal contraband up from the beach and into the original mansion."

"'The original mansion'?" Tan echoed. "So Iniki wiped out the property?"

"Only part of it. The mansion's had several additions and renovations since then. After a freak lightning strike took the east part of the house in the early nineteen twenties, the owners rebuilt a sizable new kitchen and boarded up the entrance from the cave for good. A few years later, they had the tunnel closed from the beach side, as well. The good little prohibitionists were aghast at finding the passage being secretly used for illegal whiskey storage.

"When the Kails bought the house in the sixties, I doubt they even knew about the tunnel, though it's remained structurally sound. You can imagine how intrigued *we* were to find it while looking at the property as a potential resort commodity for the main company. Requesting architectural surveys and geologic studies is a normal part of that process. My partner recognized the strategic importance of the discovery and has led a very quiet project to clear the tunnel once more. He's been vital to the process of securing a legal purchase of the ranch."

Kell bared his seething teeth at the wall now. No wonder Benson had been able to cause such a major clusterfuck with Lani's efforts at securing the new permits for the B and B. He had help. From the goddamn *partner*.

"And that deal is happening soon, then?" Tan queried.

Benson straightened his stance and folded his arms, clearly more confident in the conversation's direction. "Every building-permit official, down to the minimum wage clerks, is in our pocket. Our lovely friend Miss Kail started playing with the notion of going all the way to Honolulu with her case, but everyone in that office is on our payroll now, as well."

"Your thoroughness is impressive." The Asian picked up one of the paperweight rocks and turned it over in his hand. "Yet so is Kail's determination."

Kellan stared at that rock and envisioned using it to clobber the man. Something in the way Tan referred to Lani, the sensual stress he put on every syllable of "determination," was a reminder of how a cobra danced before sinking its fangs into prey.

"She'll be out of the picture within a few weeks." Benson tapped a thigh with a nervous index finger. "The woman's not going to have any financial choice but to take our offer."

"Hmmm." The man's mien changed in such a subtle way Kell doubted anyone noticed it but him and Tait—but damn did they notice, especially when Tan shifted his stance to disguise the small jerks of his cock. "What a pity," he murmured, "that she can't be part of the package."

Red. It gained terrible meaning when it became the color of a man's rage. Kellan had never known such a violent version of the feeling, lashing its way through every drop of his blood, tethering itself to every tendon in his limbs. He didn't have to look at Tait for the assurance that his friend shared the fury. He felt the energy of it spewing from T's hiding space.

Mr. Tan, you officially just signed your kill order.

"Fascinating." Benson had the nerve to sound like the guy had simply asked for fries with his burger. "So you've seen her?"

"We have been performing our own surveillance of the ranch for the last few days. Discreetly, of course." Tan set the rock back down and kept his gaze fixed on the blueprints. "So yes, I've seen her. Her beauty is...extraordinary."

Another sensation joined the anger. It wasn't so easy for Kell to identify. In many ways, it was similar to the acrimony, burning and unforgiving, but now it gained a strange urgency, relentlessly gripping the center of his chest.

The Koreans had been watching the ranch. For several days. That meant watching all of them. Him and Tait. Lani and Leo. He suddenly wished for the ability to sprout wings, jet plane himself to the school, scoop them both up, and take them far, far away from Tan and his oil slick of a stare—and his disgusting way of drawing out every syllable of "extraordinary."

Benson shifted toward the man by one careful step. "A word of advice, my friend? That beauty comes with a bite. *A lot* of bite."

Tan gave a subtle chuckle. "I like biting. It's always nice, for a start." He traced a finger along the edge of the table. "Let's say I enjoy things on the rougher side."

Benson shrugged. "Nothing wrong with that. You're a man who enjoys working hard then playing hard."

"Yes, well...playing hard tended to land me in spots of trouble, so I've been on the wagon for a while now. Used to have a bloke who kept me supplied with plenty of fresh toys for 'play,' but King managed to get himself killed. In Seattle, of all places. I actually think it was a sting of some sort, involving those bothersome Special Forces boys."

Unbelievably, the turn in the conversation finally made Benson squirm. He visibly sweated in his Armani though attempted a wry laugh at Tan's comment. In the end, the guy appeared constipated more than anything, not lending a speck of charm to his comeback.

"If it's quality 'toys' you're requesting, Tan, I'm happy to email a catalog of our most circumspect ladies of the island. Hokulani Kail is regarded as a sister by Captain Franzen, making her a tougher add-on for the package."

Tan shot out another heavy sound that served proxy for a real laugh. "Saying things like that only entices me greater, Gunter." He added a seamless shrug. "And weren't you the chap telling me that the woman hasn't given you a contract signature yet? Your plan might proceed more smoothly by lashing down the woman into a commitment, if you know what I mean." The man turned, now fully revealing the erection punching at his designer crotch. "It's astounding what a woman will agree to, once her own blood is flowing from your whip strokes."

Benson didn't appear stopped-up anymore. He paled in blatant nausea. "That...that's—"

"Got to be one of the best ideas I've heard all week."

The statement wasn't issued by any of the henchmen, including Tan's hulk. There was another person in the cave who had maintained a shadow-silent presence until now. He remained in darkness, though his voice was eerily familiar to Kellan. The mystery was unsettling. Where had he heard that quarterback baritone before? And why, as he searched his memory banks for the answer, did all the possibilities make his neck hairs do the goddamn hokey-pokey with each other again?

The moment the man came forward, both those answers dropped into place with disgusting certainty.

The last time Kellan had seen that spiky blond hair, that rugged but youthful face, and that casual but graceful lope, he'd been watching Luna Lawrence blow Ephraim Lor to the terrorist hell he deserved. As Lor flew six feet across a Hollywood sound stage, the partner with whom the monster had been working, a demon who'd taken lots of Lor's money to aid his attempt at turning the West Coast into a nuclear wasteland, had fled the scene, never to be seen again.

Until now.

The reason for the latter half of the Benstock name. A fugitive on the FBI's Top Ten Wanted list. One of the criminals responsible for Luna's death and now a man who didn't flinch at the proposal of using Lani as a pawn in his next sick scheme, again taking money from more people who intended to seriously damage the country.

Cameron Stock.

CHAPTER NINETEEN

Fury? Yeah, Tait knew the shit, all right—more intimately than he'd ever wanted. But nothing—*nothing*—in his life had prepared him for this raw, roaring craving to tear apart everything in sight with his bare hands, including the cave he'd just allowed a piece of walking dick lice to leave. The shit was so intense that it manifested through his body in ice instead of fire, giving him new understanding of why some people got locked in padded rooms.

Kellan's quiet footsteps approached the crevice where he still stood, frozen in place. He'd let the guy take care of a sweep through the cave after Tan, Benson, and Stock left, planning Lani's captivity and extortion as if they were running logistics on a fucking fraternity prank. He'd admitted that if *he* moved, he'd chase the shits down and bury his knife in Stock's throat before the henchmen put him down in similar fashion. That would alert the cocksuckers that Kell was likely nearby. He'd be killed too. Then they'd declare it open hunting season on Lani, with Leo as their extra insurance policy.

"Cut the fuse, T-Bomb." Kell's voice was a welcome salve on his senses. "You have to keep it together, man."

"I know." His emphasizing huffs bounced off the walls, taunting him. "I...know."

"*Tait.*" Kellan clamped a hand to his shoulder. "Eyes here, dude." His buddy's gaze waited for him, dark as moonless midnight with its steeled determination. "We *will* drop the

ANGEL PAYNE

bastard this time. I promise. Okay?"

He forced a tight nod. "Yeah. Okay."

"Our priority right now is getting to Lani and Leo. We only have the rental car to use, since they took Lani's jeep to the school."

"Shit. And the rental's back at Franzen's place."

They locked stares again, though it was only for a second. Thank fuck they were still on the same mental page.

We need to move. Now.

Though using the road would've gotten them to Franz's faster, they knew the beach route would be less conspicuous. On the other hand, running without a hundred pounds of gear on one's back did speed up the pace. And the thought of Stock getting to Lani first? Tait would have sprinted to the summit of Kawaikini and back to keep that disaster from happening.

Every second was vital.

Despite that fact, Tait commemorated their arrival at the house by tossing the keys at Kell. Though he was certain the guy already read his intention in the action, it was too damn important for the ether of telepathy.

"Grab the Remington. And all the ammo you brought for it."

* * * * *

Less than two hours later, it was back to head-banging-against-the-wall mode.

Tait glared over at Kellan, who wore an empathizing look. The cause of their mutual ire was once again the growling baritone from the phone on the lanai table between them. This time, the phone was a burner unit they'd bought during a fast supplies stop in Kekaha, so Franzen was only represented by a string of numbers with the country code for Indonesia. That did little to impersonalize their exasperation at their captain, despite the strings he'd pulled to get them, along with Lani and Leo, into one of the beachside cottages at the Pacific Missile Range Facility base.

Different phone. Different lanai. Different breathtaking beach view.

Same helpless fury.

"Franz." Kellan leaned forward, planting elbows on his knees in another attempt to reason with the man. "We're not saying that we don't understand—"

"Of course you're not," their CO countered. "You're just saying that neither of you *want* to understand."

Tait burst to his feet. "Maybe we have a translation problem here. We're telling you that Benson is all but sucking Cameron Stock's dick and that, as we speak, they're drawing up a contract to accept upwards of seventy million dollars from the North Koreans—with Lani tossed in as the signing bonus."

"Damn it," the man boomed. "You don't think I hear you loud and clear, Bommer? And you don't think that I wish to fuck I was there beside you to deal with this, instead of here with the responsibility of this battalion and these men?" A long pause was filled with his peeved exhalation. "But commit *this* to that dense gray matter of yours, Sergeant: the logistics of this wouldn't change even if I *was* there. This scenario calls for intelligence and deliberation, not impatience and drama. There are only two of you, wanting to stage an operation with little else but that rifle and a couple of knives, on a property twice as big as the Bin Laden compound. There were nearly thirty personnel and a dog on that op."

Kell shook his head while pitching to his feet. "*Psshh.* Thirty navy guys, two army guys; same difference."

Franz cut off Tait's chuckle before he could get it started. "You two aren't just being impractical; you're being stupid. For the time being, both those adjectives are deleted from your vocabulary in favor of a fun *new* concept I have. It's called safety."

Kellan stopped and slammed his hands to his waist. Tait let his head fall back. Franz was smart enough to interpret the huffs they attached to the actions. He sent back a commanding grunt, not budging his position.

Tait swung forward again. "The Kails aren't going to be any safer than a cottage on a missile testing base."

Franzen gave way to another growl. "I'm talking about *your* safety, shit-for-brains. I can't be there, but I'm sending the next best thing. The Fifth SFGA had a team ready to launch on a mission that was aborted; they've already been reassigned and were airborne forty-five minutes ago. They'll be landing at the base in about sixteen hours, and you *will* await then assist them."

Sixteen hours!

Tait stopped himself from punching out one of the lanai supports only because Kellan expressed their outrage by kicking a chair down the porch. "Captain, with a shit ton of respect, we don't have sixteen hours. When Lani and Leo don't return to the ranch tonight, Stock and Benson will start a hunt without hesitation."

"Which means they'll check my place next. You thought about that and left the lights on when you left, right?"

"Affirmative," Kell put in. "But eventually they'll connect the dots and realize we're on to them."

Tait coiled his hands into fists. "Then they'll be desperate for a chance to escape. They'll rush to finalize things with Tan and the Koreans."

"Which they can't facilitate without Lani."

"It's easy enough to forge her signature on the property docs."

"But Tan doesn't just want her signature." The comeback came from Kellan. With every step he took back toward the table, the storm on his face gave way to resignation. "And T, that means the captain's right. Our most important duty right now is hunkering down here, making sure Lani and Leo are secure and safe."

A satisfied huff came from the phone. "At last, the light of common sense shines upon the shores of my native land."

The urge to smash something to dust blasted once more through Tait's limbs. He spun to make his way back inside the cottage but was stopped by a stare of luminous silver light, belonging to the woman who stood in tense silence beneath the doorframe. Without granting him mercy from her gaze, Lani called toward the phone, "Glad you called, Johnny. Somebody had to pound some sense into these guys."

"Johnny?" Kell actually grinned, ready to move in for the kill shot on the tease.

Franzen let it slide. "Hoku-hulu-baby!" he cried in delight. "How're you holding up, *kaikuahine*? And how's Leo?"

Her features crumpled a little. Then a lot. Tait's chest imploded. He hated seeing how frightened she was. He hated watching her fingers tremble as she tucked her hair behind an ear. Most of all, he hated how she stiffened against the arm he tried to wrap around her in comfort. "We've...errmm...had better days," she finally stated with forced brightness. "Leo's okay, considering the circumstances. He's retreated to his room with his earbuds and music."

"A saner plan than what my bullet ninjas were planning."

"No shit," she agreed. "Wishing I could follow my *kaikaina*'s example and do the same, but I think I'm still in shock. Gunter Benson's douche quotient is bigger than I ever imagined."

"It won't be for much longer," Franz assured. "Some of the Big Green Machine's finest are on their way. I just got an inbox from our friends with the navy, as well. Guess they caught wind of the fun you're all going to have and are trying to round up a few SEALs to help out with the op."

Kellan gritted his teeth through a fake smile. "Gee, Franz, want to make our night even better by announcing we get poi with dinner?"

Tait laughed as Lani jabbed the guy in honor of their running joke. Personally, he loved the native Hawaiian dish, made of crushed taro root. Kell's opinion of the stuff ran the exact opposite.

"Enough," Franz protested. "You're making me homesick!"

Kellan groaned, which made Lani giggle again. Tait tried to stir some matching humor once more, but the feelings waned as Kell signed off with Franz, confirming he'd drop a text as soon as the battalion from the Fifth arrived at the base.

This wasn't right. Every minute they waited was another minute wasted. And there wasn't a damn thing he could do about it.

Tait turned and headed down the lanai steps. In another dozen strides, he was on the shore itself, pacing hard in an effort to work off his urgent ire.

"T-Bomb."

He kept walking. Kell would get the point in another second or two and back off. Though only a half circle in the sky, the moon was brilliant tonight. It turned the beach into something from a goddamn romance movie, pissing him off more. Where was a depressing storm when he needed one? The fuckers happened every five minutes on this island, didn't they?

"Tait."

He didn't stop.

"Bommer, for fuck's sake!"

He gave the guy a pity stop. Nobody liked watching a man playing needy puppy with another, no matter what the circumstances were. "Not in the mood, Slash-rific. Don't you have to go look for your misplaced balls anyway?"

The man jutted his jaw. "You know I don't like this waiting game any more than you. You know I'd be jumping in the car right next to you if I thought it made sense. But if you dig deep, you also know that once those assholes get it that we're on to them, which will be any second now, they won't leave a pebble of this island unturned to try to find her."

He pointed to the runway a few thousand feet away. "Hate to repeat the obvious, but this place is a bit fortified. And staffed by people who know a thing or two about defense systems and weapons."

"And any one of them could *also* be in Stock's back pocket. You heard the conversation in the cave as clearly as I did. The guy has bought off most of the local governments on this island *and* Oahu. Who's to say he hasn't found a few folks on the take on the base? That's before we consider Tan's influence, as well. The man was in cahoots with that bastard King, who damn near snatched Sage away from Hawk again and had paid minions all over Lewis-McChord. Fruit on the same tree. Just as rotten, just as poisonous, just as important a factor to consider here."

Tait stabbed his hands into his pockets. His logic heard the words, even agreed with them, but his heart screamed louder. The memories returned, taunting and bitter, of the weeks after Luna's death. The revenge he'd craved, the fury of knowing Stock still roamed the earth, living like a king off Lor's payoff money...and the helplessness of accepting he'd likely never be found. It all slapped Tait anew, stinging a hundred times worse now that he'd peeled back the shields on his soul and allowed so many of his scars to be seen—scars that were ripped open all over again. He knew exactly where to find Stock now yet was leashed from doing a single thing about it. *Un-fucking-acceptable.*

He stabbed a foot at the sand, sending the shit flying into the water, where it plunked in the foamy shallows. "You promised me we were going to take him down this time." He didn't bother to hide the accusation beneath it.

"And we will." Kell squared his shoulders. "We *will*, Tait—when we have the support to do it the right way."

"Sure." He whipped a glower at the guy. "Because doing it 'the right way' helped us so much during the op in LA. You need a refresher on how that panned out, my friend? On how Stock disappeared off the grid less than twenty-four hours after that fun little showdown?"

"This is different and you know it."

"Why? Because you think Stock will stick around for the money?" When Kell's silence confirmed that, Tait emitted a scoffing snort. "Sticking around for it and staying exposed because of it are two different things. The guy knows how to sever himself from that poison tree faster than you can say

Johnny Appleseed. Then he'll hide himself in all the other ugly fruit on the ground. Our window on finding him narrows another inch for every minute we wait. When this shit goes down, the only one taking the bullet will be Benson."

"And Tan."

"Yeah. Tan. Who's really the big fish here, right? Which is the real reason we're waiting on the fucking Fifth. It's not for Stock, who's going to waltz free again. Who, less than twelve hours from now, will be sipping something with an umbrella in it while Luna's ashes still feed the fish in Puget Sound." Another freezing fist ground into his gut. "It's not fair. It's *not* fucking fair!"

Kellan blew out a heavy breath. "T, don't do this. You've finally started to fly on the right side of the envelope again. Now grab the goddamn stick and correct your angle."

He wheeled around. While his gut was ice cold, his face burned with fury. "*Correct my angle?*" He slammed it into hard air quotes. "Seriously? When that filth who calls himself a human wouldn't recognize *correct* if it chomped off his cock?"

His friend nodded slowly. "I know how you—"

"Don't." He surged and grabbed Kellan by the neck of his T-shirt. "Don't you *dare* tell me that you know how I feel!"

Kellan's mien barely changed. His serenity was infuriating. "All right, then let me tell you how *I* feel. There's a lot at stake here. People who are still alive, who need us, people you're willing to neglect for the sake of chasing an empty revenge."

His arm shook with rage. He twisted his grip tighter. "Not empty." The words shook. "*Not* empty!"

Kell clamped a hand around his forearm. "She told you to move on. Lani's voice, but Luna's words. She told you to—"

"She died in my arms!" It ripped out of him, a bellow of

wrath and grief and frustration. "She used her last fucking breath to kiss me!"

"I know," Kellan countered. "I know, man."

"No," he snarled, "you don't. You have no goddamn idea what I'm talking about." He looked down between their bodies to the sand. Why the hell was he clinging to this guy, even in anger? Kellan called him a brother, but he wondered if the guy knew what that meant. The very nature of Kell's job required an emotional detachment that lots of guys struggled with—but never Kell. Made sense now, didn't it? With a disgusted snort, he shoved away. "Feelings are convenient accessories for you, Kellan, and nothing more. I'd pay for a full fireworks show if you ever let someone in to the point that they terrify you."

Kellan's eyes, already dark in the night, descended to the shade of pure pitch. "Fetch your checkbook, dickwad—if you can pull your head out of your self-centered ass long enough to notice."

Tait snickered. Then sobered. "Lani? Are you kidding me?"

Kellan stood his ground and spread his arms. "Do I look like I'm kidding? Or feeling anything except fear about how those assholes plan to use her?"

Tait studied him. Everything about the guy screamed sincerity, but acknowledging that meant looking in the mirror at how thoroughly the woman had come to fill *his* heart too. He fought back by snarling, "I don't believe you. This is a half-assed ploy to get me to back off going for Stock. You should be ashamed of yourself, Slash-a-drama."

He'd stomped only a couple of steps back toward the cottage before Kell stopped him short—with a fist to his stomach. "Nah," the guy growled, "let me show you something

I'd really be ashamed of."

Before Tait could consider a retaliation, Kell slammed a foot against his backside, treating him to a "Kaua'i kiss," Barking Sands style. Tait spat dirt and rolled over, tangling his calves around Kell's ankles, bringing him down. The guy grunted while landing flat on his back, a position worth taking immediate advantage of. With fury tearing up his throat, he dug a knee between Kell's lungs and swung his fist up. "Shiner blue always *was* your color, asshole."

Kellan's hand seemed to come out of nowhere, latching on Tait's face like a crazed spider. He landed one finger in an eye and another two in Tait's nostrils. The impromptu sinus cleanse distracted him for the second Kell needed to unseat him, though he wasn't going tits-up without a fight. Letting his frustration feed the sound, he threw his buddy over with a vicious roar. Kellan echoed the bellow, turning his action into a full barrel roll. They wrestled through three revolutions one way then two the next, before Kellan tried the spider face attack again.

"Honestly?" Tait spat as they both gained their feet again. "You fight like a fucking girl, Slash-arina."

"No more than you, Beach Fun Gidget."

"*Stop.*"

The plea was desperate and sweet but came from so far away, Tait shoved it from his mind. He drove his head into Kell's chest before grabbing the guy's thigh. Time to make this takedown stick. "How 'bout some dirt with your poi for dinner, honey?"

"How 'bout my fist up your ass, dollface?"

"*Stop!*" There was no mistaking the scream this time. And its beseeching need. And its underline of tears. "Stop it, both of you!"

Tait stumbled backward, thrown off-balance as he and Kell released each other. Kellan's stability wasn't much better. He gave a victorious grunt. The guy was definitely breathing harder than him. They were only eight months apart in age, but he never let that stop him from writing Kell off as the old man.

The "old man" Lani chose to run for first.

Another knot of lead twisted in his stomach—until she rammed a punch into Kell's shoulder. Tait only got halfway into a laugh before she whirled and repeated the treatment on him.

"*He aha no la kou ano?* What the *hell* is wrong with you?" She hit Kell again. "*Both* of you!"

"He started it." The protest spilled from them in tandem murmurs.

"I don't care if Saint Peter himself floated down from heaven and started it!" She pushed at them with another chuffed word in her language. He got the upshot of it and was certain Kell did too. "Three hours ago, I was thinking about the future, trying to talk Leo into going to the University of Hawaii. Believe it or not, the kid wanted to talk to the guys at the West Point table. I actually let him! Now, I've found out that 'the future' may consist of my home, complete with its custom weapons smuggling cave, being sold out from under me to the damn North Koreans. And oh yeah, there's that part about *me* being their signing bonus on the package. So where are the two *elite soldiers* who are supposedly helping to prevent this disaster? Here they are, fancying themselves as the Teenage Mutant Ninja Turtles. *Hupos!*"

She threw up both arms before whirling to stomp away.

Her huffs didn't stop the wind from carrying her wrenching sobs back to them.

Tait backhanded some sand off his face. "You know that book we keep thinking of writing?" he muttered.

"Yeah?" Kell grumbled.

"I think I have our title."

"The Idiot's Guide to Being an Idiot?"

"I was thinking more *Fifty Shades of Idiocy*, but yours works too."

Thankfully, Kell didn't milk it any further. He did what Tait hoped he would. Went after her. With willing steps but a gut dipped in remorse, he followed.

She tromped back toward the cottage with furious footsteps. He and Kellan maintained a respectful—and careful—distance. Whether he wanted to admit it or not, he was going to bruise where she'd landed that punch. He greatly preferred dealing the marks, not getting them. With more pleasurable results for all.

Not the time for thoughts like that, Bommer. No matter how luscious her ass looked in that frothy floral skirt or how delicious and demure the pink sweater set that topped it.

She stomped into the cottage without altering her pace. He and Kellan followed but stopped in the living room as Lani proceeded through to the cottage's second bedroom. All the complex's three-bedroom cottages were snapped up for the summer, but that had been all right by Kell and him. They'd resolved themselves to swapping nap sprints on the couch tonight, if either of them was even in the mood for sleeping. The probability of that had dropped into the realm of "highly unlikely," especially now.

When Lani stood in the open doorway to the bedroom,

eyeing them both with her iridescent stare, it was clear she shared that mind-set. A firm fling of her head, all but decreeing them into the room with her, had Tait gaping in slack-jawed shock—and open-season lust. A glance at Kellan showed the same reactions on his face.

"Can she...errr...do that?" his buddy stammered. "There's a term for that, isn't there? Topping from the bottom?"

Tait eyed him. "You really want to go there right now?"

"Excellent point." He didn't say anything else as he let Tait lead the way down the hall.

Her bedroom was the larger of the two in the cottage, decorated in comfortable but functional furniture covered in subdued tropical shades. In short, the army's version of resort accommodations. Though Tait glanced hopefully at the bed, he ordered all follow-up thoughts into retreat. A bed in the room didn't always trump a woman's wrath. Even *this* woman.

She shut the door by backing up against it. After the thing clicked shut, she stayed there, hands behind her back, throwing her brilliant glare between the two of them. Tears still threatened to manifest in her eyes, frying his gut in remorse again.

He guessed a little levity couldn't hurt. "Well, you can't order us to go to our room."

"Shut up."

Or maybe it could.

Kellan tried his own approach, gentle but firm. "Okay, we're a couple of jerks. You know it's just because we both care about—"

Her sharp laugh sliced him short. "You care about me? Really? And this is how you show it?" She shoved off the door, pushed between them, and turned with her fists slammed on her hips. "I was tired of breaking you two up after the first two times I did it." She nodded hard at Tait. "Though it helps that you can walk a straight line on your own this time."

It wasn't a real joke. Wisely, Tait knew it. "Truce declared, okay? We'll keep our hands off each other."

She dropped her hands but sustained her suspicious glower. "Prove it."

He swung back an awkward glance. "Okay, I'll take first watch outside. Kell, why don't you grab some dinner, and—"

"No," she cut in again. "Not good enough."

He traded a glimpse with Kellan. *Let's make her happy and shake on it.* With a resigned breath, he reached out a hand. But Kell never got close with his return extension. Lani grabbed both their wrists and slammed their hands against her body, forcing them into a sudden, joint breast grope. Before either of them could process their shock enough to act, she pushed their grips harder against her beautiful mounds. Tait joined his buddy in a hiss when her nipples instantly beaded and pushed against her sweater.

"Keep your hands off each other by putting them on me." Her whisper was as urgent as her gaze, jumping between them with the intensity of lightning. "Please, just help me to forget about all of it for a little while. I need the strength of you both... the care of you both...the passion of you both. I just...need you both. Please?"

CHAPTER TWENTY

It was a night for crazy circumstances. And even crazier actions.

Lani was still spitting pissed at both of them, despite how deeply she understood their shoreline antics. Their emotions had been ripped out of the typical sockets today as harshly as hers. Taking out their follow-up rage on the safe targets of each other was a logical progression on the psychological ladder. In the end, it would be a skirmish that meant nothing.

In the end.

An end that was approaching with the subtlety of a freight train. A conclusion to this horrible episode with Benson that would go one of two ways. Tait, Kell, and the guys from the Fifth would either be in time to surprise the Benstock boys and the Koreans, or they wouldn't. Neither scenario was a promise she'd ever see her ranch—or both her men—again.

This was all the time they had left. Their only remaining moments to stamp the magic of their triad on the ribbon of time and memory.

She let out a tight cry, trying to beat the thought down as melodrama, but one look up at the guys, and the deep purpose in their rugged faces, confirmed it as the bitter truth.

No. She wouldn't concentrate on bitterness right now. Or goodbyes. She'd only soak up their heat, their passion, and their adoration. Make them fill her one more time. One last time.

She swallowed hard and meshed her fingers tighter with theirs. Before she could take another breath, Kellan twisted his free hand in her hair, yanking her head back for Tait's crushing kiss. Both the guys groaned as Tait sank his tongue deep. She joined her needy groan to the mix when they both pinched her breasts through her clothes.

"Yin needs a turn too." Kellan growled it as he drew her from Tait's mouth and replaced it with his own. He tasted like the wind and sea, musky and salty, a heady combination with Tait's woodsy scent hitting her from behind as he pressed against her there.

"Is Leo still tuning out with his music?" came Tait's query at her ear. She nodded, not an easy feat considering the man already lifted her skirt, glided both hands beneath her panties, and palmed her ass with his bare palms. "Hmm," he replied in a sensual snarl. "That's good to know."

Kellan's gaze was a breathtaking gray storm as he pulled away from her mouth. "But not entirely helpful," he added. "We both know how our girl loves to scream."

"Won't that make it fun for her to try whispers and silence, then?" He gave her the challenge just as he trailed a finger at the rim of her anus, causing her to gasp and writhe. "Bite it back, babe," he directed. "Whispers"—he worked in another finger—"and silence."

"Damn." Kellan met her stare directly, brushing the hair off her face. "Look at what that did to these eyes." He leaned in and kissed her nose. "You like this, Starshine? Does it make you hot to know we control every sound off your lips now, every breath you take in and release?"

Gods. She was going to be a puddle of nothing in just a few minutes. Already feeling like her mind detached from her body, she gave Kellan an eager nod. "Yes. Ohhhh yes, Sir."

Tait stepped around and stood next to his friend again. After giving her a soft kiss on the forehead, he murmured, "You said that so beautifully, dreamgirl." A smile curled his lips. "Now we're going to give you a few minutes to reflect on it."

Kellan beat her to the punch in an open display of confusion. "What?"

Tait arched his brows at his friend. "Don't you think it's time to go get the Boy Scout ready pack from the car?"

Kellan chuckled. "I officially hand over the dominant honor badge to you now."

Tait turned and took both of her hands in his. "And this is Lani's chance to earn the matching submissive one."

She let her smile grow. "I'd like that."

"And we're both pleased." Tait lifted a long-fingered hand to one side of her face. "While we're gone, we want you to prepare yourself for our pleasure. Make your body ready by stripping naked then washing your pussy and ass for us. After that, center your mind by kneeling in the middle of the bed, legs spread, posture straight, and hands still. This tells us, both your Sirs, that you entrust us with your power tonight. That you know we'll use it to push you a little...fuck you a lot...and gratify you even more."

Had he asked for half the pineapples on the island along with that, she would've found a way to comply. Luckily, her breathy "Yes, Sirs" seemed to suffice. He and Kellan took turns kissing her before quietly leaving the room, which spurred her into instant motion. She had a minute, maybe two at most, to ready herself as Tait had instructed.

Sure enough, she'd just gotten onto the bed and was crawling toward its center when the guys came back in. She froze in place, feeling fifteen again, caught by Mom as she sneaked back into the house after making out on the beach with Troy Keweha. Only she hadn't been totally nude then. Or feeling every nerve ending in her body ignite from just the sound of the opening door.

"Hmmm." She didn't have to look up to know the dark panther purr was Kellan's. A new instinct even picked up the tiny bite of sadistic pleasure in it, curling an answering desire deep in her pussy. "What do we have here?" he added to that while walking to the foot of the bed. She watched from the fringe of her lashes as Tait joined him, turning them into a pair of muscled sentinels who drenched her body with their hot gazes.

"Looks like someone who didn't get into position fast enough."

Every note of Tait's tone, so full of predatory serenity, brought out baby bumps of awareness along her skin. Nevertheless, she flashed him a dirty look. She'd *be* in position, if they hadn't given her all of sixty seconds to do their bidding.

"But I'm enjoying *this* position, buddy."

"Must agree. It's nice."

"Look at that perfect curve of her ass...and the silhouette of her nipples...all that hair cascading to the mattress like a waterfall..."

"Roger on everything, man. It doesn't suck one bit."

"Maybe that can be fixed."

Their commentary made her feel beautiful and special, like a precious piece of art—until Kellan's remark turned her to hot goo. She craved the praise of their flesh, not just their eyes. She whimpered and licked her lips, hoping he was serious about the intent of the words. The man's harsh grunt indicated that he was. Thank the gods.

Tait chuckled. "Looks like she wouldn't mind that 'fix' at all, brother."

"You don't mind?"

Tait tapped something with his hand. It sounded like the leather of Kellan's well-stocked supply pouch. "I've got some prep work to keep me busy, but don't think I won't enjoy things as I do. Watching this girl's lips go to work on a cock, even if it isn't mine, is up there on my *Wonders of the World* list."

She couldn't help a giggle. And an eye roll. "Sir, with all due respect, you are full of crap."

Tait, now standing next to the bed behind her, snorted. "Thanks for the deference, dreamgirl, but you'll still accept a small punishment for that, as *you* are full of shit."

She tossed a coy pout. "Oh, dear. Guess you forgot about the whole thing about Leo being in the next room? Silence and whispers tonight, *not* smacks and screams, remember? I suppose that makes punishments a little...umm...impossible?"

Tait looked at her, incredulity stamped on his lips— before he traded a confident laugh with Kellan. Lani felt the certainty fade from her face. If she'd just given the punch line, she wondered what the hell the joke was. She was tempted to fire that exact line at the two of them, but the bed trembled as Kellan climbed up beside her, kneeling so his crotch was directly in front of her face.

"Silence is golden in many different forms, sweetheart." He ran his knuckles along her cheeks, bringing blissful trails of heat, before shifting his hands to his fly. "Your little lip workout gave me a great idea for one."

She answered with an adoring sigh as he unzipped with a brusque jerk, letting his swelling flesh burst free, veins standing out along the length of his crimson stalk.

"Kiss it," he ordered quietly. The moment she did, his dark purple head erupted with a shimmering white drop. "Now suck that off."

She moaned, all too eager to obey. Kellan hissed and bucked his hips. "Good, Sir?" she whispered.

"It's a damn good start, Starshine."

His growl turned her senses into a thousand forms of lust. Since the beginning, Kellan had been a lover beyond compare, forceful and passionate, who enjoyed being on top in so many senses of the word. But Tait's guidance had drawn out the stricter, sexier side of him, a dominant in desire who curled her toes, spun her senses, and drenched her sex in need. Tonight, she needed that leader more than anything, and he was *not* letting her down.

Kellan raked a hand through her hair, gathering most of it around his fist. He pulled her forward, guiding her lips back to the broad crown now dotted with more drops of precome. "Open your throat, sweet girl. I want to fuck it good before I bury myself in your pussy."

He fed her his cock with one hot surge, consuming every corner of her mouth with his hot girth. Lani felt him shake and swallow, holding down his groan. She forced back her answering cry with a long breath.

Within seconds, she learned that the sound containment ricocheted all the arousal back down through her body, five times more potent than before. Her whole sex quaked. She inhaled again, reveling in a repeat of the sweet tremors in her deepest folds, assuaging the lust by sucking harder on Kell's cock. A hot breath left him. He threw back his head. They taunted each other in that silent, sexy game for many hot minutes. Who would be the first to snap their silence, even with a whimper?

Lani dared an exultant stare up Kellan's torso, into his eyes. She was, after all, the one who had the most sensitive part of his body at the back of her throat. Piece of cake.

She'd underestimated how well these two men knew their cake.

In the second before she was certain Kellan would crack, there was a shocking pain near *her* crack. Were those Tait's *teeth*? Was the man biting her on the ass?

No. Not "biting." *Biting*. The digs weren't a few love nips. He dived in at both her cheeks like they'd turned into chocolate frosted donuts *with* sprinkles. With every sink of his teeth and lips, she twisted the bedspread harder from the exquisite pain.

After five bites, she surrendered the silence contest to Kellan, mewling around his cock. He countered with a gentle shush, though his thrusts in her mouth became more deep and demanding. At the same time, Tait grabbed her back cheeks and pulled them wide, using that new valley as a gateway to seek her sex with his mouth.

In the room, it was so quiet that the ticks of the gaudy red eighties alarm clock could be heard. Inside, Lani was panting, gasping, and shouting for mercy from her two-sided assault of pulsing male desire. In her mouth, Kellan's cock burned and throbbed. Between her thighs, Tait's mouth pulled and licked. *Aue*. They were relentless. Tireless. And perfect. She curled her fists tighter into the bedding, struggling not to scream from their hungry torment. It was so good. So slick and sizzling and hot. She swallowed hard. Again. It didn't help. A cry bubbled in her throat...

"Don't." Kellan's murmur, sounding strained itself, wove

through all her senses. "Don't do it, sweetheart. Your voice still belongs to us, and we haven't untied it yet." When she gave an incensed growl, he released her hair in order to caress her jaw. "Focus it all here. Take what Tait's giving you and then funnel it back to me. Suck me harder, Lani. Deeper. Holy fuck, yes. Yessss!"

Hearing what she did for him, feeling it in every throbbing vein of his cock, unfurled a deep fulfillment in her heart. She loved serving him like this, knowing she affected him like this. Every grunt from his lips and tremble of his body brought a surge of power and a wash of gratitude. This bond was like nothing she'd ever had with another person before—and doubted she would again.

As Tait rode her clit more intensely with his tongue, she knew those cords of connection wound to him too. After her confession in the garden yesterday, it felt damn near decreed by the angels themselves, if not one in particular. Just as Kellan had entwined himself in her heart, Tait had sewn himself into her soul.

How the *hell* was she going to let them go?

She wasn't allowed to consider an answer for that. Tait, taking his turn at the mind-reading thing, assured that by taunting her with only the tip of his tongue now. She gasped as he flicked it back and forth, teasing her clit like a bee after nectar. Her sex responded with plenty of thick, warm honey. Her muscles clenched. Her thighs ached. She couldn't stop the wave of heat, rushing at her faster. *Faster...*

"Tait, she's going over. Do it now, man!"

Confusion collided with her passion. *Do* what *now*?

In the moments before her pussy exploded, Kell pulled back from her mouth. No, *she* was hauled from *him*, flattened onto her back in one mighty move from the soldier who'd just been paving her way into heaven with his tongue. Suddenly, Tait was the man who filled her vision with his naked glory and guided his condom-covered cock to her needy, wet entrance. She had no idea when he'd found the seconds to strip and didn't bother asking. As he entered her in a single thrust, she clung to his shoulders with a sigh of gratitude, letting him spread her wider with powerful slams of his hands.

"Lani," he whispered into her ear. "Let me feel that explosion, baby." He added a bite to the skin just below her lobe while withdrawing and then plunging all the way in again. "Let every inch of my cock know how hard you're coming for me."

Her clit, unfolded and unprotected, was sensitive to every damn breeze in the room. It trembled from the power of his words, making her body grip his ramming cock, driving her toward the shimmering peak of her passion.

"That's it, dreamgirl. Give it up. Let it go."

She bit into the meat of his shoulder to quell the scream from the climax, bashing her body and senses with unexpected force. Without thinking, she clawed a hand into his dark gold waves, likely ripping a handful of his scalp out with the action. To her delicious shock, Tait reacted with a growl of arousal, leading into the sharper lunges that gave up his own hot release.

He pulled away all too soon, but she cracked open her eyes to find he was being pushed away. Kellan, now breathtakingly nude with his own sheathed erection, moved to fit himself between her thighs. "Number two, sweetheart. You ready?"

She shot him a stare like he'd just chugged the insanity milkshake, but as the man leaned to take her mouth in a luxurious kiss, her body begged for a taste of the drink, too.

Kellan stroked himself a few times before thrusting into her with a determined stab, seating himself deep. His heavy breath of passion mingled with hers.

"Damn," she rasped. "Oh, damn. Th-Thank you, Sir."

"Thank *you*, Starshine." He kissed her more tenderly this time, rolling his hips to set up a steady, urgent pace for their bodies. "Your cunt is so hot. T warmed you up well for me."

"Speak of the devil." The crack came from Tait, who rolled back onto the bed as Kellan twisted to his side, keeping his body inside hers by pulling her leg around his waist.

"Indeed." Kellan flashed a wry smirk at his buddy over her shoulder.

"Speaking of warming her up..."

The guys exchanged one of their spidey power stares, making Lani's stomach roll like taking the first climb on a monster roller coaster. A thrill lay ahead. And lots of fear too. Tait's own kiss, delivered to the middle of her back, didn't help the former win out over the latter. Neither did his whispered command for her to relax.

As soon as he reached down and spread her ass a little wider, she determined the reason why. "Oh!" she cried, unable to help herself. Kellan subdued the sound with his mouth.

"Sshhh, sweetheart," he murmured. "He's going to make it better." As he brushed her hair back with big, gentle strokes, Tait turned in order to get a better view of...things. There was a discernible squirt of lube, followed by the cold infusion of the liquid to her back hole. Kellan kept up his sensual rhythm as Tait worked the lube into her ass, rolling his fingers in masterful swoops. Everything below her navel started vibrating again. Clenching in all the right ways again.

"Oh." She repeated it in a whisper this time. "*Kamaha`o*...

that's..."

Incredible. Unbearable. Wonderful. So damn wonderful.

Kellan kissed away her voice once more. "We know. You don't need to say anything. Just open your senses and experience it, Starshine."

She nodded, smiling to give him a sign of her trust in him. In them both. After the climax Tait had brought her to, she didn't think her body would bear much more pleasure...

But oh, how she was wrong.

"Ahhhh!"

It was a high gasp that likely drove all the dogs within earshot crazy, but her two hunks only gave cocky chuckles. Of course. They'd been totally in league about this. About how Tait would slide the thin steel rod into her ass in place of his fingers and flip a switch to make the damn thing start vibrating. They'd known exactly what the treatment would do to every inch of her vagina, just beyond the thin membrane of her anus, to the walls that gripped Kellan's cock...then on to every sensitive inch of her pussy. They knew it would stimulate her in ways that yesterday's "fun" hadn't, pulling her into a vortex of lust completely different from what she'd experienced with Tait.

Through it all, Kellan never stopped giving her every inch of his cock. With each long, intense stroke, it was clear he longed to saturate her in pleasure. His body was bronze and beautiful, his smile wide and wicked, and his adoration open and obvious. "You enjoying that, sweetheart?"

"Wh-What—" She shook her head, trying to form words. "Wh-Where did you—"

"A little present we picked up for you along with the takeout last night."

Tait chuckled. "You ever notice the store that's four doors down from the Chinese joint?"

"That's a *really* interesting strip mall," Kellan cracked. "Pun thoroughly intended."

"W-Well...this is a hell of a lot better...than chow m-m-m—"

She stammered into inarticulate silence when Tait clicked the remote for the wand again. Her sex flared in pure bliss. She was going to scream. It wasn't a matter of *if* but *when*. She stabbed a pleading stare across the pillow at Kellan. *Help me!*

He gazed back at her, smile now gone, replaced by angles of domination and passion. Without wavering his eyes or the pace of his body, he grated, "T. Come over here. Now."

Tait's face appeared in her line of vision. "What is it? What's wrong?"

"Not a damn thing." Kellan gentled his lunges long enough to thread some fingers through her hair. "We've simply made our girl feel so good, she wants to scream—and we're going to let her."

Tait grinned again. "Outstanding."

She threw a questioning stare at them both—until the control module for the wand appeared again in Tait's grip. Her stare turned to a glare, she was certain of it. *Were they serious?*

Tait answered her question with one of his own. "Do you trust us, Hokulani?"

She closed her eyes. And nodded a slow *yes*.

"Dear fuck." Tait murmured it this time. "Your submission is so gorgeous, baby."

Kellan didn't add anything to that. His body became a piston, hard and sculpted as his face, as he built up the rhythm of his thrusts again. Within seconds, the tension in her pussy coiled tighter. That forced her anus to constrict, doubling the pleasure of the wand's pulsations. She looked up at Kellan with the same pleading look. *You want me to scream? Well, here it comes, buddy.*

Kellan curled his darkest satyr's smile. "Muffle her, T-Bomb."

His friend complied by clamping his big hand over her mouth, sealing her lips in as tight as duct tape. She was still able to breathe through her nose, but being held down by him like this came as a sudden shock. A flagrant subjugation.

A turn-on like she'd never known.

"That's good, baby," Tait praised. "You're making me hard all over again, just with the power of your incredible eyes."

Kellan gripped her thigh, wrapping it harder against his muscled waits. "Now I want to hear her scream."

"On the same page, brother."

"Hit the wand again."

The second Tait flipped the switch, Lani gave them what they wanted. The wand sounded like a small mixer, forcing Tait to slam down a pillow to drown its naughty grinds as it flailed her ass, vagina, and clit with a thousand pulses of fire. The magnificent torment tore through her body, ripping her throat open on a shriek of raw passion. A tidal wave of sensation slammed, threatening to rip her mind from the moorings of reality itself. She reached out, needing them both as anchors, gripping Tait's neck with one hand and Kellan's with the other. Their gazes darkened yet warmed at the same time. She could happily drown in the magic of their eyes.

"Good girl," Tait murmured. "You're our very good girl, Lani. You're taking it so well, baby. Goddamn, your whole ass is vibrating. Kell, I wish you could feel this."

"Who says I'm not?" Kellan opened his lips enough to let her see his clamped teeth. "Goddamn, Starshine. My cock's never felt anything like this before."

Tait, the bastard, started pumping the wand in and out in time to Kellan's plunges. Lani screamed harder against his hand. "Ohhhh, yeah," he whispered. "That's it, baby. Come for us one more time. Give it all to us."

As if the walls of her vagina simply awaited his clearance, they thrummed and pounded, squeezing that special button inside that set off her orgasm like a subsonic boom. Lani ground her fingers into the guys' necks as her heart stopped, her lungs seized, her mind flew, and her pussy detonated. Just a few seconds later, Kellan reached back and pulled the wand free in order to grab her ass with both his hands, leveraging her tunnel for his deepest drive. His orgasm started with his tight grunt and continued with tremors that shook every inch of his massive frame. At last he crushed her mouth in a kiss, pulling free the final knots on what little was left of her emotional composure.

The tears came, silent and potent, as she gazed up into the faces of the men who'd taken her body, her spirit, and her mind to places she'd never dreamed possible. Who'd forced her to shirk the silver domes, to befriend the voices on the wind, to unleash the wildest passions in her body. Who'd taught her that in her submission and softness, she could be her strongest. They were her two demons yet her matched angels. Her tormenters yet her rescuers. Her gray and gold. Her yin and yang.

Her heart and her soul.

The tears came harder. The realization wasn't fair. Its

timing was a more hideous injustice. Why did she have to recognize her feelings *now*, just hours from the moment that they'd leave this cottage to fight *her* battle?

All right, so the army wasn't flying in a whole battalion just because of her. The security of the whole country hinged on who triumphed at Hale Anelas, and she was confident the US would be that victor—but at what price? Had destiny brought her Kellan and Tait only to take them from her on the steps they'd defended last week?

"Lani?" Kell pulled his body from hers, tossed the condom aside, and stretched out beside her, mirroring Tait's posture. "Sweetheart, are you all right?"

Tait scraped the hair away from her face. "We didn't hurt you, did we?"

"Was there something you didn't like?"

"You should've said something—"

She cut them off with a misty laugh. "Excuse me, security? I need to file a report. Someone's taken my two Doms and replaced them with these fourteen-year-old girls." After they fell into a sulky silence, she reached to the thick waves on both their heads and tugged hard. "Okay, how's this for screwed-up teenager? I'm... I'm falling in love with you." She sniffed to fill their thick silence. "Yeah, *both* of you. Feel better now?"

Kellan was the first to move. With a gaze luminous as spring mist, he leaned and claimed her lips beneath his in a tender caress. "Save room at the end of that drop, sweetheart, because here I come too."

She couldn't let that one go without sobbing again. After Kell kissed her a few more times, she turned a tender smile toward Tait. He twisted his lips, clearly at war with himself about what to say. She pressed a protesting finger on the middle of all those sexy angles, ordering a halt to his battle. "It's okay," she said. "There's no gold stars here for forced words. Just acceptance for the honesty in your eyes."

He lifted his head in order to catch that finger between his lips. After tenderly suckling it, he flicked his gaze to his friend. "Hey, Kell?"

"Hmmm?"

"Did we do something seriously awesome on a mission and forget about it? Otherwise, I don't get how a couple of dorks like us got gifted with a star like this."

The lush curves of Kellan's mouth gave way to their own smile. "I don't think we should tempt the universe with that question, dude."

Lani shot him a frown. "Why not?"

"Because it might realize it made a mistake."

She stuck out her chin. "Well, it can't do that."

"Oh, no?" Tait kicked up his brows. "In our line of work, babe, you learn real fast about the universe."

"The sadistic bastard," Kellan put in.

"Gets his kicks on random take-backs."

"Word." Kellan swung a sideways fist into the air over her head. Tait met the bump, only to drop out of it to land his hand directly on her left breast. Not shockingly, Kell's hand ended up in the same position on her right breast. "Damn," he muttered. "Sorry about that. It has a will of its own sometimes."

"Yeah," Tait added. "Mine too. Guess my hands just crave to touch things of beauty."

While Lani giggled, Kellan gave a whistle of approval. "Nice save, brother."

She took advantage of the chance to slide her hands up both their arms, savoring some beauty of her own in the form of their muscled landscapes before cupping both their prominent jaws once more. "Maybe I don't want to be saved."

They answered that with tandem growls, interrupting themselves long enough to take turns in kissing damn near every thought out of her mind.

Except for the truth behind her words.

I don't want to be saved.

They were both here, in this shitty and dangerous situation, because of her. Because of the duty they felt to save her. She didn't blame them for it. She didn't even fault their profession for it. Gods, these two had probably spent their baby years "guarding" their teddy bears from the "evil force" of the washing machine. Protectiveness was branded into their DNA. Though maddening, it was simply another amazing fragment of why she loved them both.

That didn't mean she couldn't circumvent it. Especially when it was completely in her power to do so.

This entire situation would go away—if the caves beneath the ranch did.

Her heart cracked. But the fissure was wide enough to allow clarity in, along with its friend, determination. An added encouragement: the plot would be ridiculously easy to carry out. Swiftly, quietly, and alone. By the time the guys woke up and figured out what she was up to, the damage would be done. The tunnel, and nearly everything on top of it, would be gone.

It wouldn't keep Kellan and Tait out of danger forever. *Aue*, every line of their job descriptions started with the word. It only meant that they wouldn't be killed because of her. Not at the will of maggots like Cameron Stock and Gunter Benson. Not outside her front door.

Over the last few days, she'd heard them both lecturing

Leo about making right choices. *This* was the right choice. Though the two men in her arms would never see it that way, her heart and soul voiced their firm approval to her plans. The heart and soul that hadn't just been captured by these two amazing warriors but transformed by them. Changed from insecurity and suspicion to confidence and trust. Guided to becoming more of the person she wanted to be.

She owed them so much—and had no idea how she'd ever show them the real depths of her gratitude.

But she could start to try.

★ ★ ★ ★ ★

As she'd hoped, they both fell asleep. Yeah, they'd been slinging their macho soldier shit about taking turns for naps, but that was before both of them had their heads on real pillows and their bodies in a real bed, after working their toned asses off to give her some mind-bending orgasms in said bed.

They'd be out deep for only a few minutes. After the years they'd spent on missions, their minds were trained to pop in and out of REM sleep faster than most people changed TV channels. Even with that working for her, slipping out from between them wasn't easy. Tait roused enough to loop her by the waist with a groggy protest about keeping her close. He called her "Hoku-lulu" this time, instead of "Luna," which she wryly considered a step in the right direction, before telling him it wouldn't be pretty if she didn't pee soon. He'd let her go with no more objection and then fallen right back to sleep, thank the gods.

After that, she made a quick stop in the dining room with paper and pen in hand. She owed Leo an explanation, though she already knew he'd understand what she was about to do. In his way, her little brother had fallen just as hard for "T-Boner" and "Slash-gasm" as she had.

Now she stood outside the cottage with the keys to their rental car in hand. Though she'd followed them here in the jeep, the rental ran quieter. Still, she vacillated. What if the guys heard her starting the car? Her ass, perhaps more, would be marked for the punishment of her life.

She huffed. "Who are you kidding, Hokulani? The second you drive out of here, the punishment's a sure thing." And every bone in her body told her Tait and Kell could make punishments as bad as they were good...

A shiver vibrated down to the soles of her feet.

"Knock it off," she chastised herself. "You have the means to make this *all* go away—so get this party started and *do it*, damn it."

Without another backward glance at the cottage, she marched to the rental, got in, and drove off the base as quietly as she could.

Once she got to the highway, she opened up the engine— relatively speaking. The rental had the pickup power of three donkeys and a gopher, but it got the job done in getting her to the turn-off near Kaipo's market. The store was dark. Not a surprise. The eighties alarm clock at the cottage had done a glaringly good job of telling her what time she got out of bed, meaning that by now, it was well past midnight. The big Samoan had long ago hung the Closed sign, probably a little early in order to take advantage of the great surfing weather, before going home to his gorgeous wife and three rambunctious boys.

For a tiny moment, she tried to imagine herself in the same kind of situation. A home full of laughter. Healthy, happy kids. A husband who worshipped the ground she walked on...

That was where the dream fell apart. Trying to envision Tait *or* Kellan in that role, without the other, shattered her fantasy. She didn't want to dream of a life without loving them. She didn't want to think of an earth without them on it. Which was why she was going through with this plan.

She filled in for Kaipo at the store when he wanted to treat Natia and the boys to special trips, so it was easy to let herself into the store in order to retrieve the items she'd need. She left cash on the counter for the fire starter, flashlight, and batteries, and then locked up and made her way to the car.

Where Luna decided to pay her a fun little visit.

She shook her head to clear it of the presence, so recognizable now, who wafted into the fabric of her mind like a wisp of cool wind. Given the muggy heat of the night, she likely would've welcomed the intrusion under other circumstances. But she had a good idea of why the woman's spirit had chased her down here and now. Unlike the first two occurrences, the timing on this one sucked like rain on a Sunday.

I'm not that easy to get rid of, girlfriend.

Lani sighed. "Are you here to lecture me about how they're trained Special Forces professionals who confront danger like this every day?"

Why would I waste time on that? You already know it and are ignoring it. But I get that. I did the same thing for the exact same reason. You think this could be the op where they won't get lucky—and thank God you're here to save them from their fatal date with destiny.

She smiled into the darkness. Since she knew every rut and bump in the road between here and home, she purposely left the car's lights off, just in case Benson and Stock decided to stake an early claim on the ranch. "So you do understand," she murmured.

Sure I do.

"Thank you."

I also understand that if you get yourself captured or killed on this crazy stunt, it'll destroy Kellan.

"Damn it."

And Tait too.

"You can go away now."

Thankfully, her mind was silent after that.

Fortune smiled on her again; everything at the ranch was equally quiet.

After driving up the main road and passing the mansion, she turned down the truck road to the barn. The dirt lane was a mire of mud due to the heavier rains lately, making her doubt the decision not to take Kaipo's delivery truck for this, but she knew if Benson and his "friends" were sneaking around, the rental would lend her the most anonymity. As an extra precaution, she snagged Tait's Seahawks cap and tucked her hair beneath it. Now she appeared like every other island girl...who sneaked around a barn in the middle of the night... proclaiming her devotion to the Seahawks.

Maybe this *was* a little crazy.

But fortune didn't favor the sane. And sometimes, not even the brave. That was a good thing, because she didn't feel a lot of either as she twirled the combo lock for the barn and then opened the big red door. Clutching the flashlight for an extra dose of nerve, she made her way to the big iron storage locker that took up a good chunk of the opposite wall. The cabinet was secured with another combination lock. After she clicked in those digits and popped the shackle, the door swung back with a creak she was certain they could hear in Lihue.

She let her nervous grimace give way to a smile when the boxes she was seeking were right where she'd hoped. She flashed on the afternoon, so long ago now, when she'd found the wooden crates while cleaning out the pantry with Dad. How old had she been? Thirteen? Fourteen? No. She'd still been rocking the orthodontics, so it'd been earlier, eleven or twelve. She and Dad had snickered at seeing the red block letters, *TNT*, straight out of a Bugs Bunny cartoon, though they'd shared a thrill when they looked inside, discovering the containers really did contain the distinctive red blocks. It had been like searching a castle and finding a hidey-hole with a princess's diary inside. Where had the stuff come from? Who left it there? And why?

Their moment of glory hadn't lasted long. Mom had *not* shared their delight. She'd ordered the explosives out of the house and into the barn, where they'd remained ever since.

In the years since, Lani had always been curious about that anomaly. Three boxes of explosives stored so close to the mansion's kitchen, of all places. After what Kellan and Tait had shared with her today, the dots started to connect. The new kitchen had been built over what was known as the ranch's "first pantry," now a term she knew as code for the entry point into the house from the cave. The *TNT* was brought here as a drastic "Plan B" by the outlaws who'd used the tunnel, as a means of burying their tracks—literally—in case of pursuit by enemies.

Tonight, she was going to honor the scalawags' brilliant thinking.

She had no illusions about the damage she was about to wield. Judging from what Tait and Kell relayed about where they found the mouth of the cave, as well as the "hollow" parts of the kitchen floor that had always made her so curious, she guessed that the tunnel ran right under the observation cliff. Once the cave was imploded, the hill would crumble. Most of the orchard and rose gardens would be taken out by the slide, as well a good length of the beach access path. The explosion would also destroy half, if not all, of the main house. The barn and paddock were far enough away to be spared. Everything else would take years to rebuild. But somehow, they *would* rebuild.

And Tait and Kellan would still be alive.

As she returned to the house and offloaded the explosives to the back lanai, she paused once a minute to eavesdrop on every molecule of the night's air. All was still, the atmosphere broken only by the occasional breeze off the lazy ocean, for which she sent silent thanks to the gods. If a car came up the drive or a "visitor" approached from the beach, she'd definitely know it.

By the time she slid her key into the lock on the back door, her heartbeat eased into a tango beat instead of a salsa. She didn't use the reprieve as an excuse to let down her guard. After toeing off her shoes, she took pliant steps through the kitchen, across the dining room, and into the living room, and then held her breath to listen once more. All seemed normal. The shadows in the rooms were the same as always. The windows sighed softly from the wind, also completely normal.

She exhaled in relief.

And just as quickly girded herself with another long breath in. She'd caught a lot of lucky breaks so far, nothing to take for granted. "Surreptitious" continued to be her middle name while heaving the first box of explosives out of the car and into the house.

As she set the container down, she was richly rewarded for her mouse act.

Gunter's lord-of-the-manor baritone filtered up through the floorboards, stirring fresh bile in her stomach. He barked an order of some sort, causing a lot of frantic boot scuffles in response. She curled a tight hand to her middle and let out a conflicted rasp.

Damn it.

Why hadn't she included the possibility of people being in the tunnel when she unleashed the fire and brimstone on it? Worse, why hadn't she anticipated hitting this dilemma about turning them all into human cake batter?

All right, yes, they all worked for Gunter Benson. And if the floorboards were figuratively flipped, Gunter wouldn't waste a second on lighting the fuses for *her* doom. In many senses, he already had. Promising her as a use-and-dispose "toy" for his North Korean friend required an infusion of evil she honestly hadn't imagined in him. Maybe that was her problem. Maybe *she'd* bought the designer suit sham in a few ways, too, and now couldn't see that taking out the man and a few of his goons would be seen by some as a favor for the world.

She moaned softly and dropped her head. Her conscience had the worst timing in the world.

"Well, hello there."

The greeting, quiet even against the stillness of the house, knocked her on her butt. "Shit," she gasped, scuffling to slam her back against the wall. *"Shit."* She raised her gape at a man who looked like the cover of Asian *GQ*. "Wh-Who are—"

He interrupted her with a laugh the texture of creamed cocoa. "Gunter was right." Make that creamed tea. His voice lilted with an accent right out of Buckingham Palace. "You're quite lovely when you're—how did he phrase it?—full of sass and spit." He unbuttoned the coat of his perfectly fitted ivory suit in order to crouch in front of her. "And they say midnight snacks aren't worth the trouble."

His voice was London proper, but his gaze was raw jungle predator.

"Get out of my house," Lani spat. In the position he was in, it wouldn't be easy to get her heel into his balls, but she'd find a way.

The man released a string of cultured *tsks*. "Now, now, darling. Perhaps we've charged through the china shop prematurely." He held out a hand with elegant ease. "My name is Ayaan Tan. Now your turn."

"I know who you are, asshole. And I know why you're here." She kicked his hand away. "*Don't* come near me."

Tan gave a soft snort before pulling out a linen handkerchief and wiping his hands. He rose, stuffed the square into his breast pocket, and then clapped those hands once. Within seconds, the kitchen was blasted with light and filled with six Koreans the size of rhinos. After a flick of Tan's wrist, the men descended on her. Before Lani could think of letting out her first scream, Tan replied to her charge, in his calmest tea-hour tone, "I have no intentions of touching you, my little snack cake. Not yet, at least."

CHAPTER TWENTY-ONE

"When I get my hands on that woman's ass again, it's going to get stripped, spanked, and flogged into a couple of red, throbbing—"

Kellan cut into Tait's tirade with a harsh grunt. When his friend stopped trying to turn the sand in front of the cottage into glass with his heated pacing, Kell jerked his head up at the lanai. A groggy-eyed Leo stood on the porch.

"What the hell's going on?" the teen moaned. "Sounds like you two are doing a damn *hula p'iumauma* out here."

Kellan lifted a scowl at the kid. There was no sense in sugarcoating this. "If that means wanting to throttle your sister, then you just nailed it."

Leo stopped rubbing his eyes. "Shit. Where is she?"

Tait stomped up the stairs and thrust the note at the kid. "Sorry we poached it out of your room, but when we couldn't find her, we thought she may have gone to check on you."

Leo studied the letter with a face that widened in surprise and then darkened in dread. Kell imagined Tait's face and his must've carried the same expression five minutes ago, during their own stunned reading.

Mafileokaveka...my brother Leo...

This isn't easy for me to write, but you more than everyone else can understand I've given this a lot of thought. Dangerous men want to get their hands on Hale Anelas, people who are only going to start on you and me before they try to destroy the whole country, using our island and our home as their command post. Tait, Kellan, and their friends from the 5th SFGA are convinced they'll be able to stop these monsters, but the thought of more death in the air at the ranch, especially theirs, is a horror I couldn't bear. If I destroy what Benson and his friends want the most, the access tunnel from the beach, the core of their treasure will be gone, and we'll be free from their awful plans.

I'm going to use the explosives from the barn to do this. You know what this means for the majority of the ranch as we know it. I'd beg you to forgive me for destroying our home, but in reality, all I'm blowing up is our ranch. Home is the place in our hearts that's always reserved for each other. Whether we rebuild here or our life's journey takes us elsewhere, you are always my kaikaina, my beloved brother.

I won't ask you to keep this a secret from Tait and Kell. There's a good chance they've taken it from your room and read it by now anyways. They have taught me a great deal about trusting the wisdom in people, no matter how insane that might feel. Maybe it's time for the teachers to revisit their own lesson.

I'll see all three of you again soon. I promise.

~Lani

When Leo looked up from the note, his gaze carried a thousand questions and a shit ton of shock. "Is she fucking serious?"

Neither he nor Tait chastened the kid for the language.

Five minutes ago, they'd been spouting much more colorful expressions.

"Our rental car is gone," Kellan admitted. "And we can only assume she hasn't gone for a soda run to the market."

Leo fell against the wall. The note shook in his hands. "I can't lose her too, you guys."

Tait hauled the boy into a hug. "We're not going to let that happen, dude." He followed it up by swinging a damning stare at Kell. "This wouldn't be happening if I'd gone after Stock three hours ago."

Kellan didn't know whether to pick incredulous or enraged as a reaction. What the fuck, why choose? "Let me get this straight. As your best friend, I *wasn't* supposed to talk you out of one of the most dumbass decisions of your life?"

Tait stomped to the edge of the lanai and stabbed a finger downward. "If I was out there right now, instead of her—"

"It'd still be an idiot's move made by your pride and ego instead of your reason and good sense." He planted his feet and curled his fists. Last time he checked, his call sign wasn't Scapegoat. "You want to swing the flogger at her, man? Be sure to smack your own ass first, you fucking hypocrite."

"What the hell does that mean?"

Kell narrowed his eyes. "It's a pod called stupid—and the two peas mashed in it are my best friend and the love of my life." He tossed an uncomfortable glance at the kid still propped against the wall. "Sorry, Leo. I pictured telling you under really different conditions."

The kid flung back his normal wise-ass grimace. "Why? 'Cause you think I didn't figure it out already?" He jerked his chin at Tait. "I got your number too, T-Boner. You moon at Lani worse than he does."

Tait kicked at the wall and growled, "Fuck."

"Shut it," Leo retorted. "You both make her happy, and that makes *me* happy. But you're both wasting time acting my age instead of yours. What the hell are we going to do? Should we call Franzen again?"

"*No.*" Kellan's bellow coordinated note-for-note with Tait's. Franz would go ballistic from the news. Literally. Within minutes, he'd have every active-duty police cruiser on the island barreling at Hale Anelas, destroying the requirement for subterfuge still needed here.

By instinct, they followed up the command by locking stares. Kellan instantly read Tait's mind—and now his heart, as well—and also recognized how deeply T understood his.

They had to get to the ranch as fast as possible.

Best-case scenario: they found the woman before she attempted a technical-as-shit explosives operation, preventing her from an unintended suicide mission.

Worst-case scenario number one: they came upon the ranch already in flames, without a sighting of Lani.

Worst-case scenario number two: they didn't find flames *or* Lani, meaning Stock and Tan had gotten to her first.

No matter what "prize" fate held in store, their shared stare confirmed a single, unalterable reality. If they didn't work together, they would fail at the single most important mission of their lives.

CHAPTER TWENTY-TWO

Why the fuck couldn't he remember how to breathe?

Tait slammed his eyes shut for a moment, consciously calling up the relaxation techniques that were normally as natural as breathing to him, especially during a high-intensity op. *Slow your heart rate. Calmness flows in; tension pours out. Center your gravity and your thoughts.*

Fuck relaxation.

He drove a fist into the ranch's kitchen wall, just in case the universe needed to be clear on his viewpoint. Three feet away, Kellan and Leo crouched near the box of *TNT*, still unopened, in the middle of the floor. A foot away from that, in the middle of the scuff marks on the floor that could have only been made by battle-grade boots, was Lani's cell phone, purposefully crushed by one of those boots.

"Fuck." Leo visibly trembled once more. "Wh-What the hell happened?"

Tait let Kellan attempt an answer to that. "You remember the asshat we told you about? Gunter Benson's silent business partner?"

"Cameron Stock?"

"Yeah." Kell used the excuse of getting in a nod in order to scramble his composure. "It looks like he might have been waiting here for her, and—"

"Now he's got her."

The teen uttered it with finality, having clearly expected

this possibility. Tait's gut turned over. He personally knew what it was like to have half a world of pain shoved down your throat before hitting sixteen, but fate was force-feeding Leo the other half. He twisted his fist against the wall to keep from going to the kid and pulling him into a hug. He had no doubt Leo would be fine at holding together the waterworks; he just didn't trust his own shit right now.

"Yeah." Kell attended the dirty work of making the confession. "He's probably got her."

"And we have no idea where they've gone."

"No. We don't."

Kell practically retched the words. Tait could empathize. Despite the chaos in his gut, he reached to clap his friend on the shoulder. Might as well fuck every mission protocol they could, right? But he wasn't going to stand on "suggested procedure" when those three words, more than any whisper the man had given Lani in the bedroom, told him exactly how deeply Kellan had fallen for the woman—and how thoroughly his heart was breaking now.

Leo snapped his head up. "Hey," he grated. "Do you guys hear—"

Kell cut him off by slashing across his throat with one finger. He motioned Tait to kill the lights with the other. Not needed. Tait was already at the switch, plunging them into darkness as the sounds got closer. Boot stomps, at least six pairs. Male grunts. And a woman's terrified whimpers.

Lani.

Leo jolted to his feet, a battle grimace already plastered on his face. Thankfully, not all Tait's training had deserted him. With barely a sound, he subdued the kid and flattened him to the wall. If Stock, Benson, Tan, and their men were headed back here, the only advantage they'd have on the crowd was the element of surprise.

The party seemed to be coming closer. Tait regulated his breaths and noticed Kell doing the same. They exchanged a grim look. If the shit went down in here, they'd end up having to Bruce Lee their way through these assholes. It'd be bloody, messy, and dirty.

It sounded like the posse was nearly on top of them now. *But where were they?* Kell narrowed his gaze in perplexity. Tait threw back the look, until Leo caught their attention with a wave. The kid stabbed a finger at the floorboards. Tait dropped his jaw as comprehension hit.

The bad guys weren't on top of them. They were below.

In wordless tandem with Kell, he dropped to the floor. With his ear locked to the boards, he could tell Lani had been gagged or duct-taped. The anger beneath her whines filled him with both pride and terror. The heat of the first and the chill of the second made his jaw clench and his nerves race, but he forced his body to comply with the focus of his mind. On the Indonesian op, he'd made a huge mistake because of misplaced emotions, and an innocent had bled. The penance for his sin this time would be Lani's life.

He concentrated on the men's voices. Their exact words were fuzzy because of the boards, but he discerned Stock's gruff baritone as well as Tan's tearoom lilt. There was a third voice in the conversation. It wasn't Benson's arrogant tone, though something about it rang familiar in his gut.

He glanced at Kell, wondering if his friend recognized the speaker. The guy's hunched brows told him he wrestled with the same bafflement.

Without a sound, he rolled to Leo. Into the kid's ear, he

whispered, "Tell me there's at least one loose board in this floor."

Pay dirt. Leo was able to indicate a board nearby. Two of its rusty nails were gone. If they could loosen the other two, they'd be able to lift the board out and have a visual into the cavern below. The goal gained more urgency during the minutes it took for Kellan to slither into the kitchen, grab a butter knife as a makeshift screwdriver, and return. During that gap, Lani's whimpers fell into silence. *Not* a great development. On top of that, the strange nag in Tait's senses worsened. Why did his senses react so strongly to the third voice in the cave? Who did that familiar timbre belong to?

Luck was their lady one more time. Kell started working in earnest at the rusty nails, not having to worry about any wayward sounds from his efforts due to an argument that flared between Stock and Tan.

"Has anyone checked the entrance lately?" Stock's initial bark seemed directed at his men. "What the fuck am I paying you come-stains for? Everyone afraid they'll get their pretty boots all dirty?"

"Don't stress, Cam." The reply came from *that* voice. Tait strained to listen harder, but when mystery man finished, he'd paced at least ten feet down the tunnel. "I'm on it."

"Thanks, man." Stock still sounded more stressed than grateful. He trundled back toward the area where Tan seemed to be positioned. "Okay, where the hell were we? Oh, yeah. You were going to tell me why you're being so goddamn intractable."

Tan erupted in a fierce snarl to preface his comeback. "Big and impressive words, Cameron, but they don't accomplish a bloody thing." He unfurled a dark growl. "I am awash in disappointment by the turn of all these events and by you in particular this evening. Less than twenty-four hours ago, you met me here and supported my approach. Now, you don't have half the water for it."

"There's nothing wrong with my goddamn 'water,' you Korean kook. Glare in the mirror if you're calling anyone's nerve into question. This crazy cluster—"

"Would not even be a 'cluster' had you and Gunter done your jobs. Tonight, the man has become a feast for the sharks as his payment for the mess. But you've been valuable to me in the past, and I'd like to benefit from your special gifts in the future, as well."

"Then take the benefit of my advice now, goddamnit. This bitch's stubborn streak is longer than her hair. You can beat her and fuck her six ways until Sunday, but all that'll get you is a couple of wasted hours. She's not going to sign until you let me use my contacts at the base to grab that guppy brother of hers. Once you bring him back here, cut off a few of his fingers, and threaten to do the same to his balls. I guarantee she'll sign anything you want, including her own suicide note. How's that for my *boiling* water, buddy?"

Kellan finally popped the nails from the board. On his nod, Tait helped him lift the wood out, securing them a window that measured about three feet long by six inches wide—just in time for them to witness what Stock's threat did to Lani's face.

And to flood Tait's soul with the lust to kill the man for it.

They could only see her eyes and nose due to the duct tape wrapped around her head and across her mouth, but that was enough to know that their girl was past terrified. She shivered from head to toe despite being sandwiched between two burly guards who held her by the elbows, probably the same assholes who'd stripped her to nothing but her black bra and panties.

Her wrists were bound together in an expert bondage shackle, and her ankles were encased in leather cuffs with O rings. It didn't take a big leap of imagination for Tait to construe why.

Fuck, fuck, fuck.

In an instant, all the threats he'd promised for her ass were wiped from his mind. For all her fire and fanfare, Lani possessed one of the most pure and open souls he knew. She had no concept about the wickedness that thrived in the world, in the form of vermin like Stock. It tore at Tait's spirit to watch her get a hideous dose of that lesson now, demonstrated in her horror-filled eyes and flaring, frantic nostrils. One glance at Kell confirmed he sailed in the same boat of dread.

Tan paced back into their line of vision. His face looked gaunt, thinned by anger and waning patience. "Tell me, then. How long will it take to activate these 'contacts' of yours at the base?"

Stock stepped forward. "A couple of hours at most." His hands were clasped like a priest about to hear confession or a waiter attending a wine order. Either way, the pose added to the weirdness of the evil being conspired below. Tait scowled at Kellan, who nodded his agreement. They'd wisely kept Leo back against the wall and planned on keeping things that way until they determined what their plan would be from here.

"I see," Tan returned. His own hands rested in the pockets of his ivory suit, which remained pristine despite the grungy surroundings. Maybe the man *had* signed a pact with the devil. "And in those two hours, you don't think that her two soldier friends will have gotten half a clue about what's going on? You believe the two idiots will just invite your mates in for a beer before they snatch up Leo for the road?"

Stock rocked from foot to foot, clearly conceding the point

to Tan. As he did, Tait looked again to Kellan. His buddy's face reflected the dark concern creeping through his own veins. The slur didn't matter. They'd been called worse than idiots before, and being underestimated was actually a favor. But they also could have used the extra two hours that Stock's plan would have afforded. Now they'd be lucky to get two minutes.

If Tan's will prevailed, it would be even less. The man left their angle of vision for a long moment. When he walked back into view, he carried a bullwhip at least five feet long. In serene silence, he let the leather unfurl. With even more grace, he brought the handle back and let the leather fly with a fluid coordination of his elbow and wrist. The popper *smacked* the air directly over Lani's head, causing even her two henchmen to flinch. Lani's eyes widened. A violent quiver claimed her whole body.

Tait swallowed hard as nausea seared his stomach once more. Had he been witnessing a Dom in the Bastille dungeon back at home, he would have labeled Tan's expertise a thing of beauty, but in the cavern below, the monster provided proof of how easily Dominance could be perverted into abuse. Once more, Tan drew back the whip. When the leather dropped this time, it took a sharp nick at Lani's waist. Her scream pushed at the duct tape, and she started breathing harder.

"As you can tell, Miss Kail, I'm a bit of an enthusiast when it comes to beautifully made long tails...and the ways I can paint a woman's skin with them." Tan glided his fingers down the braided leather as he strolled over to personally inspect his handiwork. He ran a thumb across the bloom of blood he'd induced and then sucked the stuff off with a sigh of pleasure. As Lani sagged like she was going to be sick, the man added, "But I am also a fair man, darling. Sign the papers now, turning over all of Hale Anelas to Benstock as a free-and-clear gift from your generous heart, and this single stroke will be the only kiss you get from my kangaroo hide. It would sadden me to give up the pleasure of playing with you tonight, but I've been assured my hunger will be sated with other willing ladies on the island. As they say, the choice rests in your hands."

It was torment to watch Lani's reaction, but Tait forced himself to the task, hoping she could feel his gaze, his support, and his longing to tear up these boards and leap on Tan with his knife at the ready. The misery on her face tore him apart. The tears pouring from her closed eyes were like silver prayers before a death she'd clearly resigned herself to. Why would she think otherwise? Tan intended on killing her, no matter what. He'd simply let her decide whether he whipped and raped her first. She'd escape the torment of the assault by accepting the agony of signing over her home.

"Damn it, dreamgirl." His whisper came from the depths of his soul. "Don't give up!"

Thank every one of her gods, she somehow found that fortitude. He and Kellan watched, grins growing, as she suddenly straightened her spine and jerked from the hold of the guard to her right. In the seconds it took the guy to realize what she'd done, she rammed her bound hands up into Tan's nose. The two grunts she issued with it were delivered with the emphasis unique to only one insult.

"No, darling," Tan returned with a bitter laugh, "fuck *you*—which is what I'll be very happy to do, once I've taken a few layers of skin off your pretty body."

During the exchange, Tait felt Leo moving closer to their peephole. Though it ravaged his heart to let the kid stay, it would be even more wrong to shove him back like some five-year-old. Kellan didn't object, either, though the guy had to smash a hand over Leo's mouth when the teen went ballistic at Tan's declaration. Kell gripped the back of the kid's neck, forcing Leo to stay locked to his dictatorial stare. He mouthed two words. *Not helping.*

"Strip her," Tan ordered his guards below. "Then secure her to the post. There's a spreader bar on the table; clip her ankles onto that. Make sure it's pinned at the widest setting."

Leo's chest pumped in furious heaves. He flung Kell's hand away and zapped a glare of silver rage at them both. "How much longer are we going to sit here?" His whisper was harsh. "He's going to peel off her skin with that thing! And then screw her like a whore!"

Tait jabbed a finger toward the main part of the kitchen, wordlessly ordering Leo and Kell to follow him there. They had a half wall and the refrigerator helping to muffle their exchange from Tan.

"Leo, we copy you on the concern, but—"

"But what?" the kid seethed. "We're standing around with our dicks in our hands while Lani—"

In one sweep, Kell pinned the teen to the refrigerator. "Take a chill, Simba. We know the goddamn circumstances. But in case you weren't looking, the man has an army of guard apes. We charge in there with nothing but our battle cries and Bowie knives, you'll end up watching your sister get tortured and killed on the mound of our carcasses."

Tait stepped over, giving Kellan a let-me-give-it-a-try look. "You remember the day we first met?" he challenged Leo. "And the issues you were having with Isis? You remember how we worked together, did it smarter instead of harder?"

Leo mashed together his lips but finally returned, "Fine.

So do you guys have anything 'smarter, not harder' in mind?"

Tait looked to Kell. The guy's face was stone, but he wasn't capable of hiding the anguish in his eyes as Lani's panicked cries filtered up to them. Things were going to get worse, in a very fast way, if they didn't do something soon.

As in right now.

Shit. Karma had a sick sense of humor. He was asking Kell to totally separate head and heart, a task he'd totally screwed the pooch on in Indonesia. But now the stakes were higher. Lani's life was on the line. He prayed that his friend could reach deeper inside than he'd been capable of during the failure in Indonesia. *Become* my *hero now, Slash—and hers. I swear to you I'm here a hundred percent this time.*

Thank fuck. The universe was listening this time, and so was Kell's spirit. Between one blink and the next, the guy narrowed his gaze, squared his jaw, and turned into Tait's mission-centric buddy again. "The Remington's still in the trunk of the rental car," he stated in a bullet-hard tone. Tait was a little surprised Kell hadn't called the rifle by its nickname, "sweet baby." The guy had worked so extensively with the weapon, he could shoot a flea off a dog from a thousand yards away. "All we need to do is flush the bastard out of the tunnels," Kellan supplied. "If he hits the beach where we were last night, I'll have no trouble picking him up on my night scope."

"You can stage up on the cliff," Leo interjected. "Yeah. It'd give you perfect height and invisibility."

Tait turned with a fast glance of appraisal. The kid's aspirations to West Point didn't sound so cray-cray anymore.

"But getting him out is still the boner killer." Kell frowned. "As much as I love Lani for leaving enough fire power to turn this place into a mile-wide kill zone, the goal here is to save her, not seal her in with those asstards."

"I can help with that one." Leo was still a glowing isotope of impatience, but now his energy had direction. "We have a compost bin off the back lanai. After all the rain we've had lately, everything in there is going to be really damp. Light that shit on fire, and we've got instant smoke."

"Instant *putrid* smoke," Tait elaborated.

"Excellent," Kell concluded. "Make it happen, kid."

Leo had bounded three steps across the kitchen before stopping in his tracks and throwing them a scowl. "What if that asshole flees but leaves Lani in the cave?"

Kellan, fully fortified in the steely shell of ops mind-set, shook his head. "Not going to happen unless Tan's a complete nimrod. He'll know Lani's his insurance policy out of the trap and use her as a human shield. But just in case the guy did eat paint chips for dinner, you're going to stay here and serve as eyes and ears at this end." He leveled a stern stare at the kid. "If any of those choads finds their way out through here, you kick the bin over, turn them into flaming compost casserole, then get your ass down to the barn and hide there until one of us comes for you. Got it?"

"Yeah." The teen's face lit up with a mix of excitement and anxiety. "Got it."

"You sure? This isn't normal procedure, but I need T-Bomb on that ridge with me, so we have to rely on you, Leo. If you dick around, your sister will have *our* gonads diced, pickled, and put in a jar on display next to the kitchen fruit bowl."

The kid's face sobered. The consequence Kellan painted was closer to the truth than all three of them cared to admit. "I'm sure, Slash." No "gasm" as an addendum this time. "You can count on me."

"All right," Tait ordered. "Let's roll."

Once they were outside, he told himself to shove Lani, and the first lashes she was likely getting from Tan, from his mind. It was harder than he thought. No, it was fucking impossible. Somewhere between moving the explosives outside, helping Leo haul in the compost bin, and assisting Kell with the rifle load-up, the realization hit. He was in love with Hokulani Kail as much as Kellan was.

And he may never have the chance to tell her.

Focus. You can't afford not to, Bommer.

"Okay." Now standing in the kitchen again, he handed over the fire starter to Leo. "Is your phone on voice radio mode?"

"Yes, sir," the kid answered.

"There's no time to brief you on all the shit you're being called to keep track of, so your common sense and your brain are going to be your best friends right now." He tapped the teen's forehead. "Use this"—and then tapped his chest—"and not this. Got it?"

"Yeah." Leo was admirably solemn. "Yeah, I got it."

"Cool fries."

He reached out to fist bump the kid. Leo didn't meet the gesture. "Hey. Give one more thing to me straight-up."

Tait nodded, also somber. "Sure."

"If that scumsucker is using Lani as a shield, then Kellan has to be damn accurate with the kill shot, right?"

Tait clapped a hand on Leo's shoulder again. "I'm his spotter. We do this all the time, Leo." Well, they *had* been doing it all the time. They hadn't succeeded at a challenge shot like this in well over a year. But the synchronicity they'd shared lately, burnished to perfection by their partnership in loving

Lani, was in its best form ever. Had either of them expected to put it to the test this soon? In a situation like this? The answer was obvious. Of course not. But sometimes in life, especially their lives, there wasn't a choice about being ready for the big test. You simply had to plow deep and find that readiness.

"I get that." Leo clearly excavated his gut for his own courage. "But it's two in the morning. And that beach is dark. Is...is Slash-gasm that good?"

Tait might have been unsure about how to answer the kid's first question, but his reply now was a no-brainer. "Yeah, Leo. He's that good."

CHAPTER TWENTY-THREE

Lani's eyes burned with tears. Her throat burned from screaming. Her ass and back burned with pain. Tan was only three strokes in to his promise of stripping the flesh off her body, one whip lash at a time, and she wondered how many more of his terrible grunts, followed by the whir of the leather and the fire on her flesh, would come before his goal was accomplished.

Something else burned now too. Her lungs.

"What the fuck?" The guard standing nearest to her, who'd been enjoying Tan's show with a prominent hard-on, pushed off the cave wall. Lani blinked at him, only to wonder what was going wrong with her vision. Everything was covered in a weird gray haze that thickened by the second. "Christ almighty, what's that stench?"

As if cued to do so, the rest of Tan's henchmen began coughing and wheezing. Lani ducked her head, trying to take shallow breaths herself. It smelled like the cave had contracted the flu and now hurled on all of them. The camp lanterns looked like glowing chunks of puke as the guards grabbed them in desperate efforts to locate the source of the stench.

"I think it's coming from above," one of the men called. "Someone's in the mansion, and they know damn well that we're here!"

"Let me drill their ass with lead, Tan. This'll be fun."

"Idiot," Tan snarled. "It will also be suicide. If you break the wrong supports to that kitchen, we'll be buried down here."

"Shit."

"In a word, yes." The man raised his voice into a shout. "Everyone out! Now!"

Lani couldn't contain her reacting sob. She'd take the smoke and stench over Tan's new proximity, less than a foot away from her. She flinched as he unfastened her ankles from the spreader. He made her worst nightmare come true by unhooking her wrists from the posts and then yanking her back against him.

"Just a wild guess, darling, but I'd say your boyfriends want to join our little party." His growl was low and menacing as he latched a possessive hand on to one of her bare breasts. "So let's make sure their favorite guest makes an appearance."

His brutal hold intensified her pain, but she clung to a new hope. This twist had Tait's and Kellan's ingenuity written all over it. Had they truly bucked their orders from Franz? Were they really here? She could almost feel their presence on the air. Maybe if she set her mind free a little more and tried to hear an assurance from that cool wind of a voice again... *Aue.* Who the hell was she kidding? If Luna *had* returned, Lani couldn't hear past the hammers of pain in her body, the heavy grunts of her captor, and the cavernous echoes of their steps through the long black tunnel.

When they burst out onto the beach, a thousand feelings blasted at once. She wanted to weep at the sky, having given up on ever seeing its splendor again. But she wobbled, suddenly cold, as the wind slammed her nakedness and bit into her wounds. She also peered around in confusion. Not a single one of Tan's goons had waited for him. But there was no sign of Tait, Kellan, or any police or military support, either.

Only two people stood there: Cameron Stock and the man who'd replaced Gunter in their scheme. Just as young and well-tailored as Gunter, Shane—who was so trendy, he apparently had no last name—wore his chestnut hair a little longer and his suits a little looser but shared Gunter's vigilant gaze and Gatsby-like indifference to everything that didn't pertain to their plan. In short, he was a perfectly pretty successor to Gunter—and Lani hoped he met the same fate too. The sharks could always use some extra dinner.

"What the hell are you still doing with her?" Shane barked. "We need to cut liabilities, *all* of them, right now."

"He's right," Stock added. "The car's waiting next to the sand around the next bend. My contacts at the base have arranged for a private transport to get us to LA, where I've got a thousand corners for us to hide in. Let her go and let's get the fuck out of here."

Lani prayed Tan would see their logic, despite its roots in five hundred versions of evil, and toss her aside. "I-I won't say anything," she croaked. "I-I promise."

"Oh, there's nothing for you to say, honey." Stock's tone was smooth and snide. "They'd only need you for picking us out in a lineup, which is never going to happen."

Dread crashed through her as Tan let out a roar and twisted his hold tighter. "No! She has one more purpose to us, and I'm going to take full advantage of it!"

Stock huffed. "What the hell are you—"

"Those two Special Forces wankers are going to pay for what they've cost me—in the most devastating manner their poor little hearts can imagine."

Lani shivered harder. This time, her quivers had nothing to do with the wind and everything to do with raw terror. Tan made sure that point stuck when slamming his pistol to her temple.

No, no, no!

"Wait." Shane's voice punched through her mental and physical ice. "Her two 'soldier' friends are *Spec Ops*?" The man stomped over and yanked at Tan. The Korean almost fell backward, decimating Lani's own balance. She only stayed upright through the desperate force of Tan's grip, clawing furiously into her flesh. "Tan, you have to ditch this bitch and move on *right* now," Shane commanded. "I guarantee there are rifle coordinates being dialed in on your skull as we speak."

Tan laughed with urbane glee. "Is that so, sweet Shane? My, my, you get a little hot under the collar when talking about those boys in uniform. Did you know one, perhaps? Did you put on your *dress blues* for him? Did he tell you about his *secret missions* and show you his *special guns*?"

Lani prayed Shane's patience had a breaking point and Tan had just breached it. A skirmish between the two men would be perfect in so many ways. If Shane's allegation was true, Kellan and Tait *were* here, waiting on the cliffs for their perfect chance to take Tan down for good. The sooner she could get out of their way, the better.

But damn it, Shane had to be as emotionally untouchable as she'd originally assumed.

"Drop her, Tan." The man's stance was as rigid as his voice. "You've poked worse than a hornet's nest, and you're not going to win."

"He's right," Stock growled. "If you want a voice of firsthand experience as validation, let me be it. Lor and I were ten minutes out from success on our plan in LA, and those Spec Ops motherfuckers dropped in on us like a machine."

"Shut up," Tan snapped. "Just shut the bloody hell up, Cameron!"

Stock shook his head and blew out a hard breath. "I'll do you one better, you insane asswipe. I'm out of here."

"He's right." Shane rushed up again. "You're being insane, Tan. You can't do this. Let Cameron get you off the island and into LA, and we'll regroup on a new plan. Killing this woman in cold blood isn't going to help a fucking thing."

Tan's grip slipped a little. With a rush of relief, Lani collapsed to her knees, only to be held captive again by the monster's hand twisting a fistful of her hair. Tan jerked her head back until her vision was filled with nothing but the stars—and the barrel of his gun between her eyes.

"Poor, stupid Shane," he muttered. "You're mistaken. This does help. So many things."

Lani's limbs went numb. Her blood ran with ice. But suddenly, strangely, she was warm again. The stars reached down to her, bringing the light and fire of two special stars with them. The first, with his gray gaze and fierce devotion, she slipped into her heart. The second, with his golden eyes and open spirit, she dropped into her soul.

She smiled.

Right before a single shot pierced the night.

She took a breath, bracing for the burst of white light to welcome her through the veils of existence. It didn't come. Instead, her senses resounded a deep, anguished cry—her own. Only blackness and stillness surrounded her.

But then she noticed the stars again. And the sea. And the trees, flittering softly in the wind. And then the man, Shane, kneeling next to her—only he wasn't himself. Soft concern lit up his caramel-colored eyes with tiny gold flecks. His mouth lifted at her in a gentle smile.

Even though Ayaan Tan lay flat in the sand next to her, with a bullet hole in his head.

"Oh, my God." She pushed away from him. "Oh, my God."

"Ssshhh. Careful." Shane cupped her shoulders. His hands were shockingly warm. Strong. And caring? He stripped off his suit jacket and folded it around her. "You okay?"

"Y-Yeah." Her breath left her in stunned spurts. "What the hell happ—"

A loud *zzzzzzz* cut her short. Appearing in the trees just a hundred feet away, riding the Hale Anelas recreational zip line like a pro, was Kellan. The sight of him made her heart surge and her body hum despite all its physical agony. He hit the landing platform and started shimmying down the ladder, preceding Tait by only a fast minute. His sniper Remington rifle was still strapped to his back.

"Shit." Shane spewed the word as he shot to his feet.

"Wh-What?" Lani questioned. "What's wrong?"

Kellan arrived, having sprinted across the sand to her. He shucked his gun and hit his knees in the sand, grabbing her with the fervency of a starving man who'd arrived at an oasis. Lani sighed into his mouth as he kissed her with matching hunger, finally letting her go in order to lift his eyes to Shane.

"You should seriously get out of here," he told the guy.

"Yeah," Shane said. "Probably."

"What the hell?" Lani queried. "Why?"

Tait arrived now, also at a top-speed run—that he continued into a full body check against Shane. Lani shrieked, confused and stunned, as the two men rolled into the sand. Shane's kindness, although brief, stirred her enough to try to pull Tait up. Wasn't happening. Tait was lost to a haze of rage.

He pulled back his arm, curled a fist, and drove it into Shane's face before she could stop him.

"Tait," she screamed. "*Lawa!* Enough!"

The man ignored her, preparing to punch Shane again.

"Tait!" Shane yelled. "Listen!"

The air left her lungs. Her jaw dropped. She snapped her gape toward Kellan. "How does he know who Tait is?"

"It was you," Tait roared, "wasn't it? In the cave, with Stock and Tan. 'Handling things' for them. *Working* with them!"

Tait went in for two more blows, but Shane successfully dodged both. It was clear to Lani now; the guy had a lot of experience fighting Tait, able to interpret and evade each of his moves. That expertise would've been gleaned by a friend of Tait's, not a fashionista criminal boy working for a creep like Cameron Stock.

What was going on?

Finally, Shane crawled free and popped to his feet. Tait didn't give up. He snarled and readied to rush Shane again.

"Don't think it, T." He issued the words from gritted teeth. "I *will* drop you. We both know I can."

"What. The. Hell?" Lani blurted again.

Her words didn't falter Tait by an inch. With his chest heaving and his eyes blazing, he seethed. "I should just let you do it. Drop me and pummel me, you asshole, because that'll give me perfect justification for killing *you* with my bare hands!"

Shane wiped blood off his lip with the back of his hand. "Neither is going to happen."

"No? And why the fuck not?" Tait's hands turned into white-capped fists at his sides. "You're working with *Cameron Stock*—and with the man who had a gun at the head of the woman I love!" He pushed his head forward, staring hard at Shane. "Does that concept even get to you anymore? Do you remember the hell I went through after Luna, how I despaired of ever *feeling* anything again, let alone knowing love? Well, God's brought me another miracle—and tonight, she almost died as I watched. As *you* watched, goddamnit!"

Lani grabbed the edges of Shane's coat and pulled them tighter as tears came again. She bowed her head, needing to be alone with this crazy moment. *Tait loved her.* Yet he stood there, trembling from the effort of reining back his murderous rage at Shane.

"I wouldn't have let that happen," Shane leveled, "and damn it, you know it." While Tait flung back only a bitter silence, the man slowly straightened and brushed off his pants. "I have to leave now, Tait. And you're going to let me."

Tait chuffed. "Right. You have to leave. Because Cameron fucking Stock is waiting for you, isn't he?"

Shane clenched his jaw. Sharper lights intensified in his eyes, almost turning them pure gold with his anger. "There's more at play here than you understand. You're going to have to trust me."

The guy didn't say anything else. Lani gawked again at Kellan as Tait visibly shook, clearly abhorring himself for every step Shane took back up the beach. Tait stayed that way even after the man disappeared around the curve in the shore. Lani stepped toward him, but Kellan shook his head a little, indicating Tait had to wage his own battle with this particular demon—who, in the end, hadn't been much of a monster at all. She ran her knuckles down one collar of Shane's jacket. It smelled a lot like the cave, at least before the universe started to barf inside it, with a faint touch of cedar and citrus.

"Tait?" she finally murmured. "Talk to me...please. What's going on? Do you know Shane?"

Tait lowered to the sand next to her. His gaze was still fixed at the darkness that had swallowed up Shane. "Yeah," he stated. "I do know him. But his name's not Shane. It's Shay. Shay Bommer. He's my brother."

CHAPTER TWENTY-FOUR

"I never thought six weeks could feel like six years."

Though Lani meant every woeful note of it, all she got in the way of sympathy from Franz was a snort and a long eye roll. "Heaven help us," he muttered, keeping half an eye on the baseball game playing on his new widescreen TV. "Little sister's gotten herself some regular kissin' on the *kahakai*, and now we all have to deal with the moony-faced fallout."

"*Psshh*." Leo flopped onto the couch next to him. "You've only been here a few days. Try living with the *wahine*. And no, the new kitchen remodel *isn't* keeping her occupied enough."

Franzen chuffed. "Better you than me, little broheim."

"Hey." She locked hands to her hips and flashed an accusing glare. "Who's made all the Johnny Franzen favorites for dinner tonight?"

Franz rolled his eyes the other way. "Only because they happen to be Bommer and Rush's favorites, as well."

"*Bah*." Lani tossed a dish towel at them as she moved through the living room but was unable to prevent a playful smile from breaking through.

"There she goes again," Leo mumbled.

"Yeah," Franz concurred. He cocked his head at her. "And it's always worse when she walks this way." His eyes widened. "Heeyyy... The three of you didn't do anything crazy on my couch back in July, did you?"

"Crazy like what?" Leo scowled and took a sip of his

soda—before choking on the liquid and leaping to his feet again. "Oh *yeezuss*, no! I do *not* need a visual on that shit."

Lani snapped her fingers. "*Language.*"

"Seriously? After what *you* did on this couch?"

She was saved from the downward spiral of the conversation by a crunch of tires in the drive. "They're here." She didn't intend it to sound like a teenybopper squeal, but she wasn't going to waste time on an apology, either. "They're here, they're here, they're—"

She was cut off first by Tait, who swept her up into his arms and mashed her lips in a tongue-twister of a kiss. Kellan barely gave her a moment to breathe before he swept in, repeating the assault with fierce hunger. She finally pulled back to stare at them both, a little stunned to see them still wearing their BDUs, complete with boots, dog tags, and regulation caps.

"Errr...wow. I didn't realize your side trip to Honolulu meant you'd be working."

When they'd last been on Skype together, the guys told her that they'd be returning to the island a few days after Franzen, due to a "necessary stopover" they had to take in the state's capital. She'd been giddy with the news, thinking they'd gotten word from Kellan's buddy at the permits office that at last cleared Hale Anelas for B and B status. Her pleas to Franz for information had been met with the man's smirking silence. He only revealed that the guys had a damn great surprise for her, an offering that went a long way toward earning his approval on their "unique" situation. He'd stopped short of confessing they'd won his complete sanction, but Lani deduced that story would be the same if she brought home the Dalai Lama on one arm and the Pope on the other.

By noon today, she'd been *very* ready for her surprise.

The BDUs were *not* what she'd expected.

"Sorry about the work threads," Tait murmured.

"We didn't want to waste the time on changing them," Kellan added.

"We had more pressing reasons to get home."

"Well, one."

Silver lights of mischief danced in Kell's eyes. Tait countered that with a mocking scowl, twisting his lips into extremely kissable angles. "And technically, we're not 'home.'"

Lani forced herself to ignore his lips in favor of a chastising glare. "That's because you guys told me to meet you *here*, remember? And if you tell me it's because you want to spend the evening watching Johnny's new widescreen, you can even forget dinner."

"We don't give a shit about the TV, Starshine."

Kellan emphasized it by leaning and nuzzling her neck. When he pulled back, they traded a fast version of the broheim-sneaky-spidey look, resulting in their matched set of devious grins.

Tait explained, "We asked you to meet us here because we wanted to see your face when you walk back home...with this."

Lani followed the direction of his nodding head to the sheet of paper now in Kellan's grasp. The Hawaii state seal gleamed on top.

Lani gasped and then screamed. She brushed back tears, hardly believing the sheet was real. Their grins grew as she took it with both hands, reading every boring word as if they were a magical incantation.

"State of Hawaii...official permit...recognition of historical bed-and-breakfast..." She hopped up and down and then tried to jump them both. Neither man complained, since the awkward lunges gave them chances to "steady" her with their hands all over her anatomy. "Thank you," she sobbed. "Thank you, thank you, thank you!" She looked up to see her brother strolling out of the lanai, pretending to barf all over Franz because of their open affection. "*Kaikaina!* Look; look! It's finally happening!"

Her brother kicked up his chin at Tait and then Kell. "Congratulations, Sergeants," he drawled. "You've turned my sister into a squee'ing ball of joy, and you haven't even gotten to the good part yet."

As wonderful as their chests felt under her hands, she pushed off and planted herself between them. "The 'good part'?" she charged. Sure enough, they answered with indulgent but secretive smirks. "Assuring I can keep my home *isn't* the good part?"

Kellan took one of her hands. "What if we could make it *our* home?"

She gave back a perplexed frown. "It's already our home, my Sirs. You know that. I'm well aware of the demands that your job carries, and that's okay. This miracle that the gods have given us...it's worth it. Whenever you two can make it back here, Hale Anelas will be waiting for you. *I'll* be waiting for you." Tears stung her eyes anew. She didn't try to hide them. "In the two of you, the gods have given me my *mau loa*... my forever love. My home is yours, my bed is yours, and my heart is yours...always."

Kellan lifted her hand to his mouth and captured her knuckles beneath his lips. "Thank you, my love." As he did that, Tait tilted her face up and gave her his thanks with a languorous kiss that had her head swirling and her body swaying.

"*Bleggghh.*" Leo's exclamation coincided with a low roll

of thunder from overhead. "Can we get past the sucking face part, *please*?"

"Hold on to your panties." Kellan chuckled. "We're getting there."

"Right." Lani bounced on her toes, throwing a curious stare between the two of them. "'The good part.' You're 'getting there.' Wherever 'there' is."

Her grin dropped a little when Franzen came out and joined Leo. There was a fresh beer in his hand, yet he looked a little sad. Maybe more than a little.

Tait slipped one of his hands into hers now too. "The reason we're in work gear is because we were at the base at Pearl Harbor. For...job interviews."

She squeezed his hand without thinking. Kellan's too. No matter how many times she flashed her disbelieving gawk between the two of them, neither cut loose with a single teasing snicker. "What the hell do you mean?"

"This latest episode with Tan fleshed out a big concern on the part of the Joint Operations Special Command," Tait went on. "Hawaii's viability as an insertion point to the country, by *any* terrorist state or organization, can't be ignored anymore. Think about the famous attack on Pearl Harbor. If the Japanese decimated us that thoroughly using nineteen forties equipment, think about the possibilities our enemies have today, with modern technology at their disposal."

What he said made sense. Lani nodded her understanding.

Kellan continued the explanation. "After our debrief in Pearl Harbor about the episode with Tan, JSOC approached us about a new elite team that they're putting together here, based out of Pearl Harbor. It's going to be a composite crew under JSOC's direct command, the *best of the best* from all the branches: Marine Spec Ops, Navy SEALs, Rangers, and"—he cracked a lopsided smile—"us."

Lani probed him with a long stare. "You...how?"

"Doing what we do best," Tait filled in. "The bullet ninjas sniper team. At first it'll be just training and development, but we'll also be assigned to protect Hawaii as if we've been deployed here." His lips looked even more delectable as he curled them into a shit-eating smirk. "Our job will be, quite literally, to protect *your* ass."

"Along with a million and a half others," Kell muttered.

"Yeah, but hers is the most important."

"Duh."

Though Tait maintained his grin, the corners of his eyes tightened. "In an even crazier twist of coincidence, part of our job will be to help the FBI in following up on Stock's whereabouts. Hopefully we'll land the puzzle pieces behind Shay's shenanigans."

Kellan winced. "Did you really just say 'shenanigans'?"

"You want me to use something else? *Sleeping with the enemy*, perhaps? While on paper, he's still deployed in South America somewhere?"

"Fine. Use 'shenanigans.' Just not any more tonight."

The clouds brought a few scattered raindrops, plopping on the ground around them in the same way that understanding began to splash in her mind...and her heart. "So...you're telling me that..."

"We're going to be around a little more." Tait's eyes gleamed with golden joy again. "As in, hanging around on most weekends and maybe a few weeknights when we can catch a lift over to Barking Sands."

"Don't forget the bed part." Kellan's features smoldered as

he leaned in to assert it. "You *did* mention the bed, Starshine."

"Yeah, I did." The last of it got lost beneath a soft sob. As she expected, the two of them bunched over her, one on each side.

"Shit," Tait gritted. "We made her cry."

"I told you not to bring up Shay."

"Like that had anything to do with it, asshat."

"Shut up." It tumbled from her on a giggle, which made her tears come even harder.

"Sweetheart, we're sorry. It was too much to dump on you all at once."

"We can ease into things. We'll keep most of our stuff at the base. We don't have to have drawers in the dresser or anything."

"Well...we'll need *one* drawer."

"Why?"

"Toy storage?" Kell's voice dipped, conscious of the fifteen-year-old standing ten feet away. "Floggers? Lube? Rope?"

That snapped her head *way* up. She grinned at Kellan. "Yes, please!" she whispered eagerly. Neither of them had put their Dominant hat back on since the night they'd taken such beautiful control of her in the cottage at Barking Sands. She was crawling out of her skin with need for their hands—and their lips, and other body parts—all over her like that once more.

Tait's features were still cautious. "We can take it slow, baby." He ran a hand through her hair. "We have our whole lives to pleasure you, to love you. This doesn't have to happen to—"

She jammed all four of her main fingers over his lips.

"Shut. Up. Right. Now." She swung her head around, including Kellan in her glower. "Listen to me. *Both* of you. I haven't just been waiting six weeks for you two. I've been waiting my whole life for you. I've been seeing my therapist regularly since the shit went down with Tan. My mind is good. My body is healed. The only thing I need right now is you—*and* you—in my bed, in my body, in as many drawers as you want and need...

"But most of all, in my life. Forever."

"And ever." Kellan lifted her face for a kiss as silken as his voice.

"And ever." Tait's echo possessed more gravel, weighted by the gratitude that shined from his eyes. As he claimed her lips, a palpable breeze glided over Lani's spirit. A smile washed over her soul as she felt Luna dance to her lips, transforming her breath into a sigh of connection and joy. The answering sound from Tait's chest, resonant and rough with his deep emotion, conveyed how he'd felt it too. When they pulled apart, he worked his lips, trying to form words. Lani shook her head. Sometimes miracles were best without labels.

"Are you three going to stand there in the rain playing smoochy hoochey all night?"

As they laughed at Leo's charge, the sprinkles turned into a steady downfall. Lani tilted an impish smile at her brother. "Maybe we will," she teased.

"In that case, I'm staying with Franz tonight."

Franzen chuckled. "That's just fine by me, kid. I'll introduce you to the magic of Stephen Schwartz. You can pick from *Pippin, Wicked,* or *Godspell.*" As Leo's groan echoed out to them, Franzen looked to Tait and Kellan, the sadness clinging to his gaze. "It's going to suck to replace you two, despite your blatant middle finger to my orders the last time you were here."

Lani arched both eyebrows. "A decision that saved my life, Johnny." In more ways than the man would ever realize.

"Yeah," the man drawled. "That's why they lived to brag about it." He replaced his sarcasm with a respectful tilt of his beer bottle. "On a more serious note, I'm proud as hell of you both at being tagged for the JSOC venture. Congrats, Sergeants."

The guys conveyed their thanks for the praise before Franzen returned to the house. The rain kept coming down, soaking all three of them, turning the steamy Hawaiian twilight into a brilliant baptism for their new life together. Lani laughed and lifted her face, rejoicing in the shower from the sky the same way she finally accepted what destiny had brought in the form of these two incredible men. All it had asked in return was her openness, her passion, her courage to embrace it all. It bade the same of both Kellan and Tait, in overcoming their own walls: for Kell, in recognizing he even *had* walls, and for Tait, in realizing that Luna wanted him to be truly happy again.

They'd all come so far.

Yet it was only the beginning.

The rain surely masked her tears now, but somehow she knew the guys could tell the difference anyway. She peered up at them through the mist of her happiness and whispered, "Let's go home."

None of them turned back toward the car. Arm-in-arm, they took the beach route back to Hale Anelas. As they started to walk along the sand, the last rays of the sunset burst through the clouds and across the sea, guiding Lani and her warriors through the rain with a perfect symbol of the spirits' blessing on their love.

A triple rainbow.

Continue the Honor Bound Series with Book Six

Hot

Available Now
Keep reading for an excerpt!

EXCERPT FROM *HOT*

BOOK SIX IN THE HONOR BOUND SERIES

Damn it.

Zoe almost spat the words aloud, despite risking another heart-halting look from Mr. Shane Burnett. She could ignore her animal-level attraction to everything else about the man—his thick chestnut hair, sinful gold eyes, model-perfect jaw, and linebacker-wide shoulders—but when he turned on *the look*, something strange happened to her bloodstream.

Strange. And magical. And terrifying.

It had been a long time since she'd had some scary magic in her life.

Too long to be projecting such feelings onto a stranger in an airport bar.

She'd first seen him use the look on his phone, glowering at the thing as if willing the texts on it into submission. He'd likely succeeded, too. God knew how *her* knees went weak, surrendering to the heat that flowed between them and the most tender folds of her body, from just watching him. *Caramba*, the man was all her favorite flavors, and none of them were vanilla. She would've bet her favorite shoes he was a lifestyle Dominant—and imagining him in a Dom's skintight leathers, holding a flogger in his hand instead of a phone... approaching her across a dungeon with *that look* on his face...

Ohhhh, yes.

Ohhhh, *no*.

She couldn't foster that fantasy again. Ever. The near-disaster with Bryce had taught her that much. Her submissive dreams were doomed to be just that. Dreams. If she had a drop of truly submissive blood in her body, fate had dried it up well before she could do anything about it.

No, it wasn't even fate's fault. When Mom died, *Papi* had fallen apart. Someone had to take care of Ava, and Zoe was the obvious choice. Maybe the angels had forgotten about her being only eleven years old. She'd been livid with them for a while, of course, but now saw it gave her a stubborn strength she was proud of.

Most of the time.

On other occasions, she opted for full retreat. Seemed the easiest route tonight with Mr. Sexy Scowl. She'd gone for duck and cover, sipping her water and checking her phone, praying El and Brynn would get a clue about the man's polite rebuffs. Before that could happen, Ellie had become Sleeping Beauty on the bar. Then the man himself had gained a name. He was no longer anonymous-fantasy-Dom-to-ignore but Shane Burnett, a businessman with endless patience for her friends, a smile more captivating than his scowl, and a protective streak as huge as the arms in which he now held Ellie.

And one more little thing.

A presence that pulled on her like the moon did the tides.

Which was why she could muster nothing but a prissy huff before following him out of the terminal and into the cab.

What the *hell* was she doing? She was easily the only sober one left in the company tonight. She had to take care of the others, not just El and Brynn, yet she let Burnett load the three of them into the cab. She was aware, perhaps better than most, that dominant men could also be assholes, even abusers. Though Burnett directed the driver to the Hilton, what plans did he have for the three of them after he got them to the room? Images blared to mind of tomorrow's headlines, relaying the news that she, El, and Brynn had been beaten to death by an unknown attacker...

She shook her head free of the melodrama. Resolve time. She simply wouldn't let him get past the lobby elevators.

For the time being, he offered a true favor. El was down for the count, and Brynn was still more than a bit blasted. Handling them by herself really would have been a bitch. The ride was only four blocks, but every inch of it was going to be hell. In all the most tantalizing, torturous ways.

Zoe realized it the second Burnett slid into the car and closed the door. Even after he unloaded El, letting her head slide down into Zoe's lap, he seemed to consume the taxi's back seat. With Brynn opting to grab shotgun in front, Zoe found herself the sole object of the man's concentration, a focus he drilled into her without mercy. Or apology.

The car's confines seemed to shrink more. She breathed deeply, battling to calm her racing nerves, but his scent drenched her senses. Earthy strength, woodsy spice. An escape to the forest in the middle of Century Boulevard. *Wow*.

Time for Plan B. But returning the man's stare with a scrutiny of her own was another failure. Why did he keep studying her like the rest of the world didn't exist? The neon signs of the airport district whizzed by—Girls on Fire, Strip-A-Rama, Boobalicious Beauties—but the temptations could have been dust mites for how weakly they dragged his attention from her.

Ohhh, God.

Wait.

Maybe he was gay.

The possibility was such a relief, she smiled for a second. That was all the time he gave her to enjoy the feeling. As he extended his arm along the top of the seat and then dropped two fingers to her nape, the inquiry on his face intensified. He added a third finger to the pressure, his gaze again a wordless query, seeming to question whether she'd welcome him or shirk him.

Before she could help it, a long sigh spilled from her lips.

Burnett's alluring mouth parted a little. His jaw undulated in quiet assessment, flashing with a small tic of muscle.

Her whole body zinged with awareness.

Crap.

Not gay.

She scrambled for a logical argument. This was insane. Unreal. Serendipity that only happened in movies, to people who had perfect lives and all the right lines prewritten for them. Not someone like her, who'd made a *desastre* of her last "relationship" and now must have a tattoo on her forehead, visible to men only. *Hit on me; I haven't had sex in almost a year.* People who could summon a drop of moisture to their mouths instead of letting their tongue turn to cotton from the simple press of a man's fingertips.

"You're tense."

He murmured it between a couple of El's snores. Wait. That wasn't El. It was Brynn, who slumped against the window like she'd pricked her finger on the same enchanted spinning wheel as Ellie.

Great.

She pulled in another breath. And was hit by another arousing wave of his fresh forest smell. *Vaya*, it was nice. Why did a guy in a designer suit smell like he'd just stepped off an alpine hiking trail? Further, why did she sense he'd ditch the suit for the trail in a second? With that jaw, that hair, and those eyes, he was stunning enough to fill one of the Rolex watch ads on the billboards overhead, yet he claimed he was in the airport for business. Now he was stuck in a dingy city cab, in the middle of a freak LA fog bank, with two women who might rouse from their drunken stupors any second just to barf on him—and a third who'd gone dizzy from the effort of resisting his smoke-dark stare.

She finally managed to answer, "And you, Mr. Burnett, are nearly a stranger."

One corner of his mouth lifted. "A nice one"—he trailed his fingers up the back of her neck—"unless you ask me not to be."

This story continues in Hot: *Honor Bound Book Six!*

ALSO BY ANGEL PAYNE

The Misadventures Series:
Misadventures with a Super Hero

Honor Bound:
Saved
Cuffed
Seduced
Wild
Wet
Hot
Masked
Mastered (Coming Soon)
Conquered (Coming Soon)
Ruled (Coming Soon)

Secrets of Stone Series:
No Prince Charming
No More Masquerade
No Perfect Princess
No Magic Moment
No Lucky Number
No Simple Sacrifice
No Broken Bond
No White Knight

**For a full list of Angel's other titles,
visit her at www.angelpayne.com**

ABOUT ANGEL PAYNE

USA Today bestselling romance author Angel Payne loves to focus on high-heat romance starring memorable alpha men and the women who love them. She has numerous book series to her credit, including the Suited for Sin series, the Cimarron Saga, the Temptation Court series, the Secrets of Stone series, the Lords of Sin historicals, and the popular Honor Bound series, as well as several standalone titles.

Angel is a native Southern Californian, leading to her love of being in the outdoors, where she often reads and writes. She still lives in Southern California with her soul-mate husband and beautiful daughter, to whom she is a proud cosplay/culture con mom. Her passions also include whisky tasting, shoe shopping, and travel.

Visit her here:
www.angelpayne.com